THIS WASTED LAND

KENTON KILGORE

Copyright © 2018 Kenton Kilgore
All rights reserved.
ISBN-13: 978-1-7311-0713-8

This story's for the misfit kids,
and the ones who rock it old school.
And it's for Liz.

Also by Kenton Kilgore:
- **For young adults (and adults who are still young):**
    o *Dragontamer's Daughters*
    o *Lost Dogs*
- **For children (and their parents):**
    o *Our Wild Place* (with Patrick Eibel)
- **Non-fiction:**
    o *Hand-Selling Books: Making Money & Winning Fans*

Residents of Kent County and Queen Anne's County, MD will note that I have taken some artistic license in the depiction of certain sites. For this, I beg their indulgence.

My thanks to John George for permission to use **George's Song Shop** (albeit a fictional location in Stevensville, MD) for the setting of most of Track 4, *Sign of the Gypsy Queen*.

Most of the characters appearing in this work are fictitious, and any resemblance by them to real persons or dogs, living or dead, is purely coincidental. However, to provide a greater sense of verisimilitude to the story, some public figures are referenced or make cameos.

But just so you know: "Sally," the Beagle mix? Totally real.

Alyx's Playlist

TRACK 1. YOU COULD BE MINE 1
TRACK 2. THE WANTON SONG 7
TRACK 3. LADIES ROOM 13
TRACK 4. SIGN OF THE GYPSY QUEEN 21
TRACK 5. NO ONE LIKE YOU 35
TRACK 6. IN THE DARK 46
TRACK 7. PLUSH 55
TRACK 8. SIXES AND SEVENS 67
TRACK 9. ATOMIC PUNK 74
TRACK 10. PARANOID 83

TRACK 11. TOYS IN THE ATTIC 97
TRACK 12. DO YOU WANNA TOUCH ME (OH YEAH) 109
TRACK 13. THE THING THAT SHOULD NOT BE 125
TRACK 14. WHERE HAVE ALL THE GOOD TIMES GONE 138
TRACK 15. SICK AGAIN 147
TRACK 16. DON'T KNOW WHAT YOU GOT 159
TRACK 17. DUST N' BONES 169
TRACK 18. PLOWED 185
TRACK 19. HUMANS BEING 194

TRACK 20. INNUENDO 204
TRACK 21. IN THE EVENING 215
TRACK 22. I'M GONNA CRAWL 226
TRACK 23. WHY CAN'T THIS BE LOVE 233
TRACK 24. WOULD 249
TRACK 25. FOOLIN' 261
TRACK 26. LOVE LIES BLEEDING 271
TRACK 27. AIN'T TALKIN' 'BOUT LOVE 285
TRACK 28. STILL LOVING YOU 292
TRACK 29. DON'T CRY 302

TRACK 30. PHOTOGRAPH 310
TRACK 31. LIGHTS OUT 321
TRACK 32. ESTRANGED 335
TRACK 33. MASTER OF PUPPETS 343
TRACK 34. TOO LATE FOR LOVE 353
TRACK 35. GOD OF THUNDER 359
TRACK 36. HEAVY METAL (TAKIN' A RIDE) 369
TRACK 37. LITTLE BY LITTLE 379
TRACK 38. LOVE SONG 392
DISCOGRAPHY/LINER NOTES 400
IF I MAY ASK A FAVOR 404

Track 1. You Could Be Mine

"Hold on!" I tell Sam.

His arms wrap tight around me. The bike—a red Ninja 250R—screeches as I go through the gears, feathering the hand brake as we skid to a stop less than a foot from the bumper of the white Ford Fusion in front of us.

About a hundred yards ahead, a semi laying on its side across both lanes of Route 213. Blue and red lights: police, fire trucks, EMT ambulance. Must be like twenty cars backed up in front of us.

"You were going too fast!" Sam shouts, over the bike's engine.

"I like going too fast!" I shout back. Wasn't even doing 70, so I don't know what he's bitching about.

The sun's almost all the way down, and we're on our way back to Sam's house on Kent Island, coming from Fairmore Farm, where he does therapy riding. I can't wrap my head around how he's cool with getting up on a stupid horse, but a bike freaks him out. Whatever. We just got through Centreville, and were headed for the ramp to take us onto 301, but now it looks like we're not going anywhere.

I give the bike a smidge of gas, start to ootch us out onto the shoulder. Maryland state trooper up there by the wreck sees me, shakes his head, waves for me to get back onto the road. I stop, shrug, point past the truck. He shakes his head again, mouths *No*, waves me back, more insistent this time. Another asshole, just like all the Maryland state troopers. I give him the finger, then pull back in behind the Fusion.

I kill the bike. "Crap!" Sam says. "My mom's gonna be pissed."

I flip up my helmet's visor. "Can't help it." I want some water from the bottle in the mesh sleeve on my backpack, but I don't feel like asking Sam for it. He's already stressing out about being late—because of course he is—and if I ask him for shit right now, he'll probably go off on me. So annoying when he does that.

Headlights from the cars stopped behind us. He's tapping his phone. "I'll text her we'll be late."

I peel off my gloves, drape them over the gas tank, take out my phone from the jacket sleeve pocket where I keep it and a little LED flashlight. I ask Siri like three times for another way to Sam's house, but she keeps wanting me to take 50. Never mind. I hit Waze.

"What's up?" he asks.

C'mon. C'mon. Find us already. So slow, out here in Nowhere, Maryland. "Hold on." I type in his address.

He stands up on the foot pegs, steadies himself, his hand on my shoulder. "Damn, we are *so* close to 50. Can't we go around?"

"Didn't you see? That shithead cop won't let us." There. Got it. A road off 213, not even a quarter-mile back from where we are. It'll run us west and north, and then we can catch another road south and west, back to 301. A little out of the way, but it beats sitting here.

"Let's go," I tell him, stashing my phone. "There's another way." I pull on my gloves, fire up the bike, slap down my visor.

We do a u-ie, head back up 213. Just past the shopping center with the McDonald's, I tap his thigh, point left. Vincent Drive. I slow down, turn that way. The woman stopped in the gray Honda beside us, in the other lane, backs up enough for me to slip the bike through. Sam waves to her. Thanks, lady.

Full-on dark now. I hit the high beam and crank the bike, first gear, second, third, the Ninja whining and buzzing when it wants me to shift. Fourth gear, and I hear Sam my head, yelling to slow down, but it's just my imagination: we're not telepathic, or anything.

Chilly—I feel it through my jeans, on my knees and the tops of my thighs. Two-lane road: no cars around. It's too loud to tell Sam to lean with me, but he knows to do it anyway as we take a curve.

When we come out of it, I clutch and shift again, and we're in fifth gear, 60-something miles an hour.

He wiggles around on the back pad, trying to get comfortable. A Ninja 250's not really made for doubling up, but neither of us are big. Me especially, cuz I'm a girl and Korean—half, anyway.

The road runs straight for a while, then bends right, straight, right again. Straight. A low bridge over a creek. Straight. Left. Lefting again, a tight bend this time. I pull in the clutch, ease up on the throttle.

His arms squeeze tight. I yank the hand brake, stamp the foot brake, back end fishtails let off the brake still too fast tap tap tap with my foot, front's locking up let it go long enough to downshift downshift feather the clutch, bike's screaming. Jam to a stop a few yards before we can hit.

Train in front of us, going slow. *klgg klgg klgg klgg klgg*

"Are you kidding me?" Sam snaps.

The train keeps rolling—no end to it. We passed some other roads off this one—any of them go back to 50? Not that I remember from Waze. I pop my visor, shut off the bike. Take off gloves, get out my phone.

"She is going to be totally mad," Sam says.

"I thought you texted her."

"I did."

"What'd she say?"

He checks. "She hasn't texted back."

"Maybe she hasn't noticed."

"Well, she's going to notice. I'm supposed to be back home in twenty minutes."

"Well, she's going to have to get over it, cuz there's not a damn thing we can do about that."

"Easy for you to say."

"Don't get all pissy." Honest to God, sometimes he makes me

crazy. I check my phone. Waze is even slower this time—I've got one bar.

klgg klgg klgg klgg klgg

"We're just sitting here."

"What'd ya want me to do?"

"Find another way."

Waze has finished loading. I show him. "There's no other way. Unless we go back."

"That's not right."

"Yeah, it is."

"You pulled up the wrong road."

"Did not." I zoom out, show him my phone again so he can see the names of the roads. "That's 213," I tell him, pointing. "That's Vincent." I take the phone back, zoom in, hold it out to him again. "Here we are."

He takes the phone. Looks at it. Looks around. "No, it's not."

"Yeah, it is. Don't be dense."

"There aren't any railroad tracks on the map."

"So, the map is wrong."

"No, we're on the wrong road," he says, giving me back my phone. "Who's dense now?"

"Damn it, Sam, the ma—"

Then the bike spills, falls to the road, my leg under it ow ow ow! my head bounces off the asphalt thank God I still have my helmet on. Sam sprawled next to me. The hell just happened, car hit us? No, no headlights, no car here ow ow ow my ribs my side I scraped my hands DAMN IT that hurts. Sam—is he okay?

Oh, good God, what's that smell it's like—

EEEEEEEEEEE shrieking right here right on top of me it's an old woman gray tattered dress long scraggly white hair wrinkled face like a rotten apple when they get mushy and horrible, it's her, she's what smells so bad, like a garbage dumpster on a hot day. Jesus what's going on? She leans over me her eyes are silver where they should be brown or blue or whatever.

"Alyx," Sam gasps, trying to get up. The old woman grabs my helmet—both hands long skinny fingers yellow ragged nails—starts to pull me off the ground by it no no no don't do that don't do that it hurts it HURTS my neck, my back. Grab her arms; she's yanking me up from under the bike. My boot catches on the handlebar for a second—OW OW OW—then it's loose and I kick her. Nothing. She jerks me close to her. God, she smells so damn bad.

EEEEEEEEEEE she screams, right in my face, her mouth is dribbling blood and her teeth are actual pieces of broken glass. She bites through my plastic face visor and I freak and I kick her in the guts and the crotch and the chest where it should hurt her but she's got no tits. I punch her on the side of her head and in her face and she's snapping, bites my hand, it hurts it hurts but don't care don't care I punch and kick and she slams me to the ground—legs, hips, shoulders, neck, back, everything on fire. My hand's bleeding where she bit me. Sam, Sam, are you okay the hell is this

"Alyx..." he gasps, like he got the wind knocked out of him. That crazy old smelly bitch is dragging him by his foot away from the bike, toward the train.

I get to my feet, everything spinning around me. Right side's tight, hard to breathe, did she break my ribs? Never mind deal with it ignore it. Lean over, almost fall, pull my knife from my boot. Straighten up. Toward them. Sam Sam he's hurt he's bad. Blood on him. His? Mine?

She notices me, turns around, lets go of him. Lurches over like there's something wrong with her, like she can't walk too good, like Sam. She grabs my wrist, bends it back toward me, gonna stab me with my own knife. Trying to fight. Can't. She's too strong.

I drop the knife before she can cut me and I tromp on her foot again and again and again. I can't tell if she feels it. She tosses me a few yards. I hit the ground and it hurts everywhere. When I can look up again, she's got the back tire and she's picking up the whole bike, over her head. Three hundred pounds.

She's going to kill me. For real, kill me.

She grabs the frame with her other hand, swings the bike, and I roll mostly out of the way as she smashes it down, pieces of it breaking, flying off. Part of the engine hits my foot; the boot takes most of it, but it still hurts so bad I scream, though I don't want to. Want to get away get Sam get out of here. I start to scramble to get up. Behind her. Sam, hobbling toward where my knife fell.

She drops what's left of the bike on me. I'm down again.

Sam calling my name over and over. Everything going dark. Hurt. Only hurt. I can't. I'm done.

She grabs him by the hair before he can take the knife, pulls him—kicking, thrashing—toward the train.

Black train. Black.

Black.

Track 2. The Wanton Song

The world comes back. Pieces of the bike all around me: shattered headlight, snapped handlebars, torn cables. It's still dark. The train's still going, so I couldn't have been out too long—a few seconds? A minute?

klgg klgg klgg klgg klgg

I'm not dead. My riding gear—padded leather jacket, boots, full helmet—saved me. But I'm bad. There's blood under me, mostly from my hand, where she bit me. Never mind. I crawl out from what's left of the bike.

Get up. It takes me a while.

The knife's still there, on the road, where I dropped it. Stagger to it. It takes a few tries before I can pick it up. Hands won't stop shaking. Doesn't matter. The knife's got a clip on it; I hitch it to the inside of my boot.

Where's Sam? Gone. Him and that crazy old bitch.

klgg klgg klgg klgg klgg

Knees wobbling—don't! Don't! Too late. Legs give out from under me. I crumple to the pavement. Wheezing—hard to take a breath. I fumble with the chinstrap, tug at my helmet. Broken visor where she bit it, like she's half shark. Yank it off, let it drop; it rolls a foot or so, then stops. Breathe. I can breathe.

Lie there for a while. How long, I don't know.

Train still going. Slow, really slow. *klgg klgg klgg klgg klgg*

Better. Hands not shaking, heart not racing anymore. Phone. Where's my phone? Was holding it. Yes. Showing him the map. He said we weren't on the right road. He said there were no train tracks on the map. Have to find my phone.

Try again, get up on my hands and knees. Jeans torn, left knee's scraped—s'okay. Up, get to my feet. Lift my head. The world spins, just a little. Close my eyes until it stops.

Okay. Okay. Do this. Open my eyes. Look around. No streetlights, no moon, only stars in the dark. There.

Boots dragging as I go to it. Bend—everything's spinning again. Sink to the asphalt. Phone's in a little puddle of blood. Doesn't matter. Wipe my hand dry on my jacket. Pick it up.

Screen's cracked. Tap it. Lights up. Still works. Screw you, you crazy old bitch. Swipe the screen. EMERGENCY, right there at the top. Tap it.

Rings.

Rings.

Come *on*.

klgg klgg klgg klgg klgg

A woman on the line. "Nine-one-one operator. What is your emergency?"

For a second, nothing comes out of me. Then, "I've...we've been...someone attacked us. Me and my boyfriend."

I hear her typing. "Where are you?"

"We're...I'm at Griffiths Road, by the train tracks."

"Is anyone hurt?"

"Yeah, um...I'm...pretty messed up."

"You say you're on Griffiths Road? Near Centreville?"

"Yeah. Centreville."

"And you say you're by the railroad tracks?"

"Yeah."

"I'm not seeing where any railroad tracks cross Griffiths."

"Well, there are, and there's a train on them right now."

klgg klgg klgg klgg klgg

"I'll check again. What's your name?"

"Alyx. Alyx Williams." Easier to talk now.

"And is that short for 'Alexandria?'"

"Alex*andra*."

"What's your boyfriend's name?"

"Sam Patterson. Samuel."

"Is Sam ok? Is he hurt?"

"He's..." Chest heaves, eyes start filling up. Something ripping from the inside, trying to get out. I won't let it. Keep it together. Keep it together. "He's gone. She took him."

"Who is 'she?' Who took Sam?"

"This...woman. I don't know who she is."

"What did she look like?"

I can't tell her it was an old woman with silver eyes and jagged glass for teeth, who can pick up a Kawasaki. "I don't...I don't know for sure. She had white hair—long white hair. And a gray dress. It was all torn up."

"And she took Sam?"

"Yeah."

"How? Did she have a weapon?"

"No, I..." No sirens, no lights. "When is someone going to get here?"

"Help is on the way, but there's a big accident in Centre—"

"I know."

"—and a lot of units are tied up there. We're having an issue with your location. There aren't any railroad tracks on that road you gave us. Are you sure you're on Griffiths?"

"Yeah, I'm sure." *klgg klgg klgg klgg klgg* How long is this train?

"This woman—did she have a weapon?"

I wipe my face; my hand's stopped bleeding. "No, she didn't. She just beat me up and took him. Took Sam." I'm not going to cry. I'm not going to cry.

"Was she on foot, or did she have a vehicle?"

"She..." I look around. "I don't know. I never saw a car."

"Is anyone else around who might have seen this woman?"

"No, no one. Just me." The last train car goes by, still going slow. *klgg klgg klgg klgg klgg*

"She got on the train," I tell the 911 lady. "She grabbed him and put him on the train." I start after it, stumbling down the tracks. "You have to stop the train."

Nothing for a second. Then: "The officer's there and he says there are no railroad tracks and nobody's around. He doesn't see you."

"There's no cop here." I'm going faster now, limping after the train. Foot and ankle hurt where the bike clipped it. Never mind. Keep going. Don't let it get away.

"Alexandra, look around. Can you see the officer or his car?"

"She's on the train," I growl, and then I'm hobbling as fast as I can—isn't much—not listening to the phone, hands swinging at my sides. Trees on each side of the tracks now. Running. Breathing's ragged. Doesn't matter. Have to get him. Have to get the train.

klgg klgg klgg klgg klgg

I run alongside the last car. There's a big sliding metal door—open—and a handrail. I tuck the phone in my pocket, grab the rail, try to pull myself up.

Fall. Pointed gray rocks alongside the tracks. Hands, elbows, knees, hurt like hell. Ignore it, get up, run. Phone buzzing in my pocket. Ignore it. Run. Run, damn it.

klgg klgg klgg klgg klgg

Grab the rail again, both hands this time. Swing one leg up. My back seizes, spasms—it hurts deep everywhere. Other leg dangling, hopping along. If I fall and slip under the wheels, they'll cut me in half. Don't think about it. Pull on the rail. Pull.

Get the other leg up. Roll all the way into the empty car. Gasping. Back and legs ruined. Rest. Gotta rest.

I lie there in the dark. Nothing but the trains' wheels, faster now. *klggklggklggklggklggklggklgg* Laying there, listening. Just for a minute. Another. Another.

What the actual hell is happening?

Something tearing at me again, like a rat trying to eat its way out of my chest. Hands shaking again. Stop it. Stop it. Keep it together. Hold on. Hold on.

Okay. I'm okay.

I sit up. It smells like a portapotty in here. My right sleeve pocket—there's one of those little LED flashlights. Unzip, take it out. Please let it still work.

It does. Look around the car.

Empty except for a basket laying on the floor of the car. It's made of wire and metal scraps and trash and animal bones, all stuck together with some sorta dried yellow goop. It's about two feet long, kinda oval-shaped. It's got a big hole in it, at one end. That's where the stench is coming from.

The air's gotten cold. I see my breath in the flashlight's beam. The train's going even faster now—*klggklggklggklggklggklgg klggklggklggklggklggklggklggklggklgg*—the car jerks and bumps and sways.

I get up, go closer to the basket, to about an arm's length away. No way am I going to put my hand in that big hole, or my face by it. Just going to take a peek with the flashlight. That's all. It reeks of piss and shit and that rotten wet smell that some food makes when it's been left too long in the fridge. My throat tightens. This—

mhurrrr from the basket. I don't move.

mhurrr again. It's like a cat or some other small animal, but one that's hurt or sick or has something wrong with it.

mhurr

But then, sort of not like an animal at all. Almost like it's—

I get my phone from my pocket, have to call someone, anyone, right now. EMERGENCY, all right. Need the cops, need EMT's, need—

The screen: it's just gray and scratchy. The phone buzzes stupidly, for no reason, again and again in my hand. Come on. I tap the button for 911. Static from the speaker, the call's not going through. Try it again. The screen goes out. Work, damn it, work!

Phone slapped out of my hand. It hits the steel floor, spins around and around, useless bings and bongs and chirps as ringtones go off. The crazy old bitch—where'd she come from how'd she get here?—grabs my jacket, yanks me away from the cage, that's what it is, it's a *cage*, not a basket, and—

"It's not yours," she hisses, low and raspy.

"Where's Sam?" Hand wrapped around the flashlight, I'm punching her in the face, in the head, but she doesn't seem to feel it. "Give me back Sam! Let him go!"

"He's not yours, either," she says, and then her eyes and nose and mouth are gone, stalks like a snail's sprouting out of her head, each of them with dozens of tiny mouths with broken-glass teeth, and I scream I can't stop and I try to get away but she's too strong and she jerks me towards the stalks with jaws full of glass shards and I kick and punch and writhe and one clamps down on my arm, tearing, shredding my jacket, and I lean back kick her in the throat and suddenly I'm falling she's let me go and I'm out of the car and I hit HARD and bounce and roll roll can't stop myself finally do and the train goes by *klggklggklggklggklggklggklggklggklggklggklggklggklgg*.

I lift my head. She's put herself back together, and she's leaning out of the door of the car, watching me. The train keeps pulling away, and then she's gone. And Sam's gone, too.

I look around. Nowhere anyplace like where I was before. Not even close.

Track 3. Ladies Room

The sky is all wrong. When I got on the train, it was dark but clear. I could see the stars. Now it's brighter: the sun's hanging just over the horizon, a ball of weak white light behind thick gray clouds that go from one end of the sky to the other.

That just can't be. I was only on the train for a few minutes, so, how can it not be night?

"Maryland is like a mini-America," Sam once told me. *"We have hills and mountains, we have wetlands and forests and plains, big cities, small towns, and suburbs. Lakes and rivers and the Bay and the ocean. We have everything you can find anywhere else in America."*

"You don't have deserts," I said.

"Okay, you're right: we don't have deserts. But who wants deserts, anyway?"

"I like deserts."

"You're weird."

"Like you're not?" I punched him in the arm, hard enough to sting.

"Ow!"

"You like me because I'm weird."

He laughed. *"Fact."*

Maryland doesn't have deserts. But here I am in one.

Tiny flecks of gray and black gravel under me. Gray dust in my hair, all over my face. Gray pebbles and rocks. Weeds—gray or black, not green. Broken glass, paper scraps, twisted bits of wire, snips of rusty metal. Near me, where I'm laying, is an old, dented can, its label faded and yellow, peeling off. Next to it, an empty, clear plastic bottle, buckled and cracked. It's like I'm at one of those places where they dump the garbage and then bury it forever.

Not a sound, except faintly, very faintly, the wind whistling far away.

Slowly—it hurts—I bend my legs, get my hands out in front of me. Start pushing myself off the ground. God, it hurts. Get to my knees. Breathe. Breathe. Head up. Look around—not too fast. Light flickers at the edges of my eyes—is that what they mean by *seeing stars*? Close them. Breathe. Okay. Open my eyes.

Look that way: low, blunted hills not too far from here. The other way: train tracks running into the gray haze.

My phone. It's on the damned train. If it isn't broken into a million pieces.

One leg up, foot on the ground. Push. Hands out, steadying myself. Other foot up. Wobbling. Hold it. Okay. Okay. I'm up.

Now what?

The wind howls by, just for a few seconds, dust and gravel flying. I cover my face with my hands until it's gone.

"This is impossible," I whisper.

I shrug off my backpack. The water bottle in the mesh pocket on the side is still there. I take it out, take a swig. About half of it left. I put it back, open the pack, remind myself what's there. Sketch pad and pencils. Pens and a comp book. That novel—*The Sun Also Rises*—that we're reading in Mrs. Humphreys' class. Some napkins that me and Sam snagged from Ledo's last Sunday. Hand sanitizer. Lip balm. Mascara. An opened box of Always Infinity pads, and a little bottle of Midol, because it's going to be that time soon. The little amber-colored prescription bottle with my meds. A baggie with a few Goldfish crackers left over from lunch.

It's all I got. And I have no idea where I am. I put everything back and put the pack on again.

Whatever she is, she's on the train, and she has Sam. So, let's go catch a train.

I start following the tracks in the direction the train went. At first, I walk between the rails, on the wooden beams between. It occurs to me that another train might come soon, so I walk alongside.

Damn, it's cold. I thought deserts were supposed to be hot. Doesn't make any sense. None of this does.

No birds. No animals. No plants except more gray weeds. I think—no, I *know*—that all plants are green. They have to be to live: it's how they make their food. From the sun.

The sun. I look behind me. It hasn't moved or gotten any stronger. The wind comes back again. Pull my jacket tighter around me until the gust's over. Keep following the tracks.

I walk. And walk. Nothing else moves. Nothing else makes a sound.

Where are the cops? They were coming—that's what the dispatcher at 911 said. And I told her that the crazy bitch took Sam on the train. Wouldn't the cops follow the tracks? So why haven't I seen them? Why aren't they here by now?

Maybe they went the wrong way.

Wouldn't some of them go one way, some the other? Maybe. But how would they? Drive on the tracks? Next to them? What if they couldn't? Too many trees or something.

But the lady at 911 said the cops couldn't find the tracks. Or me.

Then they're not coming?

My feet hurt. I stop, lean over, hands on my thighs. What am I doing? Where am I going? How am I supposed to find Sam?

I straighten up. This can't be happening. It just can't.

"SAM!" Hands cupped by my mouth. "SAM!"

Nothing. Not even the wind. Stupid of me. No one's out here.

No one.

I look around. Not a sound. No roads, no cars, no lights. No buildings anywhere. Nothing but cold, gray desert and trash.

Sam, where the hell are we? And where are you?

Where these tracks go: that's where he is. Somewhere.

I start following them again.

Sam. Why does she want him? What's she going to do to him? Is she hurting him? Is she going to kill him?

My hands ball into fists. I walk faster.

What *is* she? Not human. Some kinda monster. Which is insane. There aren't any monsters. Not real ones. I'm too old to believe in them.

Walking.

Walking.

Walking.

After a while, something there, up ahead, along the tracks. A house?

Maybe. Maybe someone's there. Maybe they'll let me use their phone, call the cops, stop the train. Get Sam.

I run. It hurts: my feet, my legs, my chest, my back. Ignore it. Keep going.

Run.

Run.

Almost there. I slow down—walking again. Breath coming out in big clouds. I'm not cold anymore.

It's not a house. Smaller, squat, on a concrete slab. I get closer. Empty window frames. Over them, broken letters that probably used to light up in neon: **T C ETS**.

An old train station platform. I look into the ticket booth. It's just one room, nothing but gravel and trash that's blown in. No one there. No phone.

The tracks keep going, but a little ways behind the platform is another building, same design, but it's long and low. Two doors, next to each other. I go see what they are.

Restrooms. WOMEN'S and the triangle lady on one door; MEN'S and the round-headed guy on the other. Hell yeah, I could pee.

The door squeals and sticks as I shove it open. A stench like someone—or a lot of someones—pissed all over the floor. Shadowy in here: some busted windows near the ceiling. The fluorescents don't work, so I get out my flashlight. Rusted pipes overhead, some sand and junk on the floor, but not much. Sinks against one wall, a long mirror, cracked in places, over them.

Pick the stall that doesn't look quite as filthy as the others. A smashed window about six feet up, on the back wall. Some gray dust on the seat, but no bugs or bird crap or people crap or anything else nasty. No water in the toilet, but that's okay.

Lock the stall door. Brush off the seat; the bathroom's piss smell is even worse when I lean over. Keep my backpack on—don't want to set it on this nasty floor. Stash my flashlight. Ease my jeans down past my knees. Long bruises on the front and outsides of my thighs. No idea what the backs or the rest of my legs look like, but they've gotta be bad.

Hover over the seat and pee. And pee. And pee.

That feels so damn good.

I finish. No toilet paper, so I take off my backpack, get some of the napkins. Wipe up, drop them in the toilet. Put the pack on, start pulling up my jeans.

skeeeeeeee of the women's room door opening. I freeze.

Slow, shuffling footsteps. Is it the crazy old bitch? She didn't walk very good, from what I saw.

Quiet as I can, I yank up my jeans, button them. Sit on the seat and pull up my feet so whoever it is can't see them.

Little boy? he asks. At least I think it's a he. Deep voice, sorta slurred, more like croaking than talking. Slow, panting, like talking wasn't easy.

Shuffling. More slow panting.

Little boy?

There's no little boy here, you freak. Why would there be one in the women's bathroom?

Shuffling, coming closer. Did he see me? Hear me?

Are you there?

Stops in front of my stall. In the dim, I see scuffed and battered men's dress shoes, one brown, one black, different styles. Ragged gray pinstripe pants, like from a suit.

Pulls on the stall door. The latch goes *khk*. It doesn't open.

Little boy, he sighs.

I don't breathe.

Pulls on the door again.

Huhh, he pants. **Huhh. Huhh.**

I slip the knife from my boot.

I want you, little boy.

"Go away."

The panting pauses.

"I'm not a little boy." Stronger now. "And I've got a gun." Let him think that. "I'll hurt you if I have to."

I won't hurt you.

The knife shakes. "Leave me alone."

I want you.

Something slaps the top of the stall door. It's coming from a tattered black suit jacket sleeve with a ripped cuff, but it's not a hand. Wide and round, sorta shaped like the end of a shovel, yellowy pale. It grabs the top of the door and starts slowly jerking it back and forth, back and forth, the latch rattling.

Little boy…little boy…

What do I do what do I do it's not a guy it's not a pervert it's a monster a for real monster like that crazy old bitch—

dmmdmmdmmdmmdmmdmmdmm goes the door—he's trying to yank it open. Then another paw or whatever like the first one slaps across the bottom of the door and starts shaking it and the door keeps going *dmmdmmdmm dmmdmmdmm*

I lurch off the toilet seat and jab the knife at the not-hand on top and I miss and the point goes *jkxx* bouncing off the metal door and this time I slice all the way across the paw, one end to the other, but no blood, nothing comes out, and the door goes *dmmdmmdmmdmmdmmdmm*

I stab the paw right in the middle and I twist, but it won't let go it won't stop pulling on the door and the hinges start cracking, they're rusty and old and I stab again and again and still nothing comes out, but the paw at the bottom of the door grabs my leg.

Burns it burns so bad I jerk back but the paw sticks to my jeans and I scream, yank my leg away, crash into the back corner of the stall, toilet hits my elbow it goes numb all at once and ow ow ow my jeans are ripped, a scrap of it sticking to the paw, and then he shakes it off, reaches with the pad again, its palm covered in hundreds—thousands—of tiny, spiky, sticky-looking black hairs that twitch and wiggle like feelers on bugs. I look at my calf where my pant leg's torn and I'm bleeding from dozens and dozens of tiny holes. The paw flaps, trying to grab me again. I jam my back against the cinderblock wall and wrench myself to my feet so he can't get me.

The paw goes away. The other one disappears behind the top of the door. Squeaking rubber as he staggers away. I hurt him I hurt him I—

Little boy…I want you…in my mouth….

BMM as he slams in the door and the latch jiggles, nearly pops open and he stumbles back *BMM* into the door again and I throw myself at it, arms out, "Go away! Go away! Go away!"

The paws come back, over and under the door again, flailing for me. I jump for the toilet seat: one foot slips, boot tromps inside the bowl, *BMM* he hits the door again. Leap up to the windowsill, miss it, catch the side wall of the stall slam against it. *BMM.* I jump again, grab the windowsill, pull, pull up, push off the side wall and the toilet, *BMM* and a paw tugs my boot as I fall through the window, knocking pieces of glass out of the frame, thank God for my jacket. Hands and wrists slam onto the ground, then the rest of me crashes onto cold gray gravel and sand.

Roll over, look up. Nothing there. Nothing coming out the window after me.

Little boy?

I get up and run as fast as I can. Run. Don't know where, except away. Run. Run.

Until I can't.

I slow, stumbling. Look back. The station and the bathrooms are tiny bumps. Nothing's following me, but I keep going, staggering on. Keep looking back.

Finally crumple to my knees.

Sam. Sam, what is this? I don't know. I don't know. I don't—

Crying. Don't want to, but I do.

Track 4. Sign of the Gypsy Queen

Walking. I don't know where to, so long as it's not toward that restroom. I got away, and right now, that's all that matters.

Can't think about it, any of it. Can't think about where I am, or the...*thing* in the bathroom. Can't think about the train or what was in the basket, or *her*.

Or Sam.

Oh, God.

Oh, God.

No no no no no

Think about something else. Something good.

* * *

GEORGE'S SONG SHOP STEVENSVILLE. Gold letters painted on the front window. Under that was AMERICA'S OLDEST RECORD STORE—NOW ON THE EASTERN SHORE! An old house someone—George, I guessed—had converted into a business.

It looked more interesting than the antique stores and the fancy Italian restaurant—Amalfi Coast—here in the town center. Had to be cooler inside—hot and muggy out, like every summer day around here, I'd learned. *August in Maryland is like being in the mouth of a very big dog*, my uncle had told me.

I took off my backpack, turned the door knob, went in. AC was cranked, thank God. Music blasted over the speakers in the corners of the ceiling. Sounded like Eighties, all keyboards and horns and bass, not much guitar. An old-time record player spun on the counter, by the cash register.

Guy my age—white kid, short brown hair, kinda geeky-looking—by the record player. No one else in the store, but then, it was a Tuesday. He looked up from what he was reading, smiled, waved, started to say something. Reached under the counter, and the music wasn't so loud anymore. "Hi, can I help you find anything?"

"No, I'm good." I put my bag down just inside the door, kept my sunglasses on cuz I hate how my eyes look. I'd never seen so much vinyl in my life. Bins and racks and shelves—big, tall shelves, toward the back—of albums, cassettes, and CDs. How many?

It's like he read my mind. "We have two floors, and about ten thousand records."

"Thanks." I turned my back to him, went over to the far wall, to the rock section, started flipping through albums. Almost all of them were used, with scuffed covers, or creased corners, or the plastic wrap torn or missing. Original copies from back when they were first released. Where did "George" get all these? Yard sales? Record conventions? Don't know.

"What do you like to listen to?"

Jesus, you dudes are all the same. I didn't turn around: that would only encourage him. "Just…stuff." Now shut up and leave me alone.

"If you're looking for new releases, they're around this end of the counter. We just got Taylor Swi—"

"I hate her." Not really. Just tired of being hit on by losers.

"Okay, uh…we also have Dra—"

"Hip hop sucks." Some of it's okay.

"Yeah…I'm more into older stuff, you know?"

Kept flipping through records. AC/DC—I already had all those. Aerosmith—no *Toys in the Attic?* That's their best one. Alice Cooper. Allman Brothers—do they actually have anything decent in this store?

I heard him coming out from behind the counter. Dude, buy a clue, will you? I pulled out an album, checked out the cover. In the upper left corner: APRIL WINE. Must be the band's name. At the bottom, the album title: THE NATURE OF THE BEAST. The rest of it was a big photo of a guitarist rocking out, but instead of being a normal guy, he had a tiger's head.

"You want me to play that one for you?"

"Sure." Whatever. I turned around. That's when I saw.

* * *

Cold. So cold. Wish I had my gloves. I took them off to check my phone. Put them on the gas tank. They fell off when she knocked us off the bike. Must still be on the ground back there. Wherever that is from here.

Don't think about it. Walk. Just keep walking.

* * *

He had a crutch and he kinda lurched when he walked, almost looked like his left leg was buckling under him and he was gonna fall on his ass. What's wrong with him?

I handed him the album. "You okay?" I asked.

"Yeah." Nodded. "I'm all right."

I looked down at his leg. "An accident?"

He shook his head. "Shark attack, last summer in Ocean City when I was surfing. Bit my leg off right below the knee. They tell me it might have been a hammerhead, but nobody really saw anything with all the blood in the water. This is just a temporary prosthesis—next week, I get my permanent one from Shriners Hospital."

"For real?"

"No, I'm kidding. Cerebral palsy. Happened as I was born."

"What's that?"

"Something went wrong during delivery, my brain didn't get

enough oxygen, and it messed up the muscles in my arm and my leg. The rest of me's fine, though. I'm lucky. A lot of people with CP come out with all kinds of issues."

"Oh." Great, just great. Could I have said anything more stupid than *oh*?

"It's okay." He smiled. I tried to. "I don't mind that you asked. I'm used to it, you know?"

I nodded. "Yeah." Okay. Okay. That didn't come out totally terrible. He turned around, started heading back for the counter. "You can let this one finish playing," I told him. "It's pretty good, whatever it is."

He went behind the counter, held up an album cover. Burgundy background, a few thin lines going across part of it. Smiling woman with white—I mean, *white*—skin, black hair, green eyes, red lips, long-ass tapering purple earrings. DURAN DURAN, it said at the top. Then, under that, RIO.

"Heard of them?" he asked.

"No."

"My mom listens to them." So uncool. He seemed to notice.

"I like old stuff, too, but metal, you know?"

He nodded. "Like, uh…Led Zeppelin?"

"I'm mostly into Eighties, but some Seventies stuff is cool. Not so much Nineties. So, GnR, or Skid Row, or Scorpions."

"What about Def Leppard?"

"They're awesome. Metallica, too. I really like them."

"What else do you like?"

"Queensryche. UFO. Priest."

"Van Halen?"

"Love Van Halen."

"Dave, or Sammy? That's my name, by the way. Sam."

"I'm Alyx. I like them both."

"Bon Jovi?"

"Bon Jovi's not metal. They just think they are."

"Some of their stuff is good." I bet his mom likes them, too. "So, how come you like all that old music?"

"Because it's loud and crazy and fun. *Wild*. It's how music should be. It's how life should be."

"I'm not really into hard rock."

"What d'ya like?"

"Eighties New Wave, like Talking Heads, Devo, Blondie, and The Cars. I really like The Police, and Depeche Mode. B-52's."

I pointed to the speakers. "Are they New Wave?"

"Duran Duran? Yeah."

"So, you probably like them, too."

He grinned, nodded. "You got me. They're my favorite."

"You blush easy."

He shrugged, still smiling. "Got me again."

* * *

Cold. How long have I been walking? Feels like hours. This place, wherever I am—gravel and rocks and weeds and trash—it just goes on forever.

There's something out there, a ways off. Just sorta sticking up out of the ground. I don't know what it is, but it's a little bit bigger than a person, I guess. And it's not moving. Maybe it's something that'll help.

I go see.

* * *

I went down an aisle, looking at the albums, but not really. "This is a big place."

"The original store in Johnstown is even bigger."

"Yeah?"

"That's what Mr. George tells me. He was my history teacher in sixth grade. His dad owns these stores. My teacher—well, he's not my teacher anymore—he runs this shop. His dad still runs the other one."

"In Johnstown."

"Yeah." I got to the end of the aisle, went around the corner, started coming back the other side, flipping through records as I went. Harry Connick, Jr. The Contours. Sam Cooke—hey, another Sam. "So, are you visiting from somewhere?" he asked me. "I haven't seen you around before."

"I just moved here about a week ago."

"Where'd you come from?" He blushed again. "Sorry. I mean, where did you live before?"

"Why'd you say 'sorry?'"

"Well, because I didn't mean to ask 'Where are you from?' you know, like you're not American or something. I didn't mean anything by it."

"It's okay, I didn't take it that way." He grinned, obviously relieved. White boys. I swear. "Pennsylvania. King of Prussia. It's near Philly. My dad was military. My mom's Korean. Like, just off the boat."

"Do you speak Korean?"

"No, not really." Fluent, actually. I don't like to, but Mom doesn't know much English.

"And your dad—what branch was he in?"

"Army."

"I guess you all moved around a lot."

"We used to, when I was little. My dad left us about six years ago. Haven't heard from him since."

"That sucks. Sorry to hear that."

"I don't care. When he took off, we were up there in King of Prussia, so we stayed. My mom cleans houses. Well, she used to."

"What made you come here?"

"A couple months back, my mom got an e-mail from her sister about a job in her husband's new business, refurbishing phones. She wanted us to move to Daegu, in Korea, but I didn't want to, so I came to live with my uncle. He has a house off Route 8."

"Your mom's going to Korea?"

"Already left."

"And you're just not?"

"Nope."

"That's badass! Aren't you going to miss her?"

"We don't get along."

"Your uncle must be so cool."

"He's okay. He's my dad's oldest brother, and he's always helped us out when he can. I guess he feels responsible for us."

"Because of your dad just…. So you never see him? Your dad?"

"No. It's no big deal." I was still flipping through records. Found more good stuff. "It's not like he was 'World's Best Father' or something."

"Has your uncle lived here a long time?"

"Yeah, but he's not always here. He has houses in Maine and Florida, too."

"What does he do?"

"He owns two or three used-car places in Ohio, and some Eat'n Parks around Pittsburgh and Altoona."

"What's 'Eat'n Park?'"

"You don't know what Eat'n Park is?"

He shook his head. "We don't have those around here."

"It's like Denny's, but way better. They have these awesome smiley face cookies. So, what grade are you going into?"

"Senior."

"Me, too."

"Kent Island?"

"What?"

"Are you going to Kent Island High School, or a private one?"

"Kent Island."

"Do you know who you have for English?"

"Mrs. Humphreys."

"Jean Humphreys? I had her for British Lit. You are going to love her. She is soooo cool and so funny. What else are you taking?"

"You know, the usual. Spanish. Math." I didn't tell him it was only Algebra 2. He'd think I was an idiot.

"Do you know who you have for math?"

"Ms. Jung." I say it the Korean way, with the "J."

"She pronounces it 'Young,' and she's a complete bitch. I had her for pre-calc."

"Great."

"Seriously, you need to switch classes. She's nuts, and she can't teach for crap. What's your other class?"

"Art. It's the only thing I like about school."

"That's cool. What kind of art do you do?"

"I draw."

"I wish I could. Do you carry around a pad of paper and pencils and randomly sketch things, like artists are supposed to?"

"Sometimes." Okay, all of the time.

"Could you show me some of what you've drawn?"

"I don't have anything right now." Not totally true—my pad was in my backpack. There was just nothing I wanted to show anyone. "What classes are you taking?"

"AP Bio, AP English, AP Calc, French V and Band. Trombone, believe it or not."

I smirked. "You look like you're in band."

"I'm sure as hell not on the football team. Which is excellent, by the way. We went to the playoffs for the sixth time in a row last year. You do any sports?"

"Sports are bullshit."

"You don't watch football?"

"God, no."

"I'm a huuuuge Ravens fan. We have seas—"

Then the door opened and this girl walked in, and Sam was all about her.

* * *

Wait—is that what I think it is?

It's like a skinny closet, with a metal frame and glass sides, some of them cracked. An old phone booth, the kind you go inside. I've only ever seen one in movies. What the hell is it doing out here, in the middle of nowhere?

The door doesn't want to work. I yank on it, yank it again, slowly drag it open, sand scraping down at the bottom, in the track. I get it about halfway open before it won't go anymore. I squeeze inside.

Not quite as cold in here. Newspapers all over the floor. Graffiti—scratched or drawn—all over, some of it I can read (and some of that's pretty crude), most of it I can't. Are those even letters? The phone's that ancient kind where you poke your finger in a wheel and turn it just to dial a number. At least, that's what they did in the movies. A cord wrapped in metal going to the…I don't know what you call it. The part you hold up to your ear and your mouth. I pick it up.

It hums.

I just stand there, holding it. It keeps humming, like those old phones are supposed to.

No way.

I put my finger in the hole for "9." Twirl the dial—there's this kinda grinding noise—all the way until my finger hits the little metal bar on the edge. Take my finger out, and the wheel clacks its way back to where it was.

"1"

"1" again.

Put it up to my ear. It's ringing. C'mon. C'mon. Pick up.

Rings.

Rings.

Rings.

Rings.

I stand there for a long while, until it just stops.

You have *gotta* be kidding me.

Nothing. Just silence.

I hang the phone back on its metal hook.

Take the phone down. It hums. Dial the numbers again.

C'mon. C'mon.

Same thing.

Hang it up again.

I try my uncle's house number. Nothing happens. No ringing. Stupid thing's broken.

I read the label right over the dial. I'm a dumbass. I dig in my pockets, find a dime. Pick up the phone, drop it in the slot at the top. Dial the number again. He's in Fort Myers, but maybe Mrs. Sullivan's there?

Rings.

Rings.

Rings.

I hang up.

I hear my dime drop down into the part with the little door. I push it open, get my dime back. Drop it in again.

Dial Sam's number.

Rings.

C'mon.

Rings.

Rings.

Please. God, someone—please.

Rings.

I don't hang up. But after a while, it just goes silent. Like it did when I tried 911.

Lean back against the glass, still holding the phone to my ear. Waiting. Waiting for him to answer.

* * *

"Hey, what's up?" Sam asked the girl who had just walked in. Looked like she was early twenties. Strawberry blond, freckles, blue eyes a little darker than mine. Her mouth and nose were a little wide, her eyebrows a little bushy, but she was pretty, just not in a cheerleader/supermodel way. She looked natural.

"Mom wanted me to come get you," she said.

"Crap." He looked at his phone. "You're early. Josh doesn't come in for another twenty minutes. I can't leave 'til he does."

She sighed, twirling her keychain around her finger. "I'm the only one here," Sam continued.

"Well, text Mom and let her know."

"Can't you?" he said, looking at me. "I have a customer."

"It's cool," I said. "I should probably head out."

"I like your hair," she said. I couldn't tell if she meant it or not. I had dyed the front part purple the day before yesterday.

"You didn't get a chance to listen to this," he said, holding up the April Wine album.

"You know what? I'll just get it. I'm sure it'll be awesome."

"You sure?"

"Yeah. How much is it?"

He rang me up on the cash register. "Fifteen eighty-nine." I glanced over at the girl while I got out my money. She was scrolling on her phone.

"That's my sister, Cynthia."

She didn't look up as she did a half-wave.

"You don't look alike," I said.

She smirked. "That's the nicest thing anyone's ever told me."

"If she knew you better, she wouldn't have bothered." He handed me the plastic bag with the album in it. I went to the door, got my backpack where I left it on the floor. Crouched, started to unzip it. If I was careful, it would just fit without breaking. "I guess I'll see you around school?" he asked.

"Yeah." I zipped my pack, stood up, put it on.

"Hey, do you need a ride?" he asked. Cynthia glared at him.

"Nah, I'm good. I got my bike."

"You mean that red motorcycle there?" Cynthia asked, pointing out the front window. "Cool bike and cool hair. You go, Punk Rock Girl."

Was she trying to make fun of me? I didn't tell her I don't like punk rock. Instead, I said, "See ya, Sam," and left. It was only a million and three degrees outside.

An old man—white, of course; it's Crackerville on this

island—came down the street with a dog. The dog saw me, strained on the leash, tail wagging like mad. Beagle, I think. I crouched, and she got up on her back legs, put both front paws against my knees, started licking my hands.

"Sally! Behave yourself!" The old guy shook his head. "I'm sorry, she just really loves everybody."

"It's okay. I like dogs." Pretty. White coat with big brown patches, some black ones, too. Big, floppy ears. Huge brown eyes. Spots on her legs. "Dogs don't judge you. They just like you no matter who you are. Or what."

"That's true. My name's Roy, by the way."

"I'm Alyx." I stroked Sally's head and her back. "What kind is she?" I leaned over, and she licked my nose, my cheeks, my chin.

"I think she's a mix of Beagle and Basset Hound. She was a stray I picked up on the side of the road last fall. We just came from the groomers." He tugged gently on the leash. "C'mon, Sally, we have to get back home to Mama." Looked up at me. "That's my wife, Amanda. It's our anniversary today. Forty-six years. Our daughter Karen's taking us to dinner."

"Nice," I said. "Bye, Sally." Sweet doggie. I stood up, and they headed down the sidewalk to a black pickup truck parked two spaces in front of my bike.

I took the keys from my jeans pocket, got my helmet from where I had left it between the handlebars. Got on and started up the bike. All the way to my uncle's house, I thought about Sally and Sam and his sister and the way-cool record store.

This new place might be all right after all.

* * *

Sitting on the newspapers on the floor of the phone booth, back against the glass. Elbows on my knees. Head in my hands. Outside, the wind goes *skkrriiiiiiiiiiiiiiiiiiiiiiiiiiiiiiiiii* for a second or two, and then it's gone.

The sun still hasn't moved.

Nothing.

Nothing.

I look up, at the phone, hanging there on its hook.

Nothing.

Nothing.

Then it rings.

I don't move. What? Who?

It rings again.

I scramble to my feet, yank the phone off the hook, hold it to my ear. "Hello? Hello?"

Nothing. No, that's not true. Someone's there. I can hear them. I can *feel* them.

"Sam? Sam, is that you?" Stupid. Why would it be Sam? Why would it be anyone who knows me? They don't know where I am. *I* don't know where I am.

"Hello?" I ask. "Hello? Please, whoever it is, say something. Please, help me. Please."

"Sam. Mine. My own." A raspy whisper, like her throat's full of gunk. "I do like my sweet, sweet Sammy."

"Who is this?" But I know.

"I'm bringing a basket to Ōth." She says that last bit like the word for a promise. "Something sweet for him, too. And should I bring him a girl? If you come along, I will."

She hangs up.

"No! No!"

The dial tone's hum.

I hang up the phone. Stand by it. Wait for it.

Wait.

Nothing.

Nothing.

Track 5. No One Like You

I know I'm dreaming, cuz I'm back on the train. Except in the dream, I'm not me, I'm Sam, but not really. I look like him, but inside, it's me.

Sam's sitting in a chair. He—I—can't look left or right, can't turn my head—Sam's head, really—but somehow, in that dream sorta way, I know that there are lots of other chairs, rows of them, and that they're all full, though I can't see anyone else.

Sam's hands are stuck to the armrest. I want to move them, but I can't. There's something sticky cementing them down, and I wonder if it's like the goo that the basket in the other car was made with. Sam's feet are stuck to the floor, and something—the sticky stuff—is all over Sam's neck and mouth, so he can't turn his head and he can't talk. I don't like it; Sam doesn't like it, either. I feel him try to rock back and forth, side to side in his chair. I feel him trying to talk, straining to open his mouth. But he can't.

I don't like not being able to move. And I can't see well through his eyes: everything's blurry. Something hazy, like a big plastic tarp, or gauze or some not quite sheer fabric, is a few inches from Sam's face.

The train's going fast. Through his seat, I can feel the wheels thump, thump, thump. All around, over the *klggklggklggklggklgg* of the train, I hear the other passengers. Groaning, sighing, puffing, moaning. Somehow, I know that they can't move, can't talk, either. That they're stuck to their chairs, too.

Footsteps. A shape—hunched, huge hooked nose—leans over him. Smells like wet, rotting garbage, like dog crap. It's her. I know it is. A jagged yellow fingernail pokes through the hazy thing that's in front of Sam. Bent, knobby finger, wriggling around, widening the hole. Then it slides out, and I feel Sam panting, trying to jerk away, heart drumming in his chest. Or is that me?

An eye, peeking through the hole at him. Silver where it should be brown or blue or green.

"There's my boy." She sounds like her throat's full of gunk.

I feel his eyes open wide, not blinking. He doesn't dare close them. I just want to look away.

Her eye, gone, a flash of her wrinkled, dirty cheek. Then the pointed tip of her tongue slowly slides through the hole. Waggles up and down. It's gray, like a piece of meat left out too long, and there are little lumps here and there, and there's something small and white—is that a tooth?—sticking to the underside of it.

Something burning in Sam's throat. I taste his barf as he fights it down.

Her tongue slides out. The eye comes back.

"Would you like, sweet Sammy?"

Something like a laugh—and then the silver eye squinches. Presses up against the hazy thing—it has to be some kinda tarp. Stares right at Sam. Stares right at me.

"Who's there?" she whispers. "Is that you, little girl?"

Oh, God, she sees me. I don't know how, but she does. I try to scream and Sam tries, too, but I can't, I can't, my mouth won't open, it won't. I can't scream, I can't breathe, can't move, I can't I can't I—

I jerk awake, chest heaving. I'm laying on the floor of the telephone booth, my pack beside me. I must have fallen asleep, but I'm okay. I'm okay. It was just a dream. Just a dream.

Just outside the phone booth, a little black cat, not much more than a kitten. Thin, its tail a bit too long for its body, huge yellow eyes, round irises. It sees me, opens its mouth, but nothing more than a squeak comes out.

I sit up, reach out, steady myself on the cold, damp glass sides. Takes me a minute—everything aches—but I stand. Slide open the door. The cat freezes.

"It's okay, kitty. I won't hurt you." Slip back down to the floor. Unzip my backpack. Nothing for a starving cat in there. Unless....

I get out the sandwich baggie of Goldfish crackers, pour them into my hand. Hold them out. "Do you want some? Come here, kitty. Have some."

She—I've decided the cat's a she—bounds toward me, into the phone booth, climbs into my lap and starts gobbling down the Goldfish, purring real loud.

I ease the door shut with my foot and stroke her head, her neck, her back as she eats, and she purrs louder. It's all the food I have, but I don't care. I cuddle her for a while until we both fall asleep.

* * *

When I wake up again, the cat's gone, which is impossible, cuz the door's still shut, and she couldn't have opened it. Maybe I dreamed her, that she wasn't real?

Look down at my shirt, covered in black hair. Okay, so she really was here. Start brushing myself off. I guess she must of woken me up at some point and I let her out and went back to sleep and forgot all about it.

The newspapers on the floor. Most of them are old, yellowing, ripped. One's familiar.

THE KENT ISLAND BAY TIMES. It comes every Wednesday; when it rains, it's in a clear, green cellophane sleeve. On my way back from school, I always put the bike in neutral and stop where Uncle Tony's really long driveway meets the road. I get the paper out of its blue plastic box, glance at the front, fold it, stuff it in my jacket, put the bike in gear again.

Usually, it's stories about who volunteered where, or what new housing development they're building, or what road they're fixing before summer, when all the *lemmings*, like Uncle Tony calls them, drive across the Bay Bridge and Kent Island on their way either to or from Ocean City, a couple hours down Route 50. Sometimes, there'll be photos of kids from high school in an important football game, or a lacrosse tournament, or wrestling, or some bullshit like that. Every so often, a big car accident. But not this time.

On the front page, it's me and Sam, our yearbook photos, him in a tux, me in that stupid white drape that they make all the girls wear. The headline above, in big letters going all the way across the page: KI Teens Missing After Motorcycle Crash.

The paper's dated April 10, a week after that witch took Sam. It says that cuz how smashed up my bike was, Sheriff Hoffman thinks that we were speeding, lost control, hit a tree. It says they found blood at the scene, but they don't know what happened to us next, where we are. A shot of the bike, in pieces. My helmet, the visor shattered where she bit it. But no railroad tracks. Nothing in the article about them, either. And—

Something looming outside the booth.

Pale. Gray. Naked. Not much taller than me. It stands on two split feet with no toes. Something forked squirms, wiggles as it dangles from its crotch. Claws at the end of long arms—five, six, seven of them?—sprouting from its shoulders, its chest, its back. Flat face, a row of jagged points hanging down where its mouth should be, and right above them, in the middle of its face, three red slits, like cuts.

Shit shit shit shit shit oh my God oh Jesus what the hell is that what am I gonna do no way out of here I'm trapped it's gonna get me kill me eat me!

It stares at me, its slits sort of pulsing, getting thicker, then thinner. It shambles closer, presses its forehead against the booth. I press my feet against the bottom of the door, like that's not going to stop it from shoving the door open—or just breaking the glass and yanking me out with all its freaky arms.

The knife's in my boot. All I gotta do is pull my knee toward me, reach, get it out. But if I move, what will it do? Maybe it doesn't really see me, at least not well. Maybe it's actually blind, and it doesn't know I'm here, maybe it heard me or smelled me or—

It turns and stamps off.

I wait for a long time—how long, I don't know—before I move again, finally getting my knife in case it comes back. The monster.

A monster. Like, a for-real monster, out of a movie. Not the same one as back in the bathroom, and not that crazy old bitch who took Sam. No, another one.

That's un-frickin'-possible. All of this is. It's crazy. Just—

It's crazy, or *I'm crazy*?

Like I don't know the answer to that.

I unzip my pack, dig around for my amber pill bottle. Open it, shake out white triangles. Lamotrigine, 100 milligrams each, from Walgreens. Generic for Lamictal. Mood stabilizer. The label says *can cause drowsiness*. TAKING THIS MEDICINE ALONE OR WITH ALCOHOL MAY LESSEN YOUR ABILITY TO DRIVE OR PERFORM HAZARDOUS TASKS. Nothing about losing your mind and hallucinating monsters.

Seventeen of them. I pour all but one of them back in, take the one with a sip of water, like I'm supposed to every day. The label says I have two refills left. Not sure how that's gonna work out.

I put the pills back in the bottle, close up my pack. Get up, look around. Nothing out there. Slip out of the booth, and run before there can be anything.

* * *

I shouldn't have come.

I should have waited, stayed by the bike until the cops got there. Then I could have told them what had happened, and I could have come with them when they stopped the train and found Sam. And then we could have gone home. If I had done that, I wouldn't be wherever I am. I wouldn't be hurt and lost and alone. I wouldn't be wondering where to go, how to find him.

But I had to do something. I couldn't just let him go. Let her just take him. So, I had to come.

Damn, it's cold.

The ground is rockier now, not as much sand or pebbles. Lots and lots of boulders, each about as big as Sally the Beagle: black stones, with holes and pits in them. It's not as flat as it was, either. It's more uneven, little rises and ridges and dips and depressions. Not as many of the weird gray weeds; now there are lots of thin grass shooting up here and there, none of it taller than my calf, none having any color. Lots of trash still.

I have to crap so bad. There's nothing around that looks like a restroom, and even if there was, I wouldn't go in. Who the hell knows what might be there. So I find a particularly big rock—it's almost as tall as I am—pull down my pants, lean against it, and squat.

So gross, and my ass is so cold. I pee, too, then wipe with the last of the napkins from my backpack. I just leave it all on the ground, like I'm some kinda savage. What else am I supposed to do? Could bury it, I guess. No way I'm gonna do that without a shovel. And it better have a long handle.

Thank God for hand sanitizer.

As I walk away, I check again what I have in my pack. Mascara, pads, Midol—maybe I don't have to hurt all over. Dumbass. Should have thought of this earlier. I get two pills, use a small sip from my water bottle to wash them down. I'm really damn thirsty. Make myself stop after a big swig. Just a little bit left.

I'm hungry, too, but still okay with letting the cat have my Goldfish. I saw once on TV that if you're lost in the middle of nowhere, you're supposed to stay in one place until someone rescues you. But with nothing to eat and not much to drink, I don't see that working out. I saw on another show that you're supposed to walk downhill until you get to a stream or river, and then you're supposed to follow it, because sooner or later, you'll find people. Except there's no water anywhere. So I just keep walking. Which sucks.

To stop thinking about how cold I am, and how hungry and thirsty I am, and how everywhere on me is either bruised or cut or both, I start paying attention to the trash I walk by.

Shreds of old newspapers.

Cigarette butts.

Empty cans. Some of them ripped open, some of them rusty. Some both.

Bits of glass. Sometimes bottles, most of them cracked or partly broken.

Dirty scraps of clothes.

Old shoes. Just one at a time, never a pair.

A smashed vinyl record. Nothing left of the label, so I don't know what it was. Nothing good, I hope.

Metal or plastic broken bits of parts from machines. I don't know what kind. One of them looks like….

I squat, pick it up. It's a black metal right-hand glove, the middle finger broken off at the knuckle, wires sticking out of it. Not as big as that gauntlet-thing the purple bad guy had in that Avengers movie, more sleeker, and no funky jewels on it. But sorta like that. I turn it over. On the underneath of each finger, a groove with a thin metal thing in it.

Slip my hand into the glove and try to close my hand. The glove's stiff and doesn't want to. Wiggle my fingers, arch my palm. The metal things in the grooves ooze out slow, like they've been stuck for a long time. Curved blades, like claws. Two of them are chipped here and there. None of them are sharp; I try them with my thumb.

Okay, it's kinda cool, but it's still junk, and no damn use to me. I pull it off, drop it, stand up and keep going.

Lots of plastic bags, most of them ripped.

More papers. More clothes. More broken machinery.

A big hunk of a billboard, laying face down on the ground. I don't bother flipping it over to see what, if anything, it still says.

Another can, dented, part of the label scratched off, but still sealed. I—

I stop. Crouch down next to it. Pick it up, turn it over. HORMEL CHILI WITH BEANS, it says.

No way.

I look around. Nothing and no one coming—should be safe. I sit down, on the ground—it's cold—cross my legs. Hold the can and study it. Stomach's growling.

So, how do I get this open?

Wish I had one of those Swiss-army knives, with all the special attachments, like a can opener. My uncle keeps one in his pocket all the time. Says you never know when you might need it. Tell me about it. I take my knife out of my boot. It's just one short blade, and definitely not as useful, but what the hell, I bought it at a gas station last year.

For a while, I poke at the can with my knife, along the top, then the bottom, then the part where it's dented. Try to pry or cut or mess with it, something to get it open. Nothing.

I turn it over and over in my hands. BEST BEFORE FEB 17 1999, it says on the bottom. Doesn't stuff in cans stay good forever? Whatever. First, I have to get it open.

Put it on the ground. Get a rock, one almost as big as my fist. Hold the can tight. Hit it. Nothing. Again. Nothing. Keep beating on it, harder now.

C'mon.

C'mon.

Rock slips off the can, scrapes my knuckles, God DAMN it, it hurts! Stop, let go. Bleeding. Suck my fingers for a second, then shake, shake, shake my hand, shake it off. Hurts. Damn it. Ow ow ow

Take the can again. Hold the rock down. Beat the can against the rock. Again. Again.

C'mon.

C'mon.

Me banging on the can is the only sound. I stop, breathing hard. Echoes of the rock and the can; wonder if anyone else hears that. Look around. No one. Nothing.

Check the can. Scuffed in a lot of places. Label almost all gone. Still doesn't look like it's going to open. Have to try something else, because this bashing it thing isn't working. Think. Think.

Okay, how do they even put stuff in cans? Because if I know that, then maybe I can figure out how to get it open.

So, cans. They make them in factories, with machines. They take metal and wrap around itself and that makes the sides. And then they take another piece of metal and what?—weld it?—to make the bottom. Or maybe they make the sides and the bottom all out of one piece, like you make a clay pot on a wheel in art class. I don't know.

But however they do it, the can's gotta be open so they can put in the food, and *then* they put the top on, like a lid. And that's where a can opener does what it does. So that's its weakest point. That's where it's most likely to open.

Not much light—the sun still hasn't gone up or down. I hold up the can, look real close at it. Inside where the lid meets the side of the can, there's a little tear. Not much. But maybe just enough.

I look at my knife. I could use that little tear, try again to poke a hole in the lid. But I'm worried that the tip or the blade will snap. I squeeze the can so hard, my hands hurt. It squishes a little, not much. The tear gets a smidge longer.

I try squeezing, letting go, squeezing, letting go, and the tear gets a little longer—not much—each time. But it's killing my hands; after a while, I have to stop. I'm just not strong enough to keep doing this.

My stomach growls again. This better be some damn good chili if I get this open. Not *if*, just *when*. Stay positive.

Tap the top of the can against the rock while I think about it. It goes *dtt dtt dtt dtt*.

I could try bashing it on the rock again, but even if I get it open, it'd just spill all over the ground. I need to open it slowly, somehow. But how? Maybe...

Maybe I could *grind* it? So that if it opens, it wouldn't just spray out everywhere?

I turn the can over, rub the top on the rock. Rub rub rub rub rub rub rub rub. Stop. Check it out. The top's worn down some, the tear is bigger, and it wasn't that hard to do. I think this might work.

Rub rub rub rub rub rub rub rub. Now the rock's getting a little wet. Stop. Look at it again. The tear's much bigger. Stick the end of my knife in it. Bend up, gently. Squeeze the can, pry it up some more with the blade. Keep doing it.

I get most of the lid off. I don't have a spoon, so I use my fingers. The chili's cold and tastes funny, a little metallic—maybe shavings from the can fell in it. It's salty, so I finish my water. I don't care. It's good. I'm good. Yay, me.

* * *

I take the rock with me: it's flat and smooth on one side, and it'll be perfect for doing this trick again if I have to, but I hope I don't. For a second, I have a stupid thought where I feel guilty just leaving the empty can where I found it, because littering's bad, but then I remind myself of all the other trash laying around. Where did all this junk come from, anyway?

I'm walking along, not full, but feeling better. Still wish I had more to drink. Gatorade—that yellow kind, cuz all the other flavors are nasty—that'd be good. Or Vanilla Coke. Damn, I love me some Vanilla Coke. And none of that diet crap, either.

Ahead, the air ripples like it does just above asphalt when it's really hot. A gust of wind—*ooouuuuuu ooouuuuuuu ooooooooo UUUU-UUoooo*. My feet start twitching, jerking, shaking, and as soon as I notice that, then it's my ankles, my knees, both my legs. I fall on my butt, bang my head on a rock—ow ow ow ow damn it! All of me's juking, and for a second, I think it's a seizure. Then I see the pebbles nearby bouncing, watch the broken end of a bottle jump jump jump.

In the distance, where the air keeps rippling, something huge and black comes rumbling, growling out of the ground, spitting rocks out of its way: one as big as my head crashes down by me. I squinch tight into a ball, cover my ears, but it doesn't help; the crushing and smashing rattles through me. Sand and gravel and little pieces of glass and other trash rain on me. It goes on for a long time—how long, I don't know.

Then everything goes still. Rumbles echoing, fading, dying. I lie there for a while, straining to breathe. When I can, I roll over, sit up. Stand.

Out there, where the air was rippling but isn't anymore, where there had been just rocks and garbage, is a ship—an enormous one—laying on its side.

Track 6. In The Dark

I wade through water up to my ankles; my boots squish into newly-made mud. The ship has these holes in it and a big jagged part where I guess something tore it in two, and water's gushing out of it. I reach down, scoop some up, slurp it out of my hand. Cold and clean and good. I stoop, suck double handfuls of it while the ground—more thirsty than I am—soaks up the rest. Now I really feel like a savage.

I drink what I can until it oozes away. Gray goo clumps on my boots, tugs at them, tries to pull them off. Slowly, I high-knee it toward the ship, looking around as I go. This can't be happening, can't be real, but there it is: a big-ass boat, big as a building, right in front of me, doing the beached-whale thing.

Tiny rocks, thousands—maybe actual millions of them—laying where they spilled out the ship's split middle. I crouch, eyes up, watching for anything moving. Pluck a few from the ground. They're round, mostly, each about as big as a blueberry. Glistening, dark, almost black because they're wet, but as I roll them around in my hand, they start drying quick, and they fade to dull grayish-red.

I drop them, stand, brushing off my hands. Millions of worthless rocks. Why would a ship be carrying these? They make crunching *kssh kssh kssh* noises under my boots as I go closer.

The ship's hull is dingy white along the top and halfway down, faded red after that, including the bottom. The back part of the boat is partway on one side; the front sticks out of the ground at an angle.

There's this gap between the front part and the back, big enough to drive a bunch of cars through side-by-side. At least you could, if it weren't for all the tiny rocks flooding it. I tramp my way over the rocks until I get to the gash that goes from one side of the ship to the other.

Laying there mostly tipped over, the ship's as tall as a tree. Inside, so far as I can see, it's just a huge empty space, where I guess they kept all those little stones. I get out my flashlight. Yep, more rocks in there, and the cargo hold—I'm guessing that's it—goes back even farther than I thought.

I want to climb inside and see what's there, but I'm afraid of what I might find.

Ships need people to run them, and people need food. And some ships take long trips, so the food is probably in cans. And damn, if I'm not hungry.

But when a wrecked ship just shoots out of the ground in the middle of a desert that shouldn't even be here...well, there's no telling what freaky-ass shit might happen next. And my day does not need to include being chased by zombie sailors.

I walk around the back end of the boat, thinking about it. There's this thin layer of greenish-yellow slime on the outside of the hull, and under that, the metal's nubby, not smooth. I don't really know why—don't like minerals and stuff settle on shipwrecks? I thought I saw that once in a photo of the Titanic, the real one, not the movie. If that's so, then this boat sank a long time ago.

Not a sound except my boots squishing in the mud. As I go around the back part, I come to the top of it, the deck and the cabins or whatnot, where the crew used to go inside. There were windows here, but the glass is gone, only empty black spaces left.

I could crawl through one, if I want to. Poke around, maybe find something to eat, or something useful—who knows, maybe a phone that works? Then get the hell out of there. Wouldn't be hard.

But if there's something *bad*...

I stand there, looking at the big empty rectangle that used to be a window. The frame is wet and slimy; there aren't even any pieces of glass left. Just a hole as big as I am. The sun's on the other side of the boat, so it's dark here, and the hole is even darker: I can't see anything inside it.

Could use my flashlight again. Makes sense. But if there are zombies or something even worse on this ship, it'd be right here, right inside the cabins. And my flashlight would show it—them?—right where I am.

Assuming, of course, it—they?—hasn't already heard me crunching around the pebbles or slopping through the mud. Assuming it—they?—isn't watching me right now, from one of these windows.

I take my flashlight out of my pocket. I don't turn it on. Squeeze it tight in my fist, at my side.

Come on. Come on. Just do it.

I don't.

Come on. Nothing to be afraid of.

Yeah: *right*. Been to a bathroom lately?

A low *ooooooooo* and I jerk the way it came and I swear I almost pee myself until I realize it's just the stupid wind. Damn it! "I hate this, I hate this, I *hate* this," I whisper.

Fine. Whatever. I lift the flashlight up to my shoulder, thumb the button.

A room, and the rusty remains of old chairs and stools, tangled on the floor near the window. A tabletop, warped and swollen by water, in one corner; I don't know what happened to its legs. I go a little closer. Looks like this was where people used to eat. Not like a big dining room or anything, but just someplace they could sit down for a meal.

Which means that the kitchen—*galley*, right? Isn't that what it's called? The galley must be right next to it. And if it is, which it should be, then there might be food in there.

Or rats.

Rats? In a sunken ship? Don't be stupid. There won't be any rats. They need air to breathe, and this thing has been underwater for a crapload of a long time.

Okay, then, crabs. Like the kind they have in the Bay, except bigger. Sam said they eat anything.

This Wasted Land

Yeah, well Sam eats crabs, just like everybody else on the Eastern Shore, and if he does, I can, too. So yeah, bring on some giant, girl-eating crabs.

I pull out my knife, hold it in front of me, flashlight in the other hand. All right. We're doing this. We're doing this right *now*.

Bend, duck my head, step through the window frame. The floor's tilted and muddy and really slippery. Lots of shells the size of my fingernails, white and brown stripes, here and there on the walls, the floor, the ceiling, what's left of the furniture. Are those barnacles? I don't know. Smells wet and damp in here, but it's not too bad.

At the other end of the room, a wooden door with a round window, glass still in it. Just like something you'd see in a movie, except the door is slimy black and most of it's covered with hundreds of those tiny striped shells. I pull the handle, but it doesn't open. Not locked: the wood's just soaked up too much water. I shine the flashlight through the window, glance in. Looks like a kitchen, but I don't take too long a look, in case there's something else.

I hold still, listen. Nothing. Okay. Okay.

I put the flashlight in my teeth. Hold the knife with one hand. Take the handle with the other. It's so cold. Wish I had my gloves.

Let's do this.

I work the handle, pull on the door. Nothing. I tug on it, harder. It doesn't budge. Damn it.

Slip the knife back into the sheath in my boot. Keep the flashlight in my teeth, though I hate that metal taste. Both hands on the handle this time, jerk my whole body. The door moves a little. Okay, that's something.

Lean back with all my weight, yank, yank, yank, yank. Puffing around the flashlight, can hardly see anything as the light flashes back, forth, back, forth. Hands raw, shoulders burning—keep at it, keep fighting.

The door shudders open. A really gross smell, like rotten fish. Something inside goes *ssssschffff*.

Flick off the flashlight, throw myself against the wall behind the door, hand over my mouth to stifle my panting. Stupid. Like whatever's in there isn't going to find me hiding here. It's so dark, I actually can't see anything: it's the same black with my eyes open or shut. I slide the knife out, hold it ready.

Nothing.

Nothing.

Then *irrrrrr* and something lightly nudges my boot.

Hold my breath, move my foot over. Gently set my heel down so it doesn't make any noise.

Something quietly goes *irrrrrr* and nudges my boot again. Presses against it.

I feel the knife shaking. I don't move, don't do anything. Just wait for whatever it is to do whatever it's going to do.

Nothing except resting against my foot. Not moving, not making a sound.

Because—I finally realize—it's only the door. It had slowly swung open and made that creaking *irrrrrr* noise and bumped against my foot. And when I moved my foot, it swung open some more and touched my boot again. I'm such a dumbass.

I'm halfway to getting on my feet when it occurs to me that first, there was another noise, one that went *sssssschffff*. And it came from inside the galley. No big deal: probably some kitchen stuff shifting around. I go around the door, switch on the flashlight again.

The dead man has no eyes and no legs.

He's slopped onto the floor, laying there like a wet sack. That's what the noise was: him sliding because of how the ship's tipped. Everything that's left of him—his arms, his neck, his bald head, his shirt and jacket—are stained mud brown, with streaks of gray-black. Below the elbows, each arm is just two thick bones. He has no hands, no hair, no nose, no lips. One ear is still there. But there's nothing of him below the waist.

I stagger back a few steps, but I keep the light on him. I've never seen a dead body before, not a real one. It's nothing like TV and the movies. He's not some actor laying there, maybe with their eyes half-open, maybe with some fake blood on them, trying not to let their chest move when they breathe. He doesn't even look like a person anymore: he's just...some *thing*, a gross hunk of soggy rotten meat.

Seeing him makes me wonder what happened to the ship. Was there a storm? Did it run aground? Did—I don't know—one of the engines blow up or something? It must have been quick, because he was here in the galley when it happened. No chance to get to a life boat, or even to put on one of those vests that's supposed to save you from drowning.

It's narrow here, I can't go around the body, so I step waaaay over it, making sure not to touch it. Him. Whatever. I open the cabinets. Not much on the shelves, just a few cans, the labels soaked off a long time ago. I stuff them in my pack, figure I'll take my chances on what's in them.

Rummage through the drawers. Nothing much left there, either, just a few forks and spoons. I take some. Another cabinet, down low: a couple metal bowls, paint faded or chipped off in places. Might need one. Different drawers: ladles and spatulas and rotten wooden cooking spoons. Look for a can opener, either an electric one, or the old kind that you do by hand, like my mom got from the dollar store. Don't find one. Of course not. That would be helpful.

No water, but a few glass bottles of pop still aren't broken. They're smaller than the ones from machines. No batteries I could take for my flashlight. Everything else I can think of taking is either missing, too waterlogged, or no use to me. Not that I have much more room in my pack, but that's a good problem. I wrestle with the zipper, sling it on my back; a lot heavier now.

Stop by the window I came through and listen for a minute. Nothing but the wind. Peek outside without the flashlight, so it doesn't give me away. Nothing moving. I duck back outside, scamper down from the deck.

Back to the middle of the ship, crunching across the millions of tiny rocks. All right, not *millions,* but lots. Still don't know what they're for. I look up at the front half, coming up out of the ground like that tower—isn't it in France?—that they built crooked. Or maybe they built it right and then it started leaning over later. I don't remember.

At the other end of the boat, way in the air, is the room where they drove it from: the *bridge?* Don't know if that's what it's really called, or if there's anything useful in there. But there might be, and from up there, maybe I could see where I need to go. Spot the train tracks or...I don't know. Something.

It'd be an awfully steep climb, but I can get onto the deck no problem, and on the side, there's a guardrail I can use. Hard to do with this heavy backpack, but I'm not about leaving it here. Don't want anyone or anything taking off with it. Besides, I might need something from it once I get up there.

Well, if I'm going to do it, I'd better just do it now. I go over, put one boot on the slanted deck, grab the metal guardrail with both hands. It's cold as all hell, just like the door handle was—damn it, why did I have to lose my gloves? Maybe there'll be a pair up there on the bridge. Doubt it.

I put my other foot on the deck, just ahead of the first one, strain my arms and shoulders to hold on. This is hard already. I take another step, pull myself along the rail, do it again, breathing hard. Glance over my shoulder: I'm maybe six feet off the ground. Look up and ahead. The deck of the ship is like the world's longest waterslide. There's no way I can do this.

I keep doing it, anyway, hand over hand, one foot after the other. I have to stop and rest every few yards, leaning on the rail, hoping it hasn't rusted out somewhere and that it won't break under me. Once, I slip, fall to my knees, lose my grip, slide back a few feet before I can stop myself, grab the rail, stand up again.

About halfway up—I'm maybe a hundred or so feet in the air—it occurs to me that if the ship tips over, crashes down for whatever reason, I'm absolutely for-real going to die.

I stop, look around. I'm so high up, all the tiny rocks the boat was carrying look like one huge, solid wave of reddish-gray that splashed out of the middle. I feel wobbly, dizzy—I'm panting. Clench my fists around the guardrail and lean back, away from the edge, close my eyes. "Okay," I whisper. "Okay. Don't look. Let's just not do that again."

Stay there for a few minutes, hanging on, struggling to slow down my breathing and the pounding in my chest. You don't have to do this, I remind myself. You can just go back down. This is not worth it.

I keep climbing anyway. It takes forever.

When I reach the bridge or the pilot house or whatever it's called, I wrench open the door and duck inside, collapse against the nearest wall. The floor's wet—I feel it through my jeans—but I don't care. I just sit there, eyes shut, head in my hands, elbows on my knees.

After a while, I'm not so tired. I get up, look around. I'm expecting to find what you see in movies: a big wooden wheel coming out of the floor, with spokes and handles all around it. Instead, there's just a little metal one, like the steering wheel on a car, and it's at a console with some dinky video screens not much bigger than my hands. Lots of knobs and dials and buttons and those old-time gauges with needles.

There are a couple other consoles like that, too, with more ancient stuff. Swivel chairs that've rolled to the back of the room. Broken coffee mugs, a couple ashtrays—people smoked in here? Gross. Not much else. Nothing useful.

I go back outside, careful not to slip, careful not to get too close to the rail. I thought it would be windy up here, like that time my dad took us to the top of the Empire State Building, but it isn't. Still just as cold, though.

I must be about two hundred feet up, maybe more. Sam said—and I've found out by riding around—that the Eastern Shore is flat. From here, I should be able to see where the hell I am. At the very least, all I have to do is find the bridges, both of them, over the Chesapeake Bay. They're big and they're right next to each other, so it should be easy to spot them. Then I can climb down and start walking that way. I'll come to a road, then maybe a gas station or a McDonald's or something. Then I can call the cops and bring them back here, and we'll get Sam, wherever he is. And I hope the cops shoot that bitch right through the head.

I puff out a couple quick, deep breaths. It's gonna be okay. It's gonna be okay. Just walk out to the edge there, and take the rail. Don't let go of it. Take it slow and don't look down, just look out. See what you can see. Find the bridges. It'll only take a minute.

Half-crouched to keep my balance, I take a step. Another. Keep my eyes on my hand as I reach for the rail. It's rusty—some of it crumbles as I grasp it, but underneath, it's solid. I hold tight. Take another step. Breathe. Breathe. It's okay. I look up, look out.

Nothing but gray desert and rocks and hills. Look right. The same. Left. The same. Slowly, so I don't fall, I turn halfway, still holding on to the rail. The same.

No farms. No trees. No buildings. No towns. No cars. No roads. No rivers. No Bay. No bridges.

I turn back around, look to my right again at the pale sun below me, still where it's always been, just over the horizon. Not moving. Not rising. Not setting. No matter how long I've been here.

I don't want to think it, haven't thought about it, maybe on purpose. Maybe I've known for a while, just didn't want to come out and admit it, say it to myself. Because it's insane, actually for-real insane. But it's the only thing that makes sense.

I'm not on the Eastern Shore. I'm not in Maryland. I'm not even anywhere on Earth.

I'm somewhere else. And I'm alone.

Track 7. Plush

It's cold, leaning up against the outside of the pilot house, but I don't think about it. I'm trying not to think of anything. I'm just sketching. That's all.

I have my pad and a pencil from my pack. I'm drawing the rail, the same rail where I was standing a little while ago, when I saw…when I saw that I wasn't where I thought I was. The rail's not that interesting, but it's all I can see from here, and I need to draw something. I need to make some sense of it, make some sense of…everything.

My stomach hurts and my hands shake, just a little. It's not from being hungry. It's not from being cold.

Don't think. Just sketch.

This usually works. When I'm bummed, when I can't sleep, when I can't care about anything, I sketch. If school sucks, or someone pisses me off, or if Mom and I are bitching at each other, I sketch. It's hard to think about whatever crap's bothering me when I'm focused on what I'm drawing. Almost always. But not now.

Because I'm on a wrecked ship with a dead guy, and I'm stuck in the middle of a desert on another world, and my boyfriend's been kidnapped by a for-real monster. So, yeah, I can't think why drawing stupid pictures isn't doing anything for me.

Keep at it. Go over the top rail again—needs to be straighter. Better. Some lines and shading for the rusted parts. How am I going to do the corrosion on the bolts where it attaches to the deck? Don't know. Just keep moving the pencil. Don't stop. Don't think about it. Just—

I drop the pencil, try to grab it, fail. It bounces off my shoe, tumbles end-over-end, then rolls rolls rolls all the way down the long, slanted deck, until I can't see it anymore, just hear it going *rrrr rrrr rrrr* and then *pnng* when it hits something and then *rrrr* again as it rolls some more until it goes *pnng* again, and then I guess it stops.

Stupid. Goddamn stupid. It's gone and I'll probably never find it again, and I liked that one. It fit really well into my hand. My hands—

My hands are shaking real bad.

Reach for my backpack next to me. Careful not to knock it over and have stuff spill out—don't want to lose anything else. Dig around in the front pocket for another pencil. It's dull. Get the sharpener and twirl, twirl, stop, take it out, look at it. Put it back in, twirl it some more, take it out, look at it. Little bit more. There. That'll do. Put the sharpener back. Start sketching again.

What am I going to do? Like, what the actual hell am I supposed to do?

Don't think about it—not right now. Just draw. Keep drawing. Don't stop. Don't think about it. Think about something else. Think about better things.

* * *

A soft pretzel with big hunks of salt stuck to it. A can of Vanilla Coke. A little warm, but okay. That's what I was having for lunch.

The cafeteria is a huge open space with the food line at one end, vending machines along the sides, tables and chairs in the middle, and another open space at the other end that goes to the auditorium and the gym and the rest of the school. There are stairs up to the second floor there, too. That's where I was, again, sitting almost all the way at the top. Earbuds in, Stone Temple Pilots playing on my phone. Not much into Nineties, but I like them, cuz they kick ass.

Most people eat lunch at the tables. Some of them go outside, but you have to be honor roll to do that. I don't know how anyone's supposed to know that you aren't—what are the administrators going to do: ask for your report card? But nobody eats on the stairs, which is why I do. The first few times, some people would look at me funny. I just stared back at them until they stopped. It's been a few weeks; now nobody looks.

I had my pad in my lap, sketching with one hand, pretzel in the other. I usually drew whatever was around: the pop machine—they call it *soda* in Maryland (except the one here at school only sells bottled water)—or one of the tables, maybe a chair. This time, it was the top of the Coke can, next to me on the step. I do things, not people. People are too hard.

I took another bite, looked around. Sam was in his usual spot, not too far away, sitting at a table with some other guys. They were playing cards. He saw me and waved. I just went back to my pad. He's said, "Hi" to me whenever we pass each other in the halls, and sometimes I've said "Hi" back, but we don't have any classes together.

I kept sketching, STP kept playing. I finished my pretzel, and the drawing was turning out okay. Then I heard the hall tone go off, meaning that lunch was over, and as I was slipping my pad into my backpack, Sam came partway up the stairs. He smiled, acted like he didn't notice my gross blue eyes.

I plucked out my earbuds. "What's up?" I asked.

"Not much. What're you drawing?"

"Nothing. Just doodling."

"Cool! Can I see?"

"No, it's not that good." I stood up, put on my pack.

"Okay." Paused a second, like he was trying to remember a line he'd rehearsed. "Hey, you know, you don't have to sit up here all by yourself. You can come eat with me and my friends. They're cool. I mean, most of them are band geeks, but they're all right."

"I like sitting by myself."

"You might like this," he said, holding up a card. It wasn't the usual, like the kind with spades and hearts and numbers and kings. The top half of it was a drawing of this dude with a tiger's head, and he was holding a sword. Under the picture was written something about an opponent and targeting and cards and a graveyard, and it didn't make any sense to me.

"What's this?"

"It's Magic."

"Whaddya mean, 'magic?'"

"It's a fantasy game called Magic: The Gathering. You use these cards to play, and they all have cool artwork. It's what we do at lunch every day. I thought you might like to see."

I turned the card over; on the back was the game's logo. Turned it over again, read it closer. The card said that the tiger-guy was a "rakshasa," whatever that is. Some kinda monster, I guess. It **was** pretty cool.

"It reminded me of that record you bought at the store," he said. "You know, the cover."

"Yeah," I said. "It is like that."

"You can keep the card, if you want."

"You don't need it for your game?"

"No, I have two more just like it."

"Okay." I slipped it into the back pocket of my jeans.

"So I guess you like it."

"Yeah, I guess I do."

He smiled a little. "Okay, cool. See you around. I gotta get to class. English."

"Yeah, I'm headed for Ms. Jung's. You weren't kidding about her."

"Told you." He headed down the stairs.

I headed up. "Thanks for the card," I said, over my shoulder.

"See you at lunch tomorrow?"

I didn't answer.

* * *

I'm cold—more than usual—and my butt hurts, and my sketch of the rail looks like crap. I close my pad, put it and my pencil in my pack, wriggle it onto my back. Slowly, I stand up, making sure I don't fall and slide all the way down the deck and maybe kill myself at the bottom on all those stupid little rocks.

I got nothing. Complete nothing. Everything I know, everyone I've ever known, they're all gone. It's like they died, only they didn't. I did, in a way.

Maybe that's it. Maybe I *did* die. I don't know when—maybe when she dropped the bike on me and I blacked out for a second? Or thought I blacked out? Except for real, I died, and this is Hell or something? That's why it's nasty and cold and spooky here, and there are monsters, and I can't find any way back to where I was before?

Bullshit. If I'm dead, how come I don't feel any different? How come I still have to sleep and eat and take a crap? If I jump off that rail, I bet I won't get back up off the ground when I hit. *Then* I'd be dead. But I'm not dead now, and this...this doesn't seem much like Hell.

Listen to me. Like I even believe in Hell.

So, where am I then, and how am I going to get back?

I make myself go to the rail again, but I don't look down, because if I do, I swear I might puke or pass out or both. Breathe. Breathe. Just pretend I'm on a balcony somewhere, looking out at the view. That's all. Just looking at the view.

The same gray desert, nothing moving, not a sound except a quiet little bit of wind way far off.

Okay. Okay. Keep looking. I don't know for what. Just keep looking, keep breathing, stay chill.

Gray rocks and hills and the ground's all uneven, and the only thing that grows are those gray weeds and grass and some shrubs here and there. That's it. That's all there is.

No, that's not all.

There's a long, straight black line going left to right, as far as I can see in either direction. It doesn't move, and it doesn't go up and down hills, it just looks like it either goes past them or right through them—I can't tell. What is it? Is a road or something, or—

Or…wait.

It's the train tracks.

I grab the rail tighter, lean over it—not too far. Squinch my eyes. No, really: that's the tracks. I look down the line as far as I can. I don't see the train station or the bathrooms, but that's it. That's them. I'm sure of it.

If I can get down from here without breaking my ass, if I can head that way and not get turned around or go in the wrong direction, then I can get to those tracks. And then I can follow them—I don't know which way, I'll figure it out. And then maybe I can find Sam.

And then…then we'll work on getting back home.

Let's do this.

* * *

I thought that tiger stripes would be easy, but they're not. Lots of cartoonists draw them as really long triangles, but they're not actually like that: they taper. Some are long, some are short, some are thin, some are thick, some split in two, some split and then come back together to make like a teardrop in the middle of the stripe.

I had my phone in one hand, Googling tiger stripes, comparing them to the ones on Sam's card, in my other hand. The artist did a pretty good job. No, I wasn't paying any attention to Ms. Jung and her boring-ass linear equations. Like I gave a crap.

Everybody else in class was either freshmen or sophomores; I was the only senior in here, and when I walked in on the first day, all the others stared at me. Maybe it was because of the purple in my hair. Anyway, I sat in the back so they couldn't look at me. I'd been sitting there ever since.

Even though Kent Island is Whitey McWhite-White Land, there are some other Asians here, most of them girls. One or two of them are Korean. I know at least one's Vietnamese. The rest are Chinese—one's like honest to God off the boat, doesn't speak a lot of English—and they're the only ones who hang with each other. None of them—not even the other Koreans—like me. Me, the blue-eyed mongrel.

I clicked off my phone, looked up. Ms. Jung and her uber-short lesbian haircut, still going over the worksheets she had given us yesterday. I had done maybe half the problems. I got out my sketch pad, put it on my lap. What did Sam say this dude on the card was? A *rakshoso* or something? Couldn't be too hard to do, right?

I worked on it with pencil for a while. The snout was coming out too long, and the ears weren't round enough. It looked more like he had the head of a fox or a coyote than a tiger. Damn.

Then Ms. Jung snatched the card off the desk. "Hey!" I said.

"You can have this back later." She started walking up the aisle. Everyone was looking at me again.

"You can't take that! It's not mine!" Not true, but, like I cared.

"So, if we know that the slope is 5, then—"

My chair fell over *bkkkk* against the floor as I stood. "Bitch, give me that card back!"

She stopped, turned around. Put one hand on her fat hip, held up the card with the other one. "You can have it back after detention."

I came up the aisle. "Give me that!"

"Perhaps you'd like to go to the office."

Somebody snickered. "Girlfriend's crazy," someone else muttered.

"Give me that back, or I'll kick your fat ass!"

"I don't appreciate threats, Alexandra, but two can play at that." She pinched the card with both hands, like she was going to tear it.

"Don't call me that! And give me that goddamn card, cunt!"

She ripped it in two. "Take your seat, Miss Williams."

"'Take your seat,'" someone sneered, in that bitchy, mocking tone of voice.

"Yeah, 'take your seat.'" Shane Myers, who lets everyone know that he plays varsity football with all the other assholes, even though he's only a sophomore.

I turned around, looked at my chair laying there on the floor. People giggled, especially that stupid blonde whore from the dance team.

I'll take my goddamn seat. That was the last thing that went through my head before I picked up my chair and threw it at Ms. Jung.

I don't remember what happened right after that. I was so mad that I blanked. It's happened before. The next thing I was aware of was laying on the carpet of the principal's office with my hands zip-tied behind me, and Ginger Cop was standing over me. Everyone calls her that because of her hair: she's the sheriff's deputy who's assigned to the school. She helped me get up and into a chair, and she talked to me the whole time we waited for my uncle to show up. Don't recall anything she said.

They let my uncle know that I was suspended for a week, but that Ms. Jung wasn't going to press charges. They took the zip ties off me and let him take me home. When we got in the car, he asked, "Did you really hit her with a chair?"

"They told me I missed." Clipped Shane Myers, though, on the forehead, made him bleed. At least there was that.

* * *

There's what's left of an old truck up ahead. It's rusted and grimy, and the windows are broken. The tires are scraps of rubber hanging on the wheels. I go over, take a closer look. The headlights are just bowls, empty except for a little bit of wire poking out from the back. The tailgate's down, and the rear end kinda sags. There's nothing in the cab: the seats and the dash and the floor and everything just aren't there anymore. Most of the paint's gone, but what's left—not much—under the salt and ash and rust is robin's egg blue.

I don't know how it got here. All I know is that my feet and my legs hurt. I test out the tailgate—the chains hold. I slide myself onto it to rest for a while.

I get a bottle of pop from my backpack. It's glass, and there's enough left of the soggy label for me to see it's RC Cola. Never heard of it. And the real pain in the ass is that the cap isn't twist-off. There's a bottle opener on my keychain, but my keys are in the ignition of what's left of my bike. Which is in a whole different world from here.

I mess with it for a while, try to twist it off anyway, but it just hurts my hands. So now what do I do? Maybe I could tap the top of it on a rock until the glass breaks. Yeah, and then I can get little pieces of glass in my pop and cut my mouth all up while I'm drinking it; that'd be a good move, dumbass. Think of something else.

I go through my pack, put stuff beside me on the tailgate. I take out the bowl, take out the cans, take out the forks and spoons. Take out my sketch pad and that book for school. Look at what's left in there. Nothing helpful. Except for the Midol, which I'd love to take, but I can't, because I don't have anything to swallow it with, because I can't get the damn bottle open.

Think. Think.

I look at the bottle cap. It has all these little grooves on the sides. What if....

I take out my knife, start poking underneath the cap, along one of the grooves. Try to push it up, bend it out a little. I get one to go, but it's hard, cuz the tip of my knife is fat. I need something skinnier, something like—

I get one of the forks, stick it under there, start prying. Much easier. I go one by one, around the cap. When I do the last one, the cap comes right off.

On the outside of the bottle, under where the cap was, is this black mold or something. I wipe it off on the end of my shirt. I'm thirsty and I just want to chug it, but I'm worried it's gonna be horrible, or make me puke, or poison me. I sniff it. Smells okay, just like Coke. I take a sip.

It's flat, and kinda thick, but it's really sweeter than what I usually drink. I swish it around, careful not to spill any, and then I take another sip. Not bad. Pretty good, actually. I'm almost done guzzling it before I remember that I wanted to take some Midol, so I stop myself and do.

I use my fork to open another one, and then I take down the flat rock from my pack and do my trick with it to open a can I got from the ship. Chicken noodle soup. There's no way to way to heat it up, so I just drink it out of the can and use a spoon to scrape out the noodles. It's salty and gooey and tastes like tin foil, but I eat it anyway, and then I wash it down with the rest of the other pop.

I toss the can away; it goes *dhkkk* when it hits. I throw one of the bottles at a big rock, and it misses—*tggg!*—and rolls into the trash under a gray bush. I throw the other and it hits the rock and explodes like *KSSH!*, and that's one of my favorite sounds. I like the noise glass makes when it breaks. Once, I told my mom that, and she said there was something wrong with me.

Pelican.

I yank my blade out of my boot, look right, left, right again, juke off the tailgate, keep looking around for whoever said that, whatever the hell that's supposed to mean.

Pelican.

There, in front of me, in the midst of some ripped up papers and some other cans and what looks like part of the rear brake of the truck. Has it been there the whole time? A little stuffed animal, a bird, but not meant to look like a real one. It's got tufts of fake blue and green and yellow hair sticking up all over it, and huge googly eyes like Cookie Monster's, and itty bitty wings, and big, flappy orange feet. And its yellow beak opens and shuts when it says, again, harsh, and kinda buzzy:

Pelican.

Okay. Okay. Just a toy with a voicebox, like that Furby my dad gave me. God, I hated that thing. If you so much as touched it just the slightest bit, it'd wake up and start talking and never shut up. I slide back onto the tailgate, clip my knife to the inside of my boot.

The stuffed bird is dirty and worn in spots, and looks like maybe a dog or some critter chewed on it. Not, I'm pretty sure, that it was anything but butt-ugly when it was new at the dollar store. Who would buy this for a kid?

Pelican.

That's already annoying. Aren't pelicans those big sea birds with the pouch under their beak? And they like, live in Florida, or something? Yeah, that's them. Is that what this is supposed to look like? Cuz it doesn't. Not at all.

Maybe it's one of those interactive toys that if you talk to it, it will say something different each time, like it's supposed to be answering you. I tell it, "You're not a pelican."

Pelican.

"Shut up, willya?"

Pelican.

Nope. I start packing my things: cans at the bottom, then my sketch pad, then the bowl, then the rest of the stuff I took out. I gotta get to those train tracks; I can't sit around here and—

It's a dumb idea, but I go with it anyway. "Hey!" I point the way I think the tracks are. "Is that how I get to—"

Pelican.

Of course. What was I expecting? "You're a stupid-ass toy, and you're gross-looking, too. No wonder you're out here in the middle of nowhere. Nobody would want to play with you."

It takes a step toward me. I jerk back all the way onto the tailgate, pulling up my feet so it can't get at me. It cocks its head and the little black discs in its eyes roll around crazily for a few seconds until they settle. Holy crap, it moves. Who was the twisted freak who thought THIS would be something they should make for little kids?

Pelican. Its wings flap, and it opens its beak as wide as it can, and it goes, *AH AH AH AH AH* like it's trying to caw like a crow or laugh or both, but doesn't know how to do either. Then it croaks:

> *I've got Sammy!*
>
> *I've got Sammy!*
>
> *I've got Sammy! Sammy! Sammy!*

I jump over the side of the truck and run like hell, its *AH AH AH AH AH AH* chasing me.

Track 8. Sixes and Sevens

I don't have my phone, and the sun still doesn't move, so I have no idea how long I've been walking. Has it been an hour, or three? More than that? Maybe only 45 minutes? I think I'm still going the right way. I keep turning around to look for the front part of that big ship, to make sure I'm not headed in the wrong direction. The ship gets smaller and smaller, so I guess I've gone a long way. You'd think I would have gotten to the train tracks by now.

* * *

When I got back from my week's "vacation," it was like nothing had ever happened. Ms. Jung didn't say anything about it, and neither did anyone else in class. But everyone in school knew. Every time I was in the halls, or in the bathroom, or walked into any of my other classes, people stared. Before, I hadn't ever raised my hand, but sometimes the teachers would call on me anyway; they didn't, anymore. Sometimes I'd hear somebody mutter something, but whenever I looked up to see who it was, then—*then*—no one would look at me.

Every Wednesday, they excused me from the second half of Algebra to go one of the quiet rooms at the media center and see Ms. Custer, a counselor. She was young and pretty, with long brown hair. She spoke really softly, and always asked me how my day was going. I'd tell her it was okay. Then she'd want to know how I was feeling, and I'd say "okay" again. Then she'd ask if there was anything I wanted to talk about, and I'd always say "no," but eventually, even if it took most of our 45 minutes, she'd get me say something.

I thought they wouldn't let me eat lunch on the steps anymore, but they did, so I did. Sam and his friends were always in their usual spot, playing their game. "Magic," he said it was called. Whenever I came into the cafeteria, Sam would look over and wave, but I just looked down. The first time I got back to class, I had asked Ms. Jung about the card Sam gave me, but instead of answering me, she had just called on that hockey kid Nathan to answer a problem. Then I asked her after class, but she said the principal had it, and that I should talk to him. No way.

So, school went on like that, for…I don't know. Weeks. September became October, and it finally stopped being so hot all the time. Other than that, nothing had changed. Not really. Until one day at lunch, Sam came back up the stairs.

I didn't see him, at first. I was sketching from memory—one of those tall heron birds that I'd seen in the creek behind my uncle's house—and listening to tunes on my earbuds. I don't know how long he'd been standing there until I noticed something in front of me moving, and then I looked up, shut off my phone.

"Hey," he said.

"Hey. What's up?"

"Nothing, just…uh…."

I looked past him. His friends were sitting at their table, looking at us. "You're not gaming?" I asked.

He looked back at them, back to me. "No, not now. Dylan's got the new Space Marine codex on his iPad, and he won't shut up about it."

I refused to do that girl thing where you're just supposed to nod your head even though you don't have a damn clue what he's talking about. "Whattya want?"

"I just…you know. Hadn't talked to you for a while. You know, uh…"

"Since I threw a chair at Ms. Jung."

"Yeah, that was, like, really—"

"I don't wanna talk about it." I picked my earbuds off my sketch pad. The bird wasn't turning out good.

"No, that was—that was pretty badass." He smiles. "Nobody's

ever done anything like that, and she totally deserves it. Everybody hates her. You know she once made Allison Denny cry, right there in class? I mean, Allison, of all people."

No idea who Allison is. "Well, I got in a crapload of trouble for it, so let's just…" I scrolled my phone, trying to start my music again.

"Hey, do you want to go to Homecoming with me?"

I looked up at him. The hell?

"The dance, not the game. You don't like football."

"You just walked up here to ask me to Homecoming?"

"Yeah."

"Why?"

"I want to go. I thought maybe you might want to go, too."

"Why would you want to go with me?"

"Because you're cool, and I like you."

"No."

He frowned. "Huh?"

"No, I don't want to go to Homecoming with you."

"Why not?"

"Dancing is bullshit."

"We don't have to dance. I mean, it's not like I'm good at it anyway. We could just hang out."

"No." I put in my earbuds, cranked my tunes.

I watched him shrug and mouth, "Okay." Then he went back down the steps, back to his friends. They looked at him, looked at me, looked at him again. He shook his head. One of them laughed.

Homecoming. You have *got* to be kidding me.

* * *

I step over the train tracks and onto one of the wooden ties between them. The ship's tiny from here, not even as big as my thumb when I hold it up next to it. I'm finally here, and finally, something's going right.

I'm tired, and my feet hurt again, and I'm thirsty, too, but I only stop long enough to look left, right, left. I don't know which way the train went, which way to go. For all I know, they're not even the same tracks. Screw it. I go right, start walking in the middle, between the rusty metal rails.

I haven't gone very far when the wind starts howling, gusting, swirling up dust and gravel. I wish I had a hood or a scarf or something to keep it off my face, out of my eyes, my hair. It's hard to see more than a few feet in front of me. I put my head down, keep walking, following the tracks.

* * *

"Who was that boy I saw with you in the cafeteria?" Ms. Custer asked me.

Huh? "When was that?"

"Yesterday, I think. You were sitting on the stairs, and he was talking to you."

"I didn't talk to anyone yesterday," I told her.

"Maybe it was Monday, then." She leaned forward, hands together on one knee, like always. Waited.

"That was Sam."

"Sam Henshaw?"

"No, Sam Patterson."

"How long have you known him?"

I sighed, leaned back in my chair. "Longer than anybody else here."

"Oh? How so?"

"I met him over the summer, right after I moved."

This Wasted Land

"At a neighbor's, or a cookout, or a pool party?"

"No, my uncle doesn't really have neighbors. His house is all the way at the end of this long driveway."

"Out somewhere else?"

"At the record store, where he works."

"It's a cool place, isn't it?"

"Yeah. I like it."

"Do you have classes together?"

"No, we don't. He's really smart."

"I'm not sure what that has to do with anything."

"He's in all, like, the brain classes, and I'm…I'm not."

"What did he want to talk about?"

"He was asking me if I was okay."

She didn't say anything. Waited.

"You know, with Ms. Jung and all."

She nodded. "I wonder why he did that."

"He likes me."

"So, he's a friend."

"I don't know."

"Why, 'I don't know?'"

"I don't have any friends."

"There's no one in any of your classes that you talk to?"

"No."

"Not even just to ask about homework, or if you need some paper or a pen?"

"No."

"Do people ever try to talk to you?"

"Not anymore."

"Since what happened with Ms. Jung?"

"Yeah."

"How about before then?"

"Sometimes."

"Once or twice?"

"Yeah."

"Maybe more than that?"

"I don't know. Not really."

"That's interesting. Why do you suppose that is?"

"I don't know."

She waited.

Waited.

Finally, she said, "Well, it's a new school for you. It might take some time."

I shook my head.

"You don't think so."

"It's not…no."

"Maybe it can be challenging for you to make friends."

Thought about it.

Nodded.

"Which is okay," she told me. "It isn't anything bad. It just means it might take a little longer before it happens. But I think it will."

I shrugged.

"But going back to what you said about not having friends. Sam likes you. Sam talks to you. Wouldn't you say Sam's a friend? Or could be?"

Thought about it. Nodded.

This Wasted Land

* * *

The wind keeps blowing for...a while. I don't know how long. Then as quick as it came, it's gone. It doesn't slow down, it just *stops*, all at once, and everything's dead quiet again. At least it's not hard to see anymore.

There's something on the tracks, way out there. Out of habit, I raise my hand over my eyes to look before I remember that I don't need to, because there's hardly any sun. Jesus, I'm stupid.

Up ahead, I can't tell how far away, just sitting there, not moving, is the end of a train. That train.

Sam.

I run, high knees, elbows flying, as fast as I can. Sam. I don't know for sure that it's the train. I don't know what I'm going to do if she's there. I don't think about any of that. I just run. Run. When my legs and chest burn and it hurts to breathe and I can't run anymore, I slow down, jog, walk, whatever, but I keep going until I can breathe again, and then I run some more.

I get to the last car of the train. It's the one I climbed up on. This is it. I found it. I found it. Sam.

"Sam!" I yell. I go around to the side of the car, by the big sliding door. "Sam!" I pull my knife from my boot, take out my flashlight. Look inside.

No basket made from wire and garbage and animal bones. No crazy old bitch. No Sam.

I look left, right. Start walking alongside the train, calling his name, looking in each car.

Empty. Empty. Empty.

No. No, no, no. "Sam!"

Something behind me goes *chkk*. I whip around, knife ready. A few yards from my face, the black hole of a pistol. Behind that, some tall, dirty, skinny dude with long hair and a big, bushy beard.

"You move, and I'll blow your damn head off," he says.

Track 9. Atomic Punk

No one's ever pointed a gun at me before. They don't freak me out: my dad had a few in the house, and once or twice, he took me to the firing range when he practiced. I know how they work and what they do. So I'm not scared, exactly, but it's not a good feeling to know that some guy, a stranger, can kill me if he feels like it—and there's nothing I can do about it.

"Drop the knife."

I should do what he says. It makes sense. But I shake my head. "No."

"Drop it!"

"No." I'm squeezing the handle so hard, my fist is trembling. "You want to shoot me, you go ahead. But I'm not letting you perv on me."

"I'm not gonna touch you, and I don't want to shoot you. Say the alphabet."

"What?"

"Say the damn alphabet."

"A, B, C, D, E, F, G, H, I, J, K—"

"Good enough. Sing the 'Itsy Bitsy Spider' song."

"What, you mean: 'The itsy bitsy spider went up the waterspout?'" Hard to do the hand thing while I got a death grip on the knife, but I do the best I can, pretending it's a spider, like little kids do. I learned it from them at school, cuz Mom didn't know it, growing up in Korea. "'Down came the rain and washed the spider out. Out came—'"

"What's the capital of the United States?"

"Washington, D.C."

"Whose face is on the three-dollar bill?"

The hell? Everyone knows there are one-dollar bills and five-dollar bills, and Uncle Tony used to send me two-dollar bills, ten of them at a time, in a card for my birthday or Christmas. I shake my head. "There isn't a three-dollar bill."

"Okay," he says. "You might really be what you look like."

"What else would I be?"

"You can't trust anything. If you've been here more than five minutes, you know what I'm talking about."

A monster. Like, an actual monster, not a figure of speech. "I'm a girl, that's all. A real girl. I'm not anything scary. My name's Alyx, and I'm looking for my boyfriend, Sam. He was on this train."

He glances at it, back at me real quick before I can move or do something else he might not like. "Where'd you come from?"

"What do you mean? Like where was I born?"

"No, stupid, like how'd you get here? Were you on the train, too?"

"Yeah, I was. But I'm not stupid."

"We'll see about that. Where'd you catch the train?"

"In Maryland. I got on in Maryland. You know where that is?"

"Of course I do. Where's your boyfriend?"

"You won't believe me."

"I already don't."

Fine. "This crazy old bitch grabbed him and pulled him on the train." His eyes narrow—I knew he wouldn't buy it. "We were going home on my bike, and we stopped at a crossing when this train was going by, and she came out of nowhere." With the hand that doesn't have the knife, I pull up my jacket's sleeve, show him the bruises. "She kicked my ass pretty bad, and then she took him on the train."

"She beat up both of you?"

"My boyfriend..." Christ, now I gotta tell him that Sam has CP. There's no way he's going to believe this. "He's got a medical condition."

The dude thinks about that for a few seconds. Then he wags the end of the pistol at a spot past my shoulder, behind me. "You go sit over there." He jerks his head back but doesn't take his eyes off me. "I'm gonna sit over here, and put this down," he says, tipping the gun away from me, "and we're gonna talk. Okay?"

What choice do I have? "Okay."

He keeps the gun on me as we back up. I go slowly, so I don't stumble, until I get to the edge of a train car. I glance over my shoulder. It has an open sliding door, like the one I was in before. I put the knife on the edge of the car's steel floor, and without turning around, I hop, plant both palms on the edge, push up with my arms, wiggle the rest of the way onto it. Pick up the knife again and let my feet dangle over the side.

He sits down on a big rock. Thumbs the safety on the pistol, but keeps it cocked. It's a .45, I think, and all black metal—my dad had one like this. He rests it on his lap, but keeps his hand on it. I don't put down the knife.

"Tell me what this 'crazy old bitch' of yours looked like," he says.

"Well, she was..." How am I going to tell him? It's insane. "She looked like she was a hundred years old. Her face was all wrinkled and she had this long, stringy white hair, and she was wearing this gray dress that was all ripped up. She had these nasty, sharp fingernails, and..." I stop. Blow my hair out of my face. Here goes. "And her teeth were...her teeth were broken glass. For real."

He doesn't say anything.

"I know it sounds like I'm making this up, but—"

"What color were her eyes?"

The hell? Why would he ask me that? Unless....

"You've seen her, haven't you?" I ask him.

This Wasted Land

He just stares at me. I stare back. His hair and his beard are shot full of gray. His clothes are torn and dirty, and they don't match: dark green pants with stains all over them; red-and-black flannel shirt; and under that, a yellowy t-shirt with a ripped collar. Long, dingy-brown coat that's way too big, sorta wrapped around him as best it can. Brown work boots, one of the soles starting to peel off at the toes. He looks like he's homeless. Which, I guess, he is.

"You tell me," I say. "What color are her eyes?"

"I asked you first."

"They're silver, all right? Do you believe me, now?"

"I suppose." He wipes his face with the back of his hand, rests it again on the gun. I set the knife next to me.

"When did you see her?" I ask.

"Only once, a long time ago."

"What happened?"

"None of your damn business."

"Okay, you're rude."

He shrugs. "I've been called worse." Puts the pistol in a pocket of his coat, crosses his arms. "So, you think this old woman still has your boyfriend."

"Yeah." I'm not gonna say anything about the freaky dream I had of Sam riding on the train, with the hazy tarp or whatever it was over him.

"And you're chasing after her to get him back."

"Yeah."

"You know where she is?"

"I was hoping she was still on this train, with Sam."

"They're not. No one's here. I checked it out."

I look around. Sigh. "Then, no, I don't know where she is."

"I guess you're S.O.L."

"What's that mean?"

"'Shit Outta Luck.'" The asshole smiles like it's funny. He's missing some teeth—what a surprise.

"Thanks," I tell him. "That's very helpful."

"If she beat you up before, how are you supposed to get your boyfriend back from her?" He points at my knife, there on the edge of the car floor. "Scare her with that?"

"I guess. I don't know."

"'I don't know.' That's the smartest thing you've said, so far. I bet you don't know 'jack' or 'squat.'"

What's that supposed to mean? "If I have to, I'll stab her." Never mind, *if I have to*. I want to. A lot of times. I've been in fights, and gotten pissed at people and thrown things at them, but I've never wanted to actually end someone before. But now I do. I really think I could. "I'll kill her."

"Yeah, I'm sure she sweats you." Slowly—it looks like it hurts—he starts to stand up. I grab the knife, jump to my feet there at the edge of the car. The other side's open; I can run through and hop down if he tries to—

He starts walking off. Where's he going? A dark gray shape nearby—another big rock? No. A beat-up duffel bag. He hefts it over his shoulder. Looks back at me. "I'm gonna go find that 'crazy old bitch' of yours and put a few bullets through her, because I owe her. Hopefully, she still has your boyfriend. Want to come along and find out?"

"I'm not going anywhere with you."

"Okay." He turns around, starts walking again.

I keep my eyes on him, keep holding the knife. He doesn't stop or look back or say anything else.

The only sound in the world is gravel crunching under his boots as he gets smaller. After a while, I can't hear him anymore.

A while after that, and he's just a dot. Good. He was creepy and dirty and nasty.

This Wasted Land

But he said he was going to kill her. What did she do to him?

Maybe he didn't mean it. Maybe he was just lying to get me to go with him, to fool me into thinking he was trying to help me get Sam back, until I let my guard down. Nice try, pal.

The black dot that's him is almost gone into the gloom.

Maybe he's crazy. How's he supposed to find her, out here in nowhere? And even if he did, sure, he's got a gun, but can he really kill her? She's not human. She's a monster. Maybe she can't be killed. Maybe she'll kill him.

Maybe she'll kill Sam.

He keeps walking, and I just sit here. But I can't do that. I have to find Sam. If he's not here on the train—if that guy was telling the truth—then where is he? How am I going to find him?

Damn.

That guy. I don't even know his name.

Damn, damn, damn, damn, damn.

I put the knife away, jump down from the train. Start running.

Run.

Run.

He hears me coming, turns. I stop, not too close. I'm gasping, but I think I can still take off if I have to. I lean over, hands on my thighs, catching my breath, but I make sure to watch him.

"I...I...changed...my mind."

"I got eyes," he says, not smiling. Jerk.

"How...are you...going...to find her?"

"I'm working on that." He starts walking again.

I walk alongside him, out of arm's reach, but he smells as bad as he looks. Sweat and dirt and foul breath: when was the last time he brushed his teeth? He *reeks*. I give him some more space.

"I'm Alyx. Like the boy's name, but with a 'y' instead of an 'e.'"

He doesn't say anything.

"What's yours?"

"Mike. Like the girl's name, but with a 'k' instead of a 'q.'"

"Why are you making fun of me?"

"It's a funny name. Your folks spelled it like that?"

"No, it's just a nickname."

"Yeah? From who?"

"Nobody. I came up with it."

"How come with a 'y'?"

"I don't know. Just to be different."

"Guess that's why part of your hair's purple, too. Just to be different."

"Yeah."

"Uh huh. Just like all the other kids at the mall."

"At least I don't look like a homeless person. Or smell like one."

"Yeah, you do. To both. Because you are."

"No, I'm not."

"You are now."

"I have a home."

"Not here, you don't."

"Where is 'here?' What is this place?"

"You know what a sink trap is?"

"No."

"It's that bend in the pipe under the sink in your bathroom. If you're washing your hands and the soap makes your ring slip off your finger, it'll wind up there instead of going all the way down to the sewer. Then you can just take off that piece of pipe and get your ring."

"Okay."

"Well, this is the world's sink trap. All kinds of stuff ends up stuck here. You'd be surprised."

I think about the train station, and the phone booth, and the ship. "I've already seen some really weird things."

"Yeah, me too. Everything except a huge pile of missing socks from the dryer. But you know what's the difference between this place and a sink trap?"

"What?"

"There's no piece of pipe that anyone can open."

"So, nobody can get us out?"

"Exactly."

Then we're stuck here. Until we die.

Be cool.

"And the monsters?" I ask. "What are they? How can they be real?"

He looks around. Shakes his head.

"How can any of this be happening?" Be cool. Be cool.

It's not working.

"None of this is in any science book," I tell him. "None of this makes any sense! This isn't Mars or Jupiter, so what the hell is up with this? Where the hell are we?"

He just keeps walking.

"Well?"

"Well, what?"

"Say something!"

"How about 'shut up'?"

"What do you mean, 'shut up'? What the hell's wrong with you? How much of a screaming asshole can you be?"

"I'm not the one who's screaming."

"So what if I am?"

"Well, you shouldn't, because the monsters you don't seem to believe in come in all sorts of shapes and sizes and colors, but most of them are drawn to loud noises."

Now I'm the one looking around.

"And if one of them pops up this second to eat your skinny, screeching ass, I'm not going to do jack to save you."

"Nice guy you are."

He stops walking. "You need to get some things straight. First off, I don't give a wet piece of dog crap what you think of me. Second, I don't care if you're torqued out about the fact that you and the boyfriend are stuck here in this shithole. Having a cow about it isn't going to change anything, so you're just going to have to get a grip."

Having a cow about it? Who talks like that?

"Third, if you want to come with me, you gotta shut up and do what I tell you, when I tell you, and don't ask me a lot of stupid questions. I don't have time for your teenybopper bullshit."

"I'm not a 'teenybopper.'" Whatever the hell that is.

"Glad to hear it. And one more thing: I don't like you, and I don't need you. You got all that, Alyx-with-a-'y'?"

"Yeah, I got that." Prick.

"Good." He starts walking again. For a couple seconds, I consider just turning around and heading the other way. But then I think about Sam, and I follow him.

Track 10. Paranoid

We walk for…I don't know how long. Neither of us says anything. The whole time, I'm telling myself that either I'm an idiot for coming with this creepy asswipe, or that I have to go with him because he's my best hope for saving Sam.

It's cold. Everything is gray sand and gravel. Scraggly weeds and bushes, the same color as the ground. Cracked and pitted black rocks. Broken glass and dented cans, paper scraps and shredded cloth, bits of rusted metal or faded plastic. We go up and down and between hills. Sometimes the wind moans and blows dust, and we tuck our heads and close our eyes until it's gone. Clouds swirl and grumble and go dark overhead, but it doesn't rain. And then there's the sun.

"Why does it always look like the sun's going down, but it never does?" I ask.

"What makes you think it's going down?"

I consider that. "Well, maybe it's coming up. But it doesn't get any higher. Or brighter."

"Maybe that's all the high and bright it gets."

"How can that be?" As soon as I ask, I regret it. He's probably going to go off on me again.

He doesn't. "There are places and times when the sun hardly comes up or goes down. Back home, I mean. In our world."

"Yeah?"

"Yeah. In summer, way up north, it's daytime for twenty, twenty-two hours or so. And at the same time, on the other side of the world, in Antarctica, it's dark almost all day."

No way. "Really?"

"Yeah, really. Don't you go to school?"

"Yeah."

"Where?"

"Maryland."

"Don't they teach anything at those schools in Maryland?"

"They do, I just didn't know that. I'm not really good at school."

"I wasn't either, but if you pay attention, you pick up stuff along the way. I've learned more being out of school than all the time I was in it."

I look back at the sun. "It never seems to move."

"It doesn't. But it gets dark. And then it stays dark for a long, long time."

"How long have you been here?"

"It's hard to tell. The whole way we keep track of time is the sun coming up and going down. But if you don't have that, what're you supposed to do?"

I shrug.

"For a while, I counted sleeps," he says. "I decided that every time I slept, that was the end of a day."

"So, how many has it been?"

"I don't know. I stopped keeping track. It wasn't important anymore."

"What number d'you get up to?"

"A couple thousand."

A couple thousand. And there are—what?—three hundred sixty-five days in a year? So that's…. I can't do the math in my head. But it's a lot. Years. "And that was a while ago?"

"Seems like it. Doesn't matter, anyway."

"How'd you survive all this time?"

"How've you?"

I think back to scrounging around in the dark of the ship. "I found stuff. So far, anyway. Cans of food, bottles of pop. It's not much."

"Beats starving to death."

The wind comes by, softer this time, a low *huuuuuuuuuuuuuuu uuuuuuuuuuuuurrrrrhhhh* that only swirls the dust. But it's cold and makes me shiver. "Does where we are—this world, whatever it is—have a name?"

"Not that I know of."

"How'd you get here?"

"Has your boyfriend ever told you that you run your mouth a lot?"

"No. Usually he talks more than me."

"Christ on a stick. You two must be quite the couple."

"He's nice."

"That's nice."

"And he's smart."

"I can't possibly care any less."

"Then why are you helping me find him?"

"I'm not. I'm letting you tag along so that when the next monster tries to eat me, I can push you in front of it and run like hell the other way."

"Ha ha."

"What makes you think I'm joking?"

"You wouldn't really do that."

"Yeah, I would."

"Then why did you tell me? Now I know what your plan is."

"I told you so that you'd think I wouldn't do it, because I told you I would."

"You are the most obnoxious person I have ever met in my life."

"You need to get out more, meet some people." He stops, stares ahead. "Hmmm." I try to see what he's looking at.

"What?" I keep walking.

He looks around—left, right, behind us, left again, right again. Points to something ahead. "Hurry." Starts running that way.

I go after him, but it's hard to keep up: his legs are long, and he's really fast, even carrying that duffel bag full of stuff. Not that I want to get out ahead of him, in case whatever it is turns out to be something bad.

He stops; I do, too. A few yards away, a pond, about the size of a swimming pool. Gray water, of course. How'd he even see it? He pulls out the pistol, keeps looking around as he sorta tiptoes toward the edge of it. "Fill up your water bottle and anything else you got," he says. He drops the duffel bag, digs around in it, takes out some canteens like you see in war movies.

"No way," I tell him. "That's too gross."

"We can filter and boil it later. Right now, shut up and get as much as you can."

I set down my backpack, take my bottle out of the mesh pocket, go to the edge of the water, where Mike's filling up a canteen without looking at it. He has the gun up by his shoulder, eyes scanning. I ask, "What's the deal?"

"Your folks ever let you watch *Mutual of Omaha's Wild Kingdom*?"

"What are you talking about?"

"I'll take that as a 'no.'" He jams the bottom of the canteen into the sand by the pond so that it can stand on its own, then screws the cap on one-handed. "In Africa, watering holes are a good place to get ambushed."

"We're not in Africa." I start filling up my bottle. The water stinks like a mechanic's old garage, where they fix cheap cars.

"I'm going to teach you a new word: 'extrapolate.'" He starts filling up another canteen, glances over at me. "Don't go too close and get your feet wet, or fall in."

"Why? Are there alligators or something in there?" I'm looking at the water to see if anything's moving. Glance down at the bottle. It's almost full, but there's this nasty yellow foam floating at the top.

"If there were, we'd know by now," he says. I pour out most of the foam, then fill the bottle. "Don't let your clothes get wet, because you'll get hypothermia. You know what that is?"

"Yeah, I know what that is. But even if I did, I could make a fire and warm up."

"Make a fire out of what? Besides, in this place, campfires are neon signs that say, 'Eat at Joe's.'"

I finish filling the bottle, put the lid on, stick it in the mesh sleeve of my backpack. Wish I hadn't thrown away those pop bottles, though I don't know how I'd close them. Maybe tap the caps back on, somehow? Doesn't matter.

"That's all you got?" he asks. "One container?" He digs through his bag again. "Here—use this." Hands me a red thermos with Snoopy and Woodstock on the side of it. White cup on top for a lid. I unscrew it, fill the thermos. It makes me feel bad. Some kid used to take this to lunch, and here I am putting disgusting pond water in it.

"Hurry up, willya?" Mr. Sensitive ties up his bag, throws it over his shoulder, stands, still looking around.

"Paranoid much?" I put the thermos in my backpack, start zipping it shut. Then I see them. Eyes.

They float up from deep in the gray water. Hundreds of them, maybe thousands. Some are smaller than my thumbnail. Some are as big as softballs. All of them round and golden yellow and shot through with dark green veins, except the veins wiggle and squirm like worms on the sidewalk after it rains. Each eyes' pupil is a black hourglass.

Alyx, something hisses from the water. *I'm here. I'm here.*

Mike's yelling something—I don't know what. There's nothing

else there, just all those eyes, floating right under the top of the water. I feel Mike grab my backpack, yank me to my feet.

Alyx, help me.

A hand—Sam's hand, I know it is—comes out of the water, then the rest of his arm. It—he—reaches for me. *Alyx, please.*

"Come on!" Mike screams, whips me around to face him. His breath makes me want to actually puke. He grabs the front of my jacket, starts pulling me away from the water. I twist in his grip to look back; Sam's hand still there.

Alyx, come back. Back here. With us.

Mike slaps me, hard, right across the face, and then he picks me up, my feet off the ground, and starts carrying me away from the edge of the pond, and while he's doing that I'm punching and kicking him, "No! Stop it! Let me go! Let me go! He's there he's there it's Sam he needs me!" and then he shoves me and I fall and hit my side and it hurts Sam Sam I have to—

But now Mike's not looking at me, he's staring at the pond, and there's something coming out of the water. It's sorta shaped like a person, but it ripples when it moves, the edges of it sorta fading in and out. It's the same gray as the water and the ground and it has two heads—one's like a man's, except it's smushed on one side, and the other head kinda looks like a cow's, but it has three huge tusks coming down from what should be its jaw—and the fingers of its hands bend backward, and its feet sorta splay out, and it's covered in all those eyes, the same eyes, and they move all over it, never holding still.

Alyx, it whispers. *We want to show you something.*

"Run!" Mike yells. He reaches down and grabs my hand and starts pulling me. Hurts—my ribs hurt—but I get my feet under me, stagger. Mike catches me before I can fall. A whining, buzzing sound as it comes closer.

She doesn't know. Did you? She doesn't have to. But she will.

Then I run, Mike behind me, screaming, yelling at me not to stop, not to look back, not to listen. We run. And run. And run. Until we can't.

This Wasted Land

* * *

"What the hell was that?"

"What do you think, dumbass?" he says.

We're sitting, resting, leaning against the wall of a shallow, dry gully. Every so often, Mike stands halfway up and pokes his head out just high enough to look around. Nothing following us. Nothing moving out there. Just the wind whistling by now and again.

"How did it know my name? How'd it make it look like Sam's arm was coming out of the water? What was it saying? What did that mean? How could it—?"

"There you go again."

"And why'd you hit me?"

"You looked like you were going to lambada with it."

"Why didn't you shoot it?"

"Because if I use all the bullets, I can't go down to the Circle K and pick more, along with a pack of smokes. Next time I tell you to run, just run. It's not that hard a concept."

For what seems to be the hundred-thousandth time, I tell myself that this can't be happening. "So, what do we do now?"

"Keep walking."

"To where?"

"There," he says, pointing.

"What's that way?"

"Lots more desert. But hopefully, your boyfriend."

"And her."

"Yeah, her too."

"Are you really going to kill her?"

He nods.

"You're not just saying that?"

Shakes his head.

"Why? What'd she do to you?"

"None of your business."

"Okay. But I want to help. You know, when you do it."

"I don't need your help. If we find them, you get yourself and your boyfriend the hell out of the way. Grab him and start running. Understand?"

"Where are we supposed to run to?"

"Well, you told me he was smart, so I guess he'll figure something out." He stands, puts his bag over his shoulder. "That's enough sitting around. We gotta go."

"I'm still worn out."

"Aw, poor little Alyx-with-a-'y.' Is you tired cuz you had to run away from the big, bad monster? It's okay. You stay here and take a nappy. Mean Uncle Mikey will go find Witchiepoo, and get Jimmy and his magic flute back for you."

What? "His name's not Jimmy, and—"

"I bet his flute ain't magic, either."

"—he plays trombone! And don't talk to me like I'm a baby!" It hurts, but I haul myself up. You want to go? Fine. We'll go, douche.

I tromp ahead of him. I can't believe I'm stuck with him. And what's the deal with *Jimmy* and a *flute*? I don't understand half the crap he says. Unless—

I look over my shoulder. He's just going along, eyes on the horizon. "You think you're funny. I wouldn't know anything about his 'magic flute,' you perv."

"Daddy will be delighted to hear that."

"Don't talk about my dad."

"Won't say another word."

And he doesn't. I don't, either. We only walk.

* * *

At first, the land is flat and dusty, like gray flour. Nothing growing here. After a while, it starts to get rocky and a little steep, and soon, we're climbing up and down and hills. At the top of a high one, I stop for a second to look around and see if I can see something, anything, but it's just more hills.

Then we come down into this valley, miles long, that's like a huge scrapyard, with what's left of what must be thousands and thousands of smashed-up cars and motorcycles and vans and trucks—pickups and delivery trucks and even tractor-trailers. So many pieces of bent, rusting metal, and twisted and broken plastic, and sheets and tiny bits of broken glass that most of the time, we can't even see the ground. We have to pick our way real slow across it so we don't fall and cut or bash ourselves.

By the time we get off that junk heap, my calves are cramping, and every time I take a step, the bottom of my feet feel like someone's poking them with something sharp. I find a big rock, sit down, take off my backpack. "I'm done. I can't go anymore."

He's a few yards ahead of me, and he doesn't even turn around. Just keeps walking.

"For real, I hurt everywhere, and I'm exhausted"—I don't think I've ever been this tired in my life—"and I can't walk any further, okay?"

He doesn't stop.

"Hey! C'mon!"

Keeps going.

"Don't be such a dick!"

"This isn't a good place to stop," he finally says.

I throw on my pack, get up, hobble after him. He waits for me. "What do you mean?" I ask.

He looks around. "We're way out in the open, too easy to be

spotted. If the wind picks up, or there's a storm, there's no cover. So, yeah, we gotta rest, but we can't just set down here."

I don't like it, but it makes sense. I nod. "Okay. You could have just said so."

"I bet I wouldn't have had to explain this to What's-His-Face. Stan."

"Sam."

"Him, too."

We keep going. I try to ignore how bad it hurts. I try to think about good things, about times with Sam, or when I was little and my mom and dad didn't fight so much—or at least I didn't notice then. Nothing works. Pretty soon, I'm limping, and I wish we would stop.

And then we do. In this empty place, we find a few of what I guess are trees. They're not very tall—not much higher than a basketball hoop—and they're skinny and gray and their scrawny branches droop almost to the ground. They have these leaves, about the size of my hand, and they're sorta irregular shaped, like what's left when you're cutting stuff out of paper. The leaves are gray and there's this greasy, smelly thick goo smeared on them. I think it comes from them.

I duck past the branches, making sure not to let any of those nasty leaves touch me, and I plop down under a tree, rest my back against its trunk. I'm half expecting it to open some eyes and try to eat me, but I'm so tired, I sincerely don't even care anymore.

"You look like crap," Mike says, putting down his bag. "Don't you have any water?"

"Just what we got at the pond."

"You haven't had any of it, have you?"

"No." I'm thirsty, but I'm not *that* thirsty.

He digs in his bag, hands me an old plastic Pepsi bottle full of clean, clear water. "Here." I gulp it down in two big swigs. "Eat something, if you've got it."

Shake my head. "I just wanna sleep."

"Go ahead. I'll wake you up if something comes along and wants to kill us."

I squirm out of my backpack, start ootching down to rest my head against it. It's lumpy and hard, but it's better than no pillow at all. "Don't try anything. I swear, I'll stab you."

"If I was into short hair and no boobs, I'd date your boyfriend. He probably has a better personality."

Like you should talk, I tell him in my head, but it never makes it out of my mouth. I close my eyes, and that's it.

* * *

I dream random stuff that never happened. Waiting in line with Kaitlyn and Nicholas, my little sister and brother (in real life, I'm an only child) to get snow cones (I don't even like them) from a stand on Coney Island (which I've heard about, but never been to). Sitting in English at Kent Island, but it's not my actual class, because the teacher is some guy I've never seen before in real life, not Mrs. Humphreys, but in the dream, he's the regular teacher, not a sub, and he's reading from some book (*The Arithmetic of Life*—what's that supposed to mean?) that's not on the syllabus.

Driving a golf cart across the huge-ass lawn behind my uncle's house. He does have a big house on a lot of land, cuz he's rich, but he doesn't golf, and he doesn't have any of those carts, either.

Walking at night, through the crowds of a big city I've never been to, two guys stopped in the middle of the sidewalk, one of them asking the other about his garden, and if his dog has dug it up.

Then I dream about Sam. I dream I *am* Sam, like before, where it's me on the inside, him on the outside. He's staggering along—gray sand and dust; black weeds; broken black boulders as big as cars—and he can't move his hands. He looks down and I see through his eyes. Wrists wrapped tight with thin gray snakeskin ribbon, coiling and writhing, always moving, made of smoke and bird spit and a woman's beard and the sound a cat makes when it walks—somehow, I know this.

"What do you want?" Sam asks. "Where are we going? Why are you doing this? Who are you?"

Behind him. "What. Where. Why. Who." Sam straining to look over his shoulder. Long tangles of thin, grimy-white hair. Skin of her face like a paper bag crumpled and then unfolded. Staring silver eyes with nothing behind them, like a fish on ice at the store. He looks away, shuts his eyes, stumbles, almost falls. Her nails digging into his jacket's sleeve, catching him, holding him.

"What. Where. Why. Who," she croaks again. He keeps his eyes closed, but I hear and smell her—she's worse than Mike—come around front of him, close, too close. The back of her other hand flicks his cheek, like she's trying to brush something off.

"You." Her voice husky, not raspy, her stench gone. Sam opens his eyes. Her dress is still gray tatters, but now her hair is full, clean, unknotted, and that pure blonde that women who aren't try to dye theirs to, but can never match it. She's not old anymore, and her teeth aren't broken glass. Her skin's smooth, with hundreds, maybe thousands, of tiny tattoos—they sorta look like letters, sorta not—everywhere. But her eyes haven't changed from silver, and her face, it's not quite right. Too smooth, too hard. Rigid, like plastic.

He shows her the ribbon around his wrists. "Let me go. I never did anything to you. I just want to go home. Please."

Her hands—nails straight, no longer claws—take his. Her eyes bore into Sam's—will she see me again, like she did in the other dream? Something from his inside jacket pocket buzzes, chimes *bpppppppppp*. Buzzes again, sings again, *bpppppppppp*. His phone's alarm, for school, probably.

She reaches deep into his pocket; I feel her fumbling against his belly. "No! No!" he tells her, struggles. She slams him to the ground, harder than my dad ever shoved me, knocks the air out of him. He lies there, gasping—I feel him not being able to breathe, and it's like I'm choking, too. She takes his phone, stares at it, her face blank, as it buzzes and chirps, buzzes and chirps until the alarm shuts off.

Slowly, his air comes back, he can breathe again; so can I. He holds his sides, rocks back and forth, back and forth in the dust.

"Oh God, oh God, oh God. God, that hurt. God, that hurt."

"An accident," she says, turning the phone over in her hand. Sam and the basket made of bones and trash are by her feet. "That's all."

"That wasn't an accident! You did that on purpose!"

"No." She shows him the screen. "She had one of these."

"Who? Alyx? You mean Alyx?"

"No, not her. The other. I don't know her. She had one, like this, and it had you."

He gets on his knees, then up on his feet. "You saw my picture on someone's phone?"

"An accident. I wasn't looking for her, or you. But then I saw. An accident brings you someone, and everything changes."

"What are you talking about?"

Crouching, she takes the basket with one hand, still holding the phone in the other. A third arm splits off the one with the phone, grabs Sam by his throat. She leans over him. Whispers, "I'll give him his feed, but not you. You're mine. My own."

"I'm not yours! Let me go!—"

Dizzying dark for a second, like he—I?—am blacking out or having a seizure or something, and now there's this terrible feeling like I've sorta come apart, like all the atoms of my body have spread out and now I'm falling through the sand and dirt and rock under me, falling into the blackness below, and I'll never stop, and when he opens eyes again, we're somewhere else in this waste land, somewhere far away, I know.

He sags to his knees, pukes again and again until there's nothing left, just burning slime trickling out of his mouth and nose.

Finally looks up. Near him, a huge rock coming out of the ground, like a finger pointing to the gray sky. Carvings and writing, big and small, all over it, too many to read.

She drops his phone to the sand next to him. He tries to take it, but she yanks him onto his feet, pushes him ahead of her, toward the rock.

"We'll walk the rest of the way, so he won't know," she tells him. "No one will."

And then Mike shakes me awake.

Track 11. Toys in the Attic

"Do you ever get weird dreams?" I ask him.

"No," Mike says.

"I do. Ever since I got here."

Mike just grunts. What's that supposed to mean?

We're walking again, but it's okay, because I slept and ate, and my feet and my legs don't hurt. Well, not much. Before he went to sleep, Mike let me borrow this filter he said he made, and he showed me how to use it to make the pond water clean. The filter's a two-liter plastic pop bottle that he had cut a hole in the bottom of, and filled it with sand and gravel and stuff. I didn't think it was gonna work, but I held it over the empty Pepsi bottle, the one that had water in it, that he gave me before I went to sleep, and I poured the pond water from the Snoopy thermos through it.

It took a long time, but it worked. Mike had said that I should boil the water first, but I was too thirsty, and besides, wasn't he the one that was all about no campfires? The water tasted like dirt, but at least it didn't smell anymore, and I didn't barf when I drank it. I took another of my happy pills. I don't know how much good they're doing, but I promised Uncle Tony I would, and anyway, taking them helps me keep track of days. So, it's been two now.

While Mike slept, I opened up a can: lima beans, which are gross, but I ate 'em. I was still hungry, but while I was trying to rub open another can with my flat a rock, I heard this freaky shrieking, like tinfoil being ripped apart, so I stopped and lay down on the ground as flat as I could until it stopped, and then I just stayed there for a while. When I finally lifted my head high enough to look around, nothing was out there. But after that, I wasn't hungry.

Mike didn't wake up for any of that.

"So, last night—well, I guess it really wasn't 'night,' was it?" I start. The sun's still in the same place. "Anyway, I dreamed about Sam, and what was weird was—"

"There is nothing more boring than when someone tells you a dream they had."

Really, dude? "That crazy old bitch we're looking for was in it."

"I dreamed about Patti McGuire. Want to hear more?"

"No." Whoever she is.

"Okay, then."

Fine. My belly tightens. "I gotta take a crap. Do you have any toilet paper?"

He gives me with this look like I just asked him for a million dollars. "Nope."

"No?"

"No."

"You've got food and water and a filter, but you don't have toilet paper? What do you use? I mean, you do use something, right?" Though judging by how bad he smells, maybe not.

"See what you can find."

"Are you kidding me?"

He doesn't say anything.

I start looking as I walk along. Here and there, newspapers and magazines and what look like reports or something from offices, most not in English. None of those look too comfortable. Rags and clothing scraps, but they're dirty. Meanwhile, I'm cramping, but at least it's not my period. Not yet, anyway.

Eventually, I find a ripped-open teddy bear. It's red, of all things, and it still has most of its stuffing. It reminds me of that creepy bird puppet-thing, but no, this is just an old toy. And that's what I tell myself as I pluck out a big wad of stuffing and use it a few minutes later, while I'm squatting behind a boulder. Just an old toy that doesn't belong to anyone. But it still makes me sad. Stupid, I know.

While I'm rubbing the sanitizer from my pack all over my hands, I notice that Mike's just kept on walking. I guess he's not too pressed about anything trying to kill me while I'm taking a dump.

I decide against running to catch up with him, because I'm so nasty, I can smell myself. Dirt and sand and dried sweat and crusted blood. This gray dust gets everywhere. *Everywhere.* When I pulled down my panties, I had to shake them out, and I'm chafed where my thighs meet my crotch. My breath must be awful. After I woke up and filtered some more water, I swished some around in my mouth and rubbed my finger across my teeth and tongue, but that only did so much.

I follow Mike. He walks faster than me, so I watch to make sure he doesn't get too far ahead, or turn and go off some different way. I don't think he actually knows where he's going, but for now, at least, any direction is just as good as any other. I guess.

I walk, and try not to think. Eventually, it works.

What seems like a few hours later, I meet up with him when he stops and squats. At first, I think he's taking a crap too, but when I get close, I see that he's digging something out of the ground with a knife.

"Nice of you to wait for me," I tell him.

"Shut up and be useful."

I sit down across from him, take out my knife and start jabbing at the dirt around a wooden corner of…something. "What is it?" I ask.

"A box, dumbass." He points with the tip of his blade. "See that line where the lid meets it? Half of being smart is paying attention to details."

"Okay, butthead, so it's a box. What's in it?"

"If I had x-ray vision, I'd be Superman."

"If you were Superman, you'd be a lot nicer."

"Superman's not real."

It doesn't take too long to dig it out. It's a box, all right, a little bigger than my backpack. We rub off the dust and dirt that's clumped to it, then pick it up and turn it over. It's heavy.

Mike looks left, right, all around us. Nothing moving out here. "Okay." He sits, crosses his legs. Squints and leans in close.

"How are we supposed to open it?" I ask. There aren't any latches or anything, like on a purse or a briefcase or luggage. No zippers or hinges. Just a line going all the way around it. "Maybe you pull off the top?"

Mike tries, but it doesn't open. He puts the box on its side between his legs, lines his fingertips along the seam, and pulls as hard as he can, squeezing his thighs so the box doesn't go anywhere. The lid doesn't budge. Tries again. Nothing. Pokes at it with his knife, to wedge the point in between and pry it open. Nope.

"Christ on a stick," he mutters. He reaches over, picks up a big rock. Starts beating hard on a corner of the box—it echoes *bkk! bkk! bkk! bkk!*

"You're gonna break it."

"That's the idea." *bkk! bkk!*

"And you'll break whatever's in there."

"Maybe." *bkk! bkk!* "But if we can't get it open, it doesn't matter, does it?"

"You're making a lot of noise—something's going to find us." I look around. Nothing, yet. "Give me that!"

"Fine." He puts down the rock, hands me the box. "Have a party."

I run my hands over it. The wood's old, dark, really smooth, no splinters, only a few scratches where Mike was trying to smash it. It must be pretty tough. No writing or markings to show how it's supposed to open. Hmmm.

There's a spot at one end where the wood's a little soft. I push on it, and the lid slides by itself away from me, stopping at the other end of the box. A musty smell. "Fancy that," Mike says, leaning in to see what's there.

A book. A knife in a leather sheath. An envelope. Two little dolls. A big pistol.

Mike reaches in, takes the gun, snaps it open—it sorta unfolds in the middle. "Here," I say, holding up one of the three smooth, shiny metal tubes, each as big as his thumb, that were in the box, under the pistol. "It's a bullet, right?"

"No." He frowns. "No, it isn't. Well, maybe. Could be a flare, or something. Yeah." He nods. "Only room for one shot: it's a flare gun. I guess."

"What's a flare gun?"

"C'mon—you don't know that?" I shake my head. "You point it up in the air and shoot, and a thing like a firework comes out. Makes a bright light for a few seconds, then it burns out. It's for signaling. Like, if you were on a boat and the motor went out, and the Coast Guard was trying to find you. Or if you got lost in the woods, and you were trying to let people know where you are."

"Oh."

"I've never seen one like this, though. It must be really old."

The flare has writing on it, along one side. BRANDSTICHTER. No idea what that's supposed to mean. Check out the other two: one of them says the same, the other says, BREEKBAR. Maybe the companies that made them?

I pick up the envelope, and the paper crumbles at the edges. Gently, I turn it over. Right in the middle, someone wrote JACK. Nothing else on the envelope. "Should I open it?"

"I don't think Jack will mind if we read his mail." He takes the knife from the box, pulls it from its sheath. Its blade is about eight inches long.

Carefully, I run my finger under the envelope's flap. It doesn't open so much as it lets go with a tiny *peh*. In the envelope is a tuft of long black...hair? Fur? Dog fur, I think. Why would som—

SHNKK! I look over, and the blade of the knife from the box has split into two, side-by-side. "Whoa," Mike says.

"How'd you do that?"

"Beats me. I was just messing with it, and it happened so fast, I could hardly see it." He twirls his wrist. "Feels the same, though."

I hold out my hand. "Let me see."

"All right. Just be careful."

It's light, not much heavier than my knife. And it looks sharp. "This is so cool." I squint at where the blades meet the handle. Some tiny writing there. KONINKRJK, ERISIA 1873. Whatever that means.

He picks up the book—it's hardcover. Flips through some of the yellowing pages. Frowns, shakes his head. "It's not in English." Snaps it shut and goes to toss it.

"Wait! I want to try." I put down the knife.

He hands the book to me. "It ain't Japanese."

"I'm not either." I turn it over. The cover's dark brown leather, and it's decorated with carved designs, like those fancy belts that guys at rodeos wear. Old-style lettering embossed into it. "It's Spanish—sorta."

"You know Spanish?"

"A little."

"How?"

"They teach Spanish at those schools in Maryland." I open it, start reading the back of the title page.

"Why is it only 'sorta' Spanish?"

"It must be some kinda dialect. Or it's just really old. 'Published in 1909 by Imperial...Imperial Press,'" I translate. "At least, I think that's what it says."

"So, what's this book about?"

I show him the cover. "'Stories of the...Diheneh.' I don't know what that means. Do you?" He shakes his head. I look through the book. "It's like…legends, I guess. Native American myths." I hold open the book and show him a full-page drawing. "Check out this dragon."

"And you were complaining about not having something to wipe your ass with."

I pull it away from him. "You can't use a book for toilet paper."

"You sure as hell can. I'd give my left nut for a copy of the L.A. Yellow Pages."

I put the book beside me while he reaches back in the box, scoops up the other flares, stashes them in a pocket. Puts the new gun inside his coat, in another one pocket, I guess. Starts to stand up. "We gotta go."

"Just a second." I turn over the dolls. They're made from corn cobs, with scraps of cloth wrapped around them for dresses, real hair glued to them, dots painted on for eyes.

"C'mon, put that crap down. We're hanging out our butts here—anything coming this way would see us for miles." I look up; he's right. It's flat here, no big boulders or shrubs to hide behind. I put the dolls back in the box, take off my pack, stuff the book in, put it back on. I take the knife and its sheath, stand up, start following him.

"Hey, I want that flare gun," I tell him.

"Hey, how does, 'hell no' grab you?"

"Why not?"

"Cuz you'll blow off your foot or something with it, that's why not."

"I know how to shoot. My dad took me a couple times."

"Well, he's 'Dad of the Year,' then. And you still can't have it. What would you do with it, anyway?"

"Shoot the next thing that tries to eat me."

"You're not going to kill anything with a flare gun."

"It would sure hurt like hell."

"You could just stick it with that," he says, pointing at the new knife.

I hold it up and look close at it again. "Weird."

"What?"

"Why does it have two blades?"

"It's made by Gillette? I don't know."

"Look." I point at the ends. "They're little triangles."

"Well, that's gonna leave a hell of a scar."

"What do you mean?"

"Knives and swords usually have flat blades. If you get stabbed, they'll make a slit in you that someone can just sew up. That one—" He points at it again. "That one will—"

"—will make triangle-shaped wounds. And those aren't as easy to fix, are they?"

He shakes his head. "No. And there's two of them, right next to each other. Could get really messy. Pretty bitchin', huh?"

I imagine stabbing it straight through that crazy old bitch, right in her gut and coming out her back. Then twisting it around inside her. Watching her eyes bug out of her head while she gasps for air and bleeds to death—slowly. It's a good thought. I like it. And then, right before she—

The two blades go *SHNKK*, startling me, and when I look down, it's a single blade again, like it was back in the box. "Shit!" Mike yells. Guess it surprised him, too. "What'd you do?"

"I don't know. I think I might have squeezed the handle a certain way."

"Well, figure out how that works. But don't wave it around me."

"Where do you think it comes from?"

"Who cares?"

"I do."

"Why?"

"Because. I've never seen a knife like this. Here, look." I stop as I hold it out to him. He stops, too, takes it.

"Look at what?"

"There's little writing on the blade, by the handle. What do you think it means?"

He peers at it, gives it back to me. "I don't see anything." Starts walking again.

I look close. No writing. I sheath the knife, slip it into the other mesh sleeve—the one that doesn't have my water bottle—on the side of my backpack. "It was there before."

"DILLIGAS."

"What?"

"'Do I Look Like I Give A Shit?'"

I catch up to him. "Well, the book's in Spanish, and the book and the knife were in the same box, so maybe they come from the same place. But the writing on the blade didn't look like Spanish."

"I've got better things to worry about."

How can he not be the least bit curious? How can he not even care? But then…. I look around. Nothing but empty gray desert. No food or water except what we have—now that I think about, damn, I'm hungry. Thirsty, too. Nowhere to go, nowhere to stay. Nobody out there but monsters. And her. And Sam.

"Yeah," I admit. "I see what you mean."

"You might have some sense, after all."

Nobody out there. "Mike, are you and me the only people here? I mean in this place. This world, if that's what it is."

"No, we're not the only ones."

"So, these other people…where are they?"

"Around. I've seen one or two them, every once in a while."

"How'd they get here?"

105

"Does it matter?"

"Yeah. Yeah, it does. Cuz if we knew how they got here, maybe we could find a way back."

"There's no going back. It's a sink trap, remember?"

"How do you know?"

"I've been here long enough."

"We could at least try."

"I've got a witch to kill first. And your boyfriend to save."

"All right, but after that."

He chuckles.

"What?"

"Nothin'."

"No, what's so funny?"

"You are."

"Why?"

"'After that.' Like we're just out running errands, marking things off our 'to-do' list. Yeah, after we walk across the desert and find her and kill her and get the love of your life back, we'll just blow this taco stand. Maybe I'll call the house and ask my wife if she wants me to pick up some diapers on the way. No big deal."

"He's not the love of my life."

"No? Well, you're going through an awful lot of trouble for some guy you're eventually gonna break up with. Unless he dumps you first."

"Sam's not gonna dump me."

"Of course not, what with your winning personality."

"You should talk. I don't even think you have a wife."

"Sorry, maybe next time I'll remember to care what you think. But isn't that your boyfriend Stan's job?"

"His name isn't Stan."

"Oh, there I go not caring again."

My God, he is so tiring. "So, do you know how any of those other people got here?"

"Never asked."

"Why not?"

"Usually too busy."

"Do you know where they are? Are they all, like, in one place?"

"No, like, they, like, totally aren't. Fer sure."

"Why do you always make fun of me?"

"Just because shooting fish in a barrel is easy, doesn't mean it isn't a good time."

I don't even wanna know. "So, where are they?"

"I told you. They're around. Here and there."

"Maybe they could help us."

"Maybe they'll buy the world a Coke and keep it company. They're not gonna help us. They can't help anybody. Most of them are sad sacks of shit who ran away from the freak show or the group home. They wandered too far from the lights and wound up here. And if we're not careful, you'll find that out firsthand."

"Why? What's wrong with them?"

"Some people, they fall into here, but they hang on. They scrounge enough so they don't starve. They find water, don't die of thirst, don't poison themselves drinking their own piss. They don't freeze, they don't get too sick, they're smart and they hide from the things out roaming around, looking for fresh meat like them. They survive just long enough."

He points to the horizon. "But they can't deal with all this…empty. The loneliness. No one to talk to, except yourself. No one to help you with the fear and the confusion and the hopelessness. And then dark comes, and it lasts longer than you thought possible, and you realize you're just gonna die here, all by yourself, and no one you care about will ever know what happened to you. And that's when stuff upstairs starts breaking," he says, tapping the side of his head. "If it hadn't already."

"We're not gonna die," I say. "We're gonna get Sam, and we're gonna go home. All three of us."

"Cuz we're special, right?" he asks. "We're the lucky ones."

"I didn't say that."

"But that's what you're thinking, isn't it? 'Nothing bad's gonna happen to me.'"

"Plenty of bad stuff's already happened."

"And it's going to get worse."

"You don't know that."

"You don't know shit. You're just a kid."

"Yeah, well, you've made it this far. You're not dead, and you haven't gone crazy."

"I got hate. It keeps me going."

"Who do you hate? Her?"

No answer.

"Why? Why do you hate her?"

His face doesn't even move. I thought maybe it would. He just keeps walking, and I follow.

Track 12. Do You Wanna Touch Me (Oh Yeah)

I waited on the steps, had my pad out, like always, but I wasn't sketching this time. When lunch was dismissed, I went down the stairs, timed it so I was a few people behind Sam and his friends. Shuffled along with the others, got closer. That kid Dylan that hangs with Sam: "—I'm like, 'How can you possibly say that splinter cannons suck? Do you know *anything* about playing Drukhari?' and he goes, 'Well—'"

I tapped Sam on the shoulder. He turned, smiled. Looked back and called out, "Later, guys!" His gamer lunch buddies kept walking, Dylan still going off on…whatever.

We came out of the way, by the big floor-to-ceiling windows here in the hall in front of the main office. "What's up?" he asked.

"Nothin'."

"Oh, okay. Just saying 'hi?'"

I nodded.

"How're your classes going? Calc is totally kicking my ass, and I didn't think it would, but —"

"Listen, I'm really not good at talking," I said. "Do you still want to go to Homecoming?"

"What? You mean, with you?"

"Yeah. Or are you going with someone else?"

He hesitated for a second or two, shook his head. "No."

"You sure? Cuz you looked like you had to think about it."

"No, I mean…" Shook his head again. "Somebody asked me, but I didn't say anything yet, so, yeah, I can go with you."

"Wait—who asked you?"

"Rachael Davis. She's in my French class. I've known her since kindergarten."

"Well, you can go with her if you want. It's no big deal."

"No, no, I'd rather go with you. Rachael's okay, but her friends are kind of annoying, and she'll want to hang with them the whole time." He frowned. "I thought you didn't want to go."

"I didn't. I still don't really want to."

"So…why are you going?"

"Ms. Custer wants me to."

"Who's that?"

"She's the therapist lady they've been making me see."

"Oh."

"She says it would be good for me. And the theme is Eighties, so at least the music should be decent."

"Yeah. Everyone's supposed to dress Eighties, too."

"What? Like it's frickin' Halloween, or something?"

"SGA's trying it because last year, the night of the dance, a bunch of parents were on Facebook bitching about how slutty a lot of the girls were dressing, and—"

"I'm not doin' that."

"Well, I am, so you have to."

"I'm not wearing spandex and legwarmers, or anything like that."

"My mom has some old concert shirts."

"Your mom doesn't even know me. She's not gonna let me borrow her clothes."

"My mom's cool—you'd like her. If we're going to the dance, then we're going to the game."

"What game?"

"The football game the night before. We're playing Parkside, and we're totally going to kick their ass. It'll be awesome."

"I don't like football."

"Everybody likes football. It's fun. We all just hang out, and stand up during the whole game, and the marching band plays the fight song after every touchdown, and Parkside sucks, so we're going to destroy them. C'mon."

"Fine. We'll go to the game on one condition: I drive us to the dance."

"I didn't know you have a car."

"I don't." Grinned really big while I pretended to rev the bike. "Vroom, vroom. Wear layers. It's gonna be cold." He looked horrified.

The bell rang—we were late to class. "Shit! Gotta go!" Sam said, and he crutched off as fast as he could. I hurried, too, because I was headed to Mrs. Humphreys', and I liked her.

* * *

That bitch Ms. Jung had just thrown Sam's ripped-up Magic card in the trash, but there were lots of pictures on Google, of course. This last sketch turned out a lot better than that first one I started in class. Holding a long, curved sword, tall and lean and muscled, perfect stripes, snout not too long, and the head was round, actually looked like a tiger. I added a bit more to the back curve of a fang, a little darker and heavier there, and then it was done. At the bottom of the sheet, I wrote, in small letters, RAKSHASA, and then put the date.

A knock on the door, and my uncle came in. Graying hair, big arms and shoulders, a lot older than my dad would be now. He stood in the doorway. "Are you busy?"

"No, I just finished something for Art class."

"May I come in?"

"It's your house."

"And this is your room."

"It's the guest room."

"No, it's yours, for the time being, anyway." He came in, sat on the bed. I turned the chair around from the desk.

"What's up?"

"On Sunday, I need to fly out of BWI to Cleveland. I'm meeting some people about going in on a few dealerships out there. I should be back by Friday."

"Okay."

"Mrs. Sullivan will come by every day to take care of Jake," – my uncle's Rottweiler—"and cook dinner for you. She'll clean up and do the laundry, of course."

"Just like every time."

"Just like every time." He leaned in closer. "Are you going to be all right while I'm gone?"

I understood. It was the first time he had gone on a business trip since I lost my shit with Ms. Jung. "Yeah, I'll be fine."

"You won't forget to take your medicine?"

"No, I won't." I reached across the desk, picked up the pill bottle of Lamictal, shook it.

"If something happens, if you need me, call my phone. If it's an emergency, and you need someone to come right away, call Mrs. Sullivan."

"I will, Uncle Tony."

"You sure?"

"Yeah. I'll be fine."

"Okay." He smiled. "If this deal works out, maybe I can take you with me on my next trip out there. You can go visit the Rock and Roll Hall of Fame while I'm signing all the papers."

"That'd be cool." Are you kidding? That'd be *awesome*.

"All right, then." He patted my arm, started to stand up.

"Uncle Tony, did you ever play for the Ravens?"

He sat back down. Puzzled look. "The Ravens? The Baltimore Ravens?"

"Yeah."

"No, they came after my time. Though the funny thing is—well, it's not *that* funny—is that the Ravens used to be the Browns."

"Your team?"

"Yeah. Until Mr. Modell, the owner, moved them to Baltimore."

"Oh. Were you guys any good?"

"No, we were terrible, though we had some great players. Brian Sipe, Lyle Alzado, Ozzie Newsome. After he retired, Ozzie became the Ravens' GM."

GM? Doesn't matter. "How about you? You must have been pretty good."

"I was okay. I mean, sure, I was better than most of the other guys at Michigan—I was a fifth-round pick—but not compared to the guys in the NFL. I was a backup right guard, spent most of my time on the bench, unless someone got injured. I started…I don't know…maybe a dozen games here and there. I lasted four seasons, then I got cut, and no one else picked me up." He chuckled. "And right after that, the Browns went to the playoffs five straight times. Go figure. Couldn't get to the big one, though."

"That's…that's kinda sad. I mean, it's a shame that all that time you played, it was for a bad team."

"Ah, I'm okay with it now. I got to make a living playing a great game, I never got hurt too bad, I saved my money, and I was able to go into business for myself. Lots of other guys I played with weren't so lucky."

I nodded. "Dad used to talk about you all the time. Said you were rich and famous."

"I was neither, but it worked out for me. And your father was just a little kid—the baby of the family—when I was playing. Your grandma doted on him. Spoiled him. That's why Don turned out the way he did. That, and he was always kind of wild. Would blow his stack over the littlest things. Runs in the family. Our father was like that, too."

"I hardly remember Grandma and Grandpa. I think we went to visit them once, at Christmas."

"You were four. All of us used to get together every year for the holidays, because that was the rule at our house: no matter where you lived, no matter how old you were, everyone came home for Thanksgiving and Christmas. That's what your grandpa insisted on. He said that's what being a family's about."

"But my dad wouldn't come?"

"Some of the time, it was because he was deployed. Other times, he just couldn't be bothered. And your grandpa and grandma let him get away with that." He shook his head. "By then, those weren't the parents that raised me: those were old people trying to get into Heaven."

"That's funny."

"It's true." He sighed. "I shouldn't be talking about your dad like that."

"It's okay. I don't like him much, either."

"Well, nothing we can do about it. He is who he is." My uncle stood up. "Don't let me keep you from your homework."

"I'm done, anyway."

"Okay." He cocked his head. "When did you start liking football?"

"I don't, but this guy Sam asked me to go to the Homecoming game. And the dance."

He nodded. "I see."

"So, I was wondering, if you have some time before your trip, if you could tell me about football. You know, like explain it."

"Wouldn't you rather just look it up online?"

"No, it sounds more interesting when you talk about it."

"Well, I have time now," he said, and sat down again. "This boy who asked you out—is he a Ravens fan?"

"Yeah."

"Ugh. Do me a favor: after the dance, dump him." I smiled. He did, too.

* * *

Third and thirteen. "Why aren't we throwing it?" I asked.

"Because our quarterback sucks," Sam said, "and Coach knows it."

David Myers—no relation to that asswipe Shane Myers from math class, the one I grazed with a chair leg—took the snap, did a pump-fake that fooled nobody, lateraled it to Kevin Early, the running back, who tried to sweep around the right side and got dropped behind the line. Over the PA system, the play-by-play guy in the booth called it a three-yard loss. Punt unit came on. Again.

"I thought you said we were excellent."

"We were last year. Then all our seniors graduated."

It was cold and my feet hurt from standing on the metal bleacher for well over an hour. We were shoulder to shoulder with at least two hundred other kids, some of them bobbing up and down to stay warm, most of them talking, a few of them paying attention to the game. Parents and younger kids sat in the other sections of our bleachers, the Parkside parents and friends across the field in the much smaller visitors' bleachers.

Four and half minutes left in the third quarter, and we were down 20-2. At least we got a safety. Bonus: Shane Myers had been on the sideline the whole time. Sam says Coach never puts him in. I don't even know why he's on the team, then.

"We were supposed to kick their ass," I reminded Sam. The punt went sailing over the Parkside returner's head, bounced around for a while before our guys downed it at the three-yard line. So there was that.

"What are you wearing tomorrow?" Sam asked. "I was thinking maybe the *Miami Vice* look for me."

I didn't even know what that was. Parkside took over, made a two-yard run. Second and eight. "I got some stuff from this consignment store by the gun place," I told him.

"I know which one you mean—just off Duke Street. My mom and Cynthia go there all the time." The Parkside QB tried a quick screen, but the receiver hadn't turned around. Incomplete. Third and eight.

"Cynthia's moving out, by the way. She got a job down in Virgi—"

Cameron Jacobs, one of our linebackers, blew through Parkside's offensive line, sacked the quarterback, who fumbled as he fell. Brandon Fellows, the left defensive end, scooped it up, ran it in for the TD, and the place exploded, everyone screaming as the marching band at the top of the bleachers played the fight song (it's the West Virginia University one, because the band teacher went there). The two-point conversion made it 20-10, and it wasn't quite the fourth quarter. We had a chance.

People fired up, screaming, pounding their feet on the bleachers. "Shut up," I told him, grinning, elbowing him in the sides. "I'm watching the game."

We won 21-20 with a last-second field goal. First game I ever watched. Best game I ever watched.

* * *

I pulled up to his house on Kimberly Way, in Cloverfields, and killed the engine. It was dark, October 22, the next to last Saturday of the month; Sam didn't know why Homecoming was super-late this year. At least it wasn't too cold or (thank God) raining. In the driveway was a U-Haul truck, one of the smaller ones, open in the back, and for a moment, I was confused, until I remembered what he had said about his sister. Cynthia, that was her name. The girl at the record store.

I peeled off my helmet, hung it on the handlebars, went up to the door. Hit the bell. Sam opened it right away, like he'd been standing by it. "Hey!" he said, big grin. He was wearing black, fake-leather pants; a black-and-white striped t-shirt; a white jacket with the sleeves pushed up. Shiny black shoes, his hair poofed up and the tips frosted blond. A little orange fluffy dog came running over, yapping, tail wagging, then jumped up and put its paws on my leg.

"Penny! Stop it! Down!" Sam said. "She doesn't bite or anything."

"It's okay." I bent down to pet her. "I like dogs."

"Come on in!" I did. Penny ran little circles around me. "Mom, this is Alyx!"

"I didn't know I was going to be meeting your mom," I muttered, but then she swept in from the kitchen, a big woman, but not too fat, dark hair cut short, arms out for a hug.

"So nice to meet you!" she said, squeezing me. I'm not a huggy person at all. "I'm Brenda." She pulled back. "Look at you! You look just like Joan Jett!"

"That was the idea, yeah." And easy to come up with. My motorcycle boots, ripped up old jeans, a red t-shirt, black vinyl jacket. My hair spiked up, lots of mascara and eyeliner, hoop earrings like she had in the video for "I Hate Myself for Loving You."

"I was such a big fan! I saw her about five or six times in concert."

"Yeah, she's pretty cool."

Penny jumped on me again. "Stop that!" Sam's mom said, and scooped her up. "I'm sorry about her. She's such a bad girl."

"It's no problem." Looked around. No dad.

Cynthia came down the stairs, carrying a big cardboard box. "Nobody told me we were playing dress-up. Get the door, Useless."

"The sooner you're gone, the better," Sam said, opening the door as she went out to the truck.

"Sibling love," Sam's mom said, stroking Penny's head. "Do

you need a ride to the dance?"

"No, uh, Alyx is driving," Sam said, glancing over at me. He totally didn't tell her about the bike, did he?

"Yeah," I said, smiling. "We should get going, then."

Cynthia came back in, and for a second, I thought she was going to say something about the bike. She just walked back upstairs, to get more stuff, I guess. "What time is the dance over?" Sam's mom asked.

"It ends at ten, but Kenny Ruppert's having a party after that, and I was hoping we could go. His house is on Ackerman."

"And what time do you have to be home?" she asked me.

I shook my head. "Whenever. My uncle's not pressed about it."

"Don't you have a provisional license?"

"Yeah." Actually, I didn't a license at all.

"So, you're not allowed to drive after midnight, right?"

"Right. Yeah, I guess so." Acted like she just reminded me. "I moved here from Pennsylvania in the summer, so it's tough to remember all the changes in the laws."

"Oh, how nice! Where in Pennsylvania?"

"Near Philly."

"Well, I hope you like it down here. We came from just outside DC, before Sam was born."

"Yeah, he told me that."

"So, can we go to the party?" Sam asked.

"Sure. Just be back here no later than eleven thirty. On the dot, mister."

"Will do," he says.

"Oh! And here's your hat." She set Penny down, then went back to the kitchen—it was one of those fancy open floorplan homes, like they have on those shows where people renovate houses—and got this wide fedora (I thought that was what kind it was). She put it on him. "Now you look just like John Taylor. Doesn't he?" she asked.

"Definitely." Whoever the hell John Taylor is.

"I had such a crush on him when I was in school." Not weird at all to say, with your son standing right there dressed like him.

Cynthia came down the stairs again, with another big cardboard box. "Good, you're still here. Get the door."

"I got it." Happy to get out of there.

"Bye! Have fun! Nice meeting you!"

I looked back, did this fake smile and a weak wave, opened the door for Cynthia. We went out on the porch, Sam shut the door behind us. No crutch for him tonight: I guess he doesn't want it.

Cynthia put the box on the edge of the truck's bed, turned to us. "You better walk the bike a few houses down before you get going, or else Mom will hear and freak out. I'll tell her I need her to get me something out of the laundry room. There's a load running in there: she won't hear anything."

"Thanks for not telling her," Sam told her.

"You owe me."

"I know."

"No, like you're going to clean the upstairs bathroom for me so I can roll out of here early tomorrow."

"Fine."

"Fiiiiiiine," she said, making fun of him.

"Thanks, Cynthia," I said.

"You go, Punk Rock Girl. Have a kickass time."

Sam watched while I got on the bike, turned the key so that the lights came on but the engine didn't, popped it into neutral, and gorilla-walked it down the street. He followed me. "So, what do I do?" he asked.

I stopped the bike, turned it off. "Go behind me and swing

119

your leg over, and sit down on that little pad behind the seat."

He stood there. "*That's* where I'm supposed to sit? How do I hang on?"

"Put your hands on my hips and just relax. Do what I do. When I lean forward, you lean forward, when I go back, you go back. When we go around corners, the bike's going to lean, so lean with it. Don't try to fight it, just go with it, because if you don't, we might wreck. You've ridden a bike before, right?" I regretted that as soon as I asked it.

"No, obviously."

"Sorry. Well, we'll be fine." Actually wasn't sure of that at all.

"How long have you been riding?"

"A few months. Back in Pennsylvania, I had a friend who had one, and we'd ride." That was Tommy, my ex, but Sam doesn't need to know that. "This is my uncle's bike. Well, his son's, but he's, like, forty-something, and lives in Oregon, but when he comes to visit he likes to ride, so he keeps it at my uncle's house. Come on, let's go! You heard what Cynthia said about your mom."

"I don't know, it looks…dangerous."

"It *is* dangerous. Go with it. Have some fun. Nothing bad's gonna happen."

"But you just said it's dangerous."

"Shut up and get on." He did.

"What about a helmet?"

Crap. I had totally forgotten to bring Doug's extra one from the garage. Stupid Maryland helmet laws. I handed him mine. "Here."

"What about you?"

"What about me?"

"What if we crash?"

"We're not gonna crash."

"You keep it," he said, handing it back to me. "Just go slow, or my hat will blow off, and my mom will be pissed if I lose it."

I pulled on the helmet. "What about cops?"

"They usually park a car out front, where people are coming in, but we could take Love Point to get to the back parking lot." He jammed his hat down on his head. "Don't drive crazy, all right?"

"I *am* crazy."

"Yeah, that's what everybody at school says." I thumbed the switch, started the bike, and we rolled.

* * *

Sam was worried that we'd be the only ones who dressed Eighties, but almost everyone did. The dance was in the cafeteria; the decorating committee had folded up and taken away the tables, put chairs at the edge of the room. They had these big posters on the walls and columns, with photos of people and events from the Eighties, with captions saying who and what they were. Ronald Reagan and Madonna and Rubik's Cube and the Space Shuttle and *Raiders of the Lost Ark* and *Cheers* and a bunch of other people and stuff, most of them I'd never heard of before.

They had a DJ, and he only did Eighties songs, but everyone danced. He played my kind of music: "Pour Some Sugar on Me," and "Jump," and "Still Loving You," and "Cum On Feel The Noize." He did stuff Sam likes: "The Reflex," and "Karma Chameleon," and "Call Me," and "Every Breath You Take."

And he did a bunch of other songs: "Purple Rain," and "Beat It," and "Footloose," and "Relax" (which is, wow, *really* skeevy if you listen to the words), and "Don't Stop Believing" (which I *hate*, cuz it's, like, the most ultimate white girl song ever). I never thought about it before, but music's really changed a lot since then.

I'm not good at dancing—I just kinda bopped back and forth. Sam's not bad, all things considered. We danced for most of the songs, cuz Sam likes all kinds of music. It must come in handy, working at a record store. When we got too hot, we got some drinks—free cans of pop—and some chips or pretzels and sat down for a while. Toward the end of the dance, I was tired and I wanted to just talk, but it was pretty loud, so we went up the stairs and down the hall, by the library.

He leaned against the wall and slid down until he was sitting on the floor. I sat next to him. "You having fun?" he asked.

"Yeah. You?"

"Oh, yeah."

"Thanks for asking me. I wouldn't have come."

"I'm glad you did."

"So, why'd you ask me?"

"I told you. Because I like you."

"I don't know why. Nobody else does."

"I like you because we're the same."

"No, we're not. You're smart, and you do all these after-school things, and you have friends. I'm...I'm not that."

"Yeah, but you're a freak, just like I am."

"You're not a freak."

"Yeah, I am. I'm crippled."

"No, you're not."

"It's okay, I don't mind. Just be honest about it."

"Okay, honestly, I don't even notice anymore."

"I do, all the time. Everybody gets to forget about me being crippled. Except me."

For a few moments, I didn't know what to say. Then, I asked, "Does anyone, like, give you shit about it? Say mean things, or make fun of you?"

"Not really, anymore. When I was little, some of the kids used to call me names, tease me. The teachers got on their asses about it, and it pretty much stopped. I've been going to school with just about everyone here since kindergarten, so they're used to me. Hardly anybody stares."

"Yeah, they all stare at me, instead."

"Well, you're the new freak."

"It's my eyes."

"I think they're cool."

"When you're Asian, blue eyes aren't cool, they just make you a freak."

"No, that's not it. You're not a freak on the outside, like I am. You're a freak on the inside."

I thought about that. "I guess you're right."

"I was born like this," he said. "How about you?"

"My family...they're all messed up." He waited for me. "When he was home—which wasn't much—my dad would drink a lot. Pick fights with my mom, beat her up just cuz he could. If I got in the way, he'd hit me, too. One time, he for real knocked me out."

"Any man who hits a girl is trash. I mean, my dad's a piece of shit and my folks are divorced, but it's not because of that. It's just that he couldn't keep it in his pants."

"Nice."

"Cynthia told me about it. He left his phone on the kitchen counter, and she started going through it, because she's nosy. She saw a photo of the chick he was cheating on my mom with. Naked selfie. She had tattoos of stars right here," he said, pointing a few inches below his belly button.

"You saw?"

"Cynthia showed it to me."

"Gross."

"Yeah. She worked for him at the law firm. They moved to Chicago, but last I heard, she dumped him for somebody with more money."

"How's your mom doing?"

"That was a few years ago, so she's over it. She's sort of going out with this guy, Chuck." He shook his head. "You know what are the saddest words in the world?"

"No. What?"

"'My mom's boyfriend.'"

I took his hand, squeezed it. He leaned over, hesitated a second. Then, a soft kiss, just lips.

Again.

And again.

A little while later, the DJ stopped, and they turned on the lights in the cafeteria, and the dance was over. We didn't go to Kenny Ruppert's party; we stayed in the parking lot, both of us leaning against my bike, watching everyone else drive away or get picked up by their parents. We talked and kissed and talked and kissed. Two freaks found each other. It felt good.

Track 13. The Thing That Should Not Be

It's a house. Well, what's left. Small, old, wooden, one floor. Broken windows, door hanging open, roof sagging. A scraggly, spiky black tree growing where one wall's fallen down. "Stay here," he tells me, taking out his pistol and sneaking toward the house. It's the first time he's spoken in hours.

I follow him anyway. He glances back at me, looks pissed. I don't care. The wind's gasping *uuuuuuuuuu* real low, and I'm not staying out here by myself.

We go to the corner of the house, the close one, not the one by the tree. He leans against the wall like he's trying to hide. "Do you ever do as you're told?" he whispers.

"You're not the boss of me."

"You should talk a little louder."

"What are we even doing?" I whisper back. "Are we going to camp here?"

"You don't 'camp' in a house."

"Okay, Mister Literal. Are we going to 'stay' here?"

"Maybe. If it's safe."

"It's just an old house."

"That's what it looks like, yeah."

"Whaddya mean?"

"You can't trust anything. Unless you want to just walk right in? In which case, ladies first."

"No thanks."

"All right, then."

"Here." I take the flashlight from my jacket pocket, hand it to him. He scrunches up his face.

"What's this?"

"What's it look like, stupid?"

"It's tiny."

"So?"

"Is it a toy, or does it actually work?"

"Yeah, it works. Why would I have a toy flashlight? They don't even make those." At least, I don't think they do.

He clicks it on, seems surprised. "Damn, that's bright."

"Well, that's the point."

He edges around the corner, goes to the nearest window. Flicks the light around inside, cuts it off. At first, I wonder why, and then I think maybe it's cuz you could probably see it shining from like a mile away.

He plucks a few chunks of glass from the frame, tosses them. Straddles it, pistol pointed inside. Waves at me with the other hand, and I come over there. "You sure you don't want to wait?" I nod. He gives me back the flashlight. "Anything jumps out at us, you keep that on it while I shoot."

"What happened to running away to save bullets?"

"Might not get the chance. But if we do, I'll make sure to trip you on my way out."

"Dick."

"No, Mike. Mike Fernandez. But my dad went by Dick."

He ducks inside, and I climb through after him. I click on the flashlight, keep it low, block it with my body so no one—or nothing—outside can see its beam. The room's small, the floor's just planks of wood, some of them missing, just dirt under there. There's a rusted bedframe in one corner, no mattress. Next to it, a wooden dresser with three drawers, something black that I hope is just mold going down one side.

"I'm not—" I start, but Mike holds his finger to his lips. Slowly—real slowly—he takes a step, then another. No noise, though he's in boots. He points down, and I shine the light on them. He's walking on the side of his feet.

Do that, he mouths. I turn my ankle, go slow, take a step. The floor creaks under me, and he scowls. I take another step, even slower. Not so loud this time. It seems to take forever to walk across the room.

There's no door, just an empty black space where it used to be. I cover most of the light with my hand, let just a little bit seep out along the floor and slowly up the wall. A narrow, dusty hall, a few doors, picture frames on the walls, a curtain half-hanging at the end.

We slink down the hall. The frames have photos—no color—of a white family. Dad, Mom, lots of kids—girls and boys—from my age to babies. Everyone dressed nice in old-timey clothes, but nobody smiling. I wonder what their names were, how long ago they lived, if any of them are still alive.

We quietly push open doors off the hallway. More empty beds, some dressers, a dry-rotting crib. Then Mike's slowly pushing aside the curtain that's just dangling there, part of it nailed to the top of the doorway.

An awful smell, like crap and vomit and that stench that old, sick people get—I remember from the one time I went to the nursing home to visit my dad's dying aunt. A wide room here, broken windows, fireplace with faintly glowing ashes. Smashed chairs—maybe someone was burning pieces of them? Two long couches, a lumpy black sheet or tarp or something draped across most of one. Mike yanks my wrist, turns the flashlight's beam on it, and something under the sheet starts to sit up.

A gurgling voice—I can't tell if it's a man's or a woman's. *The sun and the moon and the stars have grown cold, and yet you have come, hyacinth.*

"Don't move," I tell…it, "or my friend will shoot you. He will. I swear, he will."

My sister is dead, and the scarabs ingest her. Soon, they will feast on me.

Of what one should I fear?

"Talk sense," Mike says. The light quivers. I hold my wrist with my other hand to make it stop.

Whatever it is under there, it's sitting all the way up on the couch. There's a lump where its head should be, but right next to it is another one, sorta flopped over. The shape doesn't move, but there's this low rustling sound coming from under the sheet.

How long until Ōth learns that you are in his country? How long until he hangs you from the Tree?

"This place is ours now," Mike says. "You get up and take your smelly ass out of here."

"Mike, you can't—"

"Mean Uncle Mikey says it's time to shut up, Alyx-with-a-'y.'" He circles toward the fireplace, and I follow him. The lump—is that its head?—sways like a cobra, this way and that, like it's looking at him, then me, then him again.

Mike jerks the pistol barrel toward the door, behind the shape. "You heard me. Go on. Get out of here."

Maybe I will. Maybe I will find Ōth and tell him of you. And then he will send his Woman to geld you.

"What if it's a person?" I ask. "What if there's an old sick man under there, and he can't walk, and—"

"That's not a man," Mike growls.

Maybe, instead, I will look upon you.

A shriveled arm with a twisted hand comes out from under the sheet and yanks it off and Mike screams and I hear myself screaming and I can't stop, can't, can't.

He—at least part of him is a 'he'—doesn't have legs, not even stumps. He's old and naked and his skin is wrinkled and white like paper, and hundreds of black beetles, as big as my thumbs, crawl all over him. No hair and only one eye, right in the middle of his face where his nose should be, no mouth, just a long, thin tube flapping from his chin.

He—it—has another head, a woman's head—a few clumps of ratty brown hair—dangling from a swollen limp neck next to his, but she—if you can call that a 'she'—has been dead for a long while, yellow bones showing through rotting cheeks and forehead, beetles all over and inside her face, chewing her, mouth's a flappy slit with no lips the bugs the bugs they ate her lips they—

The spaces between the stars are cold, and my sister is no more, it gurgles through its wriggling tube, *but you are warm, hyacinth.*

A flat **POC** fills the room, the house, everything, then another **POC** loud as the first as Mike shoots **POC** and then *kkek kkek kkek* it's empty and the air throbs, the thing—Mike's right, it's not a man—the thing gushing brownish goo in three places locks its eye on him and Mike crashes backward against the mantel, drops the pistol, slams to the floor, twitching and shaking, eyes white, wide, staring not seeing anything. Then it looks at me and—

Black. Everything black for as long as it takes to blink, and when I can see again, I'm sprawled on the floor and the thing is over me, on top of me, standing on its hands, its muddy blood—if that's what it is—dripping on my face, and its tube shivers, *Now you will seed me,* and I rip the knife from my boot, stab stab stab it in the chest in its neck its face and it shrieks, flails, tries to get away I stab it again again again, it sags to the floor and I keep stabbing, it keeps squealing *Burning! Burning!* and the knife blade breaks and Mike grabs my arm, pulls me away as the thing thrashes, writhes, screams for too long, too long, until it finally goes still.

"Oh God oh God oh God" I sob into his chest, and he smells even worse up close but I don't care, he holds me holds me tight, strokes my hair, tells me, "It's okay, it's all right, it's gone, it's okay," until I can't cry anymore. Until I just shake and stare at the nothing that is the floor.

* * *

Blank. Just blank. I stare at my sketch pad on my lap.

On the couch—*that* couch, the one that...*it*...was laying on—Mike snorts, rolls over, pulls his coat closer around himself, doesn't wake up. I'm sitting on the stone hearth, my back to the fire. It's little, not so big that it'd be noticed from outside, Mike said, and it's warm. So there's that.

But I can't draw.

I want to. I need to. Whenever bad things happen, I draw, and when it's good, then I lose myself in it. Lose the hurt, or the hate, or the fear. Lose everything for a while, until I can come back to it, back to the world, and then everything's better, just by a little bit. Just enough so I can cope.

But not now.

Pencil twirls in my fingers. Just draw a line, I tell myself. Start with that. One line, that's all. Start with that. And then, if you want, draw another. Over it, under it, next to it: it doesn't matter.

The pencil tip to the paper.

Just one line.

It doesn't move.

This has never happened to me before. I've never not been able to draw. But, I mean, how am I supposed to? What is there, what can I do? I killed it. Him. It. A monster. I killed a monster.

Mike covered it back up with the sheet, and he dragged it outside. I don't know if he buried it. I don't think he did: he wasn't gone very long, and it's not like he has a shovel. So, I guess it's just out there, somewhere, hopefully not near the house. Laying there. Dead.

On TV and in the movies, whenever someone gets shot or stabbed, they fall down, and that's it. They just die right there and then, except if it's a good guy. If it's a good guy, he'll hang on long enough to tell the hero or the girl something important. And if the girl's the one that's dying, she'll tell the hero she loves him. And then whoever it is, their eyes will close, like they're falling asleep, and they'll be gone.

They don't roll around, bleeding out gallons, screaming from the pain, ripping their fingernails off as they claw the floor. They don't shiver and have convulsions and shit themselves. They don't move slower and slower, until they can't anymore, until they're just laying there, whimpering, straining to breathe. And when they finally die, they keep their eyes open, but something in them, some light, goes out.

Like what happened.

But it was a monster, so it's not supposed to bother me. In the movies and on TV, the hero just kills the monster, and that's it. Then he does whatever it is he's supposed to do next in the story. He doesn't freak out, he doesn't go off. His hands don't shake, he doesn't breathe really hard and really fast for a long time, until he feels like he's going to pass out. Nobody holds him and tells him, "It's okay, it's okay, you're all right, it's over, don't look at it, don't look."

Like what happened.

When Mike came back in from dragging it outside, he didn't say anything. Went from room to room, checking out the rest of the house, especially the kitchen. Gathered some trash and broken scraps of furniture and made a fire in the fireplace. I just sat here, right where I still am, knees under my chin, arms wrapped around them.

"The first time's rough," he said. And then he heated up a can of okra over the fire, and ate it, and went to sleep on the couch.

And after a while—how long, I don't know—I got my pack and took out my pad.

But I can't draw.

Okay, then. Okay. Forget sketching. Think of something good. Something happy. That's what my first counselor—this old guy, Mr. Slocum—that's what he used to tell me. Back in fourth grade. Back when all the shit with me started. No, that's not when it started: it had always been going on. That's just when I couldn't take it anymore. So, they took me out of class, and brought me to Mr. Slocum. *Think of something happy.* That's what he'd say. And that always used to work.

But now, I can't do that, either.

* * *

After what seems like a long time, Mike jerks, sits up, looks around, blinking, like he doesn't know who or where he is. Then after a few seconds, his face hardens. He grunts, joints popping, as he gets on his feet. Just like every time he wakes up.

He goes outside—to pee, I guess—and when he comes back in, he squats next to me, at the hearth, warms his hands. "Good work keeping the fire going."

"It wasn't hard."

"It would have been a bitch to light again." I vaguely remember him doing it. Something with a knife and a rock and some paper scraps.

He goes to his bag, pulls out a can, pries it open with his knife. Macaroni and cheese—it smells bad and looks slimy. He doesn't bother heating it up, just starts eating with his fingers. "You should have some food."

"I'm not hungry."

"I didn't ask if you were. You should eat anyway. Don't know when you'll get the chance again."

I shake my head.

"Okay," he replies. "No sweat off my back."

I watch him scarf it down. "I don't know how you can eat," I whisper. "Or sleep. Or do anything."

"Easy." He runs his finger around the inside of the can, slurps off the yellowy-orange sauce. "It wasn't a person. It wasn't an animal. Hell, if you hadn't seen it—if it was just something I told you about—you wouldn't even think it was real. You get all hang-dog like this every time you kill a bug?"

"No."

"Well, then think of it as a bug. A big-ass ugly bug that was going to kill us. Why, you saved our lives. Ain't you the hero? Feels good, doesn't it?"

"You're making fun of me again."

"That's what you respond to. So, if you're ready to get out of here, let go of your rocks and grab your socks, because it's time to march."

He finishes eating, throws the can in the fireplace while I stand up, have a couple sips of water, put on my pack.

* * *

We've been walking for…I don't know. This place, this desert—it all looks the same to me now, just gray that goes on forever. I don't even notice the wind unless it blows really hard, like it sometimes does, but not for very long. Mike never talks. I've just been remembering, trying not to think about what happened.

We walk. And walk. And walk.

Eventually, I ask, "How many of them have you killed?"

"Huh? What?"

"You know…monsters. How many have you killed?"

"Never kept count. No point to it."

I don't say anything.

"Lots, I guess."

"That's what I figured."

"You do it enough times, it stops meaning anything, other than just being glad that it's dead and you're not."

"What was it talking about?"

"What?"

"Back there—that thing—it said…. It said all sorts of—"

"Some of them are insane, or at least, we would think they are. Some of them talk to confuse you, make you easier to take down. Some of them just want to freak you out. It's like a game for them."

"He—it—kept saying a name. Ōth?" I pronounce it the way that thing did, like the word for when you swear to something.

"Yeah, I've heard that before."

"What does it mean?"

"Nothing. It's just a name. Like 'God.' But it's not real, either."

"It said something about a woman. Could it be her?"

"Maybe. Who knows? Doesn't change anything."

"No. I guess not."

* * *

We walk and walk and walk, and it hurts my legs and my feet and finally, my back. We stop to take turns to sleep, but not nearly long enough, and I'm too tired to dream. We eat, but not much. I'm always hungry and thirsty; it's almost all I can think about, most of the time.

We go on—walking, eating, sleeping, walking again—for…I don't know. Days, lots of days. I've lost track of how long it's been since I came here. Everything is nothing but gray sand and black rocks, plains and hills and cliffs and canyons. Wind that whispers and moans and sometimes howls and sometimes goes so quiet that I can hear myself breathe. Gray clouds that never stand still, a sun that never moves. Cold. Cold all the time.

Spiny plants, trash, and bits and pieces things—*flotsam and jetsam*, Mike calls them. Sometimes we find a can of food, or an old box of cereal that isn't crawling with bugs, or half a jar of peanut butter. Sometimes we find a pond of dirty water that we can filter, or an intact bottle of something—anything—to drink.

We hardly talk, maybe a few words every day. Talking makes me thirstier, and besides, what's to say? I don't know if Mike knows where he's going, but he seems to. If he doesn't, we'll never find Sam. I try not to think about that, or the creature on the couch, or anything else.

Pelican.

"Shit!" I stumble back, drop my pack, reach for the mesh sleeve on its side, yank out my new knife, look here, there, behind me, all around. Where is it? Oh God oh God oh God where is that creepy-ass thing?

"What the hell's wrong with you?" Mike asks.

"Didn't you hear that?"

"Hear what?"

Pelican.

"That!" It's there it's there holy crap how did it get here?

He follows my eyes. Perched on a flat rock a few yards away. Googly eyes, fake blue and green and yellow hair everywhere, orange feet, ridiculously tiny wings, yellow beak that moves when it talks. It's dirty and nasty and tattered, like the other…or is it the same one? Have I gone in a big circle? Or did it follow me?

Pelican.

Mike glances at me. "It's just a toy." He doesn't sound convinced.

"It talks, and it moves, and I found one before—" Or it found me? "—and it freaked me out."

He backs up. "We'll just walk away, and th—"

Flapping its wings, swiveling its head, it sings:

> *Where we come from*
>
> *Me not know*
>
> *Me not know*
>
> *Me not know*
>
> *Where we go to*
>
> *Me not know*
>
> *Oh! Me not know*

Then it goes still.

Mike licks his lips. "Okay. Okay." He takes another step back.

The bird-thing's head whips around to stare at him. *Da-doo!* it croaks. *Da-doo!*

"What?" Mike looks like someone's just punched him in the nuts.

DA-DOO! It opens its mouth all the way and screams just like a baby. "WHAAAAA! WHAAAAA!"

"You bitch!" Mike growls, rushing forward, grabbing it as it wails. "Where is he? WHERE IS HE?"

"Mike, no!" I grab his arm, but he's too strong. "Don't do that!"

I eat eyes, it tells him, and Mike rips off its head. Blood gushes out of it, all over his hands, spills onto the sand, so much of it, like a water balloon when it bursts.

Mike drops what's left of it, stamps on it again and again, boots and pants spattered with blood, the head rolling, cackling, calling, *Da-doo! Da-doo! Da-doo!* until Mike smashes it about a dozen times with a big rock.

He kneels there, staring at its bloody remains. For a few moments, the only sound is him gasping.

"Mike?"

Nothing.

"Mike? Are you okay?"

He shakes his head. "No. No, I'm not."

"Mike, wha—"

"C'mon," he says, standing up. Starts walking, and I follow him. He doesn't answer anything, and after a while, I quit asking.

* * *

Wondering what's going on back in the world. I'm sure the cops looked for us, and maybe they found the bike, or what's left of it. Are they searching around there, in the woods and the fields? Did they put out an AMBER Alert? Were we on the news?

What if they think we ran away? Like on TV, just some stupid teenager thing, as if we were going to Vegas to get married, and have a baby, and live happily ever after, and all that bullshit. Or maybe they think Sam killed me for some reason, I don't know what, and hid my body, and now he's disappeared. And if that's happened, his mom, and Cynthia, and Uncle Tony—what must be going through their minds?

Sam's mom. I hadn't thought of her until now. She loves him—Cynthia does too, even if she acts like she doesn't. They have to be out of their heads missing him, worrying about him, waiting for him. Must be nice having a family who gives a damn about you. All I have is Uncle Tony. He was on a business trip to Florida; Mrs. Sullivan would have called and let him know, right? And he would have come back, wouldn't he, to be there when someone found me and brought me home?

Except nobody will.

I tramp along, looking at the back of Mike's head. He's lucky. I can't imagine anybody cares about him.

* * *

There's something up ahead, coming out of the ground, like a finger pointing to the gray sky. I have this weird feeling that I've seen it before, thought this before.

"What's that?" I ask.

"Do you need glasses?" Mike replies. "It's just a big rock."

It *is* a rock, looking like it has to be twenty feet high, and way too wide for me to wrap my arms around it if I tried. We go up to it like we did the house, slowly, carefully, looking here and there, ready for anything.

Carvings and writing, big and small, all over it. *These lonely lands. Ōth lies and waits. Its presence. Hangs the tree.* More. Too many to read.

There, next to the rock, on the sand. A phone. It's Sam's.

Just like in my dream.

Track 14. Where Have All the Good Times Gone

"That's Sam's phone," I said, picking it up.

"That's a phone?" Mike asks.

"Remember, when I told you I had a weird dream? I saw this: the big rock, with writing all over it, and the phone—he dropped it, and here it is!" Mike looks at me like I'm crazy. "She had him, she's taking him somewhere, and they were here!" I kneel on the gray sand, by a big patch swarming with tiny black ants, where Sam barfed.

I pick up his phone, push the home button. The screen comes on, all gray and scratchy instead of the photo of us that he had as his background. He'd set up touch ID, but I put in his passcode—2599—and some of the icons, not all of them, come up.

Nineteen percent battery. I hit PHOTOS, and there he is, doing a selfie with Buddy, the big German Shepherd who lives on Fairmore Farm, where Sam does his therapy horseback riding.

Sam took that photo right before we got on my bike and headed for his house—except we never made it. How long ago was that? It seems like forever.

I'm not gonna cry. I'm not. Mike will make fun of me, he always makes fun of me and I can't stand it he's gone he's gone he's so far away she has him and—Damn it. Damn it.

I cry anyway, for a long time, and I don't even care about what Mike's going to say. I'm sure it'll be mean. But when I look up and wipe my nose on my jacket's sleeve, he's standing by the big rock, staring at it.

I close PHOTOS, put his phone in my jacket pocket, get up. Go over to Mike. I'm sniffling.

"What are you doing?" I ask.

"I haven't found 'Kilroy Was Here' yet," he says, pointing at what's scribbled and carved and drawn on the rock, "but I bet I will."

I don't get what he means, but it doesn't matter. I just stand next to him, reading what's there. Some of it's in English, most of it isn't. Some of it, I'm not even sure is writing, just strange little pictures and symbols. Sorta like hiero-whatevers, but not the ones the Egyptians used. As if I'd know.

"You okay?" he asks.

I nod. "I dreamed this," I said, running my hand on the rock. "I was in Sam's head, but it was still me inside. I was seeing through his eyes, and I heard and felt what he did, and I knew what he was thinking."

"It's just déjà vu."

"No, it's not. It was real. I mean, yeah, it was a dream, but it wasn't *just* a dream. I've had one like that before, about Sam on the train, with...whatever she is."

"Dreams don't mean anything."

"But he was here!" I show him the phone. "This is his! He dropped it."

He takes the phone, turns it over in his hands. "How is this a telephone?"

"Wait—are you serious?"

"Are you?"

"Of course this is a phone. Everybody knows what a phone is."

"That's not a phone where I come from."

"Where's that? Mars?"

"Arizona. Payson, in Gila County."

He's totally messing with me. I take the phone from him, put it in my pocket again. Go back to where Sam puked. There's not much of it left: the wet part must of soaked into the ground, and the bugs are taking care of the rest. So, it was a while ago when he was here. Days, I guess. Since that time we camped under the trees.

He won't know. That's what she said to Sam, in my dream. *No one will.* And then she pulled him onto his feet and pushed him.... I look around.

"She took him that way," I say, pointing ahead of us and slightly to the right.

"Uh huh," Mike replies. He's slowly circling the big rock, staring at it, eyes scrunched up.

"So, we should go that way."

He doesn't say anything.

"Did you even hear what I said?"

"What do you suppose 'the empty?' is?"

"I don't know."

"I don't know either, but it's up here different places, in three different handwritings. 'The empty at the edge,'" he reads. Moves to another. "'Past the fence, past the rock, is the empty.'" Goes back to where we were standing. "'The empty is the way out.'"

"Maybe it's like dreams: it doesn't mean anything."

"Don't be bitchy. No, maybe it doesn't mean anything, maybe it does. It might be a way to get back."

"Back...home?"

"Yeah."

These lonely lands. "'The edge,' like...the edge of the world?"

"That's what I'm thinking."

"The world doesn't have an edge. It's round. Like a ball."

"We're not in that world," he reminds me. "Maybe this one isn't round, like a ball."

"How is that possible?"

He spreads his arms. "How is any of this? Or maybe 'the edge' is a metaphor. Do they teach about metaphors at those schools in Maryland?"

"Yeah, they do." Though I don't really know the difference between them and similes. "Don't be a dick."

"So, what I propose is that after we grab Sammy and throw a bucket of water on Margaret Hamilton, we find this 'edge' or this 'empty,' and get the ripe hell out of here."

"I thought you said this is a sink trap, that there's no going back."

"I've been known to be wrong before. I hope to be wrong again."

"Well, they went that way," I tell him again, pointing.

"How do you know that?"

"I saw it in my dream."

"Riiiiiiight. We should absolutely take walking directions from a dream that Little Miss Alyx-with-a-'y' had. Because that makes perfect sense."

"You mean like looking for an 'edge' that some dude scribbled about on a big rock in the middle of nowhere? And thinking that somehow, if we find it, we can get out of here? Like that makes so much more sense."

For a second, he just gives me this look. Then he goes, "Duly noted."

* * *

We walk for what must be days: I'm just about out of my meds. We always go me in front, Mike a few paces behind. I get this feeling from him like he still doesn't actually think that what I dreamed was real, or that we're going the right way, but he's not gonna argue about it now so that he can say, *I told you so* when I give up and we don't find Sam. But I'm not going to give up. And it's not like he knows where to go, either.

I tried to keep us headed in a straight line. At first, it was easy, because it was flat and the big rock stuck way up in the air, but not too much later after we started, the rock was gone, out of sight. Now I'm just guessing.

Soon after that, the wind picked up—a lot—and it won't stop. With all the dust and sand blowing around, sometimes it's hard to see more than a few yards in front of us. It's impossible to hear anything but its screaming, and if we want to say something to each other, we have to get real close and yell. I walk with my head down to keep the sand mostly out of my eyes, only looking up every now and then. It's freezing so bad that when I try to sleep, I lie on the ground shivering, my teeth for real chattering, I can't make them quit, and that goes on for hours, until I finally black out and don't dream.

We keep on like this, through the wind and the cold and the blowing sand, until I almost walk face-first into a Jeep.

I don't know much about cars, but I do know what this one is: I saw enough ads for them when Sam and I watched the Ravens on Sundays. It's a black Wrangler, two-door, with a hard top. Windows up, tinted dark—I can't see inside. Missouri plates, registration sticker due to expire in four months. It's not old and rusted and wrecked and looking like it's been sitting there for years.

Mike stares at the Jeep like he doesn't quite believe it. Which makes sense, I guess, given all the weird crap we've come across. He circles it, not getting too close, then he looks all around, and I do, too, but I can't see anything more than swirling gray.

I drop my pack, pull the long knife, pop the double blades. Cup my free hand to my mouth. "I'm getting in!"

"The hell you are!" He starts coming toward me.

I yank on the driver's door, and as it opens, I wonder—too late—what if something horrible's in there? But there isn't. It's just a car. Black interior, cloth upholstery, chrome accessories. Smells like cigarettes, though: the ashtray's overflowing with them. Gross.

I get in, shut the door. It's cold in here, too, but so much better than out there in the wind. Passenger side opens, Mike leaves his bag outside, slides into the seat, shuts the door. I thought he was putrid before.

This Wasted Land

"Have you lost your damn mind?" he asks.

"Relax." I hit the door lock button.

He pulls the .45 from his pocket. "I'm out of bullets. If there had been some...*thing* in here, we'd have been screwed."

"And if there was, it would've gotten me first. Besides, you have that other pistol."

"It's a flare gun. Haven't you ever seen *The Breakfast Club*?"

"No. Can you turn your head the other way when you talk? You stink."

"Well, now that you bring it up, you could use some Summer's Eve, sweetie, cuz you're 'not so fresh.'" He runs his hand along the dashboard, then starts fiddling with the console controls. "This is a Jeep? Why the hell would it not have a stick shift?"

The floor's littered with Lone Star beer cans, wrappers from McDonald's and Wendy's and Taco Bell and KFC, used napkins and tissues, empty bags of Cheetos and chips. At least, I think they're empty. I bend over, pick up a pretzel bag. Crumbs in the bottom. I pour them into my mouth. So salty. So, so damn good.

Mike scrounges by his boots, then reaches behind him. I turn around, knees on my seat, lean over into the back. Scraps here and there: I luck out and find a crust, about half as long as my pinky, of stale wheat bread left over from Subway. Under a *People* magazine from last February is a clear two-liter bottle of Dr. Skipper—the Safeway generic version—with a few swigs of pop left, and we split it. It only takes us a minute or so to root through all the trash on the floor, scavenging the little that's there. It's pathetic, but it's something, even if my stomach still hurts from being so damned hungry.

Don't think about it. "This car," I say. "I don't know how it got to this place, but it hasn't been here long."

"Tell me something I didn't already know." He flips open the glove box, then that space under the center armrest, then digs in the side pocket on the passenger door. "Don't just sit there sucking down oxygen, dumbass. Look for the keys."

I hadn't thought to check, but I do now, and the fob's not by the ignition, of course. Nobody except Uncle Tony leaves it there. I feel around in the driver's side pocket. No key fob there, either. Something else, though.

I hold it up with the very edges of my fingertips. An unwrapped condom. Stretched out. Mostly dry inside.

Mike holds up both hands, shakes his head. "I got problems of my own."

I open the door, blast of sand and cold air. I toss it, slam the door shut.

"Do you know how to hotwire a car?" I ask.

"No. Do you?"

I get out Sam's phone. Still nineteen percent battery. No bars. But maybe—

"What are you doing? Calling Triple A?"

"If somehow I can get Internet, we could google how to hotwire a Jeep."

He stares at me like I'm speaking Korean. "What the hell are you talking about?"

"I know it's crazy, and probably stupid. I mean, there's no possible way we could get any reception." I think about the phone ringing back in the booth, and the ship coming out of the ground. "But maybe we'll get lucky, and I can look it up."

"I don't even know what you're saying. You can't 'look up' anything on a phone. The only thing you can do with a phone is call somebody, and there's nobody to goddamn call."

Now it's my turn to look at him like he's not making sense. And then I remember him saying, *That's not a phone where I come from.*

When he saw my flashlight. *Is it a toy, or does it actually work?*

Having a cow about it isn't going to change anything, he said. Nobody talks like that. Not anymore, anyway.

And:

How long have you been here? I asked him.

It's hard to tell, he said. *For a while, I counted sleeps. Every time I slept, that was a day.*

So, how many has it been?

A couple thousand.

I tried to divide it in my head then, but I couldn't. Still can't. But it's a long time. Though, maybe it's even longer than that.

"Mike, what day was it when you came here?"

"It was a Sunday."

"What was the date?"

"August second."

"When, Mike?"

Nothing. He's looking down, not at me. He guesses, doesn't he?

"Mike?"

His hands are in his lap, and his fingers are twitching.

"1992."

Oh, my God.

He looks up.

"Alyx?"

I shake my head.

"When did you get here, Alyx?" His eyes go left right left right left right real fast.

"April third. It was a Wednesday."

"April." He nods, just a little. Swallows. "What year was that?"

"Mike…when you came here. That was…." I bite my lip.

"How long, Alyx?"

"Like…way before I was born."

He turns his face, looks out the side window. Nothing but blowing sand.

"And you're…what?" he asks. "Fifteen?"

"Seventeen. Eighteen in July."

"Seventeen." He looks down again. "So, 1992, that was…twenty? Twenty years ago?"

I don't say anything.

"Maybe more?"

"Mike, that was a really long time ago."

He sags in his seat, leans back against the headrest. Whispers, "Shit."

For a long while, neither of us says anything. He doesn't cry. He doesn't move. He just stares at the dashboard.

I reach over, hold my hand out to him. He doesn't take it.

After a while, I tap Sam's phone, put in his passcode, hit the Google app. "I'll…I'll see if, uh…if it's gonna work, and—"

He opens the door. Gets out. Grabs his bag and starts walking.

I stash the phone. Take my stuff. Go after him.

Track 15. Sick Again

An hour, maybe a little more. It's hard to tell time here, but I know it's only been about that long. That's all it took to get from the Jeep to here, the top of a high dune, and down there, at the bottom, a motel. ROBB'S MOTOR INN, the sign says. And VACANCY.

And it's lit up.

The wind's not as strong. Sand still swirling, but we can see farther. Whispering instead of whistling as it goes by, so we don't have to shout. "We staying there?" I ask, pointing.

He shrugs.

"What if there're monsters?"

Shrugs again.

I reach over my shoulder, realize that I can grab the handle of the knife without taking off my pack. Probably a good thing to know. I take it out of the mesh sleeve, but keep it in its sheath. Nod. "Okay."

We go down the dune, kicking up sand and dust and gravel and bits of trash. Past the sign, onto the asphalt pad of the bit of parking lot that's here. No cars. No lights from the windows of the line of rooms, except one towards the middle. Which we're headed for.

Mike pulls the new gun—the one he found in that box—from inside his coat. It sorta looks like what cops use when they're running radar, to see if you're speeding. He pops it open, loads one of the flares from his pocket into it, snaps it shut. I almost remind him of what he said about it and *The Breakfast Club*, but I decide not to. Doesn't seem like he's in the mood.

The door to the room opens, and some girl—she's maybe a few years older than me—comes out. She's only wearing a dark red t-shirt (ASU SUN DEVILS) that barely comes past her crotch. At least, I think that's all she's wearing: I don't wanna look too close. On the fat side, dyed blond hair that goes just to her shoulders, dirty feet. She's staring down, fumbling with a lighter for the cigarette in her mouth. Hard to do in this wind. Then she lifts her head, sees us, jerks back. "Shit!"

Mike raises the gun. "You move, and I'll blow your head off."

She puts her hands up and yeah, she's only wearing the shirt. I did not need to know that. "Tim!" she yells, cigarette falling to the pavement. "Jess!"

This guy—mid-twenties, also plump, scraggly beard, shorts with no shirt, no shoes—and a thin, skanky-looking chick—long, straight brown hair, wearing only a too-big, plain white t-shirt—come out of the room.

"Shelby, what's—whoa!" the dude—Tim, I guess—says, and he puts his hands up, too. The skank—Jess?—just stands there, staring at us. I'm not getting the feeling that any of them were honor roll students.

"Hey, man," Tim says, "be cool. What's goin' on?"

"Say the alphabet," Mike replies.

Tim hesitates. "Are you serious, hoss?"

Don't know where's Mike going with this, but I'll play along. "Shoot him," I tell Mike. It's just a flare gun, so I know he won't. At least, I don't think he will.

"A, B, C, D, E, F, G…" Tim starts to sing. "H, I, J, K, LMNOP. Q—"

"Shut up," Mike says. Points the gun at the fat girl—Shelby? "What's the capital of Manitoba?"

"What?" she asks. "How the hell should I know?"

"Good enough. You," Mike says, wagging the gun at Jess. She's just staring at the pavement. "Hey! Miss Congeniality!" He snaps his fingers three times; she doesn't look up. Just mumbling to herself.

"She's tripping, dude," Tim says.

"Shut up, asshole," Mike replies. To Jess: "Hey! You! Over here!" She looks up, eyes half open. "Sing 'Row, Row, Row Your Boat.'"

She looks at Tim, strokes his arm. "Can we go…? My feet are…cold."

"I gave you the first five words," Mike says.

"She's high!" Shelby shouts. "She doesn't know what she's doing!"

"You gotta sing for this guy," Tim tells Jess. "Then we can go back inside. Okay? Okay?" She nods, looks at Mike. "I'll sing with you. 'Row, row, row your boat, gently down the stream.'"

She shakes her head, but joins in. "'Merrily, merrily, merrily, merrily, life is but a dream. Row, row—'"

"All right," Mike says.

"Can we go back inside?" Jess asks. "Dave's gonna be mad at me," she tells Tim.

Dave? Mike glances at me. "Who else is here?" I ask.

"Nobody," Tim says. "Just the three of us. Listen, hoss, if you want money, we ain't got—"

"We don't want your money," Mike tells him.

"Cool," Tim says. "Okay, cool. You want to come in and party with us? We got beer and all kinds of good shit." His piggy eyes run all over me. "How about you, babe? Want to have a good time?"

Ugh. "No way in hell."

"We don't want to 'party' with you," Mike says. "How'd you get here?"

"We just got lost," Shelby says. "We were driving to Reno, and we tried this shortcut, and the GPS was no help, and—"

Like Waze for me. "Did you go over any train tracks?" I ask.

Shelby shrugs, looks at Tim; Tim looks at her. "I don't think we did," he says.

"Choo! Choo!" Jess goes. "Choo! Choo!" Smiles, eyes half open. "A train! A train! A train! A train!"

"Well…maybe," Shelby says. "I was pretty buzzed."

"How long have you been here?" Mike demands.

"I don't know," Tim says. "Three…four days. We took the shortcut, and then there was all this, like, wind and sand blowing everywhere, and the car crapped out." Was that their Jeep back there? "So, we walked here, and I'm tryin' to like get somebody to come fix the car, but I can't get any—"

"You have the keys?" I ask.

"Yeah, but—" Shelby starts.

"What's wrong with the car?" Mike asks.

"It just, like, won't run," Tim says. "I don't know what its deal is."

"And you've been here the whole time?" Mike asks, looking past the three of them. Lights on in the open doorway.

"Yeah," Tim says. The other two keep their hands up. Jess starts wandering back toward the room. I nod at Mike so he knows I'm watching her.

"You have food?" Mike asks.

"Hoss, there's lots of food," Tim replies. He points a couple doors down, to our left. "The kitchen's just filled, man. There's all kinds of stuff."

Mike scowls. You'd think he'd be happy to hear that. Jess is standing in the doorway, running her hands up and down the frame and mumbling again. They weren't kidding about her: girlfriend is wasted.

"Get back in there," Mike tells them, pointing at the room. "We're going to be staying down here," he says, waving the gun at the other end of the motel, "at least for a little while. Any of you come anywhere near us, I'll kill all three of you. No joke."

"Okay, mister, it's cool," Shelby says. Still with their hands up, she and Tim start backing away. "But, you know, if you change your mind and you want to hang with us, it's all good."

"I'd rather be dipped in shit," Mike says. He keeps the gun on them as they take Jess and go in, shut the door. Tim pulls back the curtain and watches us as we head to the other end.

"Are we really going to stay here?" I ask.

"You have a better idea?"

"No. But I'm not sharing a room with you."

"Patti wouldn't let you, anyway. She's the jealous type."

"Who's Patti? Your wife?"

"No, her name's Cathy. *Was* Cathy. We're not married anymore."

"Sorry to hear that."

He stops, looks at me. "Are you?"

"Yeah. Of course I am."

He ponders that. Nods. "Thanks." We start walking again. The parking lot around the motel is empty, no cars, and most of it's covered with blowing sand.

"So, really: who's Patti?"

"I was joking around."

"Okay, so what was all that about with making them sing and do the alphabet?"

"Some monsters can make themselves look and act and talk like they're human, but they don't usually know what people do. Not even simple stuff."

"They must be pretty dumb."

"No, they're usually smart. They only don't know nursery rhymes and ABC's—the stuff everybody knows—because they're only pretending to be human; they've never lived as one. After all, do you know what the Tibetan word for the number two is?"

"No."

"Me either. Because we weren't raised there."

"But that fat chick didn't know the capital of Mani...whatever you said. Is that even a real place?"

"Manitoba? Yeah, it's in Canada. Don't feel bad. Lots of people don't know it."

"Why'd you ask her that?"

"Because if she did know it, I'd be even more suspicious. Like, maybe she's a monster that can turn herself into a person *and* can read minds."

"Are there monsters like that?"

"I don't know, but I'm not taking chances."

"So, that's why you asked me all that when we met."

"Yep."

"Now it makes sense. What *is* the capital of Manitoba?"

"Winnipeg."

"If you say so. I've never heard of it."

Mike stops in front of the last door on the row. It has an old-style knob that takes a key, not a latch with a slot for a card. He turns the knob, pushes it open. Reaches in, flicks the switch on the wall by the door. A light comes on. Two beds, made, sheets tucked in, blanket spread over them, two pillows each, at the head. Thick beige carpet. A dresser with a TV on top, a little table and two chairs. Room's clean, no dust or sand or cobwebs.

"That ain't good," he says.

"Why not?" It looks nice. Hell, after God only knows how long I've been out here in this desert, it looks great.

He puts his hand up for me to wait outside. Gun ready, he goes in. Walks to the sink in the back, where the wall's covered in a mirror. Flips on the light there. Drinking glasses upside down, wrapped in plastic. Little soaps in paper wrappers. Hair dryer plugged into the wall, next to a coffee maker. He tries the faucet—water gushes out, just like it should. He shuts it off, turns, hits another light. Steps out of sight, into the bathroom. Must be okay, because he comes right back outside. Shuts the door. Starts toward where we just came from.

"What's the problem?" I ask, following him.

He doesn't say anything. Walks past the room where Jess and Shelby and Tim are staying—they're not at the window anymore—to the front, where you would check in. Goes inside and the overhead lights come on, automatically. Warm in here. Nobody at the desk. Nobody in the office behind it. Nobody in the bathrooms.

I try the phones there. No dial tone.

He goes through the lounge—couches and loveseats and a TV on the wall—to the dining area. About a dozen small, round tables, two chairs with each. Counters where breakfast is supposed to be served. Past that is the kitchen.

He opens the big, double-door refrigerator there. "Fancy that." Steps aside so I can see.

It's full of food.

Milk and eggs and butter and liquid waffle mix in cartons, and apples and bananas and oranges and big cans of juice—including grapefruit, tomato, and cranberry—and bottles of water. The cabinet next to the fridge has boxes of oatmeal and cereal, bags of muffins and bagels and bread, cans of fruit cocktail and little plastic containers of applesauce.

"This is awesome," I tell him.

"This is some shit."

Huh? I take a loaf of bread—holy crap, it's rye, I love that stuff—and look at the "best by" date. Not for another month—I guess. Now that I think about it, I don't have the faintest idea what day it is back home. In the world. I open the wrapper, breathe in. Ohhhhh, it's sooooo good.

He opens his duffel bag, starts shoveling in food from the fridge. I do the same with my backpack, but there isn't much room. I find plastic bags under the double sink in here, fill them with some of everything. I grab a gallon of milk, start drinking it right out of the jug. Is there anything better than cold milk when you're really thirsty? I don't think so.

"C'mon," he says. He's got that squirrelly look like he had at the pond where the thing with the million eyes came out of. We grab our bags, go out of the kitchen, cross the dining room real quick, then through the lounge, out the front door. The wind's blowing hard again, really cold and loud, dust and sand everywhere. Jesus, I hate this. Being somewhere normal—in a nothing-special motel lobby—for, like, five minutes makes me remember how much all of this completely sucks.

"We gotta keep going!" he yells, trying to be heard over the wind's screech.

Is he crazy? "No! Let's stay here!"

"It's not safe!"

"Nowhere's safe!" I spread my arms. "Where the hell are we supposed to go in…THIS?"

"We could go back to the car!"

"You go back to the car! I'm staying here!" I start stomping off toward the room we looked at, down the end.

He hesitates for a few moments, then hustles after me, catches me at the door before I can go in. It's not quite as loud here, under the overhang, with the building blocking some of the wind. "You ever stayed at a motel before?" he asks.

"Yeah." For a while, me and Mom were *living* at a motel, one of those crappy places where they let you rent a room from week to week.

"And how many of them just leave the rooms unlocked?"

I think about it. "None."

"Right. Otherwise, anybody could just pull up and stay without paying. You have to check in, and then they give you a key."

"So?"

"So, it's a motel with nice rooms, lots of food, running water, electricity, and heat, and you don't need money or a key to get in."

"Yeah?"

"Yeah. And it's in the middle of this shithole."

This Wasted Land

I just stare at him. What is his issue with this? Why can't something good just happen, for once? Why does he always have to act like everything's always so awful? Why can't he just…

Wait.

"'You can't trust anything,'" I tell him. "That's what you said when we first met."

"I've told you that a couple times. You can't trust anything. Not here, not anywhere."

I want to go in. I want to sit down in a real chair and eat real food—not slop from cans—at a real table, and then I want to take a long, hot shower and wash my clothes and sleep in a real bed with real sheets and pillows, and I want to be warm and not have to try to keep a fire going by burning trash, or try to stay awake while I'm supposed to watch out for monsters when it's Mike's turn to sleep. And I want to wake up in this nice room and then go home with Sam, somehow, and have all of this be over.

"So, what is this?" I ask.

"You know how they catch lobsters?"

"No. Do you?"

"They have this wooden thing—kind of looks like a basket. They put a piece of fish at one end of it, then they drop it into the sea, all the way to the bottom, where the lobsters are. A lobster can crawl in through a part like a funnel that gets narrow at the end. Once the lobster's through the funnel and at the end, it can't get out. It's stuck there, in the trap. Until the lobsterman comes along and gets it out."

"And eats it."

"Yeah."

"And that's what you think this is? A big lobster trap, but for people."

"Uh huh. How many doors does a motel room have?" He holds up his finger. "You can get in that way, but if something bad comes, you can't get out."

"I…I don't care. I don't want to go. It's finally something here

155

that isn't horrible. It's…" Damn it. Don't cry. He'll just make fun of you.

"I know. Believe me, I know. I think the last time I had a shower—not just some rain, or rubbing a baby wipe across my ass—was back at my in-law's in Arizona. And apparently, from what you tell me, that was a really long time ago."

"Okay, but…" C'mon. C'mon, Think of something. "How does the guy know when there's a lobster in his trap?"

"It's got a rope that connects it to a float on top of the water. The guy who owns the trap comes along on his boat, pulls up the rope, and looks in it."

"What if when he does that, there aren't any lobsters?"

"Then he might check to see if there's still bait in it, and if there is, he'll just drop it into the water again, right where it was."

"If this is a big lobster trap, how about we make it look like there's nothing in it?"

He looks around. "Let's go in and talk about it. I'm done freezing my ass off out here."

We go in the room, shut the door, put down our bags. As he's about to flick on the light again, I tell him, "No," and open the curtain just enough so we can see. Then I go to the thing on the wall that blows hot or cold air, and turn the heat on all the way up.

"So, what do you mean about making it look like nothing's in the trap?" he asks.

"If we stay quiet and leave the lights off and don't come out, then maybe if a…monster"—it's still weird to say that—"shows up, it won't know we're here, and it'll go away."

"It won't go away. It'll find them," he says, jerking his thumb toward the other room. "And that's better for us. They can be the lobsters."

"No way." I shake my head. "You gotta warn them."

"No, I don't, and you shouldn't, either. If I were you, I wouldn't get within arm's reach of that slimy piece of shit and his crack whores." He goes to the window, looks out for a few seconds, comes away again so that anything that might be out there can't see him. Hopefully. "All right, we'll lay low, at least to get cleaned up and some decent sleep for once. Maybe this windstorm will ease up soon—but I got a feeling that when it does, that's when it'll be time to check the trap."

"So, we'll just have to be ready to go, whenever."

"Yeah." He frowns. "It'd be nice if I knew what was wrong with the Jeep, because if I could get it running, we'd have it made."

"You think it's theirs?"

"Gotta be."

"Doesn't matter, cuz they're not gonna give us the keys."

"You'd be surprised what people are willing to do when you point a gun at them."

"You can't do that!"

"It's almost cute how naïve you are." He picks up his bag. "I'll be next door. Come get me if you need something."

"Thanks. You, too." He just grunts, like he can't imagine needing me for anything. "We should have a password, so we know it's us knocking, and not them."

"Our friends, the burnouts, in Room 13?"

"Yeah, them or something worse." I think about it. "For the password, how about 'Sam?'"

"Does the new girlfriend know his name?"

"That's not funny."

"But does she?"

Me yelling, *Where's Sam?* and *Give me back Sam!* as I'm punching her, right before she throws me off the train. "Yeah." Her looking through the tarp-thing, in the first dream of her I had. *Is that you, little girl?* "And she might know I'm following her."

"Then we need another password, in case she comes looking for you."

"How about 'Patti?' Or 'Winnipeg?'"

"'Winnipeg,' it is," he says, opens the door. "Stay safe, kid. Don't do anything stupid."

"You're not the boss of me."

"And I'm glad, cuz no matter how much that job pays, it ain't enough." Then he goes out.

Track 16. Don't Know What You Got

I switch on the light in the bathroom, shut the door so no one outside can see, take off my boots, start the shower. Wait for it to get hot—it doesn't take long—draw back the vinyl curtain, and step into the tub, still wearing my clothes. There's plenty of water pressure, not just a trickle, and I can't believe how good it feels on my scalp and my face. I strip out of my soggy clothes and leave them on the floor of the tub.

I just stand there, head down, watching the dirt and grit wash off me, leaving a trail from my feet to the drain. I let the heat seep into my neck, my back, all of me. Little bottles of shampoo and conditioner—I use like half of each, just because I can. Then I unwrap the soap and rub it on the washcloth and scrub myself all over, even standing on one foot to get between my toes. I've showered thousands of times and never thought about it much, sometimes even being kinda pissed that I had to stop whatever I was doing to get cleaned up, but this is the best one ever. Definitely.

When I'm done, I step out onto the bathmat, lean over, flip the little toggle thing or whatever it is that stops the drain, and pour more shampoo into the water that's filling up the tub. I let the shower run a little longer, then shut it off. The room's warm, full of steam—I can't see anything in the mirror here. I dry off with a big, thick towel, then I kneel down and get to work on my clothes.

I take the washcloth and start with my jeans. I scrub and scrub, even rub some of the bar soap on the washcloth and try that. It takes a while, and the water turns brownish-gray, but my jeans get clean. I throw them over the curtain rod, let the water out, turn it back on and fill it again, add the rest of the shampoo, shut it off. Do my shirt and bra and underwear and socks. Wring them out and hang them, too.

I put a towel around me out of habit, shut off the light, go out of the bathroom. Enough light for me to see coming past the edge of the curtain. There's a wrapper by the sink with a disposable toothbrush and a tiny tube of paste. I brush for what must be like ten minutes. A mini plastic bottle of mouthwash—I swig the whole thing, swish it around and around and around until I'm sick of the fake minty taste, spit it out.

I get my pack, take out the bowl and the spoon from the ship, open a box of Total that I just got at the kitchen. Pour the milk, sit in the semi-dark on the bed closest to the heater, and start shoveling it down. If you had told me before I got here that wholegrain cereal would soon be my best and favorite meal, I would have said that you were out of your mind. I tear through one bowl, fill it again, wolf down another. I'm finishing my third when I remember what I said to Mike about being ready to get out of here whenever.

I go back to the bathroom, close the door, turn on the light. Switch on the motel's hair dryer, and wave it back and forth, back and forth, back and forth over my clothes to get them dry. The bathroom's still warm, and the hair dryer's whine gets monotonous. My jeans take forever, of course, so by the time they're done, I'm almost dozing on my feet.

The mirror's not steamed up any more; I drop the towel. Bony as hell—I've already lost weight—and I have all these old cuts and bruises all over me. Not a good look. I turn off the light as I go out of the bathroom. My jacket's on the floor, where I left it: I get Sam's phone out of the inside pocket. Peel back the covers on the bed closest to the bathroom, then slip into the crisp white sheets, leaving them and the blanket tucked in at the bottom so I'm snug.

The screen's still scratchy, the time doesn't come up, but it still works. Nineteen percent battery. I put in Sam's passcode, go to PHOTOS. Swipe through them.

Us at lunch at school with his gamer friends, Dylan and Ryan and Holden. Him and me walking the Cross Island Trail—that was in March, just last month, and it was so chilly that morning. Me sitting across from him at 5 Guys, making a face and shoving a bunch of fries in my mouth. Us posing by my bike.

Sam sick in bed on Valentine's Day—he had bronchitis—so he

held up a sheet of white notebook paper with a little red heart at the top. Under that, he had written, *Store-bought cards probably aren't your thing, so I made you this. Sorry we can't be together. I love you.*

Eighteen percent now. Photos of me playing with and snuggling Penny. Us at New Year's, in his house, and of St. Christopher's decorated for Christmas, with this huge table in the foyer (Sam calls it a *narthex*) covered in Nativity figures. The stable, of course, and Mary and Joseph, and all the barn animals. But also like the whole town around it: buildings and merchants and travelers and women cooking or washing clothes. Beggars and Roman soldiers and kids running and playing. More animals: dogs and cats and donkeys and camels and sheep and even an elephant with some rich guy and his wife riding it in this little tent thing on top.

Me grinning, leaning over the Scrabble board, pointing to QUICKLY on a Triple Word Score, which gave me enough points to finally beat him, in either the fourth or fifth time we played.

A huge-ass cruise ship—Carnival, I think it was—going under the Bay Bridge as we went over it on my bike on a chilly day. That ship was so tall, it looked like it was gonna scrape the underside of the bridge. So tall, it looked like we could just jump down onto it and sail away to Miami, or Bermuda, or Mexico, or wherever warm it was going.

Thanksgiving, all of us, including Uncle Tony, on the couch with plates on our lap, all of staring at the game on TV. Well, not all of us. Sam was taking the picture, and Penny was waiting for Brenda's mom to spill her pie onto the carpet.

*　*　*

Turkey with stuffing. Sliced roast ham. Mashed potatoes with gravy. Broccoli and cheese casserole. Sweet potatoes. Mixed veggies: corn and green beans and peas and diced carrots and asparagus tips. Cranberry sauce, but does anyone actually eat that? Pumpkin pie that Sam's mom made from scratch, with Cool Whip that Cynthia stopped and bought at a store on the way up from Virginia, where she lives now. There had been a can of whipped cream before, but last night, me and Sam cuddled on the couch watching movies, and took turns tipping the can over and squirting cream into each other's mouths, 'til it was all gone.

"Everything tastes great," Uncle Tony told Sam's mom. "Thank you again for having us, Brenda."

We were sitting in the family room, Uncle Tony in one recliner, Sam's mom in the other, and in between was the couch with me and Sam and Cynthia. Kinda squished, but okay. We were eating off thick paper plates, those really good ones, watching the Cowboys and the Packers. Penny sat on the floor, ears up, tail wagging, waiting for someone to give her a treat off their plate. That someone was usually Cynthia.

"I'm so glad you could come," Sam's mom said. "Alyx told us all about you. How exciting that you played in the NFL."

"It wasn't as glamorous as it sounds," he said.

I thought for sure when Sam told me that his mom was inviting me and Uncle Tony to Thanksgiving dinner that it would be a big fancy thing like you see in movies and magazines: people dressed up, sitting around the table, bowing their heads and all that. But Sam wasn't kidding when he said that they were huge football fans. They were all in their purple Ravens jerseys, dinner was set up as a buffet out in the kitchen so you could get what you wanted and sit in front of the TV, and they were waiting for the big Baltimore-Pittsburgh game tonight at 8:30. Ravens fans hate the Steelers; Uncle Tony doesn't like either of them, but he was making nice.

"What's your favorite team?" Cynthia asked me.

"I don't have one. I just got into football right before Homecoming."

"Would you like to come to a game with us?" Sam's mom asked.

"Yeah!" Sam said. "That'd be awesome!"

"Oh, that's nice, but I wouldn't want you to go out of your way. I mean, I bet that's massively expensive."

"It's no bother," she said. "We have season tickets for four, so we're always taking someone with us." Four tickets, but there's only three of them; Sam's dad must have been the other one. "We'd love to have you whenever you want."

"Yeah, that'd be cool," I said. I had another big forkful of the mashed potatoes: they were real, not from a box, which is all we ever had even before my dad took off. "This is sooooo delicious."

"Lots better than the hospital food," Cynthia agreed.

"You work at one?" Uncle Tony asked.

"Yeah, St. Catherine's in Richmond. I'm a pediatric nurse in the NICU."

"What's that?" I asked.

"Neonatal Intensive Care Unit," she said. "Like for preemies, or babies who are sick."

"That sounds stressful," I said.

"Nah, actually it's kind of boring. I do overnights, so hardly anything is going on."

Sam tossed a piece of the outside of the ham—it was a little burned—to Penny, who let it bounce off her nose and hit the carpet. She looked around for a second, found it, gobbled it down. "Sam, just hold it out for her," his mom said. "She doesn't catch well."

"My dog never misses anything that you toss at him," Uncle Tony said.

"What's his name?" Sam's mom asked.

"Jake. Big Rottie. Sweet boy."

Sam finished his plate and said, "I'm getting some more. Anyone want something?" Leaned forward to stand up, rocked back, tried again.

"Here, let me." I held my hand out for his plate.

"I'm good." He's touchy about being able to do stuff like normal people.

"I know, it's just I'm getting up anyway." I took his plate, stood. "What do you want?"

"The other drumstick, and some more sweet potatoes."

"That drumstick's mine, doofus," Cynthia said. "I called it."

"No way! You did not!"

"Yeah, she did," I said. "When I was getting the first one."

"When was that?" Sam asked.

"Right when Mom said it was dinner time," Cynthia told him.

"I was in the bathroom!"

"Tough," Cynthia said, standing up and heading for the kitchen. "There's the quick, and then there's the hungry."

"What do you want instead?" I asked him.

He scowled. "I guess some dark meat, if there's any left."

"I bet there is." I looked at Uncle Tony, and Sam's mom. "Either of you want anything?"

"No thanks, dear," she said.

"I'm fine," he said.

I followed Cynthia into the kitchen. She was forking white meat onto her plate. "Your uncle's nice," she told me. "If he and my mom hit it off, maybe they'll get married, or something."

"He's...ancient."

"Mom's into geezers. Our dad's fourteen years older than her. That guy, Chuck, she's been seeing is almost sixty." I didn't ask where Chuck was, just put some broccoli on Sam's plate, moved over to the turkey.

"Hey, are you and my brother screwing?"

"No!" I whispered. "We've only been going out like a month."

"So?"

"So, we're not like that."

"Is it because he's disabled?"

"No!"

"Are you, like, Mormon or something?"

"I don't even believe in God."

"Were you molested when you were little?"

"No, just...." Damn, talk about awkward. "That's not a thing with us. Not yet, anyway."

"When I was in high school, if you were going out for more than two weeks—three, tops—you were definitely doing it."

"Well, we're not like other people." I piled turkey on my plate and Sam's.

"You got that right." She went to the pumpkin pie, cut herself a slice. Looked up at me. "He's never had a girlfriend before. Not serious, I mean. Not like this."

"I haven't had a real boyfriend," I said. Okay, there was Tommy, but....

She nodded. "Just don't hurt him, all right? I give him a lot of shit, but he's a good kid."

"I know," I said. "I wouldn't ever hurt him."

She nodded again. "Okay. Cool."

"Touchdown!" Sam shouted.

"Who?" Cynthia yelled back.

"Cowboys!" Sam answered.

"Damn it," she said. "My boss is a Cowboys fan, and if they win, she won't shut up about it."

That was the best Thanksgiving I ever had.

* * *

I want to keep looking at pictures, but I don't want to run down his phone, because I left my charger cord at home that morning. The morning I went to school, took Sam to riding therapy, and never came back. I put the phone to sleep, set it on the little table next to the bed. Pull the covers up to my chin.

My period hasn't come yet, and it should have a long time ago. All the weirdness and stress and being starved and thirsty all the time must have thrown off my cycle. That's the only possible reason.

I don't notice myself falling asleep. I close my eyes for just a second, and when I open them again, I have to pee like mad, and my back's sore, and I can't feel my hands or my feet, because I haven't moved, haven't even rolled over, in what must have been hours. I sit up and shake my hands, wiggle my legs, trying to get some feeling back into them, and at first, it's just that godawful pins-and-needles thing. As soon as I can, I get out of bed, go to the bathroom, sit there forever until I'm all done. Soooo good. So much better.

I flush, wash my hands, and there's no way any of this can be real. To have toilets and showers and faucets with running water, you need pipes that go to places where they take in water and clean it and pump it to you, and you need people and electricity to do that. And to have electricity there to do the water, and here for hair dryers and heaters and lights, you need power lines that go to buildings where they generate *that*, and you need more people and energy, and there's none of that in this place. This world.

So, how does it work? Where does it come from? And when I let the water out of the tub, or flush the toilet, where does it go?

Screw it—I'm hungry again. That's how I can tell I must have slept for a long time. There's a clock on the nightstand, but it just flashes 12:00 over and over again. I didn't think to set it before I went to bed—not that I would have known what time it was then. But at least if I had, I'd know how long I was out. No dreams, at least none I remember. If I had, maybe there would have been one that would help me find Sam.

I get dressed. There's plenty of food from before, but I should save it, get some more from the kitchen. Mike said not to do anything stupid, but it'll only take a minute. I'll got the new knife: it'll be fine.

I go out, making sure the door doesn't lock behind me. The

room and the shower and the bed have been so warm that it surprises me how cold it is out here. It's not as bad as before, but the wind's still blowing something fierce, which I suppose is a good thing. Hopefully, it's keeping whatever's out there away.

As I go past Room 13, the door opens, and Jess comes out again. She's wearing Shelby's ASU t-shirt, some raggedy jeans, still nothing on her feet. She's got a cigarette and looks a lot more with it. Before the door shuts, I see Shelby and Tim passed out together on one of the beds. What the hell is wrong with some people?

"Hey," she says. Pulls a pack from her pocket. "Want one?"

"Smoking's gross."

She shrugs. "I'm Jess."

"I know who you are." I grip the knife handle, just in case. *You can't trust anything.* I sure as hell don't trust her. Or any of them. "What're you doing out here?"

"Coolin' off. Tim's got the heat cranked." She takes a drag off her cigarette. "What're *you* doin' out here?"

"None of your damn business."

"Don't gotta be that way about it." She looks past me, nods once. "That guy you were with—you two together?"

Can't believe she remembers Mike or me or anything. "No, we're not." Why's she asking? "You stay away from him."

She takes another puff. "Maybe." Shaking her head, she looks around at the gray desert and the swirling sand. "This is...wild. Where we are?"

I want to tell her, *We're in a trap. And you're gonna die.* Instead, I say, "I don't have time for this." I give her a lot of space as I go past, not taking my eye off her.

The lobby's just like before, but I pop the blades on the new knife. Go to the kitchen and get some more applesauce and bananas and some blueberry muffins. I'd love to fry some eggs—sunny-side up—but that's too long away from my room, and I already wasted enough time talking to the trailer trash. In the fridge are what might be hardboiled eggs, and if they are, that'll do. I crack one open on the counter: yep. I grab all dozen or so of them, stash them and the rest of my food in a plastic bag, start heading out.

When I get to the lounge, the TV comes on.

The news. A pretty, middle-aged woman, shoulder-length brown hair. Holy shit, is she—? Yeah, she totally is. She's standing in front of our high school.

"—*exactly two weeks to the day since they went missing, the question everyone's asking, but no one has any answers to, is 'Where are they?'*"

Cuts to a picture of me and Sam sitting together at the Ravens game against the Browns. His mom took that right before kickoff.

The broadcast goes on. Says that police and paramedics responded to my 911 call—but it doesn't say what I said about that crazy old bitch. That they found my bike—they think it crashed—but they haven't found us.

Says hundreds of people—professionals and volunteers—are out searching. That we've been on the news in the whole state, DC and Delaware. That my uncle's offering a reward—$20,000—for information that leads to getting us back. But nothing so far.

"*For WBAL-TV 11, this is Jennifer Franciotti reporting live, from Stevensville, Maryland.*"

And then it shuts off.

Oh, my God. I gotta tell Mike about this.

Nobody outside. I run to his room, bang on the door again and again and again.

From behind it, muffled. "'Say the password, onionhead.'"

I'm getting used to not getting what he says. "Winnipeg."

He undoes the chain, opens the door. It's totally not him.

Track 17. Dust n' Bones

Mike's clean and his clothes are different—he must have had them in his bag. They're clean, too. He's cut his hair super-short, like he's an Army guy or something. No beard, and he trimmed his nails. He looks completely different.

"Whoa," I say.

He looks around outside. "Get in here before something tries to kill us."

I shut the door behind me. He's got the curtains drawn tight and the bathroom door open, and the light from there is the only one on. All his stuff's spread out on one of the beds; the other's all rumpled up. He must have gotten some sleep, too. And he doesn't even smell bad. "Whaddya want?" he asks.

"You don't look like hell anymore. Lucky you, cuz that skank Jess said she'll be down here any minute to throw herself at you."

"I told you not to talk to them."

"She came out when I went to the kitchen."

"Why the hell did you go back there? Are you trying to get yourself perished?"

"Relax. Nothing happened. Nothing except when I was there, the TV in the lobby came on, and there was a news show about me and Sam being missing for, like, two weeks."

He grunts. No idea what that's supposed to mean.

"Well?"

"'Well' what? TV news is bullshit. Always has been. No point in paying any attention to anything you see on it. Especially here."

He goes over to his stuff, starts sorting through it. The water filter thing he made, cans of food, a small pot with most of the handle broken off, a few Sterno cans, a couple pair of socks, a magazine, canteens, a flashlight, some other things.

"I got some hard-boiled eggs," I tell him. You want some?"

"Absolutely."

I hold the bag open and he takes a couple, cracks one open on the table where the TV is. I nod at it. "Does it work?"

"The TV? No." He sits down on the bed, starts peeling his egg and dropping the bits of shell into the little wastebasket beside it. Points at the phone on the nightstand. "That doesn't work, either."

Crap. I just now remember that Sam's is back in my room. I don't want to have something happen to it, or forget it again and leave it here. I think about asking Mike how there can be power and water, then decide against it. He'd probably just say, *Who cares?*, or, *How is there the motel here?*, or something like that. Instead, I ask, "How'd you do your hair?"

"My knife."

"Didn't you cut yourself?"

"Yeah." He leans forward, shows me his scalp. Even in the half dark, I can see lots of places where he nicked himself. He sits back up straight, starts eating the egg. Now I notice the cuts on his chin and his jaw, too.

I sit down at the little round table by the window. "Why'd you do it?"

"Tired of looking like Bigfoot. Also, keeps the lice away."

Gross. "You had lice?"

"Not anymore."

Ugh. I peel an egg, eat it. Mike finishes his first, starts on the other. I can't get over how different he looks. "Hey," I go. "How old are you?"

"If you're not kidding me about what year it is, I'm in my fifties."

Damn, that's old. "You don't look like it."

"Yeah, I've been wondering about that. It's another reason why I shaved. Wanted to get a good look at myself." He gets up, goes to the sink, stands in front of the mirror on the back wall. "I was in my twenties when I got stuck here. I've gone through a lot since then, but even so, I don't think I look more than thirty-five." He turns around. "Which would still be twice your age, so sorry, sweetie, it's not gonna work out."

"Don't tell me, tell your meth-head girlfriend down the way."

He frowns, puzzled.

"Did they not have meth in 1992?"

"Not that I remember. It's a drug, right?"

"Only a lot. So, if you've been here forever, how come you haven't gotten much older?"

He leans back against the sink. "That's a damn good question. Maybe here, time passes slower."

"How can it do that?"

"I guess they never taught you Einstein's Theory of Relativity."

"What does that have to do with anything?"

"Well, in this case, it means that time can run faster or slower for you, depending on where you are."

"Nuh uh."

"It's more complicated than that, but yeah."

Is that why my period hasn't come? "How do you know that?"

"I used to read a lot."

"I thought you said you weren't good at school."

"I wasn't. But they had a good library when I was in the county jail."

"No way!" I start peeling another egg. "You were not in prison!"

"Yeah, I was." Crosses his arms. "Six months. Beat the hell out of the guy who was screwing my wife."

"Cathy?"

"Yeah."

"Whuuuuuuuuuuuuw," I whistle. "So that's why you're not married anymore."

"No, we stayed together, even after all that."

I wrinkle up my face. "Why? If someone cheated on me, they'd be gone."

"You're just a kid. You wouldn't understand."

"What's to understand? They cheat on you, you dump them. After you mess them up."

He shakes his head. "It's not always that easy."

"Pfft. Yeah, it is. So, how come you're not married?"

"I don't want to talk about it."

"You brought it up, Mr. 'I-Used-To-Read-A-Lot-In-Prison.'"

"It was a long time ago. Longer than I thought, apparently."

"What, you're not married because you're here and she's not? I mean, so what if it's been a long time? As soon as we get Sam and go home, you can find Cathy and—"

"She's dead."

Oh.

Oh.

Damn it, I'm such an asshole.

"Sorry."

He doesn't say anything for a minute. Then: "You know, people always expect that anything that happened a long time ago is just magically supposed to be okay now. 'Time heals all wounds,' and all that happy horseshit."

"Except it's not okay, is it?"

"No, it's not."

I'm not hungry anymore. I start to get up.

"No, don't go." Shakes his head. "It's...I didn't mean to lay all that on you. That wasn't fair. It's not your problem."

Arms still crossed, he stares at the floor. I wish I hadn't said what I did. We were just talking, and everything was cool, and we were actually getting along, and then I ruined it by saying something stupid. I should have known. I shouldn't have pressed him. I should have just minded my business, like he always tells me.

I look around the room. Nothing special, just what you'd expect. Stucco ceiling, tacky beige carpet, boring furniture. I look at the bed, at all his stuff and gear he has. I reach over, pick up the magazine.

PLAYBOY. The woman on the cover is unbuttoning her blouse from the bottom up, and...and she's gorgeous. Flat stomach, tan skin, a bit of cleavage. Long, wavy brown hair, coy half-smile. But it's her eyes that make her so beautiful. They're big, and deep brown, and they just pull you in. You could drown in them, forever, and it would be wonderful. She's perfect. Absolutely perfect. She's what guys mean when they say a woman's a *goddess*.

She's everything I'm not.

"Hey, you shouldn't be reading that," Mike says.

"I'm not. I'm just checking out the cover." One of the blurbs reads, NOW, THE REAL JIMMY CARTER ON POLITICS, RELIGION, THE PRESS... blah blah blah. The next one down: YOU AND THE STOCK MARKET—who cares? Under that, TURN ON TO OUR C.B. PLAYMATE: COVER GIRL PATTI MCGUIRE.

"So that's Patti," I say. I look closer at the cover. NOVEMBER 1976.

"Yeah. Found that a while back. For how old it is, it's in pretty good shape. Some guys say they read it for the articles, but not me." Smirks. "I just look at the pictures."

"I'll bet. Perv." I don't mean it. He knows I don't, either. I set it back on the bed. "I think my dad used to buy these."

Mike comes over, starts putting his stuff in his duffel bag. "What's your old man like?"

"My dad? He's...I don't know. He walked out on me and my

mom a long time ago. Haven't heard from him since."

"That was pretty shitty of him."

"Yeah, but I'm over it. My uncle says, 'he is who he is.' There's nothing any of us could have said or done to make him stay."

"His loss. Dumbass was lucky enough to get a wife and a kid, and he just threw that away. For what? Another woman? The bottle? Not having to be responsible for anyone but himself?"

I shrug. "Don't know. It doesn't really matter anymore."

"Guess not."

"How about you?"

"My dad? He was a great guy. Worked hard—he was a mechanic, fixed those big trucks and pavers and things they use when they're laying down roads and painting them and such. Was always good to my mom. Never raised his voice or his hand to her, never went to the titty bars, never touched another woman. Coached me and my brothers in Little League. Took us fishing off Rocky Point every summer. Liked Gilbert and Sullivan. One day at the shop, he collapsed. Died in the ambulance before they could get him to the emergency room. Aortic aneurysm."

"What's that?"

"There's a big blood vessel that runs past your stomach. You get older, and the walls of it can thin out. If it tears or pops, you bleed to death inside. No warning—just happens. The only good thing about it is it doesn't take long."

"Sorry about your dad."

"Sorry about yours." He goes to the window, pulls back the curtain a smidge to peek out. The wind's gotten much stronger. "I was nineteen when he died, and I still miss him."

It's weird to think of Mike having a dad. I mean, of course he does. Everyone does, even if their dad is dead, or they don't live with their kids anymore, or whatever. But it's still weird, cuz that makes me imagine Mike as a little kid in a uniform, out there on a baseball field somewhere, listening to his dad teach him how to throw or catch or hit or run the bases. It's hard not to think of

Mike as anything but what he is now.

I stand up, gather my bag of food. "I should get back to my room and pack my stuff, so we can go real fast if we have to."

"Good thinking," he says. "Try to get some more rest."

"You, too." Then I go out, shut the door behind me. No one and nothing in sight, just gray, blowing sand.

Back into my room. I make sure that Sam's phone is right where I left it, and I remember to set the clock on the nightstand to 12:01, just so it will start keeping time. I turn on the bathroom light, and crack the door so I can see a little better without letting anyone outside know that someone's here.

I'm not sleepy. For something to do, I take the stuff out of my pack, spread it out on the other bed, the one I hadn't slept in. Purell, Chapstick, Midol. Lamotrigine. Sketch pad, pencils, pen, a composition book. I haven't been to school in forever. If we ever get back, I'm going to have to repeat senior year.

Mascara, Always pads—don't know if I'm ever going to get my period again. The last few chapters of *The Sun Also Rises,* cuz I've been ripping out pages for toilet paper. What else am I supposed to use? Besides, it's a sucky story. Cans of fruit cocktail from the kitchen. The bowl and the forks and spoons I got from the ship. That was before I met Mike: it feels so long ago. The book in Spanish.

It's not big, but it's thick, heavy. I open it: it smells old, musty. The edges of the pages are yellow. I take it into the bathroom, shut the door. Sit on the floor by the toilet and flip through the book.

Lots of cool illustrations, all of them desert scenes. Cliffs and cactus, boulders and bushes—sorta reminds me of where we are, but nicer. Indians making fires, and using spears to hunt wild pigs, and building round houses, and doing dances, but they don't ride horses, and they don't have bows and arrows.

Monsters: a big, three-eyed toad-thing that's shooting some goo out its eyes; I think it's acid, cuz it's melting this Indian warrior guy. Another picture with this little lizard floating way up in the air in the middle of a rainstorm, fighting this long critter that's mostly like a snake, except it has six legs, and it's breathing a laser beam out of its mouth, and it's flying, too. A few pages after that, there's this really ill one of a naked woman with a coyote's head and eight breasts going down her belly, and she's ripping apart a screaming baby—blood and intestines everywhere—and she's eating him alive. Gross.

The drawings are by the same person—I can tell by the style—in thick, black ink, with all this really dense crosshatching that I'm geeking on. There have to be hundreds of little lines just in the diamond patterns on the back of the six-legged snake/dragon-thing; I can't imagine how long it took to do each diamond. There's an image of a long-eared fox that's so detailed, so realistic, it almost looks like a black-and-white photo. I got no idea how the artist did that.

When I get through finding all the pictures, I go back to the beginning and start reading. The book's a collection of short stories, and—good thing for me—it seems to be for kids, with a lot of basic Spanish words that I already know. Some of the rest, I can guess at, but even so, there's a bunch of it that I just don't get. No biggie. I'm kinda weirded out that someone would let kids read a book with drawings like the coyote-woman, or the one with these Indians in masks peeling the skin off this tied-up cowboy, but whatever.

I read, and after a while, my foot's gone numb, and I start feeling sleepy again. I shut the book, put it on the floor, stand, lift the toilet lid, strip off my jeans, pee. Wipe myself—I am totally stealing all the toilet paper. Then I get the book, and shut off the light as I go out. I pack up the book and all the stuff from the other bed, slip back into mine. The clock says 2:53.

No dreams.

* * *

It's 5:31—in the morning, or the evening? Don't know, can't tell—when I wake up. Hit the bathroom, take a crap, and when I'm done, I'm hungry again, thirsty, too. It occurs to me that the kitchen will have pop. Oh my God, would I love a Vanilla Coke right now, but that's probably way too much to ask for, cuz you can't always find it in even in our world, the real one.

But I bet they've got regular Coke.

I get dressed, pull on my jacket, stash my knife in it, like before. In horror movies, this would be the part where the Stupid Bitch gets herself killed by going Somewhere Bad by herself for No Good Reason. But it worked out fine before, so screw it.

Walk past Room 13: nothing going on there, that I can tell. Hopefully, they're still sleeping off their *partying*. Go to the lobby, into the kitchen. Nothing tries to kill me.

I make myself sunny-side-up eggs, with some toast, too, and—holy shit!—I find bacon in the back of the fridge. Fry up a bunch of *that*, too. And there's Coke, about a dozen two-liter bottles. I chug three glasses, with lots of ice, cuz it's better that way.

I leave the pan and my plate and the knife and fork in the sink: why bother washing them? I heft up a plastic-wrap package of 24 Dasani water bottles, balance an unopened bottle of Coke on top of it. Go through the lobby, look both ways as I push open the door to outside. Zero happening to the left, down at our end, either with Mike or our new pals. To the right—

To the right, a light's on that wasn't before, coming from the room at the end.

If this was a horror movie, this would be the part where everyone in the audience would be yelling at the Stupid Bitch to just go back to her room, to not go down to the one at the very far end of the motel, where the light's coming from, because OF COURSE there's going to be a Big Scary Monster in that room, and OF COURSE, it's going to kill her in a really messy way.

But maybe it's not a monster. Maybe it's someone else who wound up here in the sink trap. Not like the stoners, but someone who has their shit together. Maybe they can help me and Mike. Maybe we can help them.

I set the water and the pop down on the walkway, pull my knife. Slowly go to Room 1, stop just before I get to it. The blinds (the same shitty, white, aluminum ones in me and Mike's rooms) are shut, but the door isn't. Not quite. The wind tugs on it a little, makes it go *bhpp*...*bhpp*...*bhpp* against its frame every fifteen or twenty or thirty seconds or so, like a cat playing with it, as I stand outside and tell myself I'm an idiot, and real soon, I'm going to be a dead idiot.

I take the knob, knock on the door, slowly push it open. Wave of heat, cuz they've got it cranked. The bedstand lamp's on. The closer bed's empty. The other one, by the bathroom: someone's there.

"Is…is that you?" A woman's voice, so soft, I barely heard it over the heater. I step into the room, knife in front of me, ready.

"It is you…isn't it?" she asks. Thin, skin and bones—no, really. Her arms are as big around as a little kid's. Her bare legs are the same; knobby knees. Face all pulled in, most of her hair all fallen out, and what's left is just tufts of white here and there. She's old, wrinkled and liver-spotted everywhere, and her eyes are clouded over. Blind, I think. She's got nothing on but the thin brown blanket draped across her. She stirs a little, the blanket shifts, I get a glimpse. She's a *him*. At least, that's what Mike would say.

"Yeah," I say. "Yeah, it's me." I got no idea who this person thinks I am.

"I'm…glad…you came. Don't be…afraid. I can't…can't hurt you. It's…I'm not *her*."

"Who are you?"

"Tyra. I always liked it…that name…so, that's what I…called myself. You?"

"Alyx."

"You're a girl…with a boy's name. And…I used to be a boy…with a girl's name. Now, all I am…is dying."

"What's wrong?" Feel dumb as soon as I ask. She—he, whatever—is starving, actually starving to death. Seen photos of people in her condition, people in Africa, looking like sticks with heads. How long has it been since she ate? Weeks, I guess, maybe months? How long can you live without food, anyway? I stash the knife back in my jacket. "There's food in the kitchen, as much as you want. I can get it for you. You'll be okay."

"No…no, I won't. But if you…have water…that…that would

be nice."

"Hang on." I duck out of there real quick, run down to where I left the water. Tear open the plastic wrap, take a couple bottles, run back. Shut the door behind me and crouch between the beds, next to her. If this is a trick, if he—she—really is a monster just pretending, then I have my knife. But if not, I can't just let her suffer.

Put both bottles on the nightstand, uncap one. I lean in close, lift her head off the pillow. Slowly pour water into her mouth, a little at a time. Her lips are shredded, most of her teeth are gone. Reeks of piss.

She drinks about half the bottle. "Thank you." Sounds a little stronger.

"How did you get here?" I ask. "How long have you—"

"No." Weakly shakes her head. "Doesn't matter. You're here now."

"You asked if it was me."

"Yes. I knew you were coming. I didn't know when."

"How did you know that?"

"All my life, I've seen things. Not with my eyes. In dreams. Before they happen. They all came true. Little things. Meeting a new person. Watching someone put their keys on a desk. Cutting a piece of pie. Part of a TV show. Hearing someone say something. 'The mail always comes at 4:30.' Or, 'Tuesday would be better.' Things like that. Sometimes, I'd get a feeling about what I was seeing, happy, or sad. Like everything was okay, even if it didn't look that way. Or like everything was wrong, even if it looked fine."

Saying all that wears her out. I wait a while before I ask, "And you saw me coming?"

"A girl. Korean. Short hair. You dye it purple in front. Just the front."

"Yeah, that's me."

"I saw him, too. Boy. Twisted leg."

"Sam."

"With *her*. Her silver eyes."

I start to tell myself, *That crazy old bitch*, but she's not that, is she? "Yeah. I know who you mean."

"She's taking him. They're almost there. Big rocks, like knives sticking out of the ground. Past that's a mountain, flat on top. There's a place there. Sometimes it's one thing. Sometimes another. Palace. Temple. Hut. House."

For real? Maybe she's just imagining it all: you know, delusions. Maybe she's making it up, lying to me—but why? "That doesn't make any sense."

"No. It doesn't. Right now, it's a hospital. It's okay if you don't believe me."

"No, it's just…." Just what? Harder to believe than a motel with electricity and running water? No, it doesn't make any sense, but not much does. She might be delirious, she might be bullshitting me, but she *did* know I was coming, and she *did* know what I look like. There's no way she's faking that.

"So, where is this rock?" I ask.

"I don't know."

"You can see it, but you don't know how to get there from here? Fat lot of help that is."

She turns her milk eyes away. "I'm sorry."

Great: I just snapped at a blind, dying transperson who isn't psychic enough for me. "No, I'm sorry. I shouldn't have said that."

"It's all right. You're young. You can't help it, much."

Remember Mike telling me, not too long ago, *You're just a kid. You wouldn't understand.*

"Could I have some more water?"

"Yeah, sure." I lift her head, give it to her. "Sometimes, in my dreams, I see them, too—Sam and…*her*." Shrug. "Sometimes, anyway."

"You're close. You and this boy. You love him."

"I don't know."

She drinks until the bottle's empty. Gently, I put her head back on my lap. "Is there more?" she asks.

"Another bottle, right here, on the bedstand." I unscrew its cap of the other bottle, put it at the edge of the night stand.

Her breathing gets slow and shallow. She might live a few more hours, maybe even a few days. Part of me wants to wait with her until she goes, however long that might be. At the very least, maybe I can sit with her for a little while.

Outside, the wind starts picking up, a low, faint howl. I go to the window, peek out the blinds. Streamers of sand and ash and dust spilling onto the parking lot tarmac. Nothing else moving.

Tyra rouses, turns her face toward me. "Alyx?"

"Yeah." I come to her. The wind blows harder, faster, louder. A lot.

"You should go. Leave the water. I'll manage. Or not."

"I can't leave you."

"Yes. You can. You have to find Sam. I have to die. I don't know which will happen first." One of her hands flutters up; I take it. Feels like it would crumble if I held it too tight. "He loves you."

"Did you see that?"

"No." She squeezes my fingers. "Alyx, where you're going... nothing's real."

"You know that? Or is just a feeling?"

"Both. Don't believe what you see there."

"This guy I know says not to trust anything."

"That's not the same. You understand?"

"I...." I don't know. "I guess."

"Don't guess. Understand. You have to. It's important."

"Okay." I squeeze her hand, just a little. "Okay."

"Alyx, get Mike." I hadn't told her his name. "Get Mike and go now."

Dirt pattering against the window, the door. The light flickers. The wind, screeching. "Tyra—"

"Save Sam, or he'll kill him."

"Mike? No, he—"

"Not Mike. Ōth. Ōth will kill Sam."

"Who's—"

Something thumps against the window. The lamp goes out: shadows swallow the room.

"Go..." she whispers.

I pull open the door, look right, look left—can't see more than a few feet, flying ash and sand and grit stinging my face, my eyes, my hands as I hold them up. The wind shrieks so loud and high that I wince—and something out there, not far enough away, answers.

Shit. Shit, shit, shit.

I run, fast as I can, ignore the package of water I left outside the lobby, run, yelling, "Mike! Mike!" but I can hardly hear myself over the wind. Bang on the window and door of Room 13 as I run past, run to Mike's door, beat on it as hard and fast as I can.

He throws it open, already has his clothes, boots, coat on, his duffel bag over his shoulder. "Grab your shit and run!"

Thank God my stuff is packed. Wriggle into my jacket, grab Sam's phone off the nightstand, slip on my pack. Mike standing in the doorway, looking toward the lobby, the way I came, yells, "C'mon!"

Take the plastic bags of food, scramble for the door. Wailing wind, blowing sand, but something else, too, waves of force shuddering through me like when I went to a concert last year, and every time the bass player hit a note, I felt it press against my breastbone.

ahhhhhhhhhhhhhhhhhhhhhhhhhhhhhhhhhhhhhhhhh

Screaming, but it's just not the wind. It's Shelby—somehow, I'm sure it is. I try to look down that way, to the room where they're staying, but everything's swirling too thick, too close, too fast. I stretch out my arm and can barely see my hand.

"C'mon!" Mike grabbing my shoulder, pulling me away, out into—what? Where are we going? How can we see to get there?

A long, low moan coming out of the wind, somewhere not far, right over there, by Room 13, but somehow all around me, too. Like the wind's a living thing. Like it's pleased. Gratified.

Fulfilled.

ahhhhhhhhhhhhhhhhhhhhhhhhhhhhhhhhhhhhhhhhh

"C'mon!"

But I can't, because the screaming won't stop. She won't stop. She just keeps screaming, not just in terror and agony, but also, somehow, cuz she likes it. *Enjoys* it.

For two, three seconds and no more, the wind stops and the air clears and I see it. Jumble of gray dust and trash and black metal shards and mangled rubber chunks (it's the Jeep, it found the Jeep) and ribbons of dripping flesh—part of Tim's face an eye and some of his jaw and teeth—and splintered bones and wet sprays of red and brown, all of it swirling and splashing and crashing around and against itself, like it's a tornado, and it's ripping Shelby apart, slowly shredding her, and it gasps:

yessssssssssssssssssssssssss yesssssssssssssss

and she keeps screaming because even though there're only ragged tatters of her left, somehow, she's still alive, and tendrils of whatever this monster is crash through the room's window, smash the door, pull apart the frame and the walls, reach inside, and now it has Jess and she's screaming, arms and legs flailing as it drags her out, and then the wind comes screeching back, and Mike yanks me away and I finally turn and run.

Stumbling, hands out, sand blowing everywhere, it's in my eyes, I can't see where I'm going, what I'm doing. Mike—where is he? Behind me, I think, don't know for sure. Keep going. Which way? Don't know, doesn't matter. Have to get away, have to go, can't help them, can't hear them anymore, can't hear anything but the wind, the wind roaring, howling, the wind—

souls and skins souls and bones

Oh God, it's after us, I run faster, sand and dust and ashes blasting me, in my eyes can't see, in my hair and nose and mouth hard to breathe, something behind me, pushing me shoving me it's Mike and he's yelling and I can't hear what he's saying doesn't matter go go run run

Look back over my shoulder. It's there, the thing, huge swirl of dust and sand and trash and blood and flesh and scraps of the Jeep and broken pieces of the motel's walls and doors and windows, and they're inside it they're among it—Shelby and Tim and Jess—they're dead but they'll never die, it won't let them, they're caught in it and it won't ever let them go, and now it wants Mike, reaches for him, and he's turning, yanking the gun from his coat—stupid, just a flare gun won't do anything—he's going to die we're going to die, no, we won't, it'll keep us, eat us forever—

BWWWWWWMMMMMMM

Then everything explodes—fire, flames, screeching, it's screeching—and I'm spinning, tumbling in the air and I smash into the ground God God God it hurts so bad and I bounce and hit again and bounce and crash, face-first into the sand and—

Track 18. Plowed

I hurt everywhere.

Ears ringing.

So cold.

I'm laying at the bottom of a ditch or gully. Try to lift my head, and something stabs stabs stabs everywhere in my skull, all at once, and I put my head down and I lie there, eyes shut, shivering shuddering for a long time, how long I don't know.

I'm not dead. But I want to be.

Can't die. Sam. Sam needs me. And Mike.

Mike.

I open my eyes. See my breath floating away, vanishing. Okay. Okay. Do this. Lift my head again. It doesn't hurt as much.

Sam. Mike.

Slowly, I push myself off the ground, sit up. The world spins a little. I wait 'til it's done. Check myself out: not bleeding, nothing broken, not that I'd know what to do if I was hurt bad. God damn it, I was clean and warm, and now I'm dirty and freezing again.

"Mike?" Don't mean to, but my voice is nothing more than a whisper. Or is it? Ears still ringing, can't hardly hear anything else. I pick up a rock, bang it against another. A dull thud. It's me. I can't hardly hear. Shit. This better get better, cuz I don't wanna be half-deaf for the rest of my life. That would suck.

So, what happened? That whirlwind monster. It didn't wait until the sandstorm was over. Hell, maybe the sandstorm was *it* all along, and it was just waiting for the right time. It found Jess and Shelby and Tim, and it...it took them.

I should have warned them, should have told them it was a

trap. Mike said not to, but I should have, anyway. It's not that I liked them: Tim's eyes sliming all over me; Jess wasted, not talking sense; Shelby in nothing but her t-shirt. But still, I didn't want them to die. Didn't want—

Doesn't matter. Not anymore.

So, we ran, and it went after us. And then something exploded, threw me off my feet and into this gully. I don't care what Mike says: that's no goddamn *flare gun*.

Mike. Crap. He either blew himself up, or that tornado-demon thing got him. The gully's deep, maybe a dozen or fifteen feet or so; I have to climb out of here, find him, see what happened. See if he's alive or not.

It takes me two tries before I can stand up, and even then, my legs are shaky. The side of the gully is steep, and it's all dust and sand and gravel, like just about everywhere around here. My fingers sink into it as I try to climb. I get maybe a foot and a half before my arms and legs crap out on me and I slide back down, panting. I'm still too weak from getting tossed God knows how far and being knocked out. But I can't stay. I gotta find Mike.

Maybe he wound up down here, too. I rest for a few, get my breathing back to normal, and when I only feel like ninety-five percent shit instead of one hundred, I haul my ass up and start staggering down the gully.

I call, "Mike?" and something pinches really hard behind my eyes, but at least my voice sounds louder in my ears, so I guess I'm not going to stay part-deaf. Whisper this time: "Mike?"

Shut up or something will hear you and kill you, dumbass. Him talking, but not actually, only in my head. I'm winded already, but I keep lurching on, finally stumble, fall on my hands and knees. Puke out the eggs I had...however long ago that was. A few hours? Puke some more—comes out of my nose, too. Nothing left, just heaving. Burns all the way down.

Crumple to the ground. Lie there. Fight to not let everything go black.

Sam. Mike.

I'm sorry.

* * *

"Where the hell have you been?" he asks.

Mike's standing knee-deep—for real—in what's left of the motel: chunks of walls and doors, smashed furniture, shattered glass, scattered clothes and such. He sounds pissed, like my dad always did when he thought I'd been goofing off instead of cleaning the bathroom, or doing the laundry, or trying to make dinner for us because Mom was working and he had come home late from the bar—or from one of the skanks he met there.

"Scraping my shit together after you blew us up," I tell him. It took a long time before I could try again to get up, climb out of the gully, come back here. It's farther than I thought—maybe half a mile. It didn't feel that far when I was running away. "I hit my head really hard and I was messed up, but hey, thanks for asking how I'm doing. Where the hell have *you* been?"

"Digging through all this, trying to get the rest of our stuff. Including your teddy bear."

"And your jerk-off mag, I'm sure. Cuz that's more important than finding out what happened to me."

"I was a smidge preoccupied. Have you noticed that I'm not wearing my coat? Would you like me to illuminate you on why that is? It caught on fire when the gun went off. I was a little busy trying to put myself out. That was right after it knocked me halfway to Timbukthree."

"Just a 'flare gun,' right?"

"Your boyfriend Sammy ever tell you, you have a big mouth?" He goes back to rooting around through the junk. "I'm hoping Tom or Todd or whatever his name was had a coat or a jacket or something, or else I'm boned."

"Tim. His name was Tim."

"And I bet his mama was proud of him." He looks up. "Don't just stand there: help me look for whatever didn't get trashed by the Taz."

I don't move.

"You flat-chested *and* deaf?" he asks.

"Say the alphabet."

"I don't have time for this, Alyx-with-a-'y.'"

"Say it. Backwards. Or I'm not helping you." I show him my backpack. "I have my stuff. If you don't have yours, sucks to be you."

If he wasn't pissed before, he is now. "Fine," he sighs. "Z…Y…X…damn, this is hard. W…U—shit! W, V, U…T…S…Q—no, R, Q, P…"

"Keep going."

"How about if I sing you the 'Itsy Bitsy Spider' song? Or something else? I'm mostly into country. You ever heard of Waylon Jennings?"

"No."

"Not even from *Dukes of Hazzard*?"

"Damn, how old *are* you?"

"Look, the gun's over there," he says, pointing to his duffel bag. "If you think I'm a monster, go ahead and shoot."

"Why didn't your bag get burnt up, too?"

"Because I dropped it here before I started running for my life. Dropped my .45, too, and I can't find it anywhere."

I go there, pick up the gun. It's heavier than I thought it would be: ten, maybe even twelve pounds, like a dumbbell from gym class. I don't know a whole lot about pistols and such, but that's way more than anything my dad had laying around at home. Mike's just watching me.

I hold up the gun. "What makes you think I'm not a monster?" I ask him.

"Because if you were, you probably would have made a move by now. At the very least, pointed that at me."

"And what if I did?"

"You might pull a muscle trying to lift it with those Popsicle sticks you call arms, but that's about it." He slips his hand into his front pocket, comes out with the other rounds. Smirks.

"Good thing for you I'm not," I tell him.

"Likewise. Now give me a hand here."

I resist the urge to applaud sarcastically. Instead, I come over, start picking through the wreckage. "So, it's not a flare gun, but what is it?" I ask.

He shrugs. "It's some kind of…one-handed grenade launcher…pistol-cannon…thing. I wasn't military, but I don't think even they have something like this. At least not as of 1992."

"Where'd it come from?"

"You tell me."

"No, you tell *me*, Mr.-I-Used-To-Read-A-Lot-In-Prison." I take off my pack, pull the knife, pop the blades, give it to him. "Look at what's written there, by the handle."

"'Koninkrjk, Erisia.'" He pronounces it *ko-NIN-keerk AIR-iss-ee-ah*. "So?"

"So, I think that's a place, and this knife was made there."

"Big deal."

"Maybe it is. Have you heard of it? I haven't."

"And you're such a world traveler, at the tender age of seventeen."

"My dad was in the Army and we moved around a lot, so actually, yeah, I pretty much am."

"Yeah, but you didn't know the capital of Manitoba. This 'Koninkrjk, Erisia" could be a village or a little town or even a region in Scandinavia, or Iceland, or one of the Baltic countries, or wherever." He hands me the knife. "It doesn't even have to be a place. It could be somebody's name."

"I don't think so. And it was in the box with the gun, and the book."

"What does that have to do with anything?" Sorts through rubble again.

"I read some of the book, and…it's odd. It's kinda in Spanish, but not really. It's all these stories about Indians and the Old West, but I didn't recognize any of the tribes' names, or any of the places, and the maps are all wrong: it doesn't look anything like America."

"So, it's all made up, and whoever wrote it had quite the imagination."

"Maybe. Except we also have this gun that's like something out of a movie. And this knife from a place neither of us have heard of."

"Uh huh." He uncovers a black North Face jacket. "This must have been Tim-Bob's." Shakes out the dust and sand, brushes it off with his hand. "I hope it's a lot warmer than it looks."

"They are. That brand, I mean."

He puts it on, zips it up. Holds his arms out. "A little big, but not too bad."

"So, what do you think?"

"About what? The box with the weird things in it? I'd rather have a Ladmo Bag."

I shake my head. "I don't get half the things you say."

"I enjoy confusing you. It's like shooting fish in a barrel, but it never gets old." Starts going through motel remains again. "What exactly is your point?"

"My point is that I think the knife and the gun and the book and everything else that was in that box are from another world. Like ours, but not quite."

"One: that's ridiculous. Two: it's truly amazing how little I care."

"How is that ridiculous?"

"Three: you're not helping me find anything."

"Answer me."

"Okay, it's ridiculous because you're jumping to an outlandish conclusion. Maybe they're one-of-a-kind, custom-made pieces. Maybe they're prototypes. Maybe they're curiosities. Maybe they're props for a movie or theater production."

"The book's not any of those."

"Which leads me to my second statement: I don't care. I have bigger, more important things to worry about. Like finding what's left of our supplies and food, and seeing if we can salvage anything the burnouts had—"

"Why do you call them that? Their names were—"

"Screw what their names were. It doesn't matter. They don't matter. They never did. They're dead and we're not, and we're going to take their stuff and get out of here before something else horrible comes by and tries to kill us. Which ties in with the third thing I said: you're not doing us any good by standing around inventing wild-ass theories about random shit we found in a box."

I bend down, start digging. "Okay, I'll help, but listen, willya? There was this one time after I got here when I found this busted-up, high-tech, metal glove, with all these fiber optic wires and circuits and such, like something Iron Man would have—"

"Who the hell is Iron Man?"

"A superhero in movies." Sam's favorite. "He makes this suit of armor, and—"

"I get the idea."

"Anyway, back then, I thought it was just weird, but now I'm thinking maybe there's more to it than that. And I've found other stuff, too, that seemed like it was junk, but maybe it wasn't. Maybe they were all things from other worlds, and they wound up here, like that motel, and the house with that…whatever it was on the couch,"—the monster I killed—"and the cans and bottles and papers and trash, and all those rusted-out dead cars we come across."

He's found candy bars and Slim Jims, and he stuffs them in his pockets.

"I mean, in all this time you've been here," I say, "haven't you come across something, anything—it didn't have to be big or important—that was totally like nothing you'd ever seen? That you looked at and thought, 'What the hell is this?'"

He frowns. "Yeah," he admits. "Lots of times."

"So, it might not be that crazy or 'outlandish.' Remember what you told me about this place? That it's a sink trap? Well, maybe it's not just one for our world, but a whole bunch of them."

He nods. "Could be."

"And maybe the…creatures, maybe they're not 'monsters.' Maybe they're from those other worlds. Maybe they got lost and stuck here, like we did."

"And maybe none of that matters, because it doesn't help us get your boyfriend back from the White Witch." He straightens. "I've gone through this whole pile: I don't think we're going to find anything else. How about you?"

"No, I got nothing."

"You're right: this jacket is warm." Goes to his bag, puts it over his shoulder. "All right, let's get out of here while the getting's good. Not that we know where we're going—unless you had another one of your dreams where you saw which way to go." I can't tell if he's ragging on me or not.

"We have to find a huge rock that's flat on top. That's where she's taking him. And before we get there, there's all these big stones sticking out of the ground."

"You mean like the one we found, with all the writing on it?"

"I guess."

"You guess? Didn't you dream it?"

"Yeah," I lie. It's easier than telling him about Tyra, because that whole thing was too weird even to me. "Right."

"An enormous rock that's flat on top. Like a mesa."

"Yeah." I've never heard of a *mesa*, but if that's the same thing, okay.

This Wasted Land

He stares off into the distance. "I think I've seen that before."

"You have? Can we get there from here?"

"Maybe."

I hand him the gun. "Let's go find it."

Track 19. Humans Being

"Scope this out!" Mike shouts, pointing ahead. "Ain't that some shit!"

The wind's blowing up sand again, not nearly as bad as that time at the motel, but I can't see what's up from back here. Been walking for a few days, not that it's ever night. I used to try to keep up with Mike, but his legs are longer, and he never seems to get tired, so now I just go at my own pace, and he's always at least twenty, thirty yards ahead. I used to worry about being so far apart, in case monsters tried to pick off one of us—probably me, cuz I'm slower—but now I don't sweat it. What happens, happens.

I mentioned that, me not being pressed about what might happen, to Mike the last time we camped, and he said I was probably having the same attitude adjustment he went through not long after he got here. He said that people in constantly stressful situations like ours can't stay all worked up 24/7. Either you quit caring so much, or you go crazy. If you lose it, you might shut down: just stop somewhere, curl into a ball and hold your knees, then rock yourself until you snap out of it or you die. Or you might go off the deep end in the other direction, and act stupid and reckless, not even trying to do anything sensible or remotely cautious, just asking for something bad to happen to you. And eventually, of course, it would.

He said soldiers in a warzone go through the same sort of mind shift. At first, they're scared real bad, and it's hard for them to cope. The training they've gone through helps, and their commanders and the other guys in their unit make them keep it together, until after a while, they get over it. Mike never served, so I don't know if that's true, but it makes sense. My dad never mentioned it, but then, he was never in combat. Not that I know of.

I trudge up to him. "What?"

He rubs his jaw—his beard's growing back—points again. Up ahead, a quarter mile, maybe more. A long, light brown building, flat on top. Just for a second, when I first saw it, I thought it might be the rock we're going for. No such luck.

"What is it?" I ask.

"Let's go find out."

"There's gotta be something bad in there."

"Sure. But at the very least, we'll be out of the wind, so it should be warmer. And maybe we can scrounge."

That'd be good, cuz I'm about out of food. Mike told me to go easy on what we took from the motel, but it was hard to after being hungry for so long. No way am I gonna ask him to share what he has: I know how that would go. As in, him telling me *hell no*, and calling me *dumbass*. Again.

"Stick close," he says. Not a lot of windows on the side we're headed for, so something inside spotting us is one less thing to worry about. We move quickly, him right in front of me. He's got out the thing I keep calling a flare gun (even though it isn't), and he's loading it with a round as we hustle along. I pull my knife and snap out both blades. Glass doors up ahead, most of them broken. The building looms over us. He stops.

"Son of a bitch," he mutters. "That *is* something, isn't it?"

Over the doors are big letters—the kind that light up at night—that read CARTHAGE-MOORGATE MALL.

"You like shopping?" he asks.

"No."

"What kind of girl are you? Even lesbians like shopping."

"Did you have to take summer school classes to learn how to be such an asshole?"

"Although, come to think of it…'Sam' isn't just short for 'Samantha,' right?"

"No, it's not. Sam's a guy. And so what if he wasn't?"

"Just curious. I mean, you do wear your hair awful short, and you've been really good at keeping your hands off me."

"Can you shut up and we just go inside?"

It's almost totally dark in there. I hit my flashlight, notice it's getting a little dim. That's all kinds of not good. Beige diamond-shaped tiles on the floor, with a dark red one every so often for variety. Or at least, the tiles started out beige. There's gray sand and dust and ash here, too, of course, just like everywhere else. Trash that's blown in. Open atrium going up the second floor and then the skylights, most of the glass from them smashed, scattered in tiny bits that crunch under our boots as we slowly go farther in.

"We go through this place, shop by shop," Mike says, real quiet. "You take anything that might be useful, as much as you can carry. I keep an eye out and this ready," he says, showing me the gun.

"Okay, but we don't split up."

He shakes his head. "Not even to use the bathroom."

I want you, little boy, it said. I'm not gonna tell Mike about that. "Especially not the bathroom."

"If something jumps out and goes, 'Boo,' drop whatever you're holding, and bolt."

"I don't run very fast."

"Well, you better be faster than me." Once, I would have thought that he was serious. Once, he would have been. Not anymore.

YUDALA is the first store; I've never heard of it. Mike shrugs: him, either. The posters and signs that are still here say it's a cell phone place, or at least, it was. Nothing much left but empty racks and shelves. A few ancient, broken flip phones in a cardboard box on top of the counter. Not that they would do us any good even if they worked. It makes me want to pull out Sam's and look at his photos, but there isn't time for that. And not much battery. Maybe I can find one here.

Behind the counter, something on the floor. I flick the flashlight Mike's way: he's still standing guard at what's left of the glass doors into here. I go behind the counter, squat down. A yellow and orange piece of paper, crumpled. I pick it up, unfold it. A black guy looking past me. Under him, it reads, TWO CEDIS, whatever that means. At the top, BANK OF GHANA. It's not just paper.

I stand up, go over to Mike. "Look at this."

"Real African money. Maybe we can buy a paperclip."

"Do you think this mall's—"

bkk

Faint. Almost didn't hear it. I click off the light and we freeze. It takes a minute or so for my eyes to get used to what little light's coming in from up top.

Nothing.

Nothing.

"What was that?" I whisper.

He doesn't answer.

Nothing.

Nothing.

Then: *bkk* from far away and higher, at the other end of the mall, on the second level, I think. Still, neither of us move.

"You think something just fell over?" I whisper. "It could have been the wind."

bkk

"That's not the wind," Mike says.

I drop the bill. "Let's get out of here."

He shakes his head.

"Why not?"

"There might be something we need."

bkk

Is it closer? Sorta sounds like it, but I can't tell. "Then let's hide, until it goes away."

"You can if you want. I'm not gonna."

"That'd be splitting up."

"Then you better come along."

He goes first out of the shop, slowly, his boots hardly making any sound, staying against the closest wall. I keep the flashlight off and follow, not quite as quiet, but I'm trying. The only light is what's coming in from overhead. He's got the pistol up in both hands; I have the knife.

He peeks in store windows before we go by. I keep looking up, around, all over. In front of us, a wide staircase going up. We take it to the landing, turn and sneak up the next flight, to the mall's second level. Keep going the same direction we were before.

bkk

Louder. Closer. What are we even doing: trying to find whatever's making that noise? And then what? This is all kinds of stupid.

Mike ducks down, under and up against the sidewall of the walkway we're on, and I do, too. He holds his finger up to his lips, nods his head the way we were going. I lean out to see around him. Someone coming this way. Some one, or some thing.

He—it—is hunched over, coming out of JCPenny, shuffling toward Da Viva (whatever that is). He's dragging a bag behind him, but it hits a big piece of trash—looks like part of a display case—and what's in the bag goes *bkk* on the floor as it goes over. Any second now, he's going to see us.

I stand up, go, "Hey!" He jerks, lurches around, and then I hit him with the flashlight beam, right in the face so he can't see. He lets go of the bag, holds up his hands to shield his eyes.

"You better know what the hell you're doing," Mike says, getting to his feet, gun straight out in front of him.

"Doing what you would do," I mutter. Then, louder, "Who are you?"

What *are you?* would be a better question. He's a guy—I guess—but he's seriously freakish. It's not the ripped sheets and blankets he's draped over himself, or his feet wrapped up in rags like those dudes in the history book at school, who spent the winter with George Washington in Valley Forge. His skin is yellow—for real, yellow—like a highlighter, and so are his eyes where they should be white. All he's got for hair is a few long strands that are greasy and black and knotted. He's covered in these warts and bumps, and there's this huge lump on one side of his face, from his cheek down to under his jaw, like someone blew up a balloon under his skin. One arm's a lot longer than the other—like an extra eight inches. He's hunched over because his back is bent into a "u," not with a hump, but curved the other way, so it pushes his belly toward the floor. And he smells even worse than Mike used to, like he can't reach back there to wipe his ass. Which might be true.

Me and Mike just stare at him for a few seconds, and the weird guy stands there, trying to keep the light out of his eyes. I want to ask him what the hell is up with him, but I don't, cuz it's rude, so instead, I go, "What's your name?"

He shakes his head, doesn't answer. Maybe he doesn't speak English. *"¿Habla Espanol?"* He just keeps his hands up, doesn't try to go anywhere. I got one more thing left to try. *"Hangukmal hal jul ani?"*

"What was that?" Mike asks.

"I just asked him if he speaks Korean."

"Do you?"

"Yeah, I do, okay? Cuz I am."

"Anglandr," the guy croaks, like he can't talk too well, or maybe he hasn't talked for a long time. A foot nudges his bag toward us. "There to take," he says. "No me to hurt."

"We're not gonna hurt you," I tell him. Mike stretches out his leg, snags the bag with the toe of his boot, drags it closer. "We just want to talk." That sounds stupid, but what else am I supposed to say?

In the corner of my eye, Mike dumps out the bag, squats and starts jamming things from it into his pockets. "Hey, don't take his stuff."

"Hey, screw him," Mike replies. "I didn't survive this long by being Mr. Nice Guy."

"Light no to make," the weird guy says, wincing, hands still up in front of him.

"No, you keep that right on the Elephant Man, there," Mike insists, still sorting through the guy's stuff.

"Give those back to him."

"Shut up, Alyx-with-a-'y.' Let Mean Uncle Mikey handle this."

I point the flashlight at the floor under the weird guy's feet. "Goddamn it, Alyx," Mike growls, and I look over at him.

Mistake.

I see Mike's eyes getting real big, but by the time I turn back, the weird guy's already on me—damn, he's fast—and he slaps the knife out of my hand, almost breaks my wrist. I hit him hard as I can, right in that gross lump on the side of his face, but he punches me in my gut, and all the air goes out of me and I topple to the floor.

Then he and Mike are at each other, but I can't tell what's going on. Straining, trying to suck down air can't breathe can't breathe holy shit I can't breathe what did he do to me he's killed me I'm gonna die I'm gonna—

Grunting, panting, Mike and the weird guy fall on me, hurts like hell flattens me against the floor ow ow Jesus that hurts and then they're off me, rolling around, still fighting, and I can breathe oh God oh God I can breathe I can breathe never felt anything so good in my life, and I look over and Mike's on top of the him, whaling on him, but the weird guy ain't giving up, clubbing Mike's face and shoulders and they're rolling toward Da Viva, whatever that store's supposed to be, and the gun—

And the gun is right there, where Mike dropped it, not two feet from me.

I grab and pull it to me—Christ, I had forgotten how heavy it is—and I scramble to my feet. The guy's on top of Mike now, one hand around Mike's throat, and he's squeezing so hard that the veins are popping out on Mike's neck. I got both my hands on the gun, and I put it against the weird guy's head.

"Don't move, shitbag," I gasp. Still don't have my air all the way back, but I'm loud enough. He lets go, and Mike wriggles out from him. I back up before this dude can knock the gun away like he did my knife. If he comes at me, we're screwed, because even if I can get this thing to fire, it'll blow all of us up. But he doesn't know that. I hope.

Mike's crawling away, wheezing, hacking. He gets my knife, flips over onto his butt, leans back on his elbows. "He—" Coughs. Coughs again. "He tries anything…you waste him." Shakes his head, rubs his throat with his free hand. "You know what, I don't even give a crap." Starts to stand up. "I'm gonna cut his damn head off."

"No," I say. "Let him have his stuff back."

"Are you for real?"

"Just do it, and stop being a dick."

The weird guy stares at me. Mike thinks it over, then goes and gets the dude's bag, starts filling it with the things on the floor.

"A can of yellow beans," he says. "Bottle of Powerade. Pack of dice, box of rubbers—you going to Vegas, pal? Two toothbrushes. Three tubes of Pepsodent. Book of matches. Men's dress socks." Holds up a tangled mess of wires. "What the hell are these?"

"Earbuds," I tell him.

"Whatever. Can of yams—shit, I hate yams. Some twine—you know, most of this stuff could be really useful to us, Alyx-with-a-'y.' Band-Aids. Bastard has Band-Aids. I'm keeping those: I don't care what you say. 'Yorkie Original'—some kind of candy bar? Postage sta—"

"Candy her to have," the weird guy says, pointing to me. He looks over at Mike, points to the bag, then to me again. "Candy her to have."

"I heard you the first time." Mike reaches in, roots around, gets out the candy bar. Hands it to me. I'm pretty sure it's chocolate.

"Here you go, Dragon Lady."

"The stuff from your jacket, too," I tell him. "What'd you call me?"

"Look it up on your phone." He digs through his pockets, shoves stuff back in the bag. The last thing is a teeny little glass jar he holds up. Shakes his head. "Elderberry jam. Suck my ass." Drops it in, walks over to the weird guy. Plops the bag beside him on the floor. "Hasta lasagna, baby."

My arms are shaking, so I put the gun down, give it to Mike. The other dude takes the bag, slowly stands up, as much as he can, anyway, with that back bent all crooked like that.

"Her to..." Falters. "Her...*takk*. *Takk*." He says it *tahk*, like *talk* without the "l."

"Uh huh. Well, go *takk* yourself," Mike tells him. Taps me on the shoulder. "I gave him his stuff back, Mother Teresa, so let's go."

"Hold on." The weird guy's got a nasty-looking cut on his forehead that's bleeding bad. I point at the same spot on me, and his hand copies mine, dabs at it. If it hurts, he doesn't seem to feel it. Looks at his bloody fingers. Wipes them on the blanket he has wrapped and safety-pinned around his shoulders and chest. Nods at me.

"*Takk*," he says. I'm guessing that means *thanks* in whatever it is he speaks.

"Can you help us?" I ask. "I—we're looking for someone. A woman." He stares at me; I don't know if he gets what I'm saying or not. I point at myself, then stretch my hand over my head to show how tall that crazy old bitch is. "Scary woman." I make a mad face, clench my hands into claws, then up together by my mouth. Open and shut them like shark jaws. "Real scary. Very bad. Witch."

"Ōth," he says—that name again, the one that sounds like a promise. "Ōth's woman. Bad." He makes my mad face and claws, shakes his head. "Freydis. Very bad."

"Go tell Aunt Rhody," Mike whispers.

This Wasted Land

"She has my boyfriend," I say. "His name's Sam." Hold out my arms like I'm hugging someone, close my eyes and pretend to kiss the air in front of me. Open my eyes. "Boyfriend. She took him—" I act like I'm hugging Sam, then do my *scary woman* impersonation again, then act like he got ripped out of my arms.

"Freydis boy to take," the weird guy says, like *fray*—when your clothes are starting to wear out—and *diss*—when you talk shit to somebody. But what's that supposed to mean? Is it a name or something?

"Have you seen them? Do you know where they are? They're going to a big rock." I stand on tiptoes, put my hands up as high as I can. "Do you know which way it is? Do—"

"Paddoch to know," he replies, pointing at himself. "Freydis Sam to take. To Ōth."

Track 20. Innuendo

We're back on the ground level. Mike's made a fire out of trash, on the floor of the big atrium right in the middle of the mall, where the food court used to be. We sit around it—me and him and Paddoch, the weird guy—and eat, mostly snacks and such: bags of chips or pretzels, candy, dry cereal, cans of SpaghettiOs.

We scrounged them and some other stuff—meds and pop and glow sticks, and African newspapers and magazines for burning—from this tiny convenience store that Mike named The Murder Mart. I asked him why he called it that, and he said it reminded him of a little store at a gas station in Nogales, wherever that is. Said he saw these two Mexicans shoot this other Mexican dude right there in the middle of the day, with a bunch of people around. Drug deal gone wrong, Mike thinks. I think Mike doesn't know any stories that don't end all horrible.

I try not to look at Paddoch, but he's the ugliest person I've ever met. When I was little, I'd sit around and watch movies when I was home by myself at night when Mom was working, and there was this one Disney cartoon about the humpback of Notre Dame, and that dude was pretty ugly (but not too bad, cuz it was for kids). But he's got nothing on Paddoch. I didn't even know spines could bend that way. How is there room for his stomach? How can he even breathe? Aren't his lungs all squished?

Mike was all pissy before, but now he's in a really good mood. We didn't go through the whole mall, but in the part we did, we found the security office, and they had two Smith & Wesson 9 millimeters, and a Mossberg pump shotgun with a pistol grip. I recognize them from the range when my dad would take me. Mike gathered them into a rifle bag they had there, and now he's got one of the 9's on his lap.

We also found some Jack Daniel's, and Mike's been swigging

it. I don't know how he can drink that crap; I tried some, but it burned my throat something bad. Mike's smiling and talking, joking, laughing. Paddoch doesn't say anything, just stares at me all the time. Like he's not creepy enough.

"Hell of a day," Mike says. Sips from the bottle. "I haven't had a drink in…years, but I'm pretty sure I've earned this one."

I finish the bag of Cheetos I was munching, crumple it up and toss it in the fire. We have a whole pile of junk we have to keep throwing on the fire, because it burns awful quick. I'm sick of being cold, and Mike's busy drinking, so I take care of it. "Paddoch," I say. It sounds kinda like *pad* and *dock*, but at the end, it rhymes with *loch*, like that lake in Scotland that supposedly has a monster.

He looks up.

"The scary woman…." I say.

"Freydis," he answers.

"You said she's with Ōth." He nods. "She's…what? His girlfriend or something?"

"His bitch," Mike says.

"She Ōth to belong."

"What do you mean?"

"She Ōth's *threll*." Puts his wrists together, tries to pull them apart, pretends he can't, like he's in handcuffs or something.

"'Thrall' is the word I think he's going for," Mike says. "A slave."

Paddoch nods. "Freydis Ōth's slave to be."

"And who is Ōth?" I ask.

"He from dark," he says, pointing up. "Where lights not. Empty. He in water deep to fall." He pulls his hand down, down to the floor. "There he long to sleep."

Mike looks at me. Raises his eyebrows.

Paddoch holds up his hands. "Then he voices to hear. He to

come up. To island where *skreeoolings*." At least, that's what it sounds like. Mike frowns, confused. Paddoch notices. "They," he says, spreading his hands. "They. All they."

"People," I tell him.

He nods. "He not 'Ōth,' then. No name. He up from water they to see. They he to...." Puts his hands together, bows his head.

"Pray to," I say. "Worship."

Paddoch nods. "Then they he...*athmata*." Pretends like he's putting something in his mouth.

"Eat?" I ask.

He shakes his head, then his eyes widen. "To feed. Then they he to feed."

Not sure I get what he said, but okay. "And then what?"

He waves his hand. "Long time. Island cold, waters cold. Many snows. Then Freydis to come."

"That bitch again," Mike says. Takes another swig of the Jack.

Paddoch cups his hands, bobs them along, crossing in front of him. "On a boat," I say. "Freydis comes on a boat to the island."

"*Yow*," he answers, nodding. I suppose that means *yes*. "Freydis and he and he and he. Many he." He struggles for a second. "People. And Erikson."

Mike puts down the bottle. "Leif Erikson?" He says the first name *layf*.

"*Yow*. They and he and Freydis to come."

"Who's Leif Erikson?" I ask.

"Do they teach you anything worth knowing at those schools in Maryland? Leif Erikson was a Viking explorer who came to the New World about five hundred years before Columbus. He and his men settled in...." Pauses. "In Newfoundland—which is an island. And the Indians that lived there, those people...."

"*Skreeoolings*," Paddoch says.

"The Indians there, they were worshipping Ōth like a god," I say. "And then the Vikings came."

"They to fight. Many to kill. For fight to stop, Ōth and Erikson and Freydis to come, to talk. Freydis to give he, then Erikson and they to stay."

"I don't get it," I say.

"The Vikings landed and tried to set up shop, but the Indians weren't okay with that," Mike replies. "Leif met with Ōth to make peace, so the Vikings could stay. To seal the deal, Leif made Freydis marry Ōth."

"What do you mean, 'made Freydis marry Ōth?'"

"Happened all the time back then."

"That psycho witch is, like, a monster. How could she ever be married to anybody?"

"Lady, I just work here." Turns to Paddoch. "What happened after that?"

"Freydis he to name: 'Ōth.' She with he. Long time, *skreeoolings* and Erikson people no to fight. But then Freydis to die. Then they to fight again. Many to kill. Erikson and they to go. *Skreeoolings* Ōth to fight. They him to hurt. He here to come."

"Freydis died?" I ask. "I thought you said that Freydis is the witch—" I do my bit with the scary face and claws "—who took Sam."

Paddoch nods. "Freydis Sam to take. To Ōth."

"But Freydis is dead," I tell him.

He nods again. "Freydis dead."

"Witchiepoo's named 'Freydis,'" Mike says, "but she's not the same Freydis who died. Maybe wherever that bitch who took Sam comes from, 'Freydis' is a common name. Like 'Sue.'"

"Nobody's named 'Sue' anymore." I frown at Paddoch. "How do you even know this? Or are you just making up all of it?"

"Erikson and Freydis and Paddoch to come," he says, cupping his hands and bobbing them along. "On boat. Erikson Freydis to give. Erikson Paddoch to give. To Ōth."

"You were a slave, too," I say. He nods. "Why?"

He taps his head. "Paddoch runes to know."

"'Runes?'"

"He could read and write," Mike says. "That was a big deal back then."

Paddoch nods. "Runes *galdr* to be."

"What?" I look over at Mike. "What'd he say?" Mike shakes his head.

"*Galdr*," Paddoch replies. Thinks about it for a second. "Anglandr say 'magic.'"

"Magic," Mike says. "Vikings and Indians and magic. Yeah, right." Slugs down more Jack. "Sure, pal. Whatever you say."

"You don't believe him?"

"Fabio here is full of shit. For one thing, 'Paddoch' isn't even a Viking name."

"Like you know so much about Vikings."

"More than you."

Paddoch reaches in his bag, rummages around. Comes out with a pack of something. Tears it open, throws the trash in the fire. Holds out his hand: six white dice. Rolls them on the floor. They all come up 1's.

He looks at Mike, leans over and scoops them up. Rolls them again. They all come up 2's.

"Whoa," I say. Mike's face is blank.

Picks them up again, rolls them again. They all come up 3's.

Mike takes another sip.

Rolls again. All 4's.

"Let me see those," Mike says, holding out his hand. Paddoch gives them to him. Mike rolls them. 2, 5, 1, 6, 6, 2. Picks them up, rolls them again. 5, 6, 4, 3, 6, 1.

Paddoch holds out his hand, Mike gives them back. Rolls

them. All 5's.

Mike doesn't say anything. Paddoch does it again. All 6's.

"*Galdr*," Paddoch tells him.

"That's a pretty good trick," Mike admits. "Maybe you ought to go to Vegas after all. Pull down some cash playing craps, or start your own act. I'd pay good money to see more."

"You still don't believe he can do magic?"

"On TV, I saw David Copperfield make a plane disappear. Dice tricks don't impress me."

Paddoch puts them away. "So, why is 'Freydis' taking Sam to Ōth?" I ask him.

"She Ōth to feed," he says.

"Whaddya mean, 'feed?'"

He doesn't answer.

"Like, he's going to eat Sam?"

Nothing.

"Is Ōth some kind of vampire?" *Feed*. The hell? I stand up. "Whaddya mean?"

Paddoch doesn't look at me. "Say something, asswipe!"

Mike holds up his hand. "Alyx, why don't you take a walk? Maybe find us something more substantial than trash to put on the fire, like a wood chair or something. Me and Paddoch need to have a little man-to-man talk."

"What happened to, 'we don't split up, not even to use the bathroom?'"

He holds out one of the 9's. "You know how to use this?"

"Best thing Dad ever did for me."

He jams a clip into it, hands it to me. "Then, you'll be all right."

I stash it in my inside jacket pocket, tuck the double-blade knife in the waistband of my jeans. Point at Paddoch. "When I get back, you're gonna tell me what the hell you mean. Understand? You're gonna—"

"Alyx, give us a couple minutes," Mike says.

It's dark again as soon as I head away from the fire. Dark and cold. I go behind a column and I hear Mike. He's trying to be quiet, but he's not doing too good. "First off, stop looking at her all the time, because if you try to touch her, I'll cut your nuts off. You got me, pal? Now, what else do you know about Freydis? And don't bullshit me."

I hope he can tell Mike something, but it's hard to understand him. And what's his deal? Was what he was saying about Freydis and Ōth and the Vikings and all that true? If Mike is right—and he always is, damn it—about when that would have happened, then Paddoch must be, like, a thousand years old. Which is crazy, but not much more crazy than anything else that's happened since I stopped the bike at that train crossing.

I get out my flashlight, take out the pistol, cock it, flick on the safety, and walk. Mostly-empty stores, some of them I know: Samsung, Adidas, ShopRite, Payless. A lot of them, I don't: Roca (bathroom fixtures, like sinks and toilets and such); Mr. Bigg's (fast food); another Yudala (phones again); T.M. Lewin (men's clothes); Inglot (cosmetics); Jungle 531 (books and games).

I need to pee, but there's no way I'm going into a bathroom by myself, even with the 9. Not after what happened at the train station. I'll wait until Mike's done bitching out Paddoch, and then I'll have him come with me and wait outside. Mike, that is. No way I'm letting that pervy mutant anywhere near me.

Off the main strip of the mall is a hallway we haven't gone down. I go over, shine the flashlight that way. Nothing moving. Lots of stores. I look back the way I came. I can see the fire's reflection flickering off the walls, can hear Mike cussing. I'll go and tell them about this, and then we can check it out. Look down this new hall again.

Cynthia's hanging there.

I jump back, point the gun oh my God oh my God oh my God it can't be her, it can't be Sam's sister, but it is—her skin anyway. Just her skin.

It's like a big, empty plastic bag. Blood's seeping out of her, running down her legs, trickling onto the floor into a puddle. She's naked and her hair is all tangled and she—it—is just floating there, her toes—some of her pink nail polish is chipped—dangling a few inches over the beige tiles. Her face is flat, saggy, empty, cocked to one side like it's staring at something. Or it would, if it had eyes.

"Mike," I whisper. "Mike." Louder. Shit. Shit shit shit shit SHIT. "MIKE! MIKE!"

He won't hear you, Cynthia says, not in my ears, not with her mouth, not with her voice. Not Cynthia's anyway. It's *her.* The crazy old bitch. Freydis. Cynthia's face straightens, turns to me. Silver iris eyes appear where hers used to be.

"This isn't real," I tell her. "That's not really her. Cuz if it is, I swear to God, you truck stop whore, I'll—"

"'That's the nicest thing anyone's ever told me.'" Cynthia's voice this time, just like back in the record store, a million years ago, a million miles away.

"MIKE!" How the hell can this be happening? How can Cynthia be here? How this crazy old bitch even know about her?

I found her not long ago. Her voice again. *At the...what's the word? Hospital. With the babies. All the babies.*

"Alyx?" Mike calls, too far away. "Where are you?"

"MIKE! COME QUICK!"

I found her, and I took her...phone, she says. *That's the word. And on her phone was Sam. I found Sam.*

Panting all of a sudden, and I can't stop. Keep it together. "Why did you find him? Why did you take him? What the hell do you want with him?"

I do like my sweet, sweet Sammy.

"You can't have him!" Shit, I'm losing it. "You let him go!"

She doesn't say anything. Just looks at me, not blinking, with those freaky silver eyes.

"I'm gonna kill you, bitch." Teeth clenched. "I'm gonna cut your throat. I'm gonna cut off your tits. I'm gonna—"

No, you won't, little girl. But I'll hurt you. And I won't even have to touch you. All I'll have to do is show you Sam.

"You better not have done anything to him!"

I would never hurt him. Not like you will.

I shake my head. "What the hell are you talking about?"

You'll see. Soon. And it will...destroy. That's the word. It'll destroy you.

"I know who you were. I know where to find you. Me and Mike are coming, and we're gonna get Sam, and—"

By then, you won't even want him, and he won't want you. And why should he? You're nothing. I can be anything. I can be everything.

Boots, pounding behind me. "Alyx, what the hell?" Mike asks. She looks past me, at him. Smiles. It's like a worm twisting on the sidewalk after it rains.

You don't— she starts, but then Mike racks the shotgun **KCHK** and

BLUWWW

and Cynthia—her skin, anyway—billows, flutters, crashes to the floor, and Mike shoves me out of the way, goes past me, racks the shotgun again. He stamps one boot onto her neck, points the shotgun, uses the barrel to roll what's left of her head toward us.

One weird silver eye, staring at him. "Mike," she says, using my voice now. "I remember you."

"Where is he?" he growls.

"Did you lose him, Da-doo?"

"You give him to me!"

"'She Ōth to feed,'" she says, Paddoch's voice this time.

Mike lurches back, and

BLUWWW

and her head bursts like an egg you smashed on a counter and blood spatters the floor, the walls, the windows of the shops nearby as little pieces of Cynthia tumble away.

"Oh God oh God oh my God." I fall to my knees beside her, drop the 9. "It was Cynthia it was her it really was her oh shit oh shit oh shit." Crying and I can't stop. "She's dead she killed her Freydis killed her what the hell do we do how do I tell Sam what do I tell Sam—"

Mike picks up the pistol, puts it in his jacket pocket. "Come on." Pulls me up by my arm, starts tugging me back the way we came.

"That was Cynthia that's whose skin it was and she killed her that's Sam's sister his big sister and no no I don't I can't Mike I can't what do I Mike no I can't you killed Freydis but we don't have Sam what do I do how do I Sam his sister—"

"Get a goddamn grip." The shotgun smells like smoke and ash. "She's not dead."

"No that's her that's Cynthia she's—"

"Freydis isn't dead. But she's gonna be."

"But Cynthia Mike I gotta—"

He throws down the shotgun, grabs the front of my jacket, yanks me toward him. "I don't have time for your teenybopper, pity-party meltdown, Alyx-with-a-'y.' Now get your shit together, because you and me and Paddoch are gonna go find that bitch and your faggot boyfriend who needs a girl to rescue him."

"Shut up!" I smash my fist into his jaw: it's like punching a tree trunk. He blinks when I hit him, but it doesn't seem to bother him much. I swing again, but he shoves me to the floor. I jump back to my feet and rush him, but he grabs my wrists, spins me, slams me against a store window, pins my arms against the glass. I'm kicking, flailing, trying to knee him in the crotch, something, anything. Presses himself against me so I can't move: he's inches from my face. I try to bite him—cheek, nose, ears, whatever—and he jerks his head away. I'm thrashing, squirming, but he's too strong. Can't get free.

"Are you done yet?"

"Shut up! Don't talk about Sam like that! You're such an asshole!" I spit in his face, and he pulls me away from the window, bashes me against it, the back of my head hits, the glass doesn't break, doesn't even crack, but *damn* that hurts.

"I've had enough of your little shit fit."

"That's Sam sister, and you don't even care!"

"You're right: I don't."

Huh? What the actual hell? "What is wrong with you?" Crying again. "Why do you have to be like this? She's…" I shake my head. "She *matters!* How messed up do you have to be to not understand that?"

Nothing from him. He just stares at me.

"Say something, goddamn it!"

He lets go, backs away kinda slow. I slide down the window, crumple to the floor. My wrists are red where he squeezed, and they hurt.

Paddoch's there, watching us: Mike going over to get the shotgun and the 9; me in a heap, crying.

"You hit like a girl," Mike mutters.

"Shut up!"

"I'm packing up our stuff, and then me and Paddoch are headed out. If you want Sam, then you better drag ass and come along." He heads back the way we came.

Paddoch just stands there.

"Stop looking at me! Lemme alone."

"Alyx sad to be," he says, "but Alyx Paddoch to go. Paddoch to know Freydis to be. Paddoch Alyx to help. Paddoch Alyx to he Sam to take."

Track 21. In the Evening

Days—what would be days if we were anywhere other than here—have gone by since we left the mall. I can't keep track anymore, because my happy meds have run out. It's still cold, but there's no wind, no sounds, nothing moves. Just miles and miles of dust and trash, and black, thorny shrubs and thickets. Hills and ravines and empty stream beds, and sometimes, what used to be a hut or a shack or a house, always empty. Sometimes we rest there, sometimes for a little while, sometimes for what seems like hours. We walk (a lot), we eat (not much), we sleep (not much, either), we take turns keeping watch. Mike hardly says anything. Neither does Paddoch.

When we're packed up and about to take off after sleeping or eating or whatever, Paddoch will point which direction to go, and then we head that way. He and Mike don't even try to stay with me or with each other. I'd think they would, after all Mike's ever said, and cuz Paddoch supposedly knows where we're going, but no. Mike's always up ahead, never waiting for us. Paddoch's always behind: he limps, and not long after we start walking, he's gasping for air, so he stops a lot. I'm always in the middle, trying to keep both of them in sight, so I don't lose either of them, and in case something happens.

I think a lot about Cynthia. Was that really her? Did that crazy old bitch—Freydis—actually kill her and skin her and bring her here? Cuz if she did, if all that was for real...

I wipe my eyes with my sleeve. Damn it. Crying again. Can't help it. It's not so much that I'm sad for me: Cynthia was cool and all, but I only talked to her like maybe a half dozen times. Mostly, I'm sad for Sam.

So, how did she get Cynthia?

She found Cynthia at the hospital where she works. That's

what she told me. The dream I had about her and Sam at that big rock—what did she say then? Something about how you come across someone by accident, and then nothing's the same after that? Yeah, I think that was it. She said she hadn't been looking for Cynthia, but she found her, got her phone—I guess she took it and looked at it. And then she saw Sam's picture on it.

How did she find Sam?

Well, she's some kind of witch, right? That's what Mike calls her. Maybe she cast a spell to tell her where Sam was. Somehow—maybe another spell—she went to him, to us at that railroad crossing, the one that Sam said wasn't on Waze. I guess that was another spell, too.

If she found Sam, maybe she can find Sam's mom. And Uncle Tony.

Shit. She kills people and does magic and can change what she looks likes and she's strong enough to pick up a motorcycle and slam it on the ground. And so far, she's just been messing with me, but if she really wanted to, she could flat-out end me.

I'll hurt you, she told me. *And I won't even have to touch you. All I'll have to do is show you Sam.*

What'd she mean by that? Show me what about Sam?

Mike's stopped. It takes me a little while to catch up to him, and the whole time, he's looking ahead, then looking back, then looking ahead again, then back. His duffel bag and the bag of guns from the mall on the ground, next to him.

"What's going on?" I ask.

He points ahead of us. Something almost at the horizon. It's hard to see that far, like everything's gotten darker. I squinch my eyes to see better.

A big rock, flat on top.

"No way," I whisper.

He doesn't say anything. Just looks all around.

"Mike?"

Shakes his head.

"Mike, what's wrong?"

He stoops, grabs the bags. "C'mon." Starts running, but not toward the rock. More like diagonal to it.

I look back: Paddoch's still stumping along. I chase after Mike. "What are you doing?"

"C'mon."

"Where are you going?" He doesn't answer. "Don't leave Paddoch!"

"We don't need him anymore."

"Let's wait up!"

"Can't."

"Why not?"

"We don't have time," he says.

"Mike, this is shitty. I know he's slow and all, and I don't like him either, but—"

He points back at the sun. "See that?"

"Of course I do." It still hasn't moved.

"It's going out."

"What?"

"Out. You know, like switching off a light."

I look at it. It doesn't hurt—it never hurt to look at it, because it's always been small and faint and there've always gray clouds in front of it. But now...

Now, it looks even smaller. Weaker. And the sky around it is darker gray than it usually is. I turn around. The horizon's black.

"The hell?"

"The sun here doesn't go down," Mike says. "It just goes out." He starts running, faster this time.

I run, too. "You're kidding!"

"Nope."

"Then what?"

"Then it's dark. And colder."

"So?"

"Shut up and run."

"Mike—"

"Shut up and run!"

It *is* getting dark—fast. Behind us, the sun's half as big as it was before, and it's shrinking. Thank God that Mike's bags are heavy, cuz I'm going as fast as I can, but I'm just barely keeping up. Don't know how much longer I can do this. Don't think about, just run. Breathing hard, my side already hurts, ignore it, run, run—

Mike stumbles on a rock, crashes to the ground. The bag from the mall spills open, the guns scatter. "SHIT!"

I stop, crouch by him. It sucks he fell, but I'm glad we stopped. "You…okay?"

"Marvelous." His forehead and palms are scraped, the left knee of his pants is torn. I help him to his feet. He bends, grabs the shotgun. One of the 9's tumbled a couple yards; I pick it up, bring it over.

"Keep it," he says.

"You sure?"

"Yeah."

I peel off my pack, stash the pistol, zip up, sling it back on. He puts the other 9 in a jacket pocket, leaves the rifle bag, winces as he straightens and stands again. He's breathing hard, too.

"Where're we going?"

"There." Up ahead, what's left of a stone building, most of it fallen down, maybe a few hundred yards from us. Hard to tell. Dark's coming fast.

"What is it?" I ask.

"Doesn't matter." He takes a step, grimaces. "Son of a bitch..." Takes another. Sucks air in through his teeth. He nods toward the building. "Go on."

"I'm not gonna leave you out here."

"I'm coming, it's just going to take me a while."

"I'll stay with you."

"No, you go ahead." Smirks. "If there're any monsters in there, they'll eat you first."

"I'm not going."

"How about every once in a while, just to surprise me, you do as I goddamn tell you, okay? Now, run as fast as you can, and when you get there, shine your flashlight back this way. You still have it, right?"

"Yeah. Why do you want me to do that?"

"Would you just get the hell out of here, already?"

"Fine."

I run. Grab the straps of my pack to keep it from bouncing too much. I'm pretty sure the pistol's safety is on, but if it isn't, I don't need it going off in my bag.

It doesn't. I don't fall and break my ass, either. Nothing from a horror movie pops up and starts chasing me. I make it to the front of the building, lean over, gasping. Running sucks.

The sun's a white dot smaller than my pinkie nail. The sky is almost totally black; there aren't any stars. The dark's swallowing everything, swallowing me. I unzip the pocket on my sleeve, take out the little LED flashlight. I never did find batteries for it at the mall. Please, work. Please, please, God, let it work.

It does, barely. A faint beam of light. The building—what's left of it—is tan bricks. Twisted frames of empty double doors, shattered glass from them scattered around. On the wall by the door, a brown metal sign, white letters. PADDOCH COUNTY PUBLIC LIBRARY.

"Are you serious?" Mike'll—never mind. Figure out what it

means later. I point the flashlight the way I came. The light doesn't seem to go very far.

I wait.

I wait.

Now, it's all dark: nothing but this skinny little white beam and its glow. I can't see anything else past it. C'mon, Mike. I don't like standing around here. What'd you say about making campfires? That they tell every monster in the neighborhood where to find something to eat? Well, I'm feeling like I'm about to become a snack. So hurry up, damn it.

Real nice, Alyx-with-a-"y." He might have twisted his ankle back there, or even broken it—he's stubborn enough to keep walking on it anyway—and you're bitching abou—

khhch

Something—I don't know what it is, I don't know where it comes from. I drop my backpack, fumble with the zipper, get the gun. The flashlight's beam jitters. Oh my God. Oh my God. Shaking. C'mon, Mike. C'mon. Please. Please.

I sweep the light, pointing the 9. Nothing but the library and the dark. Nothing I can see, anyway. But can anything see me?

"Alyx?" I whip around. Mike.

"Don't move!" I flick off the safety, hold it the pistol out in front. "Don't come near me!"

He drops his bag, but not the shotgun. "What is your malfunction?"

"Say the alphabet!"

"Stop this. We gotta get inside—"

"Say the goddamn alphabet, or I'll shoot you!" I fight to hold the gun still.

"Your dad's a worthless sack of shit who ran off and left your mom to work all day and all night cleaning houses and scrubbing toilets at a truck stop in Buttscratch, Pennsylvania. You stayed in motels for a while until your mom saved up enough for a crappy apartment with roaches as big as your thumb. But it was all worth it, because at least Daddy wasn't drinking his paycheck and smacking Mommy and you around. Now you live with your uncle who made some money playing pro football, and he owns a few diners and used-car dealerships. Do you want me to keep repeating back things you've told me, or do you think it's really me?"

I lower the pistol, but keep the light on him. "What is it you always tell me? About trusting?"

"You can't trust anything."

"Yeah, it's you."

He bends, gets his bag, tosses it over his shoulder. He limps toward the doors. I show him the sign by them.

He shrugs. "Told you that wasn't a Viking name."

"So, what else did he lie about?"

"Who cares?" Steps up to the doorframes. "Shine the flashlight in there."

A big room, can't tell how far back it goes. My light's fading, just like the sun did. Gray sand and bits of smashed bricks on the carpet, and some books laying there—that much, we can see. Mike has to duck to slip through what's left of the doors; I follow. It's where you come into the library, so there's a long desk and bookshelves—some of them knocked over—behind it, and there are more books spilled all over the floor.

We go farther in. The library's a mess, and everywhere's this horrible musty smell of old books, thousands and thousands of them. Past the front desk is the main room, where most of the shelves are—or were—and in the middle of it, there's a pile, like a hill, that's way taller than Mike. More books laying all over the floor, some of them open with their pages out, some of them open and face down, and sometimes there're so many, you can't help but step on them. There were some side rooms off of here, I think, but not anymore: the roof fell in on them, and so did some of the walls.

bkk bkk bkk bkk Heavy footsteps, real close. Mike drops his duffel and we turn, I have the light, he has the shotgun. A narrow metal staircase from the basement, I guess. Someone coming up the steps.

Paddoch, with an old box lantern. Smiles with a mouth full of crooked teeth. "Alyx."

Mike keeps the gun on him. "How'd you get here before us?"

"*Galdr*," I say.

Paddoch nods. "Magic."

"Yeah, that's cute," Mike replies. "Now, how did you really?"

"Dark to come. Alyx and Mike to run. Paddoch here to *galdr*." He mimes throwing something.

Glance at Mike. He doesn't get it, either. Shake my head.

Paddoch squats, sets the lantern on the floor. Finds a hunk of brick. "Paddoch," he says, putting it down near the lantern. Picks up another bit of brick. "Alyx and Mike." Places it ahead of the other chunk—that's supposed to be us, and the other one is him. Takes a whole brick, shuffles a few steps, plunks it down way ahead of the me-and-Mike piece. "Paddoch Soontie Poo-blis Lib-rar-ree," he says.

"Here," I say, setting my pack on the floor. "The library."

He nods. "Lie-bree."

He goes back to the two pieces that are supposed to be the three of us. "Dark to come." He twists a little knob at the base of the lantern, and the flame weakens. "Alyx and Mike to run." He moves our little rock a few inches. Picks up his own. "Paddoch runes to know." Bobs it up and down, turns it in his fingers, carries it to the brick, sets it down on it.

"Paddoch lie-bree to *galdr*. To magic."

"Bullshit," Mike says.

"How else could he have gotten here before us?"

"I don't know. Maybe he's not really the same freak we left back there."

"Don't start that." I turn to Paddoch. "You've been here

before. What's your real name?"

He shakes his head. "Alyx that not to have."

"Why not?"

"Then Alyx *galdr* from Paddoch to take."

"I'll steal your magic if I know your real name?" He nods. Mike rolls his eyes.

"I'm through listening to this." Mike points at the stairs. "What's down there, Stud?"

"Paddoch here to live."

"This is your home?" I ask.

He nods again. "Lie-bree."

"Well, give us a tour," Mike says, "because we're moving in."

"Wait—what do you mean, 'moving in?'" I ask.

"We're staying here until the sun comes back."

"Okay, so we'll get some sleep, and then in the morning, we'll go."

"That'd be a whole lot of sleep, because it's going to be a long while until 'morning.'"

"How long?"

"As long as it wants to."

"Which is what? How many hours?"

"Lots."

"Like, days?"

"Well, it's hard to keep count when there's no sun. Kind of like how it's hard to do when there's no night. But, yeah: 'like, days.' Maybe 'weeks.'"

"So, what—we're just stuck here? No! We gotta go! The rock's right over there!" I'm probably not pointing the direction it is, but I don't care. "Sam's there! He's right there!"

"We can't."

"No, we gotta! It's so close!"

"It's not close, and if we try to go before it's light, we aren't going to make it."

"Yeah, we will! I got a flashlight!"

"That's some flashlight you have, that can shine all the way to that rock without being noticed by every monster in our ZIP code."

"We've walked all this way, and all this time! We can't stop now!"

"Listen, it's not like I don't want to go. It's tearing me up that—"

"Oh, yeah, it's really tearing you up! You don't give a crap about Sam! Just like you didn't give a crap about Cynthia! You don't care about anybody but you!"

"That's not true. I don't like this situation either, but you're going to have to be patient."

"Damn it, I don't want to be patient! I want Sam! And I wanna kill that bitch!"

"And we will, but not now."

"No, now! We gotta do this now!" Jab my finger at Paddoch. "You heard him: she's gonna feed Sam to Ōth, cuz he's probably a frickin' cannibal!"

"It's not like that rock's right next door, and we can just pop over. It'll take days to get there, but we won't last hours. I've been through this before, lots of times. The light goes out, and you can't see a damn thing because there aren't any stars or moon. It gets colder, like 'frostbite' colder. And to top it off, really nasty things that have been sleeping or hiding or waiting come crawling out."

"What kind of…*things*?"

"The kind that like Korean food. Or Korean girls. Or both."

I squat, yank open my pack, get the pistol, jam it in my jacket pocket and zip it. Snatch my pack and throw it on as I stand up. "I'm going."

This Wasted Land

"You do that," Mike says. "It's been swell knowing you."

Paddoch shakes his head. "Alyx not to go."

"You two wanna hang out here, you go ahead. I'm gonna get Sam."

Flick on my flashlight as I go through the doorframes. Jesus, it's already a lot more cold out here, and it doesn't help that the wind's blowing real bad. Squint to keep out the dust and sand and ash. Try to remember which way was the huge rock. Left, I think. Yeah, that's it, because it was straight ahead of us before Mike went this way. So, go left and then turn left again, then straight for, like, ever. Until I get there.

TRACK 22. I'M GONNA CRAWL

Oh my God, it's freezing. For about the millionth time, I wish I had my gloves, but they're back where Freydis got us. Got Sam. That seems like a hundred years ago, but how long has it been, actually? Don't know, can't think. Just so cold. Shivering already. Keep walking. Have to keep walking.

Flashlight's fading again. I whack it against my leg, and it gets a little stronger. Don't know what I'm gonna do if it goes out. When it goes out. I point it down, cover it with my fingers, look up, wave my other hand in front of my face. Can feel the sand stinging my cheeks, but I can't see anything, just black. Like Mike said.

Forget it. Keep going. Just keep going straight.

* * *

Walking. Walking. My fingers, my hands hurt so bad. Blow on them, but it doesn't help. Take turns stuffing them in my armpits, switching when I can't stand it anymore. Drop the flashlight, it goes out for second—shit!—comes back on, pick it up, hold it tight, tighter. The big rock was on the horizon: how far could have that been? Sam would know. What would he say? Depends on how high you are? Me and Mike were on a ridge when we saw it: how high was that? I don't know. I can't figure out how far it is. Miles, I guess. Sam could figure it out. He's smart. Lot smarter than me.

hrrrrrrrrrrrrrrrrrrrrrrrrrrrrrrrrrrrrrnnnnnn

The hell? It's not the wind, but it's almost as loud. Off to my right, somewhere. Not close. Please, God, not close.

hrrrrrrrrrrrrrrrrrrrrrrrrrrrrrrrrnnnnnnnnn

Coming this way. Oh, shit. Oh, shit.

This Wasted Land

HRRRRRRRNNNNNNNNNNN

Crashing, stamping, closer now, I can hear it over the wind. Tiny lights—two, then three, then a dozen or so, some white, some yellow-green—swirling around fifteen, maybe twenty feet off the ground. Lights. No, not lights.

Eyes.

HRRRRRRRNNNNNNN

It's seen me it sees me lights its eyes are lights light turn off the flashlight turn off the goddamn flashlight!

I switch it off, run, run run arms out can't see anything hope I don't smack into anything. Screeching behind me, lights swirling, sweeping. Thudding, thumping—its feet? Or is it slithering along on its belly? Don't know doesn't matter run run run can't see—

Falling shit falling I'm dead I'm dead I—

Slam to the ground uffff tumble roll ow! hit my head on something hard a rock I guess in movies that always knocks people out but for real it just hurts like a bitch roll now sliding down hands out flashlight my flashlight's gone I lost it shit grabbing trying to stop myself feels like it's a huge slab of stone or something stop hit bottom not falling not sliding anymore thank God thank God thank—

The lights—its eyes—way, way up over me, weaving here, there, looking, not seeing, not seeing me. I lie there, panting, gasping, trying not to, holding my hands over my mouth so it won't hear me, please don't hear me, please don't.

The lights go out. Dark again.

I sit up real slow. Hurts to move. Hurts to breathe.

Touch my face, my hands. I'm all cut and scraped. Pat my neck, my sides, arms and legs. I don't think I broke anything.

The wind again, right through me. So much colder than before. I curl up, wrap my arms around my knees. It helps, a little.

I can't see. I don't know where I am. I don't know how to get to Sam, I don't know how to get back, and I'm just gonna die. Mike—I should have listened to him. I shouldn't have gotten mad and gone off on my own, and now I'm gonna die and Sam's gonna die, too, and I'm sorry. I'm so sorry I couldn't save you, Sam. I'm sorry.

Oh, God.

Oh, God.

Hold myself and rock. Hold myself and rock.

* * *

It was just past ten on a Monday night. Sam's mom had already gone to bed. I should have been on my way back to Uncle Tony's, because I had social studies homework, but it was cold out, and it was just going to be colder on the bike. Sam and I were cuddled on the couch, watching the Ravens beat the crap out of the Texans, 24-6, at almost the end of the third quarter.

"I used to wish I was like them," Sam said.

"Like what? Rich?"

Sam gave me a funny look. "Huh?"

"My Uncle Tony says they make a lot more now than he did when he was playing."

"That's not what I meant. I wanted to be normal."

"They're not normal. Look how big that one dude next to the ref is."

"You know what I mean."

"Okay, but it doesn't matter."

"It used to, to me. When you're a guy, you're supposed to play sports, and have muscles, and be tough and stuff. A lot of guys at school are on the football team, or the lacrosse team, or they do basketball, or wrestling, or whatever. I've never played any of those—not for real, you know, just only like in gym class. And even then, it was like…" Shook his head. "Do you know how embarrassing it is to take your turn at bat in baseball, and everybody in the outfield starts walking closer because they know you can't hardly hit it past second base?"

"Who cares? Baseball is bullshit."

"That's not the point. Other guys at school, they hunt, or they volunteer at the fire department, or they're joining the military. Josh Manning got accepted to the Naval Academy. I'm never going to do any of those things."

"So what? You're not like other guys. You're really smart, and you like retro music, and you're in band, and you play that cool card game—"

"'Magic' is not cool."

"I think it's cool."

"If I could, I would have traded all that to be there," he said, pointing at the TV. "I've never scored a touchdown. I'm never going to."

"Well, me either."

"It's not the same for girls."

The third quarter ended, with the Texans second and seven on the Ravens' 48. Commercials, a crapload of them. That stupid one with old couples walking around holding hands and staring into each other's eyes while the announcer said you should see the doctor if you have an erection lasting more than four hours. Gross. I can't believe they're allowed to put that shit on TV.

A truck ad: every time they go to commercials during football games (and they do that a lot), there's always an ad for either Chevy or Ford, and I didn't care about either of them. One for Budweiser. Then some commercials for a bunch for TV shows, including that one with the hot Latina with the great hair and the big boobs.

"Look at her," I said. "I'm never gonna be like that. She's beautiful, she's famous, she's got lots of money, and every guy in the world wants to do her."

"Not Zach Willard. Or Justin Quimby."

"Who are they?"

"They're in theater. Zach was the Wizard when they did

'Wizard of Oz' last year. Justin goes out with Eli Barlow."

Eli's in Art with me. "Okay, so not gay guys."

"Kelli Peterson would definitely do her. So, it's not just dudes."

"What about you?"

"Me? That'd never happen."

"What if it did?"

"Like, what? I'm walking down Rodeo Drive in Hollywood, and she pulls up in her half-million dollar, Italian convertible sports car, and she looks over her sunglasses at me and says, in that accent, 'You. Me. Now.' You mean like that?"

Giggled. "Yeah, like that."

"Then, I'd tell her, 'The back of the line is that way, *chica*.' Just because she's all that, doesn't mean she doesn't have to wait her turn like all the other girls."

We laughed, and I ooched over a little closer to him. He held me tighter, kissed me on my forehead. The game started again. The Texans ran for four yards on second down, then threw incomplete on third. Punting team came on. Down by 18 and they're going to kick it away. Losers.

"You said, you used to wish you were like them," I reminded him. "So, you don't, anymore?"

"No." Short but high punt, Ravens let it bounce into the endzone for a touchback. "I'm never going to be like them or those other guys in school, but it's not like I don't have other things going for me. You know, like you said. So, instead of trying to do and be what somebody else thinks I ought to, I'll do and be the best I can. And I'll just be happy with myself."

More commercials. Every time the teams change possession, they go to commercials, even if they just showed a bunch of them a minute ago. That's the one thing about football I can't stand.

"The only thing I'm good at is drawing," I told him. "If I could, I'd trade that to look like Senorita *Chica*."

This Wasted Land

"You're more than just that. You like cool music, and you ride a motorcycle, and you're tough, and everyone thinks you're a badass."

"I'm not badass. I'm just messed up."

"Same thing. But if you looked like someone else and acted like someone else and did different things, you wouldn't be you."

"I don't want to be me."

"Well, if you aren't going to be you, then you better get off my couch, because if Alyx finds you here, she's going to beat the shit out of you. Girlfriend's crazy."

We laughed again. He always makes me laugh. I should have gone home earlier, but I stayed and cuddled on the couch with him until the game was over, 27-9. Froze my ass off on the way back to Uncle Tony's. Totally worth it.

* * *

Can't feel my fingers. Can't feel my feet. Doesn't matter. Crawling, hands and knees. Don't know if I'm going the right way. Just have to go some way. Any way. As long as I get to him.

Palm slaps down on something metal, round, freezing cold. Grab it—don't want to, shouldn't want to, cold oh my God it's so cold, squeeze it. Light. White light right in front of me.

My flashlight. No way. No damn way. Fingers loosen just a bit, just so I can make sure. Yes. It is.

Tears trickling warm down my cold cheeks. Thank you, God. Thank you. Please help me. Please help me get Sam. Please.

Point the light up. Next to me, a wall—natural? man-made? can't tell—of smooth gray rock, one huge chunk. That's what I slid down when I fell, when I was running in the dark, running from the thing with the eyes.

My light doesn't even go all the way up to the top of the wall. To get back to where I was, I gotta climb up there, but how am I sup—

Pelican.

Flick the light in front of me, it's there, just a few feet away. The ugly stuffed bird toy. Its wings flap, its eyes roll around, its beak snaps open and shut, open and shut. *Pelican.*

Grit my teeth to keep them from chattering with the cold. "Are…you in there? Huh? Freydis? Is that…you…you bitch?"

Something buzzing inside it as it waddles toward me. *Pelican.*

Keep the flashlight on it while my other hand goes for my jacket pocket. "Did you…send your…your toy out here…so you could…watch me…die?"

Pelican.

Fingers cold, don't want to work, make them anyway, make them unzip my pocket. Reach in. The pistol's a lump there. Slide it out.

The toy stops shambling forward. Head tilts. Eyes stare into, stare past the flashlight. Into me. Through me.

I flick off the safety, point the gun. The grip's cold—doesn't matter. Ignore it.

"I'm not…gonna die."

You'll wish he had, it squawks.

Pistol jerks in my hand the bird's head explodes no blood this time just scraps of paper, notebook paper with lines on it, like in school, and they burst into tiny flames, burn up, wink out as they swirl past my hand, past my face, and the 9 jerks again again and fire eats the rest of the bird and as it melts its beak snaps open and shut open and shut and I hear it whisper *you'll wish he had* even after the gun's thunder echoes away, even after something huge and far off roars, even when Mike is there, tugging me to my feet, wrapping a blanket around me, calling my name, calling me. Calling me.

You'll wish he had.

Track 23. Why Can't This Be Love

The wind's blowing hard again, roaring and whistling through the ground floor's broken windows, but it doesn't come down here, in the library's basement. I don't remember Mike and Paddoch bringing me back here, but I woke up a while ago, laid out on a folding table, with a blanket over me, and a Coleman lantern on the floor under the table.

Like upstairs, the basement's mostly a big open space. Rows of aluminum shelves, most of them packed with books. More books all over the concrete floor. Pieces of broken wooden furniture: chairs and cabinets and other tables. Hundreds of burning candles—some round and fat, some tall and skinny, some small, some tiny, even some of those ones in glass jars that smell really good—resting on the floor and wherever there's space on the empty shelves. It must have taken Paddoch forever to find all these. So he has to have been living here a long time.

Me and Mike are camped out at the bottom of those metal stairs that Paddoch was coming up when we first got here. Mike's lit a Sterno, and we're warming up some food. All I got's a can of creamed spinach, and it absolutely sucks.

"How'd you guys find me?"

Mike helps himself to another spoonful of Pedigree dog food. The label says chopped liver and lamb, but it looks like corned beef hash, and I swear to God, I'm just about jealous. It has to be better than what I'm having. He smirks. "'*Galdr.*'"

"'Magic?'" I wish I had saved some of those potato chips I took from The Murder Mart. "Thought you didn't buy that."

He shrugs. Sips from the bottle of Jack. There's not much left.

I gulp down a small, lukewarm wad of creamed spinach without chewing it. It's a little better that way, but not by much.

"Thanks for getting me. Bringing me back here."

"Wasn't my idea."

"You'd have let me die out there?"

"I told you not to go, but you keep saying I'm not the boss of you."

"Well, thanks anyway."

"Don't thank me. Thank Paddoch the Muppet."

I gotta wash away this awful taste in my mouth. My pack's next to me: I take out a bottle of water and the Midol, pop four of them. It's more than I usually take, but my back and legs and shoulders and neck are stiff, and everywhere on me hurts.

"So, where is he?" I ask.

"Don't know."

"He's got to be around here, right? I mean, how big is this place?"

"Not very."

I wouldn't say that. Off the main room here in the basement are halls that go down to storage rooms with more books, furniture, and junk. I think Paddoch sleeps in one of them. A janitor's closet, and a tiny bathroom, with a toilet and sink, but no running water. "Is he, like, outside?"

"Don't know. He just slips away every now and then. No idea where he goes."

I finish the spinach, swigging water after each spoonful. Might be the worst thing I've ever eaten, but it beats not eating at all. I guess.

"So, what's the deal with the sun?" I ask.

"What do you mean?"

"It just goes out?"

"What part of that didn't you grab the first time I told you?"

"How can it do that?"

"Don't you ever get tired of asking stupid questions? I don't know why you expect things to be like they are in scenic, downtown Baltimore, or wherever the hell you're from in Maryland."

"I'm not from Maryland."

"Yeah, that's really important for me to bear in mind, retard."

"Only douches say 'retard.'"

"I'm relieved to learn that skinny Oriental girls still use 'douche,' though."

Asshole. I'm not even going to get into it with him and *Oriental*. "I'm just trying to make sense of this. Does it do this because—"

"There's no sense to be made. The sun goes out when it does, and it turns back on when it does. And in the meantime, you don't want to be caught out there. As you found out the hard way. What the hell were you shooting at?"

"A creepy bird puppet thing. Like the one you ripped the head off of."

"You wasted bullets on that?"

"It was her, okay? Freydis. She was inside it, just like she was back at the mall, with Cynthia. When you went off."

"You're the one who went off." He slurps the last bit of dog-food gravy off his spoon, tosses the empty can into a corner. Takes another swig of Jack. Moves the lantern from his side to between us, for better light.

"Yeah," I tell him. "Yeah, I did."

Damn, it's cold down here. I'm glad I have the blanket to sit on. Mike must've found it here, cuz I haven't seen it before.

I watch the Sterno burn out. Sip my water. After a while, I look over at him. "So, we have to wait until the sun comes back. And then we can get Sam."

He nods.

I want to ask him again how long that'll be, but it'll just annoy him, and I know he doesn't know. "It's lucky you saw this place."

"Damned lucky. Conveniently lucky, just like lately."

"Huh?"

"All of this makes for some very nice coincidences, wouldn't you say? I traipse around the devil's ashtray here for twenty-some odd years, and don't so much as catch a glimpse of your friend and mine, Witchiepoo. Then I run into you, and she's just happens to have kidnapped your boyfriend. Oh, and you just happen to have dreams about them that just happen to turn out to be real."

What's he getting at? "And?"

"And we just happen to come across the one guy who just happens to know the shit-sucking bastard who holds that bitch's leash. And he just happens to know where to find him, and her, and your boyfriend. And then it just so happens that he's nice enough to show us the way there, even though we tried to kick his ass and take his stuff."

"That was all you. I said to give it back to him."

"The sun starts to go out, which is pretty much a death sentence, and we just happen to be in sprinting distance of this place, which just happens to be monster-free, in addition to being our new friend's home. You run off, and he just happens to have a 'magic spell' to find you before you get turned into Creature Chow. Very convenient."

I don't like where this is going.

"You know," he says, "if I were paranoid, I'd wonder if maybe you and Paddoch are actually working for Witchiepoo. That she sent you two to trick me into letting my guard down, then have you screw me over when I wouldn't see it coming. Maybe set me up so she can waste me, maybe you do it yourself while I'm asleep."

Is he kidding me? "Listen, kiss my ass, okay? I don't need you and your 'can't-trust-anything' act. All I wanna do is kill her and get Sam back, and—"

He holds up a hand. "Relax."

"—and if you think I'm on her side, you can—"

"I believe you, okay? If I didn't, I would have shot you a long time ago."

Shot you. It's weird to hear Mike say it so…casually, so matter-of-fact, after all this time we've been together. But despite that, how well do I really know him, anyway? Not a lot. Not as much as I think.

"Did anyone ever tell you, you have a problem with flying off the handle?" he asks.

"All the time."

"How does Sammy take it?"

"I don't do that with him."

"He must be special."

"He is. He gets me."

Mike nods. "If you have someone who understands you—*really* understands you—well, that's a rare thing. Don't know that I've ever had that."

"Not Cathy?"

"No."

"Why not?"

"She loved me, but she didn't get me."

"If she loved you, why'd she cheat on you?"

"It's…." Shrugs. "I'd explain, but—"

"—but I'm just a kid, so it'd go right over my head."

"I'm not saying that."

"You said it before."

"If you haven't been through it—"

"Whatever. You just think I'm dumb." I wish I had another blanket to wrap around me. So sick of being cold. I dig around in my pack for Sam's phone.

"Fine. You want to know? Then I'll tell you." Swigs from the bottle.

"Okay." My hand finds Sam's phone, and I take it out.

"You meet someone," Mike says. "You fall in love. They're your world. They're everything."

I tuck the phone inside my jacket.

"You spend time with them, you live with them, and you start to think you understand them, even if you actually don't. The rush, the excitement of falling in love wears off, but you think everything's peachy-keen. You get comfortable. They get familiar. You come to expect them, like you do with having food to eat, or clothes to wear, or someplace to live. And they might do the same with you."

"So, you count on them. What's bad about that?"

"Nothing, necessarily, if that's as far as it goes. If you don't take them for granted. If no…distance develops between you two. Know what I mean?"

"Sorta. Not really."

"After a while, if you're not careful, if you're overlooking all their good qualities because you're used to them, they can get on your nerves. Stuff about them that you didn't notice before—they pick their teeth after they eat, or they never use their turn signal, or they don't fold the towels the way you like—it starts to honk you off. And crap you do bothers them, too. A lot."

That's not me and Sam. We don't do that. Okay, there was that argument at the mall. And I was kinda annoyed with him when we were on the bike trying to get home, stopped at the train tracks, but that's cuz he was all pissy about being late and he thought I had gone the wrong way even though I hadn't, I knew where we were going.

"You try to get them to change, to stop doing all those little things that annoy you. Maybe they do, maybe they don't. Maybe they only stop with some of them. You start saying in your head, 'I can't believe that asshole does such-and-such even though I've asked him a million times not to.' Or, 'If that stupid bitch doesn't get her crap together….'"

This Wasted Land

Me thinking about Sam, *Honest to God, sometimes he makes me crazy.*

"So then, you stop paying attention to them. You don't talk as much. You don't go out and have fun together like you used to. You don't do little things for each other anymore. Helping bring in the groceries. Saying how good the dinner they made was. Writing them notes when you leave the house and they're not there, or kissing them on the cheek when you come back."

My hand squeezes the phone.

"You tune out. They tell you about their day, and you pretend like you're listening, but really, they're boring the living hell out of you. And after a while, you don't bother pretending."

"That's…" Shake my head. "That's really shitty."

He nods. "Well, it can get even worse."

I want him to stop.

"Other things, other people become more interesting. You grab lunch with a woman at work. You go out for drinks, at first maybe once a week, then more and more. One night, you're at the bar with her again, except this time, you're dancing too close, swapping spit as you put your hand in her blouse. And you don't know what's going on at home while you're not there. You don't even care. Until you find out that the person who used to be your everything is at the motel down the street with someone who isn't you."

I feel like I ate something dead I found on the road.

"You step back and remember how you started off with this person you loved so much, this person you still love despite everything, and you wonder how the hell did the two of you wind up like this? Where and when did everything so innocent and good go so wrong?"

I don't say anything. What can I?

He finishes the Jack. Turns the bottle over in his hands a few times. Chucks it into the same corner as the dog food can. I used to like the sound of glass breaking. All of a sudden, I don't.

Mike rubs his face. "That's probably more than you wanted to hear."

"No kidding."

"You asked."

"I wish I hadn't."

"There are a lot of things 'I wish I hadn't.'"

Was that Cathy at the motel? Was that him at the bar? Or was he just making all that up? I don't want to know. Not any more of this.

He cups his hands around his mouth, blows on them. "How long have you and Sam been going out?"

"About six months, I guess. Since last October."

"Six months." Nods. "You two in love?"

Shrug.

"As much as you can be, at your age."

"What's that supposed to mean?"

"Love is different at different ages, different circumstances. Maybe you'll get to find that out."

I remember him saying, *You're going through an awful lot of trouble for some guy you're eventually gonna break up with. Unless he dumps you first.* "You think just because we're kids, it's not real."

"It's real enough for you and him, at least for now."

"Whaddya mean, 'for now?'"

"Let's say you find Sam. Let's say you get him away from Witchiepoo, and the two of you somehow manage to get back to that school in Maryland."

"There's no 'let's say.' We're gonna do it."

"What then?"

"We'll…we'll be home, and together, and—"

"You think that you'll just keep wearing his class ring on a chain around your neck, and you'll go to prom together, and to the same college? Get married, have babies, all that happy horseshit?"

"Maybe...."

"You think that you won't come out of this a different person? That he won't, either? That none of what you've been through is going to change anything between you?"

"No. I mean, we...."

"Right now, you two love each other. But is that going to be enough? Is that going to hold you together?"

"Sure, it will." I guess. I don't know. I never thought of that. Why shouldn't it? "You said me and Sam have something rare."

"You do." Shakes his head. "That doesn't mean it's going to last."

"Just cuz you and Cathy were all...whatever, doesn't mean me and Sam are gonna break up." Pull his phone out. It's lit up from where my thumb hit the side button. "I don't want to talk about this."

"A little too close to home?"

"Can we just drop it?"

"Sure." Leans his back against the wall and puts his hands behind his head, all smug and pleased with himself, like he's made some kind of point. Like he enjoys being a dick and making me upset for no good reason, just cuz he can. Bastard. I'm not gonna let him see that he's bothered me.

"Paddoch," I say. "You think he made up all that stuff about Freydis and Vikings and Ōth?"

"Either that, or he's insane."

"Yeah, well, even if he is, we might as well do like he does and call her 'Freydis' instead of just 'that bitch,' or anything else. It sure beats 'Witchiepoo.' That's lame."

"You don't know who 'Witchiepoo' is? Don't they have Saturday morning cartoons anymore?"

"No."

"That sucks."

"And nobody says 'Oriental.' It's racist."

"How is that racist?"

"It just is."

"What should I be saying instead?"

"Asian."

"'Asian.' That's stupid."

"Why's that stupid?"

"Because Asia is a big place. If you say you're 'Asian,' that could mean you come from anywhere between Manila and Istanbul. It doesn't tell me anything. You say you're 'Oriental,' at least I got an idea where you're talking about."

"Don't call me Oriental. How'd you like it if I called you a Mexican?"

"Doesn't bother me. I'm not Mexican."

"Your last name's Fernandez."

"So? What's yours?"

"I'm not gonna tell you. You'd just find a way to make fun of me."

"If I wanted to make fun of you, I'd ask you when was the last time you had dog for dinner."

"I've never eaten dog, okay? That's not really a thing anymore in Korea."

Smirks. "Don't knock what you haven't tried."

"You've never eaten dog, either."

"Course not. I don't even like 'em as pets, so why the hell would I eat one?" Leans forward, points to where he threw the can. "But their food's not half bad, once you cook it a little."

"There's something wrong with you if you don't like dogs."

"There's a whole lot wrong with me, but I'm not gonna tell

you any more."

"Good." Wait—hold on. "Why not?"

"You're not a licensed therapist."

"Yeah, well, you're not funny."

"I *am* funny. You just don't have a sense of humor."

"Yeah, I do."

"No, you don't. But you are the only Asian Goth girl I've ever met."

"I'm not a Goth."

"No, of course not. You just look and act like all the others I ran into back in the Nineties."

The Nineties. That was forever ago. And he's been here since then.

For my whole life.

Longer than that. I wasn't even born yet.

"Mike?"

Shouldn't ask. Don't bother.

"Yeah?"

Screw it.

"Mike, why are you here?"

"To help you get Sam back, dumbass."

"No, that's not what I mean."

"What *do* you mean?"

"Like, why aren't you back where you lived? In our world. Why are you in this one?"

"None of your business."

"Don't say that! That's not fair. I tell you everything, and you don't tell me nothing."

"Your grammar sucks."

"Yours isn't all that, either. Don't change the subject."

"I'm here to kill Freydis."

"Why?"

"Why do you care?"

"Cuz maybe you're working for her."

"Ha ha. You know I'm not."

"Maybe you're taking me to her so she can kill me."

"If she wanted to kill you, you'd already be dead."

"How do you know that?"

"I just do."

"Be real."

He shakes his head.

What is his problem? He told me all this stuff about him and Cathy, and *now* he doesn't want to say anything?

Fine. Be like that. Jerk.

He leans back, hands behind his head again.

Nothing.

Nothing.

When did you see her? I asked him, talking about Freydis.

Only once, a long time ago, he said.

What he told me, back at the motel. *She's dead.* As in Cathy.

And, *People always expect that anything that happened a long time ago is just magically supposed to be okay now.*

The lantern's burning low.

I remember you. What Freydis—in Cynthia's skin, if that's what it really was—said to him, at the mall.

"Mike...." Forget it. He's not gonna tell me.

I remember you.

I don't want to ask. But I gotta.

"Mike, is Cathy dead because of Freydis?"

He drops his arms, crosses them. His eyes don't tell anything.

I wrap the blanket tighter around myself.

"Did she kill her?"

He nods.

"I'm—" It's stupid, but I don't know what else to say. "I'm really sorry."

He looks down. Picks at something on the floor.

Jesus. He and his wife went through all this crap, and he went to jail and they almost split up, but they stayed together. And then Freydis killed her. I thought my life sucked. No wonder he hates her. How does he keep it together? If she killed Sam—

Don't say that!

But if she did—

She is not going to kill Sam! Stop it!

Okay, she won't. She won't. But all I'm saying is that I don't know what I'd do. Cuz there can't be anything worse than losing someone you love.

Losing someone.

Freydis again. What did she ask Mike?

Did you lose him, Da-doo?

Da-doo. The horrible bird-puppet thing, the second one— Pelican, it called itself, but it wasn't one. It said *Da-doo* to Mike, and he flipped out, as much as he ever does.

You bitch, where is he? he yelled, right before he tore its head off.

And then, at the mall, with Freydis. *You give him to me,* and—

And...

"Mike?"

He climbs to his feet. "I gotta squizz like a racehorse."

"Mike, what's—"

He starts up the metal steps. "I don't want to talk about anything anymore, Alyx."

"Mike, what's 'Da-doo' mean?"

"It doesn't mean anything."

I jump up, a little too fast: I'm dizzy something fierce. Pinch the bridge of my nose and shut my eyes for second. "Yeah, it does."

"No." Still headed upstairs. "No, listen, I'm not gonna—"

"Mike." I grab the lantern, follow him.

"It's nothing."

"It's not nothing."

"It's just a nickname."

"For what?" I grab his elbow and he stops. "For 'Daddy?'"

"No." Shakes his head.

I go past him, up onto the next step. "It is, isn't it?" Hold up the lantern so I can see his face. "Mike?"

His eyes are puddling. He wipes them with the back of his hand.

"Mike. Oh my God, Mike…" I didn't think he even knew how to cry.

I lean in to hug him; he swats my arm away. The hell? "Hey, I'm just—"

He shoves me out of the way, starts going past. I punch him in the back, hard as I can. He stops again, faces me. It doesn't seem like I hurt him, but I definitely pissed him off. Jabs his finger at me.

"Don't do that again."

"Would you talk to me, already?"

"Do yourself a favor and take 'no' for an answer."

"Why are you like this? Why do you keep yourself locked

down all the time?"

"Because if I don't, I'll say and do things that I don't want to."

"You're so the typical 'guy,' like, 'Oh, I can't talk about anything, I can't have any feelings, I gotta be manly, I gotta be tough.' What are—"

"I'm only going to tell you once to shut the hell up."

"Or what? What're you gonna do? Yell at me? Hit me? Run off and leave me and never come back? Is that what you're gonna do?"

"I'm not your father."

"With your wife screwing around like that, maybe you're nobody's father."

For a second—maybe two—there's this look on his face. The only time I'd ever seen it before was back on the train, when Freydis grabbed me by the jacket, right before the stalks with the mouths came out of her head. She had that look, too. It's not anger, it's not hate. It's more like…you don't mean anything—for real, *anything*—to them. That there's no difference between you and a wad of gum stuck to the floor. So, it doesn't matter what they do to you, because you're not even a person.

Just for a second or two, and then he's back to his usual scowl. "You," he says, "are a cunt."

"Yeah, well, you're a total prick. That was low to talk about my dad. Worse than all that with me and Sam not staying together."

His eyes narrow. "Fine."

"Fine."

"His name's Jeremy. He's—he was—seventeen months old. He called me 'Da-doo' because he couldn't say 'Daddy.'"

Oh, God.

"She…" he growls. "She took him. She cut chunks out of Cathy, and then she took him. Here."

"Mike, I'm…." Again with that stupid *I'm sorry* bullshit. Is there anything more worthless to say?

His finger and thumb, an inch apart. "I'm this goddamn close, the closest I've ever been, after all this time, to getting her. And I can't. Not yet. But don't you worry your little teenybopper self, Alyx-with-a-'y.' We'll find little Sammy-boo, and you two can run off together and live happily ever after. You and your candyass *high school boyfriend*."

Track 24. Would

Fourteen percent battery. That's all that's left on Sam's phone.

I shouldn't be looking through his photos. I should be saving power (though why? It's not like I can text or call anyone, or go online). But I can't help it. This is all I have of him—maybe all I've ever have again.

Him and me and his mom and Cynthia at the Ravens game when they played the Browns last season, when Sam let me borrow his old jersey. All of us jammed into the shot, huddled together, smiling real big, our cheeks red from the cold: it was December, but sunny, at least.

* * *

Section 134, fairly close to the field and on the Ravens' side, but at the corner of an endzone. As we were walking down the concrete steps to our seats, I blurted out, "I like that all the chairs are purple." Christ, did I really go there? Could I sound any more like a chick?

I didn't have to look behind me to know that Cynthia was rolling her eyes: she's like the All-Time Maryland Champion Eye-Roller. But Sam's mom—Brenda, she wants me to call her Brenda, but there's no way I'm cool with that—turned and said, "I know, right? And it was my favorite color even before the team came along."

We got to our row, ooched our way past the other people—lots of guys, of course, but a bunch of women, too—and sat down. I looked around. Sam had stopped at the bathroom and said he'd catch up.

"I want a pretzel," Cynthia said, "and a beer." I had on

longjohns under my jeans, two pairs of thick socks, my boots, one of Sam's wifebeaters, my G'n'R t-shirt over that, my hoodie zipped all the way up, Uncle Tony's big black sweatshirt, Sam's Ray Lewis jersey, gloves, and a purple Ravens knit hat that I bought at the Big Lots yesterday, and yet I was still chilly. I couldn't imagine drinking anything cold.

"If you see the beer man, get me one, too," Brenda—Sam's mom—said. She flipped through the program. With the crowd at the entrance of the stadium where they were selling the programs, I didn't hear exactly how much it cost, but it seemed like it was a lot. Kinda dumb to pay that much for something that was only good for one day, but maybe she wanted it for a souvenir, though why she'd want that when she'd be back next week for the Colts game didn't make any sense to me.

"Excuse me. Excuse me. Thanks. Pardon me. Sorry. Thanks." Sam scooted past everyone else, slid into the empty seat next to me.

"Everything come out okay?" Cynthia asked him.

"Don't be gross," Sam's mom—I decided she was just going to be *Sam's mom*—told her.

Sam whispered to me, "My dad always used to say that." I nodded. Sam had said that his mom was over Sam's dad, but I got the feeling that wasn't entirely true.

Cynthia pointed at a photo in the program. "Hey, didn't she go to Kent Island?"

"Oh, my gosh!" Sam's mom said. Folded back the program's cover and showed Sam the page. "Do you remember her?"

"Sorta," Sam said. Pretty girl despite the big nose. Perfect teeth, long brown hair, transparent blue eyes. Those could not possibly be real. CHRISTINA something the caption said—Sam's mom yanked it back before I could finish reading her name.

"She was the Narrator in 'Joseph,' when you were in the children's choir," Sam's mom told him. "Oh, she was soooo good in that."

"Who's 'Joseph?'" I asked Sam.

"'Joseph and the Amazing Technicolor Dreamcoat,'" Sam replied. "It's a musical that Kent Island put on, and they had a bunch of kids from the elementary- and middle schools in a big chorus." Looks at his mom. "How long ago was that?"

"You were in 3rd grade," she said.

"Little Sam was cute," Cynthia assured me. "Not like…*now*." Pretended to shudder.

"You had braces," Sam reminded her.

"I was a freshman. You're not allowed to be cool when you're a freshman. But by the time you're a senior, you have to be, or they don't let you walk at graduation." Leaned over and stage-whispered in my ear. "He's not gonna walk. Not that he walks very well, anyway."

My eyes got big and my mouth hung open and I thought, *You bitch*, but Sam just laughed. I guessed the two of them were used to joking about his disability.

"It says here that after high school, she studied singing, dance, and theater in New York," Sam's mom read, "and she's been in a lot of shows around the country, and even in Europe. How exciting! Good for her! I knew she'd do well. She was soooo talented. Do you remember the production of 'Alice in Wonderland' she was in?"

"That tea party scene was funny as all hell," Cynthia said. "I still remember that. The dude who played the Mad Hatter almost made me pee myself, I was laughing so hard."

"So, why is this Christina girl in the program?" I asked. Everyone around us started standing up; Sam and Cynthia and their mom did, too. The hell? I just sat where I was.

"She's going to sing the National Anthem!" Sam's mom said. "There she is!"

I stood up. Even though we were pretty close to the field, she was still tiny (not that she was that tall to begin with), so I watched her on the Jumbotron-thing. Long black slacks, black shoes, long black wool coat buttoned all the way up. Purple scarf and matching hat and gloves with sequins.

It was just like a Kent Island football game, only bigger. All the guys took off their hats. Lots of people put their hands over their hearts. She started singing, and her voice was like a princess from those Disney movies I watched when I was little.

Everyone but me sang along with her, and when it got to the *O, say does that star-spangled banner still wave* part, everyone shouted "O!" real loud, just like they did at the Kent Island games. Sam and Cynthia and his mom did, too.

After that Christina chick was done and everyone clapped and we sat down, I asked Sam, "What the hell is that 'O' thing you all do?"

"It's for the Orioles."

"Who?"

"The baseball team," Cynthia said. "Tell me that you can't be more stupid than my brother. Even he knows that."

"I know we're at a football game," I told her. "Apparently, none of the rest of you do."

"It's a Baltimore thing," Sam said.

"It doesn't make any sense."

"Fact," Cynthia said.

"Over here, you two!" Sam's mom said, holding up her phone. Cynthia leaned way back, out of the shot; Sam squeezed up against me. We smiled. "Hang on," his mom said, "one more!" She moved over a smidge, to get another angle. "Say, 'Go Ravens!'"

"Go Ravens!" Sam yelled. I just smiled again.

"Okay, got it!" she said. Down on the field, the Browns won the coin toss and decided to receive the kickoff.

"How great would it be if I could get Christina to sign my program?" Sam's mom asked none of us in particular.

"She's probably out of here by now," Cynthia said, sitting up real tall in her chair, looking for the beer guy. The Ravens won 17-14, and everyone had a good time. I did, too, but only sorta, cuz I kinda wanted the Browns to win, for Uncle Tony.

This Wasted Land

* * *

Thirteen percent. A selfie Sam took from the end of his trombone slide, all the way out, him puffing his cheeks, eyes wide, pretending like he's blowing it real hard.

Us in DC, lots of pics. It was cloudy and only a little chilly that day. Lunch at this all-you-can eat place right off the Metro. The restaurant's Mongolian, and it's in Chinatown—I don't get that.

On the Mall, with the Capitol behind us. Then turned around, with the Washington Monument in the background—to me, it's a giant pencil. At the Natural History Museum, me standing back and sketching the big elephant they have right where you come in. Sam says it's called Henry. So, they liked it enough to give it a name, but not enough to not kill it. Makes total sense.

I wanted to see the dinosaur bones, but the hall was closed for renovations. Upstairs, posing with the Hope Diamond—it's kinda cool that it's supposed to be cursed, but jewelry doesn't do anything for me. I waited outside the insect zoo while Sam went in. He said they have live cockroaches almost as big as your palm. No thanks.

Lots of pics of me at the Korea exhibit. Pretty cool pottery and calligraphy samples, and a whole thing on traditional Korean weddings. Sam asked if it was giving me any ideas. Only that he'd look stupid in one of those funny tall black hats the grooms wear.

This statue from India. It's all white marble, and it has dark streaks through it that look like veins. It's of a god or demon or something with ten heads—seriously—with fangs coming out of its mouths, and twenty arms—no lie—and the sign next to it said his name is Ravana, and he's the bad guy in this really long poem written a thousand years ago. Sam said I should draw it, because it was cool, but I had forgotten my phone back at Uncle Tony's, so Sam took the photo for me.

Other stuff from the museum: mummies, and fake cavemen, and a life-size blue whale model, and more stuffed animals—not like the kind kids have when they were little, but like Henry the elephant in the atrium or rotunda or whatever it's called.

Out on the Mall again, where Sam got me and this really friendly Border Collie—Rex—who had one blue eye and one brown. Rex had run over to me while he and his owner—the guy's name was Rob—were playing Frisbee. Then into Air and Space, cuz Sam likes planes. About a hundred pics of them, especially the ones from World War I—they're Sam's favorite.

Twelve percent. Another photo, January, if I remember right. Me and Sam, him grinning like a crazy person, me not so much. Come to find out, it doesn't snow that often in Maryland, and hardly ever on Kent Island. But when it does, everyone heads to the K-Mart hill to go sledding. Which somehow, I'd never done in my life. But there we were.

* * *

"I don't know about this," I said.

"What?" Sam asked, looking back. It had snowed about 5 inches last night. He was sitting at the front of the sled, which was nothing but this long piece of black plastic, like if somebody had cut out and dried the tongue from that guy in KISS. We were at the top of the slope that came down from the overpass where Route 8 goes over Route 50. It's the closest thing they have to a hill on the island, and Sam said it's all of sixteen feet above sea level.

"Okay, that's awfully steep," I told him. And it was. I mean, sure, it wasn't as high as the hills they have in Pennsylvania, but still. It looked like almost a 45-degree angle where the hill ended and the rest of the ground started. And it wasn't that far from the edge of the K-Mart parking lot, so if you were going real fast, you'd slide right into a parked car. Or a moving one.

"It's nothing. I've done this since I was little."

I shook my head.

"You ride a motorcycle, but you won't get on a sled?"

"This isn't like a bike."

"You're right: it's better. C'mon!" He waved me over. "There's nothing to be scared of."

"What if we crash?"

"It's just snow. It's not gonna hurt."

I looked around. Lots of other people here. Dads with their kids, even babies. Middle-schoolers. Even some high school kids like me and Sam. Some of them had plastic sleds like us. One boy an old-fashioned wooden kind that he went down head first. A lot of them just had big pieces of cardboard.

"All right." I settled in behind him, wrapped my arms around his chest.

He got out his phone, held it up. "Smile so the authorities can identify our remains."

"Very funny." He took the picture. "How do you steer this?"

"You don't," he said, and then he pushed with his feet. The bottom of the hill rushed up to meet us, so fast that all I had time to do was think *shit shit shit shit* and then Sam dug his boots into the snow and it sprayed all over us and the sled stopped not ten feet from the grill of a parked Chevy Lumina.

"See?" Sam asked, as we got off and he picked up the sled. "Not so bad, huh?" We started tromping up the hill. "Nothing to it."

"I am *not* doing that again." But I did. A lot. We stayed out there with the others until the sleds rubbed off almost all the snow, and the K-Mart Hill turned to mud.

* * *

Me and Sam at the Duran Duran concert last month at the Capital One Arena in DC. For a bunch of old guys who play keyboards-Eighties stuff, they're not bad. I liked that one song—Sam said it was "Careless Memories"—because they finally turned the guitarist loose so he could really kick ass, and they had this cool anime playing on the screens behind them.

Sam with Pretty Boy, the horse he rides at Fairmore. Pretty Boy's all black except for this white strip, broken in three places, running down his face. Sam's therapist is this Italian guy—like, off the boat Italian, from Rome, with this thick accent—named Mr. Marco. Sam's been riding with him since he was three. Sam has to put on Pretty Boy's saddle and bridle and such by himself, and climb on with no help, and Mr. Marco gives him exercises to do while they go around the ring. Riding helps with Sam's posture, strength, and coordination, and he goes every week. I've never ridden a horse, and I wouldn't mind trying, but I always just sit with Buddy, the big German Shepherd that lives there, and I sketch.

Sam with the rest of the tech crew backstage at *The Sound of Music*, this spring's musical at school. He did lighting. I went with his mom to one of the shows (there were six). She loved it—said it was good that they ended at the wedding, because after that scene, there aren't any new songs after that, and it's all just Nazi stuff, and besides, it's long enough without that. I wasn't into it, but it was okay, I guess. A couple kids from my classes had bit parts—I know their faces, but not their names. Eh.

This one, of a sunset, pink down low, near the horizon, indigo-purple clouds above, hiding the sun as it slipped away. Sam took this picture from the roof of St. Christopher's. The hall, not the church, because the church roof was way too high and way too steep: you'd slide right off if you so much as sneezed. But the one on the hall was easy-peasy to climb up, even for Sam. Not that he was thrilled with the idea.

* * *

"We're going to get caught," he said.

"No one's going to find out," I told him. "And so what if they did? It's not really breaking the law. Well, maybe it is."

"You're a bad influence. That's what I'm going to tell the sheriff, anyway."

"Totally worth it."

Sam took a picture with his phone, one of those new ones that was supposed to have a really great camera. Like so good, that whatever you took would look like a pro did it. At least, that's what the ads said, not that I believed that. Besides, photography is bullshit. Anyone can point a phone and press a button and Photoshop it until it looks like a magazine cover. It's not art. Drawing is art.

I was sketching with colored pencils. Kinda frustrating, cuz nothing I had was the right shade of pink, but it was turning out okay anyway. "Maryland has the prettiest sunsets of any place I've been," I said.

"My dad says it's because of all the hot air coming out of D.C."

"What's that mean?"

"It's supposed to be a joke."

"I don't get it."

"Because it's not funny. How are the sunsets in Korea?"

"I wouldn't know. I've never been."

"Weren't you born there?"

"No, I was born in Georgia."

"So, you're a citizen?"

"Duh."

"Just asking. What's Georgia like?"

"I don't remember. We didn't live there long. We left when I was maybe three."

"Where did you move to?"

"Texas. Then North Carolina, I think. By then, my dad had got out of the Army. But we kept moving around. Illinois. Louisiana. All over."

"Why?"

"My mom doesn't talk about it—she never talks about anything—but my uncle Tony told me. My dad kept losing his jobs. He was always late, or hungover, or he'd just not show up at all. He'd argue with customers, or cuss out the guys he worked with, or he'd talk shit to the boss, cuz he always wanted to do things his way, even if he didn't know any better. A couple times, they caught him stealing: tools and copper wiring from one job, cash and blank checks from another. Once, he got into a fight in a parking lot for hitting on this dude's wife who worked at the same place."

"That's messed up. I guess the only good thing is that at least you got to see different places."

"Places that suck. Not like Kent Island. You're lucky. You've lived here your whole life, right?"

"Yeah."

"So, what's that like?"

"It's okay, I guess. I mean, it's not like exciting, or anything. There's really not much to do. It's this quiet little place all on its own, separate from the rest of the world, where nothing ever happens. You know, like The Shire."

"What's 'The Shire?'"

"Never mind. It'd take too long to explain."

"But you like it here?"

"Yeah, it's all right. I'm not going to stay forever, but…I belong here. At least, for now."

Belong here. What is that even supposed to mean? Like, being from somewhere, maybe the same place your parents are from? Living in the same house, or if you do move, it's just down a couple streets so you can have a place with more bedrooms and bathrooms? Knowing people their whole lives, and them knowing you, and you going to the same schools together, and doing the same things they do? Is that what *belonging here* is?

"That sounds nice."

"You could belong here."

I shook my head.

"Why not?"

I shrugged. "I don't belong anywhere."

"That's because you make yourself so…remote. You give off this vibe like you know you don't fit in, and you don't want to. Like when you used to sit all by yourself at the top of the stairs during lunch."

"I don't do that anymore."

"Yeah, now that you sit with me and my friends. But you don't talk to them."

"I'm not into gaming, and that's all they do."

"Okay, but they like you. They think it's awesome that you're an artist."

"I'm not that good."

"That's not the point. The point is that I'm the only person you hang out with—except when you don't, like when I wanted to take you to the cast party."

"I don't know anyone in theater."

"You know me, and I could have introduced you to everyone."

"Parties aren't my thing."

"They could be if you ever went. There's an Art Club at school, but you haven't joined it. You could get a job—Chick-fil-A is always hiring—"

"I'm not working at Chickaflicka."

"There are lots of other places you could apply to."

"Uncle Tony gives me gas money."

"I sing in the teen choir here at church. You could come with me and mom."

"We're at church right now."

"Real funny. You'd rather step away from anything than be part of it—doesn't that get old?"

"Stop giving me shit about what I do."

"What *do* you do, besides sketch and listen to old music and ride your bike too fast?"

"I thought you liked that about me."

"I do, but I want you to have more than just me. I want you to have friends. I want you to have fun. You say you 'don't' belong, but I think you really mean 'won't.'"

I didn't answer.

"And I don't know why you do that, because you don't have to."

The sun was sinking into the ground, and indigo deepened to black.

"Are you breaking up with me?" I asked.

"No," he said, looking at me like I'd asked him if he was going to hit himself in the balls with a hammer. "Why would you think that?"

"Cuz I don't have any friends, and I don't do anything fun, and I'm not pretty, and I'm weird, and I'm for-real crazy, and it sounds like you want me gone because you think all I have is you." I wasn't going to cry. I was not going to cry, damn it. Instead, I looked at the sun as it went. "Even though it's true. All I have *is* you."

Sam scooched closer, took my pad and set it on the rooftop. It didn't slide off, but I wouldn't have cared if it had. He held me, kissed me. Pulled away just far enough to tell me, "You have your uncle, and my mom, and you can have me as long as you want."

"You promise?"

"I promise."

Track 25. Foolin'

Sam's battery ran down to eleven percent while I was looking at the sunset photo. I put his phone in my jacket pocket, stand up. Stretch. It's gotten colder here in the basement. Mike's asleep by the stairs, sitting against the wall. I used to wonder how he could do that. Now, I don't care. It's been—I don't know, hours? A day? Who can tell?—since he lost his shit about Jeremy, and he hasn't spoken to me since. Which is fine, because I don't want to speak to him, either.

But Paddoch...him and I gotta talk. I squat, pick up the lantern—it's going dim—from the floor, straighten. I'm guessing that Paddoch's somewhere down one of these hallways going off the basement. Hopefully just him and not something horrible—but if there was, wouldn't it have come out and killed us by now?

Get out the pistol, cock it, make sure the safety's on. All I have to do is thumb the switch and it's ready. I keep the gun in one hand, and with the other, I hold the lantern high and out in front of me. Go slow into the closest hall.

Shelves of books along the wall, more books and trash—empty cans, broken bottles, shreds of food wrappers, cigarette butts, crunched-up plastic containers—ankle deep on the floor. I think I see something scurrying around under the junk and I point the pistol that way, hold still, wait for it to move again.

Nothing. Just my imagination. I creep forward. Spatters of what smells like dried piss and diarrhea and vomit down low, near the floors, on some of the walls. My foot crunches on what's left—dry-rotted wood and smudged glass and greasy, faded print—of a picture frame. As I lift the lantern again, I see there's a sliver of light ahead.

Closer. A metal door to my right. My lantern doesn't show me how far the hall keeps going, but hopefully, I don't need to find out. The light—faint, flickering—is coming from the other side of the door, and the trash near it's been pushed away, so there's just bare floor. Like someone's gone in and out of here.

I set the lantern on the bookcase behind me. Hold the gun out again, reach with my other hand. The handle's really cold. Peel the door open. It doesn't make any noise.

Candles all over the floor where Paddoch's sitting, his back to me. It's shadowy and I don't even want to look, but I can't help it. I've never seen anyone's spine bend like that. It's absolutely disgusting.

It's a couple seconds before he turns his lumpy head and notices I'm there, and it's another couple of seconds before I stop staring at his back and realize that he's totally naked. I jerk back and start to shut the door, but he grabs a blanket beside him. "For please Alyx not to go," he says, and covers himself.

I stay there, in the doorway, the gun still pointed at him, I don't know why. He looks at it, looks at me. "Paddoch Alyx not to hurt."

I can't tell if he's asking me not to hurt him, or if he's saying he won't hurt me. Or both. I lower the pistol, but don't put it away. Chest pounding, breath coming out fast, in big white clouds. Sorta scared and sick to my stomach at the same time. Seeing him like that…he's so gross, he doesn't even seem human. Like he's some…*creature*.

"Aren't you cold?" I finally manage.

His head twitches twice. *No*. Slowly, he hauls himself up, blood trickling down the back of his legs from somewhere—I don't even wanna look. I step back, put my other hand on the pistol in case I need to flick off the safety. He leaves the blanket on himself while he starts to pull on those rags he wears, and I get a better look at where he was sitting.

Tiny scratches in the concrete floor, dozens—no, hundreds—of them. Straight lines, no curves, all of them connecting to other lines, or crossing through them, to make shapes that sorta look like letters. The letters, if that's what they are, are in a circle about as big as a basketball. In the circle is this pile—about two handfuls—of red dust or powder.

"What are you doing?"

"*Galdr.*"

Doing magic bare-ass naked. And sitting in a small puddle of blood, too. Nothing creepy about that at all. "*Galdr* for what?"

He finishes getting dressed, not that he wears more than some sheets wrapped around himself. "What Alyx to want?"

"I was wondering if you could do something for me."

"Yes-no," he says. I'll take that as *maybe*.

"Sometimes, when I'm asleep, I dream that I go inside Sam's head. I see and hear the same things that he does, and I know what he's thinking. Mike doesn't believe me, but it's for real."

Paddoch doesn't say anything.

"I saw Sam on a train. Then I saw him walking along, and Freydis was with him, and then something happened, because one second, they were somewhere, and then the next second, they were by this big rock, like a finger—" I stick mine up "—coming out of the ground."

Paddoch's face doesn't move.

"But that was a while ago. Lately, nothing's happened. I've tried thinking about Sam before I went to sleep, so maybe I'd make myself dream about him, but it hasn't worked. I don't know where he is, or if he's okay, and it's really bothering me."

Paddoch just stares at me. I think he understands what I'm saying, but it's hard to tell.

"Can you do some spell or whatever so I can dream about Sam?"

He shakes his head.

"No, please don't say you can't. I mean, you did that thing with the dice, and you got here before me and Mike did, and we were running. You found me when I left here and went off by myself to get Sam—that's what Mike says, anyway. He says you did *galdr*, but

I don't know if he was just being sarcastic or what."

He doesn't answer.

"Paddoch, you gotta help. You gotta. She might have done something bad to him, or he might be dead. Anything could be going on with him. I gotta know."

Shakes his head again. "Paddoch to not."

"Are you saying you can't, or you won't?"

Doesn't look at me. "Alyx to go."

"That's not fair! You and Mike aren't fair! He says we'll get Sam back, but he won't go out there now that it's dark, even though he's got all these guns and he could just shoot anything that tried to kill us! And you said you were gonna take me to Sam, but you won't do any magic—no real magic—for me! Mike was right: it's all just tricks!" I kick over some of the candles near me. "I'm stupid to think you can do anything, you and your 'pixie dust' and your '*galdr*' and your Vikings and Indians and Freydis and Ōth and all that bullshit!"

"Alyx—"

"Shut up! You can't even talk right, you twisted, ugly-ass freak!"

"Yeah, but you're a freak, just like I am." Sam's words, what he told me back then at the Homecoming dance, but it's Paddoch saying it here and now. In Sam's voice.

Then Paddoch goes, "You're not a freak," and it's my voice this time.

"Yeah, I am. I'm crippled." Sam.

"Honestly, I don't even notice anymore." Me.

"I do, all the time." Sam again. "Everybody gets to forget about me being crippled. Except me."

At first, all I can is just stand there with my mouth for-real hanging open. Paddoch doesn't say anything else. He doesn't have to.

"How did you know that?" I feel stupid for asking.

"'Bullshit,'" he tells me. "Now Alyx to go."

"I'm sorry...I...I'm just—"

He points at the door. "Alyx to go."

Shouting. "Why won't you help me?"

He doesn't answer.

My hands, shaking. "Please, please help me." Crying. Losing it again. He just stands there and watches me. God damn him.

He holds up a hand. "Alyx." Holds up the other. "Sam." Brings them together, locks the fingers. "AlyxSam. To love."

What? No. "We haven't done th—"

"Paddoch that not to say." Shows me his hands clenched together. "AlyxSam, SamAlyx, yes? Yes. Because to love, then Alyx to dream. To dream AlyxSam, SamAlyx. Because to love."

I think I get it. He's saying that I've been having those dreams because me and Sam are so close. But is that true? "Okay, if I can see Sam in my dreams, can he see me?"

"Yes-no." Which hopefully means *maybe*.

"So, why aren't I seeing Sam anymore?"

Slowly, he pulls his hands apart. "Sam," he says, as his left drifts away. "Alyx," and his right floats the other way. "AlyxSam not."

"What do you mean? Is Sam dead?" As soon as I ask, I'm sorry I did. Not because I think that's what's happened, but because something worse might have.

Do we really love each other?

Do I actually love him?

Does he still love me?

* * *

Ten percent battery. Him and me goofing around at Mowbray

Park, swinging really high and jumping off, going down the slides head first, spinning each other almost sick on the tire chain. The little girl—Audrey, she was like four years old—that Sam helped climb up the jungle gym because she was scared. Her mom—"Gennifer with a 'g'" she said—was so glad Audrey talked to Sam, "because usually, she's so shy."

Us at the Rita's, him getting a coconut cream gelati, me with strawberry lemonade Italian ice. With Penny to the dog park, the side one for smaller dogs, not the part where the big ones go, cuz they play too rough for her, she's delicate. Him showing me around downtown Annapolis, with the brick streets and the shops and the boats and the colonial houses. Back on the island, at Ledo's, getting Hawaiian pizza.

Nine percent. Nobody but us goes to the beach in the winter. Day trip to Ocean City: walked the boardwalk, drove up and down the main drag, shopped at some of the places that had stayed open. Ate Sweet Frog froyo even though it was overcast and in the 40's. Played indoor mini golf at this place decorated like a jungle safari, with plaster elephants and zebras and crocodiles and gorillas. I did a hole-in-one on the very first hole, and Sam couldn't believe I'd never played before. Just lucky. I got a 73 on the rest of the course, he got 46, and when he first told me our scores, I thought I beat his ass. How stupid a game is golf that you're *not* supposed to get points?

Seven percent. Not sleepy yet, but I need to be. I'm laying under the steps, in the dark, wrapped in that blanket I was in when I woke up here. I tried to draw, but nothing came, and now I'm trying to ignore how hungry I am, because basically, I got nothing left to eat, and I don't think Mike's going to share. He's sitting across from the stairs, with his back against a concrete pillar, the shotgun on his lap like he's keeping guard. Which I guess he is.

Me hunched over my Early Western Civ book that time—must have been in February?—we were studying at his dining room table. I didn't know he had even taken that one. It was horrible outside that night, really cold with this icy-rain-sleet crap that they get all the time here on Kent Island. If it had been Pennsylvania, it would have been real, honest-to-God snow. No, I hadn't taken the bike; Sam drove me home. He had his license by then. Took him

This Wasted Land

long enough.

Flicking through his camera roll, starting from the top. He's got thousands of photos. Stop every so often, tap one, look at it, sometimes swipe forward or back to see some of the others with it. My bike out in the student parking lot. That line drawing I did of a dragon—it's Korean, not Chinese—that Mrs. Martin said was excellent and made me sign my name to, and put up in the Art Department display case out in the main hall, even though I asked her not to. Me sitting on the steps at lunch—that was a few weeks before he asked me to Homecoming.

I don't know how long it took me arguing with him—hours, I guess—but eventually Paddoch told me to go, but come back later. When I did, he gave me a figurine, carved out of bone, I think, covered in hundreds of tiny scratches: runes. It's in the shape of a little man. He told me to hold it in my hand and think about Sam when I went to sleep. He didn't think it will work—"yes-no-no"—but I'm going to try.

I close my eyes, cross my arms across my chest, his phone in one hand, the figurine in the other. I didn't tell Mike about it. He'd just make fun of it, and me, and I don't feel like listening to it.

Wind whipping around outside, like it always does lately. Once or twice in the past few hours, we've heard screams. I couldn't tell if they were people or not. Couldn't tell if they were real or not. Just hoping they don't come again, because when they did, I thought I might crap my pants.

Trying not to think about it, or the cold, or being hungry. Just breathe in and out, through my nose, long, deep breaths. Ms. Custer, the school psychologist, taught me that. Supposed to relax me. Sometimes, it works. Hope it does now.

Breathe. Don't think. Breathe.

Thoughts floating away.

Breathe

Far and away

breathe

float

* * *

Pale light cold sun hanging just over this world's skin. I'm floating high over the gray waste land. Floating, but I'm not scared or dizzy, like I was at the top of the ship I climbed, so it must not really be me. I'm watching from inside someone—Sam? Couldn't be. I feel the cold, hear the wind flapping my clothes, but it has to be just a regular dream. Gonna give Paddoch back that figurine when I wake up.

Drifting, toward and over a river—silver? chrome?—that doesn't move, no ripples on the water. No, not water. Somehow, the person whose eyes I'm looking with knows that it's poison, slippery, almost impossible to scoop up with your hands. So thick, so heavy, it'd hold you up, you couldn't drown if you tried to swim across. But when you got to the other side, you wouldn't make it much farther. The river's fumes don't smell, but they kill, and before they did, you'd go crazy. For-real, tear-your-fingers-off-and-chew-and-swallow-them-while-your-arms-and-legs-shake-and-you-piss-yourself crazy.

Past the river, black boulders, jagged, like knives, standing tall as trees, thousands of them, bunched together, some a few feet apart, some only inches. Maybe you could squirm through them, maybe not: they're sharp and barbed, they'd shred your clothes, stab and snare and rip the meat off your arms, your legs, your sides, your face if you weren't careful. I waft over them, look down. They make a ring, a thick fence, all around the big rock where I want to go.

An ash path winding up it, but instead I go higher, over the rock's flat top, toward something fluttering, quivering there. Sometimes it's one thing: ancient, empty house, long, but not tall, only one floor, wooden roof rotted and fallen in, rock walls crumbling, big holes in them. Sometimes it's another: thick metal bones, the skeleton of a bent, twisted skyscraper that either rusted and died, or was never born.

Sometimes it's other things—a fortress, a church, a school—but when I get close, gliding toward the entrance, it's a hospital, the big letters that are still hanging on the front saying **EM RGE CY**.

This Wasted Land

And then I'm Sam, I'm seeing from him, I'm certain, it's like always. He's in that hospital—somehow, I know that—but the room where he is doesn't look like one. It's a motel room, the exact same kind as the one where me and Mike stayed, the one with Shelby and her pervy boyfriend and what's-her-face who was high when we showed up. But it can't be the same place, can it?

It's dark and warm, and he's laying in a soft bed, under thick covers. He's clean, he's full, he's sleepy. Thank God he's all right.

Light from the bathroom, the *pssssh* of water from the shower. Why would he leave it running?

The water stops. Jangle of shower curtain hoops brushed aside. Scuffing sounds of a towel. Sam closes his eyes: all I see is black. When he opens them, she's standing at the foot of the bed.

She's not old anymore. She doesn't look like she's stiff, plastic. She's naked and beautiful. Long blond hair, almost white, that's wet and hanging to her waist. Slim, toned arms, legs, stomach. Tiny runes—I know what they are now—thousands of them, tattooed all over. Her boobs are fleshy but taut. She's every bit as gorgeous as Patti, Mike's Playboy centerfold, but I know it's her because her eyes are still silver. That bitch Freydis.

She goes to the side of the bed. Smiles. Full lips, white teeth—no broken glass. "Sam."

He's breathing hard, fast, shallow. Get out of there!

She leans over, caresses his face. It's like a fish dragging itself across my cheek. Get away from him!

"No," he whispers.

"She's not here. She's not coming. She ran away when I found you."

"No, that's not true. She didn't leave me. She wouldn't. I dream about her, I see her walking in the desert. She loves me, I know she—"

"She doesn't love you. Why would she? She's just a girl." Straightens. "She's nothing. I can be anything."

Her face shivers, thins, becomes mine, if I was pretty.

269

Glistening, deep blue eyes. No zits. Perfect, straight teeth. Coal-black hair cut short, a lock in the front dyed purple.

No. No, no, no, no. Run, Sam! Run!

His heart, hammering. She pulls back the covers. He's naked. Excited.

"I can be everything," she says.

She straddles him, kisses him, hard, tongue writhing deep in his mouth, my mouth, I feel myself gag. He closes his eyes, his hands stroking her back, her hips, her thighs.

No. Please God, no.

"Look at me." A husky whisper. "Look."

Sam opens his eyes. Her hands, cradling his face. She stares into him. Into me.

"You're there. I know so."

No. No. Just a dream. Not real wake up stop this make it stop no no Sam don't do this!

"Look at me. Look at *us*."

* * *

I wake, screaming.

Track 26. Love Lies Bleeding

This isn't happening.

It can't be real.

He wouldn't do that.

That's not who he is.

He loves me. He loves me.

That couldn't have happened.

No. God, no.

"Alyx." Mike, his arms around me. Trying to hold me still, keep me from rocking back and forth, back and forth, my knees up, arms across my chest, my hand squeezing the figurine that Paddoch gave me. The one to help me dream of Sam.

"Alyx, what's wrong? Talk to me."

Tears streaming down my face. I can't say anything. Mike glances at Paddoch, who's standing over by the folding table where they laid me when they brought me back when I ran away. "Did he touch you?" Mike whispers. "Did he do something to you?"

I shake my head. Can't talk don't talk. Tsunami in me, gotta fight it gotta hold it in hold it back if I say anything it'll crash out of me smash me tidal wave over me drown me fight it hold it back don't let go don't it out—

"I swear to God, if he hurt you, I'll kill him right now, Alyx."

No no can't hold it can't too strong I can't I can't no stop no please God help me!

Screaming can't keep from screaming no words just pain this can't be real this can't be happening he wouldn't do that he loves me he was with her I saw them I *saw*

Screaming. Mike wrenching me up off the floor, sitting me up. "Alyx! Hey! Hey! Alyx! Come back to me! Alyx!"

"No let me go it can't be it wasn't him it wasn't he wouldn't he loves me he loves me he wouldn't he doesn't love her he doesn't he doesn't love me!"

"Alyx, it's okay! You were dreaming, it's just a dream! It's nothing! It's not real!"

"It's not it's not it's real he doesn't love me he doesn't love me!" Bury my face in his chest. "Why why why doesn't he love me why was he with her what did I do? What did I do?"

"You didn't do anything! It's just a nightmare. That's all." Pulling me away, his hands on my face, like hers were on his. "Look at me—"

"No! Don't touch me leave me alone let me go let me go!" His hands off me I totter back catch myself before I fall slump against the wall it's cold everything's cold no he wouldn't why. Sliding down the wall down my forehead on the floor why why....

"Alyx, get a grip. It was just a bad—"

"Alyx Sam to see," Paddoch says.

"Mind your own goddamn business," Mike snaps.

"Sam with Freydis to be."

"Are you deformed *and* deaf? Shut up!" Crouches next to me, his hand on my shoulder. "Alyx, Sam's all right. He's fine. We're going to find him, and we'll get him, and somehow, we'll get both of you home. I promise you—"

Slap his hand away. "Don't promise me anything! Just leave me alone!"

"Alyx—"

"HE SCREWED HER!"

Mike doesn't say anything.

Sobbing. Hard to talk. "He...they were in a room...like the motel...we were in. A bed...and she was...naked, and..."

"That wasn't real."

"IT WAS REAL! I SAW IT! I SAW THEM!"

Tsunami building in me again building rising can't fight it no way I can crashes over me again floods me drowns me washes me away cold floor I curl up lie on it cry cry can't stop won't ever stop hurts oh God it hurts so bad....

I'm curled up there on the floor for a long time, how long I don't know, the hurt gushing out of me, and I don't see, don't hear, anything else....

* * *

Mike's hand, stroking my hair.

"Hey," he says, softly.

I roll over, look up at him. "Hey." A hoarse whisper.

"You okay now?"

I shake my head. "Don't...don't tell me it wasn't real. I know—"

His finger to his lips. "Maybe it was, maybe it wasn't. What do I always tell you?"

"'You can't trust anything.'"

"Right."

My eyes, seeping. Bite down on my lip, but it comes anyway. "I trusted him."

"Don't do that to yourself," he says, wiping my cheeks. "Not now. It's not the time for that. We can talk about that later, if it even turns out to be true. Right now, you can't trust what you saw, or how you feel. Because both of those might be totally wrong. Okay?"

I nod.

"Okay. So, let's go from here. We're going to do one thing at a time, and that's all we're going to think about. Not what happened, not what's going to happen. Just what we're doing right now. Sound good?"

I nod again.

"First, let's get you off this floor. You're freezing. Go over there."

In the middle of the room, a little fire made from pieces of furniture; the smoke billows to the ceiling, drifts up the stairs. Mike helps me up, gets my blanket and drapes it over me. Walks me to the fire, sits me down on another blanket beside it. Goes to his pack. Comes back, sits beside me. Hands me a metal spoon and a small plastic tub with a foil wrapper on top. Applesauce.

"Eat something. You'll feel better."

"I'm not hungry."

"Of course you're not. I wasn't either, when I found out what Cathy did. Eat it anyway."

"I don't wanna."

"I didn't ask." Takes the container from me, pulls off the foil, gives it back. "Go on. It'll help."

"Okay." He watches me dip a sliver of the spoon into it, then up to my mouth. It doesn't taste like anything. I do it again. Still nothing.

"What have you got in your hand?" The one with the spoon. I show him the figurine. He takes it, holds it up to the firelight to see it better.

"You found this?"

Shake my head. "Paddoch gave it to me."

"Did he, now?"

Nod. "He said it would help me dream. About." Can't.

"About Sam. How was it supposed to do that?"

"It's magic."

"Well, isn't that special." He tucks it into the breast pocket of his shirt. "Mr. Paddoch and I are going to have a little chat about that."

I finish the applesauce, toss the container into the flames. Give the spoon to Mike. We sit together, warming our hands.

"I thought you said campfires bring monsters," I tell him.

"They do." Pats the shotgun next to him on the floor. "But I'm in a mood to ruin someone's weekend."

I'm not in a mood to do anything. I just want to sit here. The fire makes it not quite so cold. I don't care.

"Do you want something else to eat?"

Shake my head no.

"All right. Now, I need you to clean up this place."

"Whaddya mean?'"

"Pick all the stuff off the floor and put it where it belongs. Organize it. Anything that you can't find a place for, put it in a pile in the corner so we can burn it. Find a broom and sweep up."

"Why?"

"It looks like hell in here."

"So?"

"So, you need something to do."

"No. I don't wanna."

"I know you don't, but you have to."

"It doesn't matter."

"Yes, it does. You have to stay busy and take your mind off of what's happened. Otherwise, you'll dwell on it and make yourself crazy. Trust me on that." He puts his hand under my arm, starts to stand, pulls me up with him.

"I...I can't—"

"C'mon." He goes over to where he's left his stuff, sets aside the shotgun. "Get to work. I'll give you a hand."

I squat, pick up some books, set them on the folding table.

Pick up some more books. Set them on the table, too. I look over. Mike's watching me.

"Don't...don't go anywhere, okay?" I ask him.

"I'm going to be here the whole time. Now, drag ass. I'm tired of this place looking like a shithole."

I go to it, picking up stuff, sorting it, moving it around. Mike helps me lift the bookshelves that have fallen to the floor, stand them up. With a rag I find, I dust everything. Arrange the books, alphabetical order, by title, on the shelves. Toss the trash on the fire to keep it going, put three chairs around it, stack the rest of them in a corner. Keep the folding table nearby, push the others against the walls. Take Mike with me to find the janitors' closet. Get a dustpan and broom, sweep everywhere.

Takes forever. I don't mind. Mike sings snatches of what he says are country-western songs that he tells me are from the Seventies, about not letting your babies grow up to be cowboys, and some chick named Amanda, and being on the road again, and always being on someone's mind, and going to Luckenbach, Texas, wherever that is. I've never heard of any of those. All I know is that his singing sucks.

Then *bkk bkk bkk bkk*. Familiar footsteps on the stairs. Paddoch, carrying his bag.

"Where you been, Handsome?" Mike asks. Puts down the book he was about to shelve, stalks toward him. "Another long stroll, without so much as a coat, in sub-freezing total darkness? You must have Prestone for blood, and cat's eyes to see."

"Paddoch things to find."

"Is that so?" Digs in his breast pocket. "Speaking of finding things, let's play 'Show and Tell.' I'll go first." He holds up the figurine. Paddoch glances at me.

"You gave this to her," Mike says, "and then she flipped out. Interesting coincidence, don't you think?"

"He was just trying to help."

"Let Mean Uncle Mikey handle this, Alyx." He gets up in Paddoch's face. "Now it's your turn. What is this?"

"*Galdr.*"

Mike grabs the front of the sheet that Paddoch's wrapped around himself. "Care to float that past me again, homie?"

"*Galdr.* For Sam to see."

"That she did, in a really bad way. Got any idea why that might be?"

Paddoch doesn't answer.

"Well, I do. She says she was dreaming, but I'm thinking maybe she was tripping. Which makes me wonder how that could have happened to her. Want to illuminate me on that?"

"Mike Paddoch to let go."

Shaking his head, Mike tightens his grip, shoves Paddoch. "I don't think I will. I think you're gonna level with me. Cuz you say, 'magic,' I say 'magic mushrooms,' know what I mean?"

"Mike, don't—"

"You didn't roll this around in any LSD, or peyote, or some other shit like that, did you? Something that might go through her skin, fill up her head with nastiness even uglier than you?"

"Mike, it's okay. I'm okay." No, I'm not—my insides are all shaky and none of this seems real and none of this matters and I wish Mike would stop cuz I just don't care cuz Sam, Sam was with her, she and Sam were doing it and I can't take it I can't deal with it and I just want it to stop I want everything to go away and not hurt anymore ow ow oh God oh God why is this happening?

"*Ōth?*" From upstairs, a guy, a young guy—Sam? No, it's not. Mike and Paddoch freeze.

"*Ōth?*" His voice, straining, like he's hurt. A heavy foot **bkk** on the metal step above. Mike lets go of Paddoch, crosses the room, gets the shotgun. Paddoch scurries behind me, frantically roots through his bag.

Bkk. Another heavy step. "*Meeyer dretha.*" **Bkk**. "*Vinsamlegast.*" Voice cracking. "*Vinsamlegast, Ōth....*" A growl now. "*Meeyer dretha.*"

Mike points the gun at the stairs, pushes me back toward the doorway of the hall that leads to Paddoch's room. "What's he saying?" I whisper.

Mike racks the shotgun **KCHK**. "It's Greek to me."

Paddoch still digging in his bag. "Greek is not to be. 'To kill me,' he to say. 'Please, Ōth,' he to say."

"Eg…enem…gerthee thaath effgee…." Buzzing now, doesn't sound like a person anymore. Another footfall on the stairs. **Bkk**. *"Ōth."* Something clanking. *"Vinsamlegast…thoo…sagthee…."*

Paddoch scampers in front of us, starts spilling something from a bottle onto the floor. Red dust or powder—the same as in his room? He's making a circle around all three of us. "Not to move," he whispers. "Not to talk." Paddoch's done—barely—when whatever it is tromps down off the bottom step.

"Ōth?" it gurgles. It's the shape of a person, but its skin ripples, glimmering in the firelight, hundreds and hundreds of tiny, flat, metal shards squirming up, down, across it in all different directions. Wherever it steps, it leaves silver slime.

Mike raises the shotgun. The shape looks right at us—and then lurches away.

"Wha—?" I start, but Paddoch holds up his hand.

It staggers around the room, ignoring us like we're not even here. It can't see us. That dust on the floor—some kind of magic protection?

"Ōth, thoo breyttir meeyer ee theta skrimsli. Thoo tōkst hendr meenar," it whimpers, raising its arms. It has stumps instead of hands. *"Thoo tōku a ugen a meeyer. Thoo tōkst reythr mitt. Thaad ther egkert eftir af meeyer ath taaga."*

"What's going on?" I whisper.

"Ōth him into monster make," Paddoch replies, louder than me either or Mike would want, but the thing doesn't hear. "His hands to take. His eyes to take. His…" Struggles for the word.

"His what?" I whisper. The shape stops, cocks its head. Mike scowls at me.

"Yech veeay ath thoo neeairt hyerrna. Meeyer finnst galdr thnn."

Galdr. It speaks Paddoch's language. That's how he knows what it's saying.

"He us here to know."

Huh? What's that supposed to mean? "What does it want?" I ask.

Mike mouths, *Shut the hell up!* to me and Paddoch.

It looks our way, starts slouching over. *"Meeyer dretha. Thōknanlega. Hefr thoo enga samuth, engen miskunn, eftir ull thessi arl? Hefr raithi thinn maxith eeth staath thess ath dimmd? Er art semm thoo ert barra grimmd?"*

"'To kill me,' he to say," not even trying to be quiet. "Ōth…pity not to have." It stops, stares right at him. "Not…how Anglandr to say? 'Mercy.' Many years, but not to mercy. Ōth anger more to big. Ōth…" Ponders. "'Cruel.' Ōth cruel to be."

"Thoo neeairt thartna. Meeyer dretha."

Paddoch smiles. "No, Thorvald."

"'No,' to what?" I ask, not bothering to whisper. "What did it say?" That fluttery, sick feeling inside me again. I don't know why.

The shape sinks to the floor in front of us. *"Vinsamlegast. Ferreerkafvim meeyer."*

"Yech ferreerkafvmya theeyer ekkay," Paddoch tells it, shaking his head even though it can't see us. What the hell is going on?

Mike gives me a look. He's got no idea, either. "Shoot it," I say to him.

"No," Paddoch replies. "Mike not to do."

"Kill it," I say. Tears dribbling down my cheeks, but not because of what's going on. Just—I don't know. I'm losing it. No, no. Hold it together.

It hangs its head, waits. "Go on," I tell Mike, full-on crying now. Sam. Oh, God. Sam. "Just shoot. Do it. C'mon. Look at it."

Mike lowers the shotgun. "Shells don't grow on trees around here. No need to waste one."

"Do it!"

"Alyx quiet to be."

"Shut up, asswipe!" Back to Mike. "Please. It wants to die." Sam. No, Sam. You couldn't have done that. You wouldn't do that to me. Please, God, don't let it be real, don't let it have happened.

Mike's face goes blank. "Not my problem."

Not his problem? How can he not care? How can he not give a shit? A switch flips in me. It's happened before. Like in Ms. Jung's room.

Paddoch sees it on my face. "Alyx to not—"

"I'll make it your goddamn problem!"

I sweep my foot back and forth across the ring, scattering red powder everywhere.

The shape looks up, sees us. Grinding noise from deep inside it as it springs to its feet, way faster than I thought it could, mouths ripping open from the stumps where its hands should be. Mike goes, "Shit!," swings the shotgun up, and the mouths—their teeth are jagged broken glass, just like Freydis'—spit silver slime, the same as it's dripping from its feet, all over Mike and he screams and drops the shotgun and falls to the floor rolling around screaming kicking No no no no no not Mike don't let it kill Mike shit why'd I do that it's gonna kill Mike poison him melt him with acid or something and it's all my fault!

Its mouths chomp down on Paddoch's arm, blood spatters onto the floor and it yanks him toward itself like he's just a little kid Jesus it's strong pulls him in close and black thorns jab out from where its face should be, stabbing spearing Paddoch in the chest and more blood holy shit I gotta do something I gotta I reach down grab the shotgun did Mike rack it can't remember point it at the monster no gotta get closer or I'll hit Paddoch jam the barrel against the back of its head the kick's gonna break my frickin' arm doesn't matter do it kill it pull the trigger

BLUWWW

loud as a cannon going off I'm expecting its head to burst into hundreds of soggy pieces like before, when Mike shot what I hope to God wasn't really Cynthia.

Instead, the shape just twitches when the gun goes off, seems to suck up the shot, but it's hurt, it lets go of Paddoch, slowly reels toward me, silver slime seeping out of dozens of pinpricks in its head, the black thorns cracking, dissolving, dripping more slime, bits of metal dribbling, streaming off its whole body.

"Hoonr elskar mikk efkay," one mouth rasps.

"Hoonr elskar thikk efkay," the other says. I can hardly hear from my ears ringing from the shotgun. The shape falls, splattering when it hits, silver slime drenching the concrete.

Mike. Oh, my God. Mike. I rush over, squat by him. Be okay, shit, be okay. He rolls over, shaking his head, that goop covering him. Please, be okay. He sits up, blinking.

"Are you all right?" I ask.

"Yeah." Winces. Reaches out, takes the hem of my shirt, wipes his eyes. I don't mind. "Got that shit all over my face. Felt like a hornet was raping my eyeballs. What the hell happened with you?"

He is gonna be so pissed. "I kinda...went off. Like I do. I'm sorry. I'm really sorry. I wasn't thinking, I was just mad and that was really stupid of me and please don't hate me please don't—"

"Okay, shut up," he says, getting to his feet. "The more you talk, the more pissed off I get. Where's Stud?"

Paddoch's in a heap, blood oozing out from under him. I go to him, kneel. His eyes are open. "Hey, you're hurt," I tell him. Start to roll him over. "Let me see, okay? I'll try not to move you too much."

"Alyx not to," he croaks. He sits up. He's all slashed and punctured right in the middle of his chest, where his heart and lungs should be, but he's not bleeding there anymore, even though it was spraying out when the shape was stabbing him.

"How can you not be...?" I start. Then: *"Galdr?"*

He shakes his head, starts to stand, all wobbly. Big puddle of blood under him, soaking the sheets and blankets he wears.

"You shouldn't do that," I tell him, putting my hand on his

bare shoulder. It's bumpy and cold, like that toad I caught in the woods behind the motel where we lived. "You're not okay. You gotta stay down." Ease him back onto the floor, fight not to wipe my hand on my jeans. "Mike, do we have any bandages or something?"

"No, but I'll run to the Rexall and pick some up." He's got the shotgun, and he's watching the stairs, in case something else tries to come down here. "Want me to bring you back some Sun-In and a box of press-on nails?"

"You could've quit at 'no.'" *Damn it, what am I gonna do? Turn back to Paddoch. I don't even want to ask, but I guess I gotta.* "Where are you...hurt?"

He points to his thigh. I can't see where's he's bleeding from—it's covered by his sheet—but thank God it isn't any higher. *Hold up, though: aren't there, like, big arteries and veins that run through your legs? If one of those got cut, he might be toast.*

Still keeping an eye on the stairs, Mike's nudging what's left of the shape with his boot. "Dude, bring me my backpack," I tell him. He does it without saying something smartass. For once.

Go through my bag. There they are. Paddoch watches me pull out the Infinity pads, unwrap one, unfold it, pull off the strips on the sticky part. "Okay, this is gonna be weird," I say, "but it's what we got. So, you take this," holding it flat in my hand, "and you put it where you're hurt," pretending to slide it under my thigh, "and you press it down, and it will stay there. And if this one doesn't cover all of it, we can use more."

He looks dubious, but he takes it and reaches way up under his sheet; even though I looked away, I still noticed. He either doesn't know what *leg* actually means, or he was trying not to say. "Okay, is that good? Is it on there all right?" He nods. "Do you need another one?" Shakes his head. "So, now, hold it real tight against you to make the blood stop, and—"

"Paddoch to know," he says. "Thank you. Alyx to Paddoch kind."

"You're welcome."

"Sam to Alyx kind?"

Is Sam kind to me? Is that what he's asking? My face, my stomach, all of me tightens up at the same time as something in me starts to spill out, and once it starts, it's not going to stop, just like before no please I can't take it I—

"What, are you from Oklahoma or something?" Mike standing over Paddoch. "How stupid do you have to be to ask something like that, after what she saw? And after what she just did for you? I'd kick you right in the nuts, but it might be habit-forming."

That snaps me out of it. "It's all right." Drag the back of my hand across my eyes. "I'm good."

I can tell he doesn't believe me. He grabs Paddoch by the back of the neck. "What'd you tell Satan's sock monkey when it was on its knees, begging for death?"

Paddoch doesn't answer.

Mike squats, doesn't let go. "You are really starting to honk me off mojo big-time."

I rest my hand on Paddoch's forearm, ignore how gross it feels. He glances at my hand, up at me. "It was looking for Ōth," I tell him. "Why did it think he was here?"

Paddoch shakes his head.

Mike: "Tennessee Tuxedo says, 'You gotta do better than that, Mr. Whoopee.'"

I shoot a look at him like, *chill*, and he lets go of Paddoch's shoulder. "I'm really sorry," I tell Paddoch. "I shouldn't have done what I did. I didn't mean for it to hurt you."

He nods. "Paddoch Alyx to...." Wrestles with it. "*Ferreergemah.*"

Huh?

He frowns. "To mercy. Paddoch Alyx to mercy."

"'Forgive?'" I ask. "Is that what you're trying to say?"

He doesn't get it. I lift his hand, pretend like he slaps my face. I scowl, drop his hand, make a fist with mine, pull it back like I'm going to punch him. Hold it there, shake my head. Let my face relax. Put my fist down. "'Forgive.' Do you forgive me?"

He nods, smiles. "Paddoch Alyx to 'forgive.'"

I smile back. "Thank you."

Mike rolls his eyes. Mutters, "Suck my ass."

"He to want Ōth for to forgive," Paddoch said, pointing at the silver and black puddle where the shape hit the floor. Wisps of steam or smoke or something are rising from it.

"It wanted Ōth to forgive it?" He nods. "For what?" Shrugs. "What did it say after I shot it?"

He ponders. "She he not to love," pointing again. "She Ōth not to love."

"Who?" I already know.

"Freydis. Freydis not to love. He or Ōth." Hangs his head.

"Ōth Freydis not to forgive."

Track 27. Ain't Talkin' 'bout Love

Six percent.

It's cold again; Mike let the fire die. I'm wrapped in a blanket, laying under the steps again, scrolling through more of Sam's photos. Trying not to think. Trying not to feel. It's not really working.

Me and Sam at McDonald's after one of the *Sound of Music* shows; he really wanted to go to Big Bats with the cast and the rest of the tech crew, like they always did after a performance, but I don't like crowds.

Him and Dylan and Dylan's dad, I guess, at Opening Day for the Orioles. Sam asked if I wanted to come, but baseball is bullshit.

Him in his tux, backstage with his trombone at the Spring Concert. Did I go to that? I don't think so. Where was I? Don't remember.

Sam holding his license, that he'd just got. I would have been there, but I was in detention. Mrs. Martin caught me trying to sneak some paint brushes into my bag. Said stealing art supplies wasn't something she'd tolerate. Said she was disappointed in me. I only did it cuz I needed some for home and didn't want to go all the way to the Michaels in Annapolis. I told Sam, thinking he'd get it, but he took her side and bitched me out. Said that if I hadn't done that, I could have gone to MVA with him while he took his test. Made me feel like shit.

Scrolling. A video. I recognize it as soon as it starts. I can't believe he kept it. That was only a week or two before we got here. Before she took him from me.

* * *

"What are you doing?" I asked. "Are you filming me? What the hell is your problem?"

"I don't have a problem," Sam said, behind the phone. "You do."

We were at the mall, at that landing on the second floor, outside the movie theaters, at the top of the escalators. You go down, and you're at the food court. Which is where I'd thought we were supposed to meet.

"No, seriously, put that away," I told him. "I'm not going to deal with you if you're filming me."

"I want to show you this later, after you calm down, so you can see what you're like."

"I know what I'm like."

"No, apparently you don't, because if you did, you wouldn't be this way."

"Screw you."

"Look at the camera and explain what's going on."

"No. Why don't you?"

"Sure." Some black girls in the background, by the big window overlooking the parking lot. They were watching us. Started giggling. "Okay, we were supposed to meet up here—"

"No, we were supposed to meet at 5 Guys."

"—so we could go see the 2:10 showing of the new Avengers movie. But you were late—again—and we missed it. And now you need to say you're sorry."

"No. I'm not gonna."

"Just do it."

"I got nothin' to apologize for."

"Yeah, you do."

"No, I don't, because we were supposed to meet at 5 Guys, which is where I was."

"No, we were originally going to meet at 5 Guys and get some lunch before the movie, but because you were already running late, I texted you and said to just meet me here."

"I didn't get that text for a while."

"I'm pretty sure you got it, but you didn't look at your phone until you'd already been waiting down there, getting all pissed off at me even though you were in the wrong place."

"I *was* in the right place, and anyway, while I was waiting for you, you were hanging out up here with that slut Rachel What's-Her-Face."

"This again? Really? One: Rachel is not a slut. Two: we're just friends—we've known each other our whole lives. Three: she's going out with this guy who goes to Spalding."

Jabbed my finger at him. "It's obvious she likes you."

"How? Because she and her friends were on the way to the movies, and she said 'hi' to me while I was waiting for you?"

"Why'd she take off when she saw me coming up the escalator?"

"Because it was time for her movie. And because sometimes you act like a headcase. Like now."

I gave him the finger, started off through the theater lobby for the parking garage.

"Where are you going?"

Didn't answer. He followed me.

"Alyx...."

"Shut up." Didn't look back. The phone caught people watching us, some of them smirking or whispering to each other.

"C'mon. Don't be like this."

"No, I am gonna be like this." Shoved open the double doors that go out into the garage, startling a couple not much older than us, as well as a fat middle-aged guy and his dumpy wife and two little blond boys—those people were way too old to have kids that young—on the other side. They looked at me, looked at Sam, still filming, made faces like they had no idea what was going on and didn't want to know. Sam followed me out to the garage. More people out there, all of them staring.

"Where are you going?"

"Home."

"Alyx, this is—"

Whirled on him. "LEAVE ME ALONE!" Slapped the phone out of his hand—the screen didn't crack when it hit the pavement. It kept recording. Nothing to see but the gray stone roof. Pounding of my boots as I ran off. Image jostled as Sam picked up the phone.

"Dude, is that your girlfriend?" some guy off-camera asked.

"Maybe not for much longer," Sam said, and shut off the video.

* * *

One percent. Hardly anything left.

"You okay?" Mike, arms over his head, leaning against the steps over me.

Feel a tear run down my face. Shake my head.

"Can I see that?" he asks, pointing at Sam's phone. I give it to him. He turns it over in his hands, holds it on its side, level with his eyes. "That's a phone nowadays, huh? It's skinnier than my last paycheck." Looks to see if I'll smile. I don't. Can't.

He sits down, gives the phone back to me. "When we were in the Jeep, back by the motel, you said something about 'looking up' stuff with this. What'd you mean?"

I don't want to talk, but…okay. "It's like a little computer," I tell him. "You can find out anything with it."

"How's it do that?"

Am I really gonna have to explain the Internet to him, like he's somebody's grandpa? "It can connect to all these other computers, around the world, that are hooked up to each other."

"How many computers?"

Sam might know, but hell if I do. "Um…all of them, I guess. Millions. So, if you have a question about something, you—" How am I supposed to describe Google? "—you type it in, and a computer that has that answer tells it to you, really fast, like in one second. So, you could ask, 'How do I make scrambled eggs?' and right away, it comes up on your screen."

"Go tell Aunt Rhody. So, these computers know… everything?"

"Pretty much. My uncle was a football player, and I've read about him, mostly articles from old newspapers that someone copied and put on a computer. But they don't know *everything*. They have my address, and probably my grades, and maybe my phone number, but they don't know what my favorite color is, or what I like to eat. See what I mean?"

"Yeah."

"And I'm sure there's nothing online about…wherever we are."

"No, I can't imagine there would be. So, what else does your Bat-Phone do?"

"It can play music—I've got hundreds of songs on it—and it has games, and can give you directions, and…" Texting—how do I tell him about that? "And you can type out messages and send them to people. It has a clock and a calendar and a calculator. It even has a flashlight. And it takes pictures. Lots of them."

"I'm guessing that it has photos of Sam."

I nod. "It's his phone."

"Can I see one of him?"

"There's hardly any battery left. I don't have any way to charge it back up."

"It might be helpful if I know what he looks like. In case I see him before you do."

I consider that. Press the home button. Put in Sam's passcode. Hit PHOTOS. Pull up the selfie of him and Buddy, the big German Shepherd at Fairmore Farm. Show Mike.

"He has really pointy ears, don't you think?" he asks.

Don't want to laugh. Stifling it. He's trying—not very hard—to keep a straight face. I'm trying, too.

"You're not funny," I tell him.

"I'm very funny."

"You are not. Shut up." I don't mean it. He knows it.

"It's good to see you're back to your usual bitchy teenybopper self."

"Is 'teenybopper' a real word that people in colonial times—you know, when you were born—actually used to say?"

"Oof. Picking on an old man like me. You ought to be ashamed of yourself. And to think, I used to change your diapers. Ungrateful brat."

"You're still not funny."

"Yes, I am."

"Okay, you are. Sorta." Smirk at him. "I know what you're doing."

"Oh?"

"You don't care what this phone does. If you did, you would have asked me about it a long time ago. You're getting me to talk so I won't lie here and feel shitty about Sam."

"It beats sitting around, talking to Paddoch. He sounds like Mushmouth from *Fat Albert*."

He knows I don't know what that is. "I thought you don't like him."

"We won't be exchanging Christmas cards this year, that's for sure. Even so, we've been talking."

"About what?"

"Pretty soon, I'm leaving. I'm going to find Freydis. If you want to come, you can. If you want to stay here, you can; Paddoch will make sure nothing bad happens to you. He may look like an abortion that didn't go as planned, but he likes you."

I'll bet. Every time he looks my way, his eyes squirm all over me. "Is the sun—?" I almost said *coming up*. I guess it doesn't do that, though. "Is it gonna be light again?"

"I don't know. But I'm not going to wait for the sun to come back."

"So, you're going to just…walk there, even though it's still dark and freezing out? You won't even be able see where you're going. You'll die, like I almost did."

"Maybe. Maybe not. Paddoch says he can get me to Freydis right now."

"How's he gonna do that?"

"You still have that magic gingerbread man he gave you?"

"Yeah." I dig it out of my jacket's sleeve pocket. Not sure why I kept it. Maybe the next time I sleep, it'll show me Sam again. And maybe it won't be horrible. I give it to Mike.

"I'm going to get where I'm going like this," he says.

And tosses it.

Track 28. Still Loving You

The figurine clatters *kkts* off the wall, bounces a few times on the concrete floor, vanishing into the shadows.

"Like what?" I ask. "Like how Paddoch said he got here to the library before you and I did, when the sun was going out?"

He nods.

"So...you're gonna..." Trying to remember the word they used in that X-Men movie that me and Sam watched a while back. The one with the dude who was blue and had a tail. "'Teleport?'"

"If that's what it's called."

"You said you don't believe in magic."

"I don't." He shrugs. "Whether it's magic or not, Paddoch thinks he can do it."

"Why didn't he tell us this before?"

"He says it's dangerous."

"What, like more dangerous than all that time we were walking around out there, before it got dark? More dangerous than sitting here, waiting for something else nasty to come down the stairs?"

"Apparently."

"So, he's going with you?"

"I don't know. Beats me how it works. Guess I'll find out." Rubs his chin; his beard's growing back. "Do you still want to find Sam?"

If he had asked me that yesterday, or the day before that, or any other time, it would have been a stupid question. But now... "I...I don't know." Damn it, I was happy just a few minutes ago, and he had to make me think about Sam again.

"I don't think what you thought you saw was real. Dreams don't mean anything. That one wasn't more than your brain vomiting out something that disagreed with it."

I hold up the phone. "I dreamed about this, and we found it, right where I saw it."

"That could have just been your stressed-out mind playing tricks on you, making you think you had dreamed about where the phone was, even though you actually hadn't. Like a fake memory."

"It wasn't."

"Well, then it was probably coincidence, or something else perfectly rational. But this dream about Sam—you can't trust it."

"'You can't trust anything.'"

He nods. "Right. Besides, from everything you've told me about him, he seems like a good guy."

"He—" I want to say *He is*, but I don't know that anymore. I don't know what to think about him.

"But maybe I'm wrong," Mike says. "Maybe what you saw *was* real. In which case, Sam's just a stupid, horny teenage boy who wanted to stick his dick somewhere he shouldn't."

"Mike, don't—" The thought of him, and her, together—*ugh*. It actually makes me want to puke. Smearing maggots all over myself would be less disgusting. "Don't talk like that."

"I'm just saying, if that really happened, then you're better off without him. Cut your losses. Walk away and don't look back."

"I…" Part of me wants to do just that. Part of me can't handle never seeing him again. "I don't know what to do."

Nods. "Okay. But I need to know what to do about Sam."

"Whaddya mean?"

"If you want me to bring him back, I will. If you want me to leave him where I find him, I will. If you don't even want me to look for him, I can do that, too."

"I don't know. For so long, all I wanted was get him back, but now…. Now, I don't think I could even look at him."

"Yeah, I know what that feels like."

Cathy. "I guess you do."

He starts to get up, grunting, wincing. "You okay?" I ask.

Stretches, both hands on the small of his back. "Hurt myself hitting the floor when Paddoch's friend firehosed me."

"Sorry."

"It's all right. Just think about what you want to happen. Don't take too long. I have shit to take care of, and then I'll eat, maybe try to get some sleep. Hopefully, Paddoch will be done with what he needs to do. When he is, I'm gone."

I nod.

"But for what it's worth, I don't think Sam could ever hurt you."

Biting my lip. I'm not gonna cry. "How do you know that?"

"German Shepherds are very loyal."

A chuckle ekes out of me even though I don't want it to. "That's not even that funny."

"Not as funny as you look, Alyx-with-a-'y.'" This time, I don't mind that he calls me that.

* * *

I try to stay busy while Mike's getting ready. I go through my stuff, make sure everything's still there, that nothing's broken. I still wish I had batteries for my flashlight—I need AAA's—but I haven't been able to find any. I flip through a few books down here in the basement, but most of them are technical manuals, or are about computers, or engineering, or chemistry, or some boring shit like that. I try to read more of that book I found a while back, the one with Indians and dragons and such, but translating it from that strange Spanish dialect it's in gets to be too much of a pain in the ass. I try to eat. I try to sleep. I try not to think about Sam. Or her. Or them. Or us.

I try. It doesn't work.

Mike goes upstairs; I got no clue where Paddoch is. Haven't seen him for hours. I get the lantern, make sure I have my knife, and go in the tiny bathroom down the hall. The seat's freezing, and it smells bad in here, but it beats going outside.

I'm sitting there, taking a piss, shivering cuz my pants are pulled down to my knees, and I bust out crying. One second I'm okay, the next, I'm a wreck, and I can't stop. Everything's sucked for so long, but at least I had hope that I could get Sam back. Now, it seems like he doesn't want me. Now, I don't know if I want him. And everything sucks even more.

When I finally quit bawling and come out of the bathroom, Mike and Paddoch are back here, downstairs, bent over the table. They've got my sketch pad, and from the light of the old box lantern and some candles, Paddoch's drawing something with one of my pencils.

"What the actual hell are you doing with my stuff?" I snatch the pencil out of Paddoch's hand. "Who told you you could dig around in my bag and take my shit? What is your goddamn problem?"

"We for Sam to do," Paddoch says, glancing at Mike instead of looking at me.

"What's that supposed to mean?"

"He has to draw something so we can get to Freydis," Mike says. "And your boyfriend, too."

"Stop calling him my 'boyfriend!'" Honest to God, just when I finally think Mike is for real a decent dude, he goes and says something like that.

"Rein in, okay? I'm sorry. It works better if he has something visual he can study. We needed some paper and a pen, and the first thing I thought of was your pad. I didn't know where you were, and I didn't think you'd mind."

Couldn't he hear me crying in the bathroom? Or is he just pretending so that I won't be all self-conscious? Whatever. Not like I've been sketching lately. "It's all right," I tell him. Feel like a balloon losing all its air. I give the pencil back to Paddoch. "So, what are you drawing?"

He taps the paper, shows me what he's done so far. Two tall rectangles, one near the edge of the page, one by the other. A long rectangle on top, connecting both of them. He draws a connecting line underneath the two tall rectangles. The front of a building.

He keeps going. Two squares, side by side, in the middle between the two rectangles. Doors.

Bigger squares, between the doors and the outer rectangles. Windows. Big glass windows.

"Let me see that," I tell him. He hands me the pad and the pencil and I sketch in more: the six steps going up to the doors, the doorframes, the handles, the backs of chairs and couches you could see through the windows if you were standing there, in front of it. Like I had been.

On the long rectangle up top, the capstone or whatever it is you'd call that part of a building, I write **EM RGE CY**.

I show Paddoch. "That's what you were trying to draw, isn't it?"

He nods. Mike holds out his hand; I give it to him.

"A hospital?"

"Yeah. It was in my dream. She's there, with…" Are they together? Right now? Naked—in bed?

Get a grip, don't think about that, don't lose it. "With Sam," I tell them.

"With Ōth," Paddoch says.

"That's where he lives?" Mike asks. Paddoch nods. "Well, for his sake, Ōth the Great and Powerful better be bulletproof," Mike says, giving the sketch pad to Paddoch. He tears off the paper with the drawing, rolls it up, stuffs it inside the raggedy sheets he wears. "If this works for you, let's do this," Mike tells him.

"I want to go, too," I say.

"No," Paddoch replies.

"You sure?" Mike asks me.

"Yes."

"No," Paddoch insists.

"Gear down, Lumpy," Mike tells him. Turns back to me. "I don't think you want that as much as you think you do."

I tuck the pad under my arm. "I'm getting my stuff."

"Alyx not to go!"

The hell? "Don't yell at me," I say. Never seen him this upset, even when we first met him and he and Mike were beating on each other.

"Why shouldn't she go?" Mike asks.

Paddoch takes some books off a shelf nearby, puts one at the end of the table. "Lie-bree." Walks to the other end, stacks the rest of the books there, a small one on top. "Hozz-pee-toll."

"Okay," I say. So, the one book is where we are, the others are where we're going: the mountain and the hospital.

He goes back to the side of the table with the one book. Reaches into his rags and comes out with some of the dice he had at the mall. He holds up one. "Paddoch," he says. He touches it to the top of the book, then carries the die down to the stack, rests it there. "Paddoch yes."

"You disappear from one place and reappear somewhere else, right?" I ask. He nods. "And how long does that take to happen?" He slides one of his palms across the other, real quick: does he mean no time at all?

He goes back, shows us two dice. "Paddoch Mike." Taps them on the one book, takes them to the others. Holds them a few inches over the pile. Opens his fist. The dice drop, bounce, one rolls almost to the edge of the book but doesn't fall off, the other goes over the side, hits the spine of another book, bounces onto the table. "Paddoch Mike yes-no."

Goes back, holds up three dice. "Paddoch Mike Alyx." Taps them on the *lie-bree* book, carries them to the other end. Holds his fist about a foot over the books, drops the dice. They bounce off, hit the table, roll a long ways. One of them goes off the table *pk pk pk pk* into the dark.

"Paddoch Mike Alyx yes-no-no."

"So, when you do your magic trick by yourself, it always works?" Mike asks.

"Yes."

"But if you'd try to take one of us," Mike says, "you might not wind up where you want to." Paddoch nods. "And if you'd try to take both of us, it's more likely that we won't get there." Nods again.

"What about the die that rolled off the table?" I ask, pointing where it went. "Can something like that happen? Like, you don't reappear anywhere?"

He nods.

"Would that be just one of us, or everybody?" Mike asks.

He swishes his hand around. "All. Or one. Two. Or no."

"Well," Mike says, looking at me. "Lord love a duck."

I go under the stairs. Start cramming my stuff into my pack.

"What're you doing?"

"I'm coming with."

"Did you just watch the same infomercial I did?"

"Uh huh."

Mike runs his hands over his do-it-yourself buzzcut. "Christ on a stick." Looks over at Paddoch. "Why don't you take a walk? Me and Yum-Yum need to work out some things."

Paddoch considers that for a second, nods. Takes a candle and heads off toward his room.

Mike sighs. "You mean to tell me you're okay with doing this crapshoot on Paddoch's hop, skip, and a jump to Casa de Witchiepoo?"

"As okay as you are. It's only not dangerous when he does it by himself."

"Fair enough. But even if we make it there, you don't know what we'd be walking into."

"Neither do you."

"I'm not worried about me. I'm worried about finding ourselves in wall-to-wall heinousness, and you flip out again and get both of us killed."

"I'm not gonna 'flip out.'"

"You just did a few hours ago."

"Mike, I gotta know if what I dreamed was real, cuz not knowing is making me crazy."

"And that's worth risking death for? Or worse?"

"What could be worse than dying?"

"Maybe whatever happens if you 'fall off the table.'"

What *does* happen? Are you lost forever, floating around somewhere like the Phantom Zone from that Superman movie me and Sam watched? Are you stuck as some kind of ghost, so you see and hear everything, but you can't do anything? Or do you wind up somewhere even worse than here?

I don't know, and I don't want to find out. But I do want to find Sam.

"We could wait for the sun to come back," I admit. "If it ever does. But by the time we walk to the rock and climb it and get to the hospital, Freydis might be gone, and she might have taken him with her."

"Alyx—"

"I'm going with Paddoch," I tell him. "Stop trying to talk me out of it."

Shakes his head. Sighs again. "Okay. You're a big girl: you want to go, you go."

"If you don't want to come with us, you don't have to."

"You're very kind to give me permission to take the zero, but regardless, I'm going."

"Well, good. We'll find Sam, and Jeremy, too. I'll help you."

"No. No. When—not if—the shit starts hitting the fan, remember what I told you to do."

"Which was…?"

"Get Sam and run the ever-living hell away. Comprendo?"

"But—"

"Do as you're told—for once—and save both your lives. I'll get Jeremy."

"Whatever you say."

I load the 9, make sure the safety's on, put it in my inside jacket pocket, zip it. Stand up, heft my pack. I'm wriggling it on when Paddoch comes back.

"We're going," I tell him. "All of us," pointing at him and me and Mike.

"No. Alyx not to."

I go to the table, scoop up some dice, drop them on the big stack of books. They bounce and roll all over the place, and two more of them go off the side. "If you're so worried about something bad happening, why'd you tell Mike you could do this and take us with you? Why are you even helping us at all?"

He just looks at me. I can't tell if he doesn't understand what I said, but I bet he did. He's never had any problem before.

"Why do you care?" I ask.

He sticks his hand inside his sheets again, reaches down. Winces. Takes out his hand, shows us. Blood smeared all over it.

"Holy crap, Paddoch! What—"

"Freydis," he says. "Very bad."

"She did this to you?" He nods. "When was this? Just now?"

He shakes his head, struggles with the words. "For long time. Not to away. Not to…*fix*."

"It never healed," Mike tells him. "She hurt you, and it never got any better."

Paddoch nods.

"Ain't that some shit." Mike gets the shotgun, hoists his duffel bag. "So, how do we do this? You gonna sprinkle some pixie dust, and then it's 'second star to the right and straight on 'til morning?'"

"No." Paddoch shows us a gray marble with a black cat's eye; it's covered in tiny scratches. Runes? He gets the lantern, holds out his bloody hand, with the marble in it, to me. For about the millionth time, I wish I still had my gloves. I take his hand. It's slick and warm, but the marble is cold.

Mike's got his bag and the shotgun, so he holds out his arm for me to take. "And now?"

"And now," Paddoch says. Mumbles something else I don't catch.

And now there's this terrible feeling like I've sorta come apart, like all the atoms of my body have spread out and now I'm falling through the floor, falling through the sand and dirt and rock under it, falling into the blackness below, and I'll never stop. I can't feel Paddoch's hand or Mike's I can't feel anything at all I scream and nothing comes out I scream—

Track 29. Don't Cry

I'm laying on something cold someplace cold someplace dark and ice pellets sting my face as the wind goes *hrrrrrrrrrr*. I feel like I'm going to barf, but I sit up anyway. Fumble with my jacket sleeve, get my flashlight, flick it on. Hardly any light left.

I'm outside, Mike splayed on the sand next to me. Don't see Paddoch. Sweep the light around. Still don't. Crap. Is he okay? Did he wind up somewhere else? Did he *fall off the table?*

Cup my hands to my mouth. "Paddoch!" The wind howls. "Paddoch!"

"Shut up," Mike grumbles, rolling over onto his elbows. Makes sure he has the shotgun. "Have you lost your goddamn mind?"

"He's gone."

"Tell me something I didn't already know." He leans on the gun, staggers to his feet. "Like where the hell we are." He takes his flashlight, looks around. Blowing sand and ice. "I thought we were going to some hospital."

"Me, too." I get up, switch off my light; no point.

"Maybe what you drew wasn't right."

"It was right." My stomach feels like I drank a bucket of grease.

Mike keeps shining the light around. "Any ideas?"

"Not yet."

"Well, we can't wait here for a cab."

"I know, okay?" Shit. Shit shit shit shit shit. Can't see more than a few feet in front of us cuz of all this stuff blowing around. Freezing. When we were talking about doing this, all I could think about was never reappearing, just getting lost wherever, but I hadn't really thought about winding up way far away from where we were supposed to go. Which is what I guess happened. I can't even tell how far we went.

Mike turns off his light. "We're boned."

"So, what? You're just gonna give up?"

"Nope. Just not going to advertise where we are."

"If Paddoch's around, he could see it and find us."

"Not a whole lotta chance of that. Don't have to tell you that what I said about fires goes for flashlights, too."

I know, I know: *Eat at Joe's.* "You just did." I can't see anything, not Mike, not my hand in front of me, nothing. This must be what being in a cave is like. "We should pick a direction and start walking. Beats standing here."

"Yeah, sure. When in doubt, rely on dumb luck. That always works."

"If you're gonna be a bitch about it, then give me the flashlight and I'll—"

"Hold on," Mike says. "Shut up for a second." Neither of us says anything. "Hear that?"

The wind murmurs. "Hear what?"

"Exactly." Mike flicks on the light, sweeps it around. No more ash and sand and ice and shit blowing all over the place. At least for now.

"Wait—there," I say, touching his arm, keeping him from moving the light any further. A few yards away: a stream, or something? No.

"The hell is that?"

"C'mon," I say, going toward it.

He follows, shines the light along it. A wide river of silvery chrome that doesn't move. No waves, no ripples, thick and heavy: you couldn't drown in it. But if you did swim across, you'd go crazy while the fumes you breathed in killed you.

"I've seen this before," I tell him. Not gonna bother telling him it was a dream. Don't need him second-guessing me.

"Kiss my grits," he whispers, squatting down and poking the…well, it's not water…with a stick. The end of the stick doesn't sink into it: the goo or whatever it is kinda squishes out of the way. He stands, drops the stick, wipes his hands on his pants. "It's almost like mercury—you know, what they put in thermometers—but it can't be. It doesn't come like this."

"A little ways from here there are a bunch of black rocks, like big knives sticking out of the ground. They go all around the mesa where the hospital is. So, we're close."

"*Might* be close. Those rocks could be miles from here. Who knows how long this river is?"

Damn, I hadn't thought of that. "Maybe. We could at least see if they're around here, and if they are, hopefully, they're on this side and not the other."

He shines the light across the river: nothing but boulders and shrubs and ragged dunes. The light doesn't go much farther than the bank, so how are we gonna know if the black rocks are over there? And what are we going to do if we have to cross it?

Worry about that when we get to it. At least we're not sitting on our asses, freezing to death. "Sweep it around and maybe we can—"

Something clattering *kee kee kee kee kee kee kee kee* behind us.

"Run!" Mike yells, shoving me I stumble almost fall catch myself and we're running he's right behind me the flashlight's beam wagging up and down up down up down ahead of us as we run through the dark scrambling over rocks and hunks of trash around weeds and briars *kee kee kee kee kee* closer now and "Ufff!" and a thud when Mike slams to the ground and the light goes spinning tumbling as it flies out of his hands and it hits, bounces in front of me I drop, slide, ow ow hurts never mind grab the handle point it and one of them—the flashlight shows me five—leaps and it knocks me over back of my head on a sharp stone OW OW OW GOD DAMN IT and it's slithering all over me, thin and cold and gooey and sharp and—

This Wasted Land

I'm six years old and cowering in the corner and Daddy is yelling at me because I pissed the bed again and he's hitting me with his belt on my back on my shoulders on my neck and my head with his belt and Mommy is standing there in the doorway just watching arms crossed face blank, and—

I'm twelve and it's December and it's my first day at the new school because we moved for the third time this year and Mom was late dropping me off because the morning guy didn't come in on time so she had to stay at the 7-11 where she works overnight until he finally got there and now it's already the middle of second period and I got lost finding my classroom but now I'm here and I'm walking in, bringing my note to the teacher—Mr. Schneider, and he teaches reading to the dumb kids like me who are behind our grade level—and everyone's staring at me and I hear someone whispering and I wonder if maybe they're talking about my clothes from Goodwill and someone laughs and then I know they are, and—

I'm fifteen and Tommy shoves me and I crash onto the mattress on the floor of his bedroom and he pins me down even though I keep yelling no. He's nineteen and we've been going out for almost a month and I liked him because he rides a motorcycle and had dropped out of school and I came over to his house while his folks were out and we were smoking some weed and everything was cool but now he's on top of me and he's yanking my jeans off and undoing his and he jams two fingers inside me and mashes them back and forth back and forth ow ow ow it hurts like hell and he's jacking himself, it only takes him like a minute to splash all over my belly. When he's done he says if I tell anyone he'll kill me, and when I wipe myself off on his sheets he yells at me and goes to punch me and I grab his knife from the nightstand and I swing real wild and cut him across his arm not much not deep, but he freaks out and starts screaming and crying and holding his arm cuz blood's getting everywhere and I yank up my jeans and I get the hell out of there and run home—it's only three streets down—and lock myself in the bathroom and get in the shower and stand there until the hot water's gone and I don't feel anything, and when I get out, I go to bed and Mom gets home late and she's gone to work before I leave for school, so she doesn't even see me, can't tell that something's happened to me, and I never go down Tommy's street again and I never say anything to anybody, and—

I'm eighteen and Sam's home from college—he thought he was going to go to Washington College close by, but he changed his mind and went to Rensselaer Polytech in New York, near Massachusetts, and Uncle Tony had given me a job working out of his office here on Kent Island, so I had stayed—and we're going to have Thanksgiving at his mom's house today, just like last year, but he calls me on the phone this morning and he's like, "Look, this isn't easy for me to say, but—" and he talks for maybe two or three more minutes and I don't remember much except, "I've changed a lot since I came up here," and "I think I need some time to myself," and "There's this girl Laura in my differential equations class," and when he gets off the phone, Sam's not my boyfriend anymore and I don't go to dinner at his mom's, and—

I'm twenty-six and Uncle Tony's curled up, laying on his side in this shitty hospital bed, with an IV in his arm and a feeding tube in his gut and a catheter coming out of his dick to a clear plastic bag, half-filled with piss, tied to his leg, and his gown doesn't cover his shriveled, pale ass, and other than that, all he's wearing is a pair of those blue hospital socks with the grips on the bottom and he's moaning real soft and rocking ever so slightly, his eyes open but not seeing anything, and I'm sitting next to him, holding his cold, twisted hand in this shitty hospital in Baltimore, like I've done for hours and hours and days and days, and he doesn't even know I'm here, let alone who I am or who he is, and the doctors say this is what end-stage dementia looks like, but there's nothing they can do except make him comfortable, and he might last like this for weeks, and it sucks for him because he used to be somebody, he played pro football, but now he's nobody, just a sick old man dying in a shitty hospital, and nobody but me cares about him, and it sucks for me because he's the only family I have because no one knows where my dad is or what's happened to him, and my mom hasn't talked to me since she left for Korea almost ten years ago and when Uncle Tony goes, I won't have anyone, and—

No.

No, that's not true. Not all of it. Some, but not all. I'm not six, I'm not twelve, I'm not fifteen or eighteen or twenty-six. I'm not in Pennsylvania or Kent Island or Baltimore or anywhere else I've ever lived. I'm not being beat or laughed at or raped or dumped or stuck waiting for someone to die. I'm seventeen, and I'm in a frozen waste land, and a monster is ripping my mind apart—making me remember bad things, making me imagine bad things—so it can feed off my fear and shame and hurt.

The flashlight's still in my hand; I shine it on the thing and it recoils, hissing *kee! Kee! Kee! Kee!* It's about as big and weighs about as much as Penny, Sam's Pomeranian, but it's nowhere as cute, a nasty snarl of squirming, gray, noodle-thin tendrils latched onto my scalp, my face, my neck. Another creature's stuck itself to my chest, pulsing in time with my heart.

Kicking, I thrash around, trying to shake them off me, trying to sit up, get up, but somehow, they've got me pinned. Again and again, I hit the first one with the end of the flashlight, and it goes *kooloo! Kooloo!*, and seven or eight of its arms or tentacles or whatever they are slip out of me, flailing for the flashlight, grab it, starts to pry it out of my hand. Jesus, it's strong. I let go of the light, reach for my pack next to me—it must've come off when I fell—and pull the strange knife, pop both blades. The thing on my stomach rips a bunch of tendrils off me, lashes at my arm, but before it can get a solid grip, I grab the first one with my free hand and jam the knife into it, all the way to the hilt. Something inside it pops like a water balloon, exploding gray-green greasy pus on my hair and face and neck and chest, and then the whole quivering mess goes up in flames.

"Shit!"

I toss it and roll. The other thing's let go, maybe freaked out by me killing the first one, but as I start getting to my feet, it pounces on me again—*kee! Kee! Kee!*—noodle-arms flapping, snatching the front of my jacket, the back of my head. It tries to wriggle out of my hand as I hold it, ease the knife all the way into it, through it. Its blood or brains or whatever it is gushes onto the ground, like the first did on me, and when it bursts on fire, I throw it away, too.

I get the flashlight, shine it here and there, though I can already see a little bit because the two monsters are still burning. A few yards away, Mike's jerking, quivering on the ground, eyes all white, three of them latched onto him. I kick one, but it doesn't move or let go of him, just grabs my boot and my leg, tugs me closer. I lean over, stab it careful so I don't cut Mike, use the blade to fling it off him as it catches fire. Knife the other two and kick them over by the ones that were on me.

Spare a second to watch them burn. Doesn't bother me at all. They're just like bugs. Big-ass ugly bugs that were going to kill us.

I squat next to Mike, shine the light. He's panting, fast and shallow, making little clouds in the beam's light. His eyes have come back, but they're drifting, not focusing on anything. "Mike." Shake his shoulder. "Mike." Harder. "Mike!"

His eyes lock on mine. "I... I..." Still gasping. "I... saw her...

I… saw… she was… with him… she—"

"Mike, it doesn't matter."

"And she… liked it… liked what he was doing… with her… liked… more than—"

"Mike!"

"—with me—"

"Mike, whatever you saw, whether it was you remembering it or you imagining it, none of that's real now, okay? None of it."

"None…at all?"

"No. Only what's happening now is real, okay? Only 'now' is real, get it?"

"Only now…" he says, breathing slowing down. "Yeah. Okay. Only now."

"C'mon. You gotta get up. We gotta go." I try to haul him to his feet, but he's too heavy. I settle for taking his hands, pulling him up to sit.

He looks around like he just got here. Rubs his face, his neck. Stares at the burning carcasses of the monsters that jumped us.

"Criminently," he mutters. Puts his hands under himself and totters up. "Gimme my bag, will ya?"

I give him it and the shotgun. "You all right?"

"I'm gonna be. Gimme a minute."

"I don't think we have a minute."

"Take one anyway." He points behind me. "There: scope that out."

The crawling brain-sucking spaghetti monster that I used the knife to fling off Mike happened to land in the river. It's still on fire, and now, the silver "water" under it is, too, twisting into weird, ashy snake shapes as it burns, white smoke billowing into the black sky.

"Even if that isn't mercury," Mike says, "you definitely don't want to breathe any of what's burning off. Probably poisonous vapors. If that river caught fire, it might kill everything in this area code."

In the dark, close—too close—something howls, long and loud and savage and not the least bit human:

hroooooooooooooooooooooooooo

"We gotta go," I tell him. "You good?"

"If I was good, I wouldn't have to go to church." Hands me the flashlight. "Do you know where we're going?"

"Like where the black rocks are from here? No."

hrooooooooooooooooooooooooooooooo

Closer. "Shit on toast," Mike says. "Then, pick a direction and run."

Track 30. Photograph

We don't get too far too fast. The wind again, shrieking, stinging, ripping through us. It's never going to stop. Have to keep wiping away the crud the wind throws at my eyes and nose and mouth. Can't hardly see anything. Can't hear my boots on the rocks and ice. Fingers so cold, they burn. One hand on the flashlight, the other on Mike's elbow so I don't lose him.

This sucks, and we're going to die. Either we'll walk until we can't, and then we'll freeze to death, or before then, something will come out of the dark and kill us. But not yet. Not for another minute. I count one, two, three, and when I get all the way to sixty and I'm still alive—I haven't collapsed, and a monster hasn't gotten me—then I start counting from one again, and I walk another minute. And another. And another. I don't think of her and Sam, or at least I try not to. I only walk and count.

Mike grabs my arm, shakes me, shouts, "Hey!" over the wind.

"What?" I've been walking and counting and counting and walking for so long that I didn't notice he'd stopped.

"There!" Points to our left. A white light, hanging in the air, a few feet up, coming our way. Can't tell how far away it is, but it's gotta be close. Wouldn't be able to see it otherwise, what with the blowing sand and ash. He drops his bag, racks the shotgun. I switch off the flashlight, tuck it in my jacket. Get the pistol from my pocket, pull the slide, flick off the safety.

The light comes closer, stops. Shouting over the wind. "Alyx? Mike?"

Paddoch, with his old box lantern. Mike keeps the shotgun up, but I do the safety on the 9. Cup my hands by my mouth. "What happened to you? You okay?"

"Paddoch for Alyx Mike to find! Paddoch way to show!"

Mike steps in front of me. "If it's really you, show us the drawing!"

He puts down the lantern, reaches into his sheet, pulls out a square of paper, unfolds it, holds it out. I take it, glance at it. It's the hospital I sketched.

Mike puts down his gun, and we come in closer. I fold the drawing again, stuff it in my back pocket. *"'Galdr,'* huh?" Mike asks. "How 'bout you *'galdr'* us the hell out of here?"

"Paddoch not can to do. Paddoch Alyx Mike way to show. To *tsingy.*"

Huh? *Zingee?* "To what?" I ask.

"Tsingy." He looks at me, looks at Mike. Frowns. Squats, scoops up a pitted black rock about the size of my head. Waves his hand around. "Many. Big."

"The black rocks," Mike says. "I get it."

"Why can't you just zap us there like you got us here?"

"Maybe he shot his wad for the day. Or maybe he doesn't want to push our luck and wind up in the soup by trying that again. How far is it?"

Paddoch shakes his head. Drops the rock, picks up his lantern. "Alyx Mike far not to walk. *Tsingy* near to be."

"Well, let's step lively, then," Mike tells him.

Paddoch goes first, Mike right behind him, then me. Paddoch's as slow as ever, but we're pretty slow, too, what with the cold and the wind wearing us out. Well, wearing me out, anyway. I can never tell with Mike, and Paddoch doesn't seem to feel anything.

In my head, I go one, two, three, up to sixty, start again, but now, I'm not counting how long it takes us to die. Now, I'm counting how long it takes us to get to the…zingathingy, or whatever he called it. On the ninth time that I count to seventeen, something huge and black comes into Paddoch's light.

It's as tall as a dinosaur but as thin as me and it's scarred and pockmarked and all over it are jagged spikes and blades of rock. It's not a monster, but it looks like a monster's tooth. About seven, eight inches to its left is another black stone; about a foot and a half to its right is a third. And next to them are more, and behind all of them are more. They're just like in my dream, but much bigger because I'm much closer.

"*Tsingy*," Paddoch says.

"We have to go through there?" Mike asks.

"Yeah," I tell him. "The flat mountain's past these."

"You gotta be shitting me." He goes closer.

"Watch out. They're sharp."

He reaches out, gently strokes the edge of a shard. Looks at his hand. A long cut along the palm of his glove. "You ain't just whistling' Dixie."

"Alyx Mike *tsingy* to go," Paddoch says. He holds up the lantern, turns sideways, carefully shuffles though the foot-and-a-half gap between the two big rocks in front of us. Looks back at us. "Alyx Mike to come."

The stones are so tall and so close together that it's like being in a cave, but at least they block the wind. It's so quiet I can hear my breathing, and the crunching of the frozen sand under our footsteps is too loud. If anyone or any creature is in here, they'll hear us, but they might not find us. It's like a maze.

We pick our way along, sometimes having to turn to the side, or duck, or squeeze through a narrow spot without touching any spikes or blades. Mike has to really bend and twist, and it's a good thing his duffel bag isn't much wider than me. We take it slow and try to be careful, but even so, I slice my pack and jacket a bunch of times. Like Mike does, I start covering my face with my hands when it's tight.

I can't believe, after all this time, that we're almost there. All we have to do is get through these rocks, go up the path to the top of the big flat one, and then the hospital is there. And then we'll get to Sam. And her.

Sam and her.

This Wasted Land

No, no, no, no, don't think about it, don't think about them together, no, no, that couldn't have happened, that can't be real, he's not like that, he lo—

"OW! SHIT!" Wasn't paying attention and I cut the back of my hand on a big-ass barb. "Shit shit shit damn it, that hurts!" Echoes off the rocks. Bleeding. Grab my hand with the other one, squeeze it tight.

Mike and Paddoch staring at me. "I'm okay." Am I? Look at my hand: long cut—maybe four or five inches—but not deep. Squeeze it again, hard, to make it stop. "I'm okay."

"Well, shut up already," Mike says, "before something decides to find out what your problem is."

"Yeah, I love you, too." Jam my hand in my armpit. Hurts like a bitch. This wouldn't have happened if I had my gloves. Or if Paddoch's lame *galdr* hadn't crapped the bed.

I keep following Mike. How much farther is it 'til we're out of here?

Could have been worse.

Yeah, well, could have been a lot better, too.

He said it might not work.

Yeah, but wasn't the whole point of me sketching the hospital so that it would? So that he could get an exact picture in his head where we were going?

Maybe what you drew wasn't right.

If Mike hadn't said it, Sam would've. He never thinks I can do shit, just cuz I'm not in AP Calc or AP Bio, but I can draw, okay? So kiss my ass. I'm not like that low-talent white trash Kirstin Witt, who can't get better than a "C" on any piece Mrs. Martin assigns.

Mike nicks his leg on a shard of rock sticking just above the top of his boot. Winces, swears under his breath, hobbles a little until he can shake it off. Yeah, hurts, doesn't it, you douche? I check my hand. It's stopped bleeding, so there's that.

Maybe what you drew wasn't right.

Hmm.

I stop, get my little flashlight from my jacket sleeve pocket. It won't turn on no matter how many times I click it. Whack it against the palm of my good hand. Nothing. Batteries finally died. Wonderful. But at least I knew that was coming. I put back the flashlight, take out one of the glow sticks I found at the mall. Unwrap it, snap it, shake it. Faint green for about a foot or two—good enough to see by. I get out the drawing. Unfolding it bothers me—dunno why. Take a closer look.

It's the front of the hospital. It looks like what I saw. It looks like what I drew.

But it isn't.

"Mike?" I don't see him—he's gone. "Mike!"

"What?" He must not have noticed that I'd stopped, just kept walking.

"C'mere." The paper's shaking. Be cool.

"Paddoch! Alyx wan—"

"No, it's okay, Paddoch!" Be cool. "Just wait up for us. I'll only be a second." Think of something. Think. "I need Mike to get something out of my pack." That'll work. I hope.

"For Christ's sake," Mike says, ooching between the rocks in front of me. He left his duffel bag but brought his flashlight and the shotgun. Good. "What's your—"

I hold my finger up to my lips, show him the drawing; he shines the light on it. I shake my head, whisper, "This is fake. I didn't draw it."

He frowns. Studies it.

Just now, I figure out what bugged me. "When I gave the real one to Paddoch, he rolled it up, like a tube, but when he gave it back to me a little while ago, it was all folded." I peek past Mike. No one there. "That's not Paddoch."

"Are you sure?" he whispers.

"Yes."

This Wasted Land

"Are you sure you're sure? Maybe he folded it up later on."

"Sketching's like handwriting: you know what's yours, and what's not."

"Swell." Sighs. "You still have bullets?"

"Four or five in the clip. That's it."

"Three more here," he says, taking the other 9 out of the waistband of his pants, popping out the clip, handing it to me. I stash it in my front jeans pocket. He puts the 9 back, glances at the shotgun. "I've got two shells, and two…rounds or whatever for the 'flare gun,'" he adds, tapping his jacket pocket. "But we're not going to use that in this tight space. Blow us all to hell."

He sweeps the flashlight. "I'm going first, you come right behind me, real close. I got the front, you get behind us. You see him before I do, don't wait, don't talk, just shoot. Okay?"

"Yeah." I take out the 9, keep my thumb on the safety, finger off the trigger. Pistol in my right hand, glow stick in my left, we go the way we came.

"Hey, Paddoch?" Mike calls. "Say something so we can catch up to you."

Echoes.

"Paddoch, you still there, man?" Mike shouts. We come back to his duffel bag; I go to get it, but he shakes his head, mouths *Leave it*.

"Paddoch," I say, not as loud. Whatever's pretending to be him knows that we know. That's why he won't answer. Far off, outside this maze, the wind howls. A little bit of it slithers through, tugs on the ends of my hair. "Maybe—"

Pelican.

I whip around, look down, but only tattered gray dress there and before I can shout she snatches the front of my jacket one hand picks me up over her long white hair throws, the ground hits me hard—OOOOF!—the gun pops out of my hand I hang on to the glow stick somehow look up and there's a big spike maybe an inch or two from my eye and the shotgun goes

BLUWWW

for a second or two I can't hear anything and then Mike's yelling something can't tell what and I grab the pistol get up without sticking myself on the rock that's right next to me.

His flashlight's slipped out stuck in a notch in a boulder by him her back's to me and there's a hole as big as my head all the way through her and it leaks silver goo and she yanks the shotgun out of his hands smashes him across the face with it, his head snaps back she throws the shotgun into the dark hear it clatter against a rock, can't see it, too far, I only got the glow stick, and as I'm running at her, she bends grabs him pulls him up and

chkkkk and *nnnnfffh*

and she stabs him onto the rock where the flashlight's fallen and three no four spikes come out of his chest and

I feel more than hear myself scream because the 9 kicks kicks kicks kicks kicks and Freydis—she's not young and beautiful and she doesn't look like a prettier me she's wrinkled pitted face yellow ragged claws jagged broken glass teeth—jerks and twists and staggers as my bullets crush holes in her belly her chest where her tits should be her neck her face hook nose and dead silver eye burst sticky silver splashes Mike spatters me and

She topples back skewers herself on another big boulder spear of it slices through her side more silver spouts out of her but she wrenches herself off it stumbles toward me and the gun goes *kk kk kk* it's empty drop it

Scramble back almost fall down jerk the knife from my pack pop both blades she's on me she grabs my arm my left I hold the glow stick up in her ruined face jam the knife where her eye used to be she shrieks I hurt her I hurt her she thrashes knife tumbles she lets go of me clamber away from her as she falls right by a big rock she tries to get on hands and knees and my boot stomps on her neck I bend grab the back of her head she's still trying to get up shove down hard as I can lean on her lean shove smash her face onto a big razor spur she kicks flails arms claws clutching tearing at my jeans my jacket my face and

I shove harder lean lean push her face deeper onto the spike

This Wasted Land

silver spurting she shakes convulses shudders arms legs go stiff and

Twitching trembling hands open shut

Open shut

Keep trying to grab me, get me

Slow

Slow

Flop to the ground

She goes still.

Nothing but me gasping *hnnnh hnnnh hnnnh hnnnh.* I wobble back, away from her. Hold up the glow stick. She's not moving, not breathing. I keep away, circling, quick glance for the knife, then at her, look for the knife, then at her. I find it, pick it up, don't take my eyes off her.

She doesn't move.

I run up, kick her in the side. She lurches, but that's it. Kick her again. Again. Again. Again.

Me: *Hnnnnh hnnnh hnnnh*

I lean down, right by her face. Shouldn't: I've seen enough horror movies. Grab her hair, pry her face off the stone spike. There's a great big gash, sopping wet with that silver shit that I guess is her blood, where her nose and forehead should be. I spit in the one eye she's got left.

"That's for stealing my boyfriend, you whore."

The eye rolls toward me and I jump back, hold out the knife. Her mouth yawns open, tongue oozes out, and something small and white—a tooth?—tumbles out from under it, plinks onto the stones under her.

"Sam," she croaks. "Home."

I stomp her head. Again. Again. Until she doesn't move, doesn't breathe anymore. Just me going, *Hnnnnh hnnnh hnnnh hnnnh hnnnh*

Dead. She's actually freaking dead. I killed her.

Good.

Hnnh hnnh

I keep the knife on her, squat, pick up what fell out of her mouth. Not a tooth. Hard and flat. Same shape but half the size of a piece of gum, hundreds of tiny runes etched into it. I put it in my pocket, stand.

Mike.

Oh God, Mike be okay, be okay.

Stumble back to him. He's laying on his face, blood puddling under him, big shards of rock sticking out of his back. She slammed him so hard that they broke off. "No no no no oh shit shit shit...." I kneel, roll him over. He's panting, eyes going back and forth, back and forth. His face is white and his lips are blue, so, how can he be sweating? Take his face in my hands: he's cold.

"Mike?" His eyes look at me, but they don't stop shimmying. "Mike, you're…you're hurt real bad."

"Train's still going by," he murmurs. "Cathy's in the car."

"Mike, Cathy's not here. What do I do, Mike? How do I save you?"

"Buck fifteen a gallon. Gonna shut the car off."

"Mike, you've been stabbed." And you're no help to either of us. Gotta stop the bleeding, but how am I going to do that?

Shine the flashlight back at Freydis: still dead. I go to her, cut a bunch off the bottom of her dress. Her feet are bare, calloused, dirty with gray sand and ash. Go back to Mike, start pressing down his wounds. Blood soaks the rag. Too much blood. Stupid. This isn't going to do any good.

"Where's Paddoch?" he asks.

"I don't know." Give him something to focus on. "We're gonna get this bleeding to stop, and then I'll take care of you, okay?"

"What did Sam tell you?"

What did Sam tell me about what? Forget it, he's only

babbling. In shock or something.

Mike's hand floats up, tries to take mine. Falls to the sand. "I couldn't do anything. I just stood there and let her do it to us."

Crap, the bleeding's not even slowing down, and I don't— No. Stay cool. Keep it together. "Let her do what, Mike?"

"Jeremy. When the train came. Just now."

"There's no train here. But we're going to get Jeremy, okay?"

"No, we're not." His eyes fix on mine.

"You don't know that. But you're with it again right now, so you gotta tell me what to do, cuz you're hurt and I don't—"

"Where is she?"

"Who? Freydis?"

It takes a lot of what he has left to nod. Once.

"You shot her, Mike. Right in the chest. I made sure she's dead."

Smirks. "Witchiepoo."

"Yeah, her." His eyes start going back and forth again. He's losing it. "C'mon, don't do that, help me out here."

Panting again. Blinking a lot. Is he trying to hold it together? "Don't go. Cathy, please."

I take his hand. It's freezing. "I'm not going anywhere." Doesn't matter that I'm not Cathy.

"Any more. Don't. You know that." At me, puzzled. "The dogs."

No idea. "Yeah, the dogs."

"Look down the edge of it. That's where."

On TV and in the movies, whenever someone gets shot or stabbed, they fall down, and that's it. They just die right there then, except if it's a good guy. If it's a good guy, he'll hang on long enough to tell the girl something important, and then his eyes will close, like he's falling asleep.

The good guy doesn't slowly bleed out quarts and whisper confused nonsense while the girl holds his hand. He doesn't shiver and seize up and piss himself. He doesn't lie there for what seems like hours, gasping, straining to breathe. And when he finally dies, his eyes stay open and something in them, some light, goes out.

Mike. Oh, God, Mike.

I don't know how long I sit there, my head on his chest, sobbing. Long enough that when I finally stop and look up, dust and ash and little pellets of ice have settled on his face, in his hair, in his eyes. I used to think that touching dead people would be creepy and gross, but now, I don't want to let go of his hand.

I sit there, next to him, until I finally talk myself into getting up, going to his duffel bag. Open it, go through it. Take some things: socks, a canteen, some cans of food even though I can't think of ever being hungry again. The water filter he made. Patti.

I squat next to him, slip the magazine, cover down, under his arm, against his chest. Shine the flashlight. Freydis right where I left her. No sign of the shotgun.

Back to Mike. Take the other pistol from his waistband, check it. Three bullets in the clip. Go through his jacket pockets. Band-Aids he took from Paddoch, at the mall. The flare gun and the two shots left. Reach into his shirt's breast pocket. Worn, wrinkled paper. No, not paper. I take it out.

Photograph. A toddler, a little boy, curly blond hair, brown eyes that aren't right. Down's syndrome.

Jeremy.

Track 31. Lights Out

When you're hurt bad, you go to the hospital. That must be why I'm here.

Somehow, I must have made my way through the *tsingy* without getting lost or killed. I must have found the path that goes up the big rock. And I guess I've walked for hours. Don't remember any of it. Blanked. I've done that before.

Breathing real slow and shallow. Can't stop shivering. I don't feel cold anymore, not really. But my hands have turned white and they burn. Frostbite? Don't know. Hard to think.

Mike's dead. Paddoch's gone. I'm alone. Again.

Shine the flashlight up and ahead. **EM RGE CY**. The 911 operator asked what was mine. I didn't really know what to tell her. I still wouldn't. Everything is some kind of insane nightmare.

C'mon. Get it together. Focus. Sam. I gotta find him. And he's in there.

I go up the steps, to the front doors. Go into the waiting room here in the ER, and the overhead lights come on. If anyone or anything is here or comes in here, they can't help but see me. Look all around: nothing moves except me. Click off Mike's flashlight, tuck it in my jacket's side pocket, take out the pistol. For the first time in what seems forever, I can't see my breath. Warm in here, but not so much that I wish I'd picked up a swimsuit at that mall. Rows of empty chairs; every so often, a little table with some pamphlets or magazines.

I go behind the nurses' desk, to the triage rooms. Lights snap on again, show exam tables, chairs, scales, blood pressure equipment. The cabinets are empty: no syringes, no tissues, no tongue depressors or cotton swabs or latex gloves. The actual ER room past the triage goes from pitch dark to bright white the instant I open the door.

Medical bays with sliding glass walls, carefully made beds, swing arms with monitors turned on but not tracking heartbeats or pulse or respiration. Laptops and phones and pens and notepads and clipboards and coffee cups at the long, narrow standing desk in the middle where the nurses and doctors and assistants would be between patients.

I pick up the receiver of a phone, put it to my ear. A dial tone. I punch in my uncle's number.

Right away: "You have reached a non-working number. Announcement 14 switch 18 dash 5 dash 6."

Wait—don't some places make you dial "9" first when you use one of their phones to call out? I hang up, pick up, try it like that. "You have reached a non-working number. Announcement 14 switch 18 dash 5 dash 6."

What does that last part mean? Doesn't matter. Hang up, try again, "1" first, then "9", then his number. Same thing.

Crap.

I don't have Sam's mom's number, or Cynthia's—they were in my phone. And Cynthia, she's.... No. Not gonna think about that. Her, or Sam. Not right now. Right now, I gotta call someone. Anyone.

Push three buttons.

Ring.

Ring.

Ring.

Ring.

Ring.

C'mon, how can 911 not answer?

Ring.

Ring.

Ring.

Ring.

It cuts off. I hang up, pick up again, dial it again. Doesn't even ring this time.

Something flickers: the open laptop next to me. Screen goes from pure black to solid white. Then:

Alyx

Look all around. Nothing moving. Back to the screen.

Find me

Try to type, but the keyboard's locked. Squiggle on the touchpad, no cursor. "Sam?"

Alyx help me

All the phones ring at the same time.

Please don't leave me

I pick up the phone and all the others stop. "Hello?"

A man I don't know. "Hello again, Alyx-with-a-'y.'"

I slam down the phone. They start ringing again, all at once.

The overhead lights go out. The emergency backups—pale little circles every few feet, where the walls meet the ceiling—come on, filling the room with shadows. Exit glows red there and there and there and there, too. The phones keep ringing. Speakers above crackle. The same man's voice:

Security Security Security

Big double doors at the end of the room; if they're locked, I'm screwed. Slap the metal plate on the wall near them, and they slowly swing open. Hammering in my chest. Dark corridor, spots of white emergency lights, going deeper into the hospital. Security Security Security echoing down it.

Another sound, from the end of the hall, where I can't see. *pmmpmmpm*MPMMPMMPMMPMM

What is that? Growing louder, getting closer.

PMMPMMPMMPMMPMMPMM

Running. That's what it is. Someone running this way.

Doors start to swing shut, I dash through them before they can, but then I'm stuck, don't know what to do, can't stay in the ER, gotta go toward whoever's coming, that's stupid, but I got no choice. Take off running—shit! shit! shit! shit! Does whatever it is hear me, see me? Flickering shape in the dark, headed fast for me. SECURITY SECURITY SECURITY

A shadowy hallway on my left. I take it, run, run, run! Doesn't go far, ends at a lobby, a different one. Over there, glass doors to outside. Over here, elevators. Next to them, another hallway. Over there, red EXIT sign over a side door to stairs. In front of me—

A long window and a dark room on the other side. Put my face against it, cup my hands. Balloons and flowers and metal stands of cards. Glass-front fridge, shelves of pop and juice and water inside. Racks of gum and chocolate bars and candy. I step back, find it. Glass door, gold letters painted there. LIL & ALBERT'S GIFT SHOP. Tug the handle.

PMMPMMPMMPMMPMM

Slip inside and twist the latch, locking the door behind me, then duck behind the cash register counter. Only one emergency light here, in the far corner. All dark where I am. It's going to have to be enough.

PMMPMMPMMPMMPMMPMM

It stops right outside the store. I'm breathing hard but trying not to, trying to slow down, to not let it hear me. I breathe through my nose, little puffs, tell myself to relax, to stay still, be calm.

SECURITY

I hear it pace. Is it looking for me?

Or waiting?

Don't move, don't make any noise, be cool, keep it together.

SECURITY

Running again, toward the ER. *PMMPMMPMMPMMPMM*

This Wasted Land

PMMPMmPMMPMMPMMMPMmmpmmpmm

I don't move.

SECURITY

I wait.

Far away now: SECURITY SECURITY SECURITY

Just sit.

Nothing.

Nothing.

Lean forward a little, peek out from behind the counter. No one and nothing there. Come out, slow, careful, go to the glass. Look right, left, right again as far as I can see. All good. Tuck the gun back in my jacket.

To the rack of chocolate bars—Three Musketeers and Twix and Milky Ways—and candy—Skittles and M&M's and Swedish Fish and Starburst—I tear them open, gobble them down, I'm so damn hungry. Little bags of cookies and potato chips and peanuts and Cheetos. Chug a bottle of water from the fridge, then another, holy shit they got Pepsi, I don't usually drink that, but it's been so long since I had pop that—

Krch. Plastic gears grinding.

A faint *zzrt*. I know those noises.

Pelican.

Rows of shelves on the back wall, over the wooden racks with picture stories and coloring books. Dozens of them, lined up next to each other. The closest one turns its head my way. Eyes light up yellow. Beak creaks open and shut, open and shut.

Pelican.

I don't move.

More grinding, more buzzing. Eyes light up. Heads swivel. Wings flap. Beaks open and shut. All of them.

Pelican. Pelican. Pelican. Pelican. Pelican. Pelican.

Gotta get the hell out of here. Drop the pop bottle I'm holding, whip around, no good, too slow, too late.

Pale. Gray. Naked. Not much taller than me. It stands on two split feet with no toes. Something forked squirms, wiggles as it dangles from its crotch. Claws at the end of long arms—five, six, seven of them?—sprouting from its shoulders, its chest, its back. Flat face, a row of jagged points hanging down where its mouth should be, and right above them, in the middle of its face, three red slits, like cuts.

The monster that was outside the phone booth.

Shit. Shit, shit, shit.

I take the pistol from my jacket, hold it out in front of me so the thing can see it. Hope it doesn't notice my hands trembling as I rack the slide. Point it.

The creature goes to the door, tugs at the handle *ghk*. Looks down to see why it won't open. Back up to me.

"You try coming in here, and I'll blow your damn head off." I sound more badass than I feel.

Two claws on the door handle now, and it pulls harder. *GHK*.

Go closer to the door. "You ugly *and* deaf? Take a walk, pal."

GHK.

I tell myself to do something, to don't just stand there. Shoot it, at least.

Pelican. Pelican. Pelican. Pelican. Pelican. Pelican.

Yanks again again again *GHKGHKGHK*

Okay, okay, be cool. Don't lose it. Just shoot. Shoot!

GHKGHKGHK

The birds screech louder, faster *PelicanPelicanPelicanPelicanPelican Pelican!*

C'mon!

GHKGHKGHKGHKGHKGHKGHK. The thing's like a machine, its arms jackhammering faster and faster, the door rattling in its frame. Any second now, it's gonna break the lock.

GHKGHKGHKGHKGHKGHKGHKGHK

Kill it!

PelicanPelicanPelicanPelicanPelican!

Do *something*, damn it!

POC POC POC through the door's glass, point-blank range, its chest, its throat, its head, and the monster lurches back, staggers, sinks to his knees, gasping, this black runny stuff trickling out of the wounds, its earholes on the sides of its head, its eye-slits.

My ears ringing, and all I smell is the burning from the 9. Those creepy bird toys have shut up, finally. I got him. I got him.

"Told you not to mess with me, asswipe."

It stares at me. Wobbles, five of its arms holding it up. I ought to open the door, finish it with my knife, then go—

It stands up.

Shiiiiiiiiit.

Pelican! Pelican!

One hand grabs the door, starts yanking again. Fingers of two hands jam into the holes in the glass, wiggle around, widening them, the monster not feeling or not caring about cutting itself.

PelicanPelicanPelican! PelicanPelicanPelicanPelicanPelican!

Get the hell out of here!

Glance back and to the left of me: nothing but a tall, fake potted plant. Back and to the right: wooden door, closed. I stumble back, grab the knob. It's not locked. A small office, lit by an emergency light. Go in, slam the door shut behind me, press the button in the middle of the knob. Try to slide a metal filing cabinet in front of the door, but it doesn't move, must be full.

Desk in here, chairs, more filing cabinets, water cooler, the kind with the big plastic jug on top. Phone and old-style boxy computer on the desk. No windows, two other doors. Mounted by the ceiling, a black-and-white monitor showing the inside of the shop. I shove the computer off the desk, nudge the chairs out of the way, push the desk—it's heavy as all hell, but it goes—in front of the door.

From the other room, shattering and crashing of glass. Watch on the closed-circuit camera as the monster finishes smashing its way in, goes to the office door. It looks up at the camera.

PelicanPelicanPelicanPelicanPelican!

The door knob rattles.

One of the doors on the back wall goes to a bathroom; the other's to a closet with cleaning supplies and power towels and a vacuum and a fire extinguisher, cash register tapes and boxes of merchandise, a helium tank to blow up the flat shiny balloons on the shelves next to it. No way out of either.

I climb the filing cabinet by the door, pop the ceiling tile, slide it over, stick my head in, shine Mike's light around. The real ceiling's plaster or something, and it's like three feet over the tiles. Looking left and right, there's only a big empty space stretching past the end of the flashlight beam, nothing out there, thank God, except phone wires and the metal cables the lights hang from and ribbed plastic tubes for air vents. I put my elbows on the frame that's holding up the ceiling tiles, try to push myself up. The frames bend—just thin aluminum. They're not going to hold me.

Damn it!

The monster slams itself against the door. The wall the door's on doesn't go all the way up to the real ceiling. The wall's only a few inches thick, and it looks like it's made out of gray cardboard. I pull the flare gun-launcher-whatever-it-is from my pack. I bet I could lean down and knock out the ceiling over the other side of the door and then blast that thing while it's trying to get through the door.

But we're not going to use that in this tight space, Mike had said. *Blow us all to hell.* Damn it, that's right. Stupid thing's only useful if you're a ways off from what you're shooting at. I put it back. Wish I had found Mike's shotgun.

The door's still holding, for now, but the monster keeps beating on it. Those goddamn birds have gone quiet again, but big whoop. I'm trapped here. Eventually, that thing's going to bust its way in and then it'll kill me at least I hope it kills me instead of doing anything else to me damn it damn it I wish Mike was here he'd know what to do he'd—

He'd say, *Get a grip, Alyx-with-a-'y.'*

Okay. Okay. Think. Not what I can't do, but what I can. Nothing obvious in here that looks like it'll do me any good. Nothing I can use to kill it. No other doors, no big ventilation shafts to crawl through, like you see in movies. Yeah, I got my knife, but that creature looks strong as hell and it's got all those arms and I bet it could grab me and take it away and—

Wait. Maybe there is something I can do.

Here and there, parts of the door bulge, splinter, as it starts breaking through. It keeps pounding—doesn't it ever get tired? Instead of putting back the ceiling tile that I moved to look up here, I drop it on the floor and it breaks in half and gets chalky stuff on the carpet. I jump down from the cabinet, go to the office closet, snatch the fire extinguisher off the wall. Hold it under the emergency light—please be charged up. The dial says it is. Scan the instructions on the label: yeah, that's what I thought.

Claws, arms, reaching through the door, feeling, scratching the top of the desk, searching, grasping for the knob. Gotta time this just right, only gonna have a few seconds. Let it through the door and get inside, but not too close. Breathe. Breathe. I can do this. I can do this.

Get on top of the desk, go behind the door, press myself against the wall. Point the extinguisher's nozzle down at the hole. I pull the pin while the thing rips its way through what's left of the door and the frame and even some of the gray cardboard stuff that part of the wall's made out of. As it's squirming through the hole, arms grabbing here and there, it notices the ceiling tile on the floor and looks up.

I squeeze the handle hard as I can, spraying this huge white cloud right in its face. It totters, trying to get away, trying to get me, and I jump, smash the thing in the face with the end of the canister, duck its flailing arms, wriggle through the hole it made, bolt through the shop door's empty frame, and sprint, boots pounding, like all hell down the hall, away from there, away from the way I came.

Security Security Security

Two doors at the end of the hall; I slap the metal square on the wall, spare a second to look back. The thing stumbles out of the gift shop, sees me, starts running *PMMPMMPMMPMMPMM*. I slip through the doors as they're opening, run, run, take the next right, run, an elevator on my left, piece of paper taped to the door. Out of Service. No frickin' way.

Stairs next to it, shove open the door to them, take them two at a time, up to the next floor, into the shadowy hall there, run, keep going, take a left down another hall, run, through more doors, up another flight of stairs to the next floor, run through mazes of corridors, keep looking back, can't tell if the monster's still after me, go up more stairs, out into the next floor, run, legs burning, chest heaving. Through more doors, stagger up the stairs to the very top. Heave open the door there, stumble into the dimly lit hall.

Drop to my hands and knees, gasping, thin trickle of vomit. Slump to the floor, lie there. Can't hear anything but me—for now. C'mon. Get up. Get up.

Haul myself to my feet. Sign on the wall says Maternity. Didn't Cynthia work in a ward like this? Cynthia. Shit. What am I gonna tell Sam about his sister? No, don't think about that, not now. Now, I gotta find Sam, before that thing finds me.

All down this corridor, doors with big, dark windows. I go to each, right side of the hall, left side, right side, left side, pulling, pushing on the handles, but they're all locked. Halfway down, on the right, a long, dark window. A light goes on as I go by: rows of empty bassinets. I thought they only had rooms like this in old movies.

Alyx....

Sam. He's close.

Running again, yanking on doors, all of them locked, all their windows dark. "Sam!" More rooms—they're all locked. "Sam!"

The end of the hall, in front of me, two big swinging doors, like at the ER, but over them, it says, NEONATAL INTENSIVE CARE UNIT. Women's room door on my right. Another door—no window, no sign—on my left. Storage? An office? I try the handle: it's not locked. Push it open; a light on inside.

No.

No.

Oh, God, no.

The motel room where they were. Her. And him. Sam.

I don't go in. I can't. Don't need to. From the door, I see it. The bed, sheets still messed up. Next to it, on the floor, his clothes. The ones he was wearing when she took him.

This can't be real. It can't be.

It is. It's real. It was all real. Everything I saw.

Everything.

Deep in me, the tsunami, the one from before, when I woke from the dream, just as strong, just as bad now as then. Shaking, all of me's shaking, can't stand up, can't stand it. Grab the door frame, hold it, hold on, hold myself up. Tears spilling out of me. C'mon. Don't do this. Don't wipe out.

Mike: *You can't trust anything.*

Her. Him. Right there. In front of me.

Tyra: *Alyx, where you're going...nothing's real.*

Keep it together.

Freydis: *She's nothing. I can be anything.*

Keep it together!

Freydis: *I can be everything.*

Propping myself up in the doorway, teeth clenched, panting through them, crying—can't do this now, can't stop. It was real. It was here. This is where it happened, where they were screwing, and when I saw them, everything in me—everything that *is* me—broke. They smashed me like how I'd smash empty bottles just cuz I liked the sound. And just like me, they didn't give a shit, either.

No, that's not true: maybe he didn't care, but she did. She must of thought it was funny as all hell to fuck me over while she fucked him, when I was busy chasing after his sorry ass, all the way here. To this awful place.

I hate them so goddamned much.

Panting through my teeth still, not crying anymore, just pissed. Stomp into the room. I want to flip over the bed, want to grab the clock flashing 12:00 12:00 12:00 off the nightstand and smash it, want to knock the lamp over, break that too. Want to tear, rip, shred his clothes with my knife. Want to, but don't.

What I do is crouch by his pants, pick up the phone laying face down on the carpet. It's not his phone—I still have that. It's not mine—it got busted. So, whose is it? Not that psycho bitch Freydis....

Turn it over, press the home button. On the screen, Cynthia doing a selfie of her and Sam and their mom and me at Thanksgiving.

Cynthia. So maybe all that with her at the mall was real, too.

The light goes out.

Black, totally black, like it was when I left the library by myself that one time. I jump up, whirl, stumble against the side of the bed, almost fall onto it, steady myself before I can. I'd rather dive into a swimming pool of dog shit than touch any of part of this bed with my bare hands. I fumble with the phone, don't freak out, just get the flashlight, there's a way turn it on without knowing the passcode, got it! Turn it on, shine it around. See her.

Black gown—looks like what nuns wear—flowing from the top of her head, which almost reaches the ceiling. Arms thin as broomsticks but so long that her hands—they're twice the size of mine—could touch the floor. One arm—it bends in two places, like it has extra elbows—is tugging aside the folds of the dress that cover her left breast. The other arm cradles something to herself there. It's naked and its skin is shriveled and gray, like lunchmeat that's been left out too long, and if it's a baby, it's awfully tiny, not much bigger than a cat.

Her head swivels toward me. She doesn't have eyes, or a nose, or much of a mouth, only a slit with no lip. As she glides toward me, her face starts bubbling like boiling water.

I pull my knife. Where did this freaky bitch even come from? Nobody else was in here with me. "Stay back!"

She stops. "Freydis." Her voice low, silky.

"Freydis is dead."

Slowly shakes her head. "Freydis you to be."

"I am *not* Freydis." Keep the knife on her, circle away toward the door. She moves by the window, away from me, like we're dancing. The arm holding the…child swings out to me.

"To take," she says. "To Ōth."

It *is* a baby, but its head is swollen, shaped like a balloon, and it has long tufts of stringy gray-white hair here and there. Its eyes are too small for its face, one's lower than the other and doesn't open, and the one that does rolls back and forth, back and forth. Its nose is just this twisted nub, its mouth gasps open-shut-open-shut, like fish do when you take them out of the water. Its neck is way too skinny to hold up its head, and the rest of it's way too thin, it must weigh like a pound, maybe two.

"To take," she says again. "Freydis to take."

By her feet is a big basket made of wire and metal scraps and trash and animal bones, all stuck together with some sorta dried yellow goop. The basket that was on the train. The one I thought had some kind of animal in it. But there wasn't. It was this baby.

"Freydis Ōth to feed," she says.

I bolt outta the room, run down the hall the way I came holy shit holy shit this is messed up gotta get outta here no wait can't go that way cuz up ahead a door clangs open and *PMMPMMPMMPMMP* the thing from downstairs found me it's coming turn run run back toward the ICU and it's right behind me gaining fast and

The weird woman glides out of the room and she's holding that messed up baby by one of its spindly arms, dragging it across the floor and it doesn't even cry and her dress falls open at the front and more twisted, messed-up babies dangling from her, some tied to her body or her legs by bloody, dripping bandages, some hanging on to her like monkeys do with their mothers, and one of them has claws sunk into her thigh and white goo oozes down her leg but I don't think she feels it

And the one with the claws looks up at me and even though I'm running and the thing chasing me goes *PMMPMMPMMPMMP* I can still hear the baby croak, *mama*, and the others look at me and they start to say *mama mama mama* too.

The tall creepy woman with the boiling face steps aside, and I slam into the doors to the ICU, they swing open thank God it's not locked but I trip going across the threshold, tumble into the room, door swinging shut behind me, I gotta get up gotta run they're right behind me they'll get me oh God Sam I'm sorry I tried I tried but I couldn't save you—

But instead of laying on tile floor, like in the rest of the hospital, I'm on my face in grass.

Instead of emergency lights, it's sun.

Instead of cold, it's warm.

From somewhere, not far, something goes *iiiiiiaaaaaaaaaaaaaa* in the blue sky, and it takes me a sec to remember what that is. A seagull.

Like they have on Kent Island.

Track 32. Estranged

Slowly—every part of me hurts so bad—I push myself up onto my knees, and then, slowly, I get to my feet. If it's not Kent Island, it's someplace like it. Grass. Trees. Blue sky. Gray-blue waves lapping against a black rock beach, a wooden rowboat pulled onto the shore. The water goes on forever, so it's not the Chesapeake. The ocean? Gotta be.

I look behind me. No door. No hospital. No monsters.

"Alyx." Kind of a clipped accent, don't know where it's from, but I recognize the voice: the man on the phone in the ER. A silhouette in the shade of a tree, just off the beach. I come closer.

"With a 'y.' It's good to see you again."

Paddoch.

No frickin' way.

There's a little white, wooden table on his left, a matching empty chair on his right. "Would you like to sit?"

Shake my head.

"Something to eat?" On the table's a book, some folded-up newspapers, a glass of water, a white ceramic bowl with fruit. He holds the bowl out to me. Apples. Grapes. Strawberries. Blueberries. A banana. A round, red fruit I'm not familiar with. It all looks…amazing. Despite the candy and the junk food I had, my stomach gurgles. I swallow because my mouth is for-real watering, not just like when people say that.

Shake my head again.

"Are you sure? Where I'm from, it's considered very rude not to accept hospitality."

Point my knife at him. "What the actual hell is going on?"

"Many things, which I will be glad—"

"How come you're talking regular?"

"It's a bit of a story, but I wasn't—"

"Where's Sam?"

"He's on his way, and when he gets here, we can see about sending both of you back where you belong."

Wait—what?

He must read it on my face. "That is what you want, isn't it?"

I put down the knife. "Yeah...um...I guess..."

"Then, that's what we'll do. There's a native village not far from here, and that's where he's been, since I found out about him."

"'Found out about him?'"

He shakes his head. "I never wanted Sam—or you—to come here. Freydis shouldn't have taken him. I didn't tell her to. But I am sorry that she did."

"You're...sorry?"

"Yes."

"Why did she take him?"

"That will take a while to explain." He reaches into the bowl, takes out the round red fruit, puts it on a plate. "If you don't care for this, you could have something else. At the very least, I'm sure you're thirsty."

"I'm fine." Black-winged gulls floating in the air, riding the breeze. "What is this?"

He looks out over the water. "My favorite place and time. I used to take that boat and fish in these waters, but that was when the world was younger. Now, I sit, watch the waves,"—smiles faintly—"and remember."

There's no sand, but somehow, it reminds me of a lot of Terrapin Park, where Sam and I used to go when it wasn't too cold. We'd walk on the beach, look at the boats go by and the cars crawl across the bridge. Talk. Hold hands. Kiss. Just be together. Before anything happened.

Before she happened.

There's a small blade by the plate. He starts cutting open the red fruit. "Occasionally, while I'm here, I have something to eat."

"Newfoundland," I tell him. "That's where we are, aren't we? Like how you were telling me and Mike, when we first met you. Vikings, and Indians, and Leif Erikson, and you, and Freydis."

He nods. "And it's with her that all our current difficulties began."

"But she's not the same Freydis who took Sam."

"Yes and no." He finishes cutting up the fruit, puts it on a little plate, wipes his fingers on a white napkin. I shrug off the backpack, set it on the grass in front of the chair next to him. Sit. Keep the knife on my lap.

He takes a spoon, starts plucking out little, squishy, red—I don't know what they are—from the fruit, puts them on the plate. They're like corn kernels, but not.

He notices me staring. "Pomegranates are unusual. Other fruits, you eat the—what's the word in English? The 'meat.' You eat the meat, but not the seed. Whereas with pomegranates, you eat the seed, but not the meat."

"That's what those are? Seeds?"

"Yes." Plucks out a bunch of them with a spoon, scoops some onto another little plate. Holds it out to me. "They're delicious."

"I only want Sam. Why did she take him?"

He takes back the plate, scoops out more seeds, starts on them. "Because she's the fisherman's wife."

"What?"

"From the fairy tale."

"I don't know that one." Look around. No one in sight. "How does it go?"

"I'm not going to tell you a bedtime story: you're a woman, not a little girl. Let's just say that no matter what she had, she always wanted more—and she didn't care whom she hurt to get it."

"Duh. Freaky witch monster."

"But before that, when she first came here, she was a beautiful young woman, the daughter of an Icelandic chieftain, and she was Leif Erikson's wife."

"You said Erikson gave her to Ōth."

"She gave herself, willingly."

Slut. "Cuz he had something she wanted?"

He nods. "A kingdom. This island and its people to rule over. Riches from fur trapping. And secrets."

"'Secrets?'"

"More than the smattering of rune magic she had learned growing up in her father's longhouse."

"Like what?"

"Timelessness."

"You mean, like never getting old, or dying, or whatever?"

"That, too. But when even the secrets she had learned weren't enough, she stole more. Just like how she stole Sam, brought him here, and hid him. I wish I had found out about him sooner, before she seduced him."

Him saying that punches me in the face. Something about hearing it out loud instead of in my head makes it more real, makes it hurt more.

He puts down his plate. "Not that she matters anymore, seeing as how you've killed her."

"Me and Mike did."

"That's not entirely true, but it was very kind of you to reassure him so. No one—especially when they're dying—wants to feel as if they've failed."

"Mike didn't fail."

"Yes and no. He didn't save his wife, he didn't kill Freydis, and he didn't get back his boy. What was his son's name? Jerome?"

"Jeremy."

"I don't know why Freydis took him, or what she did with him." Shakes his head. "That poor man. It must have been horrible for him. Of course, you've suffered too, because of her—and Sam."

Thanks for reminding me. I'd forgotten from like, thirty seconds ago. I swear, I just want all this to be over. "When's he gonna get here?"

"Not long. What will you say to him when he comes?"

What *am* I gonna say? *Hi?* God, that's stupid. *Are you okay?* Cuz I'm not. How about, *What the actual hell?* Or, *Did you lose your goddamn mind?* Maybe, *She beat the shit out of you and tried to kill me, so how could you stick your dick in her? What did you think that would do to me? I didn't deserve that! I didn't do any—*

Okay, don't. Don't do this to yourself. Remember what Ms. Custer said about letting yourself get all cranked up, and how it only makes you feel worse. Maybe that's what Paddoch wants—though I don't know why—so don't go along with it. Rein in. Think about something else, 'til Sam gets here, and we'll deal with it then.

Easier said than done. I blow out a big breath through my teeth. Paddoch watches me.

"How can this be Newfoundland, when back there…? I mean, this is impossible. Are we really in our world?"

"Your world, the reality you come from? No. This is another reality."

"What about the hospital? And the desert? Are they a different…reality?"

He nods. "Eight of the realities are like the branches on this tree, connected at a trunk, the trunk held in place by roots in the endless dark. But under the roots is a another, ninth, reality, not like a branch, more like a hole. The hospital, that desert, those lonely, wasted lands, are that reality, that 'hole'—and holes need filling."

"Who fills the hole?"

"It tries to fill itself by constantly reaching out, pulling in what the worlds, in their wanderings, slough off. What's broken, forgotten, discarded, lost, abandoned: things, places, people. Like me. Like you."

The ship that came out of the ground. The mall. The motel. And what Mike said: *This is the world's sink trap. All kinds of stuff ends up stuck here.*

"I didn't get pulled there, I came for Sam. I didn't have to go after him when Freydis took him."

"Didn't you? I believe you did, because, I'm guessing, that Sam touched you deeply, in your soul. And when he did, you felt joy and bliss, probably for the first time in your life. Didn't you?"

"Yes." Don't want to admit it, but I have to. "How did you know?"

"Because I've felt that, too. But when he turned away from you, he took that joy and bliss—stole it, even—and then poisoned it forever with Freydis. And now none of it is left."

My hands: they're fists. Stomach tightens. I stand up, leave the knife on the seat. God, someone, please make him stop saying that. Make him stop.

"What *is* left, Alyx? What did he leave in you? Emptiness? Hurt? Fury?"

The tsunami's building, building—I can't take this. I can't stand the pain, I can't stand how it's always there, I can't stand how whenever I think of it, I gotta fight to keep it from drowning me again and again and again.

No.

Stop.

Keep it together.

Get a grip.

You can do this. Think of something else.

"How are you going to send me and Sam back?"

Raises his eyebrows, glances left. "Let's discuss that with him."

Sam, walking toward us. Clean, new clothes, clean face, clean hair, not ragged and filthy like me. He looks good, looks taller, stronger, older. He's not limping, not holding his arm against his side, but that can't be. Can it?

He stops a few feet away. Puzzled. "Hey."

"Hey." I can't think of anything else.

Paddoch watches us.

"Alyx, how…" he starts. Looks at Paddoch. Back to me.

"Can we go somewhere?" I ask. "And, you know, talk? By ourselves?"

"What are you doing here?" Sam asks me.

"I…" What the hell *am* I doing here? "I came…for you."

He doesn't say anything.

"Sam, aren't you even happy to see me?"

"Alyx, everything's changed."

Holds up his arm, bends, flexes, turns it here and there, hand and fingers reach, pull back. It's straight and strong and it's like it was meant to be. He's healed. He's whole. He's perfect. Absolutely perfect.

I start toward him, think better of it. "How did—"

"I did," Paddoch says. "It was the least I could do, considering Freydis—"

Freydis. I am *so* sick of hearing her name. Two steps at Sam, my fist right into his belly, and he goes *ufffh*. He staggers back, my left gets him on the side of his face, not in his shiny white teeth like I wanted. He shakes it off, shoves me away; I stay on my feet.

"You hit like a girl."

"I *am* a girl! I was *your* girl! Until you and her in that motel!"

"Alyx—"

"Was she good? Huh? Was she?"

"It was just sex. It didn't mean anything."

What the actual hell? Did he really just say that? "I wake up, and the first thing I think of is you and her! I try to go to sleep, and I see you and her! And all the time in between, I try to put it out of my head, and sometimes I can, but a lot of the time, I can't, and it hurts so goddamn bad!" Crying—don't care. "It makes me feel like I'm shit, like I'm nothing, like I'm not good enough for you, like as soon as you had her, you didn't care about me anymore, that you didn't want me—"

"Alyx, grow up."

"'Grow up?' You for-real broke my heart! Was it cuz I wouldn't screw you like a whore, like she would? Is that why you didn't love me?"

"I'm not the one who wasn't in love."

"You bastard!" He's ready for me this time, catching my fists as I swing at him. I kick at him, but he sidesteps, I try yanking my arms free, but he doesn't let go.

"I wish I never met you!" I tell him, struggling to get loose. "You and your stupid 'Magic' game and your geeky friends and your ditz mother and your bitchy sister! I wish I'd never chased after you when Freydis kicked your ass and dragged you on that train! I wish I'd just let her keep you! I wish that slut had bit your dick off after she was finished with it! I hate your guts, you crippled piece of shit!"

"Alyx, we are over."

"Ya think, asshole? Let go of me!"

"I'm sorry it—"

"No, you're not!" I spit in his eyes. Sam reaches up to wipe his face and I rip myself away, stumbling backward, grasping for something. "Not yet you aren't! But you're goddamn gonna be!"

"Alyx," Paddoch says, softly. "That's enough."

I stop, stand up. I'm pointing my knife at Sam.

Track 33. Master of Puppets

I look at the knife. Didn't even register with me that I'd plucked it off the chair.

Shit. Holy shit. Almost lost it there, like I did in Ms. Jung's class, and if I had….

Paddoch's right. Gotta get a hold of myself, get it back together. Stop. Think. This is all wrong.

I drop the knife. Can't look at Sam. Murmur, "I don't want to talk to you right now."

"That might be best," Paddoch says. "Sam, why don't you give Alyx a few minutes?"

"Fine." Doesn't look at me. Starts wandering down to the beach.

Paddoch sips from his water glass. Watches. Waits. Until I finally say:

"I want you to send me back to Kent Island. Now."

"Is that where you lived?"

"Yes."

"It's farther away than you might think."

"How far?"

"Eighteen hundred of your miles, but that's the least of it."

My stomach turns inside out. "What are you talking about?"

He picks up the newspaper from the table next to him, shows me. The BAY TIMES, bottom left corner, front page. Me and Sam's yearbooks photos, dressed for the graduation we never went to. Over our pictures, a headline.

No Answers Ten Years On.

I snatch it from him, skim it. Just a few paragraphs. Talks about the bike—they still think it crashed—about us missing, about us never being found. Says there aren't any leads on what happened to us or where we are.

Says that was ten years ago.

Maybe here, where we are, time passes slower, Mike said to me, back at the motel.

Quote from Sam's mom on what a great kid he was, and how he was going to go to Loyola to study engineering. How hard it's been, because the day before the "accident" with him and me, Cynthia left work at the hospital in Richmond and nobody ever saw her again. The article says I'd been living with my uncle, but he'd never talked to the media about what happened.

The last line says that Uncle Tony died four and a half years after we vanished.

No.

No.

Crumple the paper, press it against my chest. Goddamn it, no.

I can't take this.

I can't.

Lean over, hands on my knees, sobbing, whispering, "No, no, no." Me and Sam over. Uncle Tony dead. I didn't have much before, but now it's gone.

All of it gone.

Slow footsteps, coming closer. Sam, hands in his pockets. He stops a little ways from me. Doesn't say anything.

I straighten, show him the newspaper. "Cynthia—"

"Yeah."

"—and your mom, and my uncle."

"I read it."

I want to go to him and hold him, I want him to hold me and not let go, but we both just stay where we are.

"Are you going back home?" I ask.

Shakes his head.

"Why not?"

"There's no reason to."

"Yes, there is. Your mom loves you. She lost Cynthia, and she must think she's lost you, too. She needs to know you're okay."

"It's too late. All that's over with. What am I supposed to do, just walk in to my house, say, 'Hi, mom,' and give her a big hug? Tell her I'm glad to be back?"

"Yeah. Why not?"

"Everything we had is dead. Nothing's the way it was before. Not me, not you."

You think that you won't come out of this a different person? Mike asked me. *That he won't, either? That none of what you've been through is going to change anything between you?*

I drop the newspaper on the grass. "What are you going to do?"

"I don't know. I'll figure it out."

"What about you and me? You just gonna walk away from us, too?"

"Pretty much."

"And that's just it? What am I supposed to do without you?"

"You can do whatever you want."

"Why are you like this, when you're the one who shit all over me?"

"Yeah, it's always about poor you, isn't it? It's always Alyx and her crappy childhood, and her 'screw-you' attitude, and her head full of bad chemicals. You dye your hair, and ride a motorcycle, and listen to heavy metal, and pretend you're a badass, but it's just an act. Really, you're scared shitless because you know nobody wants you, and nobody loves you, and nobody cares about you."

Crying again—still. "Why are you saying this? What did I ever do to you?"

"It's what you *didn't* do, Alyx. You didn't do enough, and you weren't enough. At first, I thought you were, because I didn't know you that well. Even later on, after I started dealing with your drama, I thought that you could be. But when I finally saw just far down your crazy goes, and just how weak and pathetic you are, I decided you weren't worth it."

Me, when he was asking me to Homecoming: *"Why would you want to go with me?"*

Him: *"Because you're cool, and I like you."*

"Sam, no. Don't be this way."

"Alyx, I never want to see you again."

Him, when we sat on the roof of the church: *"You have your uncle, and my mom, and you can have me as long as you want."*

Me: *"You promise?"*

Him: *"I promise."*

"Sam, you said we'd always be together, as long as I wanted, and I want you Sam, even after everything that's happened. Don't do this to me. Please, I'm begging you. Don't do this to us." Crying—it all comes bursting out as I stumble toward him, reach for him, try to pull us close, try to hold him and not let go, not lose him. "Please, don't leave me. Please. I'm sorry. I'm sorry I wasn't good to you. I'm sorry I only ever thought about me and my problems, and I was always in my own head, and I'm sorry for all the mean things I told you, and everything I put you through—I know it wasn't easy being with me. I'm sorry I didn't love you, but I love you now. I'm not mad at you anymore, I don't want to be that way—I won't be that way ever again, I swear. Please believe me. I love you. I do. Please just lis—"

He backs away, trying to shrug me off, I yank on him. "Sam, don't, just stay with me and—"

"Get off me, Alyx."

"—we'll make everything okay—"

"I said, get off me!"

"—we'll go home and—"

He slaps me, hard, across the face. It doesn't even hurt that much—my dad used to hit me, punch me, a lot harder—but it's just...it's....

Any man who hits a girl is trash. That's what he said. Back then.

It's like I don't even know who he is anymore.

Sink to my knees, bury my face in my hands, sobbing. Sam just stands there. God. Oh, God. This can't be happening. It can't. He's the only boy, the only person besides Uncle Tony, who gave a shit about me. And now it's all gone, not just cuz of him and Freydis, but also cuz of me and pulling the knife on him and when I went off on him at the mall, and not going to his Spring Concert, and not telling him I loved him, even though I did, and I do, but I never wanted to admit it, never wanted to say it.

We had something good, but I killed it, and he killed it. Now, we're just done. Oh, God. How did we get from me saying I'd go with him to Homecoming, to here and now, with us hitting each other and saying things we can't ever un-say?

This can't be happening.

This can't be real.

It just can't.

"Alyx," Paddoch says, "my poor girl."

I'd almost forgotten he was there, just a few feet away. Crying, I crawl on my knees to him, put my head on his lap, and he strokes my hair. It doesn't matter that I don't really know him, doesn't matter that he's so ugly. I just need someone, anyone, right now to make me feel like I'm not alone, that I'm not lost, that all those horrible things I'd gone through all that time and all the way here weren't for nothing. I want it to be Sam here, reassuring me, but it's not. It can't be.

I look up at Paddoch. He's totally different.

Mid-twenties, longish blond hair combed straight back. Trimmed moustache and beard. Nose is a little big, but straight. Cornflower blue eyes—same shade as mine. Regular clothes: long-sleeved button shirt, jacket, slacks, dress shoes. He's not hot, or drop-dead sexy, but...handsome. Like an old-time movie star, back when movies were only in black and white.

"Paddoch, what—?"

Holds up his hand. "What you saw before is not what I am, and it would take too long to explain; maybe later. For right now, I'm sorry for all the pretense, but it was necessary. Please, believe me."

Believe? How can I believe him or anything, when nothing makes sense? Mike's dead, Uncle Tony's dead, Sam hates me, and Paddoch's...I don't know what he is. I don't know what's happening to me. I just want all this hurt to go away. I want....

"I want to go home," I tell him.

"Of course you do. But where's 'home' for you, Alyx?"

"I...." I don't know. Not with my mom: we never liked each other. Not with my dad: he doesn't care about me. Uncle Tony's gone, and anyway, I wasn't his daughter, just his little brother's ugly, headcase *honhyeol* that he felt sorry for.

"Nowhere, I'm guessing," Paddoch says. "You have nothing, and now"—looks at Sam—"you have no one. But there's another way. I helped Sam, and I can help you."

I pull away from him, get on my feet. Wipe my eyes with my grimy sleeve. "Why would you do anything for me?"

"Because I've felt what you feel now: betrayal, rejection, sorrow, anger, agony, loss—devastating loss. You're alone and terrified, and the worst part is that you can't even take solace in yourself, because none of what you ever did or said or even intended has kept this from happening to you. The world you've known has come to a sudden, horrible end, and you're powerless to do anything but watch it die."

Hang my head. I don't—can't—answer. Everything in me—everything I feel and think—is just like he said.

"I can make you better," he tells me. "I can take away the pain that Sam and everyone else gave you. I can make you strong, resilient—you'll become whatever you want. And no one will ever hurt you again."

"How would you do that?"

"The easiest way to say it would be, '*galdr*.'"

"And you'd just do this?"

"Yes."

"And what would you want from me?"

"Nothing."

"Nothing?"

"I'd want nothing. But if you'd give it to me, I'd have your help from time to time."

"What sort of help?"

"Do you remember when I told you that Freydis had hurt me?"

Back at the library, before we did the thing with the marble. "Yeah. It never healed. That's what you said."

He nods.

"So, you fixed Sam, you can fix me, but not yourself?"

"The very epitome of irony, isn't it? What's even more ironic is that up until now, I relied on Freydis to bring me what I need to keep going. It's not hyperbole to say that I trusted her with my life. I'm hoping I can trust you—"

Mike: *You can't trust anything.*

"—and that you'll take care of me, like I will of you."

Take care of. Like a hospital. "Back there, before I got here, there was a...woman. With a baby—lots of babies—but they were all...twisted, and she said the baby was for you, to...feed. And that I was Freydis."

"Those were only nightmares come to a flicker of life. *Galdr* to scare off creatures that might wander here from the waste land."

It all seemed real enough, more than just nightmares, but I guess.... Doesn't matter. What *does* matter anymore? I dunno.

Tearing up again. I should hate Sam. I should want him dead. But I don't. I can't believe it's all gone, forever. That Sam's going to be gone. But then, he already is, isn't he? Because the boy standing there, scowling at me, isn't the one I met in the record shop.

No. No, he's not.

And there's a way to make sure.

"The magic that keeps the monsters from coming here," I say to Paddoch. "Does it always work?"

"Yes."

"Are you sure?"

"Yes. Why?"

Point at Sam. "Because that's not him."

Sam gives me this look like I'm retarded.

Paddoch says, "Alyx, I know you're upset—"

"It's someone or some *thing* that looks and sounds like him, but it's not."

"Oh, for God's sake..." Sam goes.

"Say the alphabet backwards," I tell him.

"Huh?"

"Say the alphabet, but start with 'z,' and work your way to 'a.'"

"No."

"You won't do it, because you can't."

"What do you mean, 'I can't?'"

"You can't, cuz you don't know the alphabet frontwards, much less backwards. Prove me wrong."

"Fine," Sam says. "Z, Y, X, W, V, U, T, S, R, Q, P—that good enough for you?"

"No." I wander toward Paddoch. "Keep going."

"O, N, M, L, K, J." He's having no problem with this. "Are you done screwing around—"

"It was you who screwed around."

"You're hilarious."

"Whatever. Keep going." I'm standing next to Paddoch now.

"I, H, G, F, E, D, C, B, A. Happy?"

"Sing the 'Itsy Bitsy Spider' song."

Paddoch looks at me, raises his eyebrows.

"No," Sam says.

"Why not?" I ask. "You know why? Cuz you don't know it."

"Yes, I do."

"Then sing it."

"I don't like to sing."

I thought he might say that.

Alyx, where you're going, Tyra told me, *nothing's real.*

Stay cool. I slip behind Paddoch, rest both hands on the back of his chair. Sam's right in front of us. "Okay, fine, don't sing it. Just tell me this: when I went to the Ravens game with you and your mom and Cynthia, what color was the Big Ben jersey I borrowed from you?"

Sam looks at me like I'm crazy. Which I am. "Black," he says. "Like ravens are."

"Yeah." I smile. "Yeah, it was black."

I yank on the chair, tip it over, slamming the back of Paddoch's head to the ground, and I jump him, stomp his head, his neck, his throat, snatch the bowl—fruit goes everywhere—from the table, smash him in the face and again and on the second hit the bowl breaks and all I'm holding is a jagged edge and I keep decking him, slashing him, bloody nose and lips and right over his eyes. He's been playing me, trying to trick me, trying to get me to say and do things I didn't want to, cuz *he's* the monster, whether he's really Paddoch or not, and now I'm gonna kill this—

"Alyx! Alyx!"

Snap my head around. The fake Sam's shimmering, rippling, vanishing. But down by the shore, where the boat was, it's Sam.

For-real Sam.

Track 34. Too Late for Love

The ground isn't grass anymore, it's broken gray rock with pale white light seeping up from the cracks. I'm somewhere shadowy and cold. The sun, the sky, the sea, the birds, all gone. Was all of that an illusion, too? Doesn't matter.

Sam.

He's wearing the clothes he had on when that crazy bitch Freydis jumped us, and they're dirty and torn, like mine. His left arm's by his side, like usual, and his left ankle is doing that bending thing it does. He doesn't look older, he doesn't look taller, he's pale and thin. Gray snakeskin ribbons made of smoke curling, wrapping, writhing around his legs and knees, wrists and elbows, shoulders and neck and face, all of them snaking back to this big rock that was where the boat was.

"SAM!" I get up, run to him, catch him as the ribbons unravel, vanish. He sags to the ground, and I go with him. "Sam oh my God Sam it's you it's really you I knew it I knew it wasn't real I knew you wouldn't be like that with me I love you I swear I do!"

His eyes are bloodshot and dark underneath them, like he hasn't slept in forever. Smiles weakly. "Back of...." A hoarse whisper: he must of used all his voice yelling to me. "Back of the line is that way, *chica*."

"Don't make me laugh and cry at the same time." Fighting to not do either. "That's not fair, goddamn it. Sam, oh Sam, I got you, I got you, I won't let go, I won't leave you."

"Alyx, I didn't do whatever hurt you. I wouldn't. I didn't say any of those things. I didn't...touch her, or anyone else. I didn't hit you just then. He...."

"It's okay. It's okay. None of that matters."

"He…"—his hand quivers as he points past me—"…it was him…."

Behind the toppled-over table—now just scraps of plain wood nailed here, and there all rickety—Paddoch struggles to get to his hands and knees. Everything's changed, but he's still got blond hair, blue eyes, an old-time movie star. He crawls to the tree, slumps against it. Moans, eyes glazed, head drooping, face bleeding.

The chairs nearby are junky, rusted black metal, not clean, white wood. Laying on the stony ground next to him, there's a bashed-up tin cup instead of the glass he was drinking from, what's left of the bowl is a grimy yellow pot, and there's no spilled fruit, just hunks of slimy raw meat that smell horrible and have wormy things squiggling all over them.

He dabs the back of his head—more blood. He's woozy, sways. "That's…my girl," he says, smiling faintly.

"She's not your girl," Sam tells him. Leans on me as I help him up.

I look around. We're in a cave wider and deeper than the stadium where the Ravens play. Instead of the ocean being gray-blue water, it's that silver chrome goo that doesn't move, the same stuff as in the river. The tree that Paddoch was sitting under's made of black iron, with metal branches drooping almost all the way to the ground, and leaves made of broken glass. It's a lot bigger than it was before, as tall and thick as one of those sequoias out in California that my mom and I went to see once, when we lived there.

I get my knife from where I dropped it, stomp over to Paddoch. Stand over him, pointing it. "Where are we?"

He starts to shake his head, thinks better of it. Mutters, "Where we've always been."

"Which is *what?*"

"This wasted land. My kingdom."

"Your 'kingdom?' What the hell, Paddoch?"

"That's not his name," Sam says, stronger now. He kneels behind him, yanks him away from the tree, wraps his good arm around Paddoch's neck. "Freydis told me who he really is. He's Ōth."

You have *got* to be kidding me. I crouch, grab the front of his shirt, growl, "Where's Paddoch?"

"There is no…'Paddoch,'" he—Ōth, think of him as Ōth—admits. "There never was."

"There was only you," I realize.

"There was only me," he says, "trying to…find…you."

"What do you want?"

"Many…things," he says. "At first…I wanted to know…more about this boy…whom Freydis had snatched…and tried to hide…from me. Then…I wanted to know…who was this girl following him…and why. Then, Alyx…once I knew more…about you, I wanted you…to come here."

"Where's 'here?'" I ask.

"Under the…*sigiriya*."

The *say-jair-i-yah*? "The big flat rock?"

He nods. Winces. Yeah, I'll bet that hurts, asshole.

"Is all this," I ask, waving the knife around, "real?"

"Yes and no."

I jam the knife under his chin; Sam tightens his grip. "Don't tell me 'yes and no.' No more games, no more bullshit, no more illusions and puppet shows."

"You're…surprisingly clever. How did you…see through it?"

"Mike said that half of being smart is paying attention to details, and you got some of them wrong. You had the fake-Sam say that he doesn't like to sing, to cover up that you don't know the Itsy-Bitsy Spider song, but Sam actually sings in his church choir."

Ōth grunts. Don't know what that's supposed to mean. Don't care.

"And you don't know shit about football," I tell him. "Big Ben doesn't play for the Ravens, he's with the Steelers, and Sam hates them. But he likes Ray Lewis. That's whose jersey I wore."

Sam nods. "Fact."

"So, tell me: is all this real, or not?"

"Everything around us…is real."

"And the hospital?"

"Real."

"And was Mike?"

"Yes."

"Is he really dead?"

"Yes."

"And was he right about that dream I had with Sam and Freydis in the motel room?"

Ōth doesn't say anything.

"Was it real? Was it?"

Nothing. I grab the back of his head, cock my arm like I'm gonna shank him right in the face. Which I might not. "Answer me!"

"No, it wasn't," he says.

"So, what's the deal with you trying to trick me into giving up Sam?"

"Alyx, if you help me—"

"I'm not helping you with shit." Keep the knife by his face. "You said you were going to send us home."

"And I will." Opens his palm. The black-and-gray marble from before.

"Time out," Sam says. "What's that?"

"It's magic," I tell him. "You hold this, think about where you want to go, and it, like, takes you there. You and whoever's with you."

"Freydis did that with me once, after we left the train, on our way here," Sam says. "It was awful."

Turn back to Ōth. "So, how does it work?"

"I'll teach you the ruling rune."

"Like a 'magic word?'" I ask.

He nods. "Something like that. It's—."

"And I can totally believe you, cuz you don't lie about stuff, like making yourself look all messed up, or calling yourself 'Paddoch,' or pretending to talk funny, or that you're a 'king' of anything."

"Believe this: I am the king of this land. I'm bound to it, and it's bound to me."

"I don't even care what that means. Right now, all I care about is how I'd know if you're actually gonna send us home and not somewhere else. Like, what if, just to be a dick, you zapped us to the other end of this sucktastic desert, or to the South Pole, or to—I don't know—Mars?"

"Why would I do something so hurtful?"

Lean in closer, the knife a couple inches from his right eye. "Are you seriously asking me that, after what you let me think about Sam and your witchy slut?"

"Alyx…" Sam goes. "Easy. Be the better person."

"I don't wanna be the 'better person.'"

"I want you to."

For a second, just one, maybe two, I think about flicking my wrist and ending Ōth's eye. Instead, I slip the photo out of my back pocket, show him. "You're gonna send us home. But first, you're gonna give us Jeremy."

"I don't know where he is."

"Don't you goddamn lie to me. You get him from wherever your psycho attack-bitch stashed him."

He looks up. I do, too. Just the iron tree, towering over us, only its lowest branches in sight.

"What?" I ask him, but right away, I hear it. Glass leaves clinking, metal branches swaying, creaking like those mechanical cranes they use in construction. Must be all kinds of windy up there, but I don't feel—

Barely juke out of the way of something spinning, falling from the tree. It hits the rocky ground right next to me—*dhkk*—bounces—*dhkk*—tumbles end over end—*dhkkdhkkdhkk*—rolls—*khkhkhkhkh*—stops. A bone, like a turkey leg, makes me think of Thanksgiving and Sam's house and watching the game with his family and Cynthia asking me if we'd done it yet and—

No, not a turkey leg. Same size, but not.

Another bone falls. Another. More. And more. Bones, none of them bigger than the first, raining out of the tree. Leg bones. Arm bones. Back bones. Bits of fingers. Bits of toes. A tiny jaw. Sam flattens himself against the trunk. I keep looking up, hand shielding my face. Ōth sits where he is, staring straight ahead. Something—a pebble?—hits me in the eye, I wince, put my head down, rub it out with my finger, look at it.

Not a pebble. A tooth. A small, square tooth.

A baby tooth.

Then a bundle of dirty carboard and flattened plastic and Styrofoam, all wrapped together in twine and tape, falls, breaks open like an egg, something squishy and rancid slops out of it onto the stone. It's a basket, like the one on the train, like the one in the room with the tall scary lady with no face, with the mutant babies hanging off her, and I don't wanna look but I do and the rotting thing that's spilled out of it oh my God oh my God no no no that's that's I can't—

Another basket falls. Another. Ōth looks at me.

"I'm sure he's here somewhere."

TRACK 35. GOD OF THUNDER

A girl shrieking as she crumples to her knees, sprinkles of scraps and flakes and bits of bone and what else she doesn't, can't think about, still falling from the tree. She screams and screams and she won't, can't stop—and then I realize that the girl is me.

Ōth gets to his feet, blood gushing down his leg, staining his pants. He pries Sam off him, tosses him about ten yards, like he doesn't weigh more than a pillow, smashing Sam onto the rocky ground by the shore of the silvery sea.

That snaps me out of it. "Sam!" Mike's flare gun-thing is my backpack, a few yards away; I lunge for it. Ōth snags my jacket's collar, flips me over, my pack goes flying, he slams me to the cave floor—ow ow ow ow pain's so bad I can't breathe can't Jesus oh Jesus. Gasping. Wheezing.

Ōth, standing over me. He crouches, grabs my hair—*shit* that hurts—yanks my face closer to his. Tiny twinkly lights at the edge of my eyes.

"You are a remarkably difficult young lady," he says, "resistant—perhaps to a fault—to persuasion. I'm glad I had the foresight to not have killed Sam yet."

"Kiss my—AUUUGGH!" He pulls me up by the hair as he stands. I'm wobbly, everything's spinning, but I stay on my feet. He leads me, stumbling, to Sam, shoves me to the ground beside him. Sam's face is bleeding, his nose broken, his mouth bloody: he must have hit pretty hard, maybe even got knocked out for a second or two, like I was when Freydis dropped the bike on me. Slowly, he rolls over, tries to push himself up to his hands and knees. Ōth kicks his arms out from under him, and Sam lands on his face again.

"I'm going to hang one of you," Ōth says, matter-of-factly—

like he's telling us what he'll do next weekend—"from the tree there." Points over his shoulder. "If it's you, Sam, you die. If it's you, Alyx, you both live."

"What…?" I ask. "That doesn't even make sense."

"It will. Whom do I hang, Alyx? You decide."

"You're not going to hang anybody," Sam says, trying again to get back up. Ōth stomps on his back, crushing him down.

"Stop!" I try kicking him, but he steps out of the way. "You said we could go back!"

"Say you'll stay with me, Alyx, and I'll send Sam home."

"Forget it." Sam, still trying to get up. Ōth backhands him across the face, sprawling him out again.

"STOP IT! STOP!" I jump to my feet—the cave spins—Ōth grabs me by the throat, holds me at arm's length. Punch and kick, can't reach him. Thrash, try to get free, but he's like a gorilla. My knife—where is it?

"So, should I hang Sam?"

"NO!"

"All right, you, then. Good girl."

He drags me to the tree, and I try not to listen, not to feel our steps crunching bones underfoot. Don't think about it, just keep it together for them, for Jeremy, for Sam. We're under the tree, and I glance down. There, by my feet, is my knife, where I dropped it when…when *they* fell out of the branches.

Long, black, metal snakes—no, not snakes, vines—wriggle down from the tree, wrap themselves round my arms, my belly, between my legs, my ankles. From the vines, skinny, stringy needles, dozens, hundreds of them, squirming through my socks, my jeans, my shirt, slipping, stinging, stabbing me dozens, hundreds of places, and I scream again. Ōth lets go of me, but the vines have me tight. I can't hardly breathe, much less move.

He picks up the knife, looks over at Sam, struggling again to get up.

Shake my head to keep the tears in. "Please, don't hurt him." Can't let us end like this, can't let him die. Have to save him. Have to. "Listen, I'll do whatever you want, just let him go."

"Alyx!" Sam calls. "Don't say that. Don't even think about it."

"No, please do think about it," Ōth says.

Sam, teetering, but on his feet. "We don't need him. We'll kill this asshole, and get out of here, and then we'll figure out some way to get back."

"Or maybe we won't," I tell him.

"What are you saying?" he asks.

"If I don't do this, maybe neither of us goes home. If I do, then at least you get to. Your mom needs you. Nobody needs me."

"Your uncle does, and I do, too."

"No, you don't. You're honor roll and NHS and college. You're gonna get a six-figure job, and someone prettier and smarter than me—someone not all screwed up—and you'll have kids, and life's gonna be perfect for you."

"How is everything with me going to be 'perfect,' knowing that the girl I love is stuck here with…whatever he is?"

"I'm a king and a god," Ōth replies, turning to him. Drops the knife. "Yet, I'm as human as you are. Perhaps more."

"Yeah, right," Sam snarls, lurching a few steps toward us. He's not going to quit until Ōth kills him. He nearly killed Mike, would have killed him if I hadn't stopped him. With the gun.

The gun.

"Sam, don't!" I yell. "He's too strong. Don't do this! I'm not worth it! Let him have me. If you don't, he'll kill you."

"Alyx—"

"I can't have that happen. I've gone through too much to watch you die. Just take the stuff from my pack, and go."

He wrinkles his brow. "Take it!" C'mon, Sam: you're smart. Figure it out. "I'm not gonna need it." Look at Ōth. "Am I?"

"No," he says, turning to me.

Gotta keep his attention on me. "Whatever you're going to do, do it now, before I change my mind."

"I've been patient with you because I like and admire you, Alyx, but it doesn't matter if you change your mind. You're mine, and you've been mine since you came to the 'hospital.' Now, put out your hand."

Wanna shout in his face that I am *not* his, but I gotta play along, gotta give Sam some time. As I stick out my left, I glance past Ōth. Sam's backed away, and he's crouched by my pack. Without taking his eyes off me, he's rummaging around in there.

Ōth grabs my wrist, wrenches it over, hard.

"Hey! What the hell?" I try to pull away, but he clutches my hand, holds it still while the iron vine or cable or whatever it is that's wrapped around my arm winds farther down.

"What is that? What's it doing?"

It twitches, and two thin needles slide out. They drip silver goo, just like the stuff in the ocean. The vine coils around my wrist, squeezes, tightens, slips the needles into me.

"Stop stop stop that hurts! No! Ow! No, please!"

It jerks me fifteen feet—maybe more, I can't tell—off the ground, dangles me, twisting, by my wrist, needles ripping from my skin and jamming back into me whenever I move. My shoulder feels like it's stretching more than it can go, like my arm's gonna come out of the socket, like my skin and muscles are shredding, like my freaking arm's gonna tear right off, and I'm gonna fall and break my back.

"Let me go! Make it stop! Please! It hurts so bad!"

"Freydis hung there for nine nights, pierced like you are. Then I brought her down, and etched into her the runes, the secrets, she wanted."

My wrist is so cold it's searing, the veins turning from blue to silver. "You made her into that *thing?*"

"We made each other what we are."

This Wasted Land

Whispered crying, sobbing, screaming, wailing all around. Beside me, above me, the leaves on the tree are jagged shards of mirror glass, but the faces in them aren't mine, they're babies, toddlers. Twisted mouths, misshaped noses, ears, chins. Eyes that don't know what they see, or don't see at all.

Thousands.

"They...." Hard to make myself say it. "Kids. She stole little kids for you."

"Only the unwanted."

"Tell that to Mike."

Scoffs. "Mike and his sheep-witted son."

"Don't talk shit about him!" Sam's found the flare-gun thing. Gotta make sure Ōth doesn't notice, but it's getting tough to breathe. Shoulder, neck, back spasming. Hurts so bad. That silver goo, seeping down my arm, inside me. Silver. What's it doing to me?

The tall, creepy woman in the hospital: *Freydis you to be.*

"You're turning me...into her?"

"Better than her. Fiercer, more ruthless. You know what it's like to be alone, don't you, Alyx?"

Like not feeling part of anyone or anything? Not fitting in? Thinking that when I try to talk to people, they don't get me? And they don't even wanna get me? "Yeah....Yeah, I do...."

"So do I. And you have hurt that won't heal. In those things, we're very alike."

Sam's broken open the gun. Loading a shot into it.

"Not gonna...take any babies...."

"You'll do that, and more. Eagerly."

Shake my head. "Kill myself...first...."

The needles in my arms, legs, everywhere sink deeper into me; I grind my teeth, squinch shut my eyes, can't keep down a long, low *uugggghh*. It hurts it hurts it Christ pain pain ow....

Behind him, Sam rising, aiming the gun. In the movies and on TV, this is the part where the good guy tells the bad guy to put his hands up and step away from the girl, to freeze and stay right where he is while the good guy and the girl get away.

Don't say anything, Sam. Just shoot. Even though you'll kill me, too. Even though I hadn't told you that. But at least you'll get away.

I shut my eyes. Do it, Sam.

"If you kill me," Ōth tells him, "you'll never go home."

I open my eyes. Ōth, standing, facing me—and yet, a double of him, connected to Ōth by their heads, their backs, their arms and legs, is stalking toward Sam, stretching apart like you could do with your bubble gum. Sam's eyes, getting huge. The fingers on the double's hands lengthen, sprout claws, then flip backwards, so they're pointed up even though its palms are down. Its face splits down the middle, making another pair of eyes and jaws, side by side. Mouths gape, ribbons of skin studded and tipped with hooks and barbs lashing from them.

I scream, "Sam, shoot!"

The Ōth in front of me—blond and handsome still—smirks.

Sam's bad arm steadies the gun.

"Shoot!"

TTMMMMHHHHHH

No enormous fireball, just a single shot hitting the demon-double right in the chest—and then both Ōths jitter, shudder as blood squirts from dozens, hundreds of tiny holes from their torsos and bellies. A roaring and screeching—it can't be the wind, cuz no air's moving—fills the cave, echoing off the walls, too loud even to hear myself gasping, sucking air through my teeth as the tree shivers, vines writhe, the needles rip their way out of me. I crash to the stone floor of the cave, feel something pop, my ankle oh my God oh my God holy shit hurts hurts did I break it did I break my goddamn ankle burns burns burns burns *burns!*

Never mind! Get up! Get up!

This Wasted Land

Plant my good leg under me, shove myself up with my arms, balance, hopping, on one foot. The tree's swaying like it's caught in a hurricane, vines flailing. The double smushes back into Ōth, blood still leaking out of him—them?—and he flops to the ground, rippling, arching his back, screaming, but the only sound is the wail that already fills the world.

The ground rumbles, shakes, bucks, almost knocks me and Sam over. The hell is happening?

I am the king of this land. I'm bound to it, and it's bound to me.

So, does what hurts him, hurts the waste land, too? Why would that be?

Doesn't matter. I hobble to Sam as he pops open the gun, dumps the casing of the bullet or the shot or whatever it was. Must have been a different type of ammo, or else this whole place would be on fire. Throw my arms around him and he pulls me close, but he's still watching Ōth as he squirms. Sam presses his cheek against mine, and I feel more than I hear him say, *I got you. I got you. Hold on.*

Then it's dead quiet again except for Ōth panting. His clothes are shredded, but he's quit bleeding, like he did when that thing went after him in the library.

"Send us back," Sam tells him. "Right now." Slips the last shot into the gun.

"She stays," Ōth says, slowly climbing to his feet. "I hang her, make her mine. I fill this lovely sweetmeat with myself, and you watch. She peels your skin off and eats it; you watch that, too. Then I hang *you* from the tree, like what should have happened after your whore mother slid you out. That's what's going to happen *right now.*"

"What the actual hell is wrong with you?" I hiss.

He frowns. "You already know that." The next time he says something, it's my voice, what I said before: "Shut up! You can't even talk right, you twisted, ugly-ass freak!"

I shake my head. "You're not a freak. I am. Sam is. You…you're a monster, even when you don't look like one."

He scowls. "I'm as human as you are."

"No, you're not. You never were. That's why Freydis didn't love you. When you figured that out, it broke you. Didn't it?"

He points to the tree. "The first thing I'll do—"

"You're not doing shit to her," Sam says, pointing the gun again. "Give us the talisman and tell us how to use it."

The gray-and-black marble appears in Ōth's hand, like he's a stage magician.

"Roll it over here," Sam says. "Last chance."

He pitches it over his shoulder, into the dark. It goes *pldd* into the sea of silver.

No! No! No no no no!

The air shimmers and Ōth the old-time movie star is gone, but instead of it being the Paddoch who I thought was my friend, it's a swelling pulsing sickly-white carcass-heap, dripping filthy muddy-brown, oozing oily yellow-white. A steady trickle of thick, gooey, dark-red, almost black blood, soggy globs suspended in it, puddles at the useless, blubbery nubs that are its legs. Still it rises, twice as tall as Ōth was, its arms long, spindly, shaggy, branching out into other, shorter arms and twitching, swollen fingers all the same length. The crusty, warty skin of its belly splits, splinters, and its face—a twisted mush of Ōth's blue eyes and blonde beard, Paddoch's crooked mouth and lumpy chin, Freydis's narrow nose, high forehead and cheekbones—waggles out.

I tell myself to do something, to don't just stand there.

Sam pulls the trigger but nothing happens, and Ōth grabs Sam's whole head, squeezes, and Sam drops the gun and screams again and again.

Do something!

You're only a deformed weakling, Ōth tells Sam, rumbling like thunder a long way off.

Don't let him kill Sam!

I grab the gun, aim, shoot, but it judders, bucking in my hand. Smoke streams from the barrel, the chamber, every seam of it. It's jammed and it's overheating—"OW!"—I drop it.

It's smoking and spinning and skittering on the stones—is it gonna go off? If it does, what happens, will it blow all of us up? What do I do what the hell do I—

Mike: *If that river caught fire, it might kill everything in this area code.*

An incidental scavenging that Freydis thought she could poach for herself, and keep from me.

The only thought I have is that for about the eighth millionth time, I wish I had my gloves. I peel off my jacket, toss it on the gun convulsing on the ground, like I'm trying to catch some small animal.

You were nothing special to her, and you won't be anything special to Alyx, after she has me inside her.

Scoop it up with both hands—SHIT it's hot even through my jacket—throw it into the silver ocean, and weird, ashy snake shapes twist and curl and white smoke billows up as the sludge it is catches fire.

Mike: *You definitely don't want to breathe any of what's burning off.*

Ōth lets go of Sam—just like I wanted him to—and shrinks away from the cloud already filling the cave. Swats at me; I fall more than dive out of the way, smacking face-first on the rocks. Doesn't matter. My knife, it's right here, where Ōth dropped it.

Do you want to die so badly you'd poison yourself?

"Don't wanna live as a monster." I scrabble underneath him, his stench stinging my eyes. Gulp what might be my mouthful of air and hold it. Please, God, just let me save Sam.

I pop the knife's blades. Stab Ōth where he's bleeding, where he's always been bleeding. Stab all the way up until both my hands are inside that wound she made, that never healed, can't ever heal. His blood spatters my arms, my chest, my hair, my face.

His howl is this world's, swallowing me and everything else. Feel myself lose it, let myself lose it, another tsunami washing over and through me, but this time, it's not hurt, not pain, though they drive it, feed it. I yank the knife back, stab again, deeper, blood drenching me.

That's for Mike, you cocksucker!

Again.

That's for Jeremy!

Again.

For Sam!

Again.

For me!

Again. Again. Again.

A stray thought over the raging flood, like a cat watching from the high branch of a tree: When he falls, he'll crush me under him and I'll for-real die.

Another thought, a bird flying from that tree: Doesn't matter.

Again. Again. Again. Again. Again!

Then, black. Only black.

Track 36. Heavy Metal (Takin' a Ride)

Sam draping my arm across his shoulders. "Lean on me," he whispers.

I have my pack and we're hobbling up a narrow, winding path toward a tunnel that I hadn't seen before in the dark. I'm lifting my hurt foot off the ground, hopping along with the other, leaning on Sam. Glance back, nothing but smothering white fumes behind and below us, something within gasping, croaking, babbling, bellowing. Within, but also all round, from nowhere and everywhere.

A dream: *The river's fumes don't smell, but they kill, and before they did, you'd go crazy. For-real, tear-your-fingers-off-and-chew-and-swallow-them-while-your-arms-and-legs-shake-and-you-piss-yourself crazy.*

"Hurry," Sam says, holding me tighter. The rest of the way up the path, then into the tunnel, the cave filling behind us filling up with white smoke. The voices trail off, go still. The air goes thick. Did we kill him?

Sam leads us out of the tunnel, back into the desert. The wind, whimpering. It's flat here. Behind us, the ring of those spiky rocks, and past them, the big, flat-topped mountain: the *sigiriya*, or whatever Ōth called it. Something hulking way up there: the hospital? Can't tell. The ground trembles under us. Overhead, the gray clouds churn.

I can see all that because the sun—low and pale, but there, on our right—has lit up again.

We go farther out, a few hundred yards, until the land ends in jagged edges of weathered, cracking, crumbling rock. A tear in the world so wide, we can't see the other side. So deep, we can't see the bottom.

We stop, me leaning on Sam. "Are you okay?" he asks.

"I...." Am I? I've got blood—already drying, though I don't

know how that can be—all over me. My ankle hurts like a bitch, but the rest of me is kinda numb. Especially inside.

"I can't tell."

I'm staring down into the dark. Just a few feet more, and the world—everything, really—comes to an end. Instead of starving to death, or dying of thirst, or—most likely—being killed by a monster, maybe it'd be better to take his hand and step off. Hold each other all the way down, to whatever's there. Maybe only rock. Maybe nothing: maybe it's like *falling off the table*.

Might be better. Definitely easier.

"Hey," he says, takes my chin, turns my face up, toward him. Snaps me out of it. "Stay with me, okay?"

I nod. "Okay."

"We're going to get out of here."

"Okay. Yeah, okay. I'm good. I'm good. It's just…just for a second, I—" Shake my head.

"Yeah, I could tell that you were starting to lose it. It's all right. Let's rest a minute." His good arm still under me, we kinda ease to the ground, me sticking out my ankle so I don't hurt it any worse than it already is.

He takes my hand. "I love you," he tells me. "Whatever comes next."

"I love you, too. I'm sorry it took me so long to get there." Make myself smile; won't let myself cry, but it's good to feel again. "Whatever comes next."

"As far as that goes, I don't know exactly what we're going to do. But somehow, we'll get back home, and then we'll take you to a hospital, a real one."

"After that, maybe you could ask me to prom."

He shakes his head. "Here we are, in all of…this"—looks around, waves his hand—"and you want to talk about *prom?*"

"It'd be nice to think about something not-horrible for a minute."

"Good point." White smoke billowing out of the tunnel, drifting off with the wind. Other than that, nothing moving. "I wasn't going to ask you, because I didn't think you'd want to go. It's not your thing."

"It's not, but it's yours. Maybe it can be mine, too, if I try. You know, like you said."

He smiles, nods. "Dylan's on the planning committee. He says the theme's 'Bollywood.'"

"I don't even know what that is."

"You'll like it."

"Well, let's go."

"Okay. Soon as we can."

I sigh. "Now we're back to thinking about horrible shit again."

Behind us, the stone knives, and the flat mountain. Right and left, ash desert. In front of us, miles and miles of literally nothing, just gray sky, going on forever, it seems. But something.... Something about this place....

"'The empty at the edge.'" I say. That huge stone with writing all over it, the one sticking out of the ground, where I found Sam's phone. "Something I read. 'Past the fence, past the rock, is the empty.' And here we are." Lean on Sam again, struggle to my feet. Sam gets up, too.

waaahn waaahn

Look around again. Wasn't there before, but is now, near where we came out of the tunnel: train tracks.

waaahn waaahn

Louder, closer, from the left. A ways off—how far, don't know—it's not a house. Smaller, squat, on a concrete slab. An old train station platform.

waaahn waaahn

And a train—*the* train, blowing its horn—is coming. Fast.

"'The empty is the way out,'" I tell him. "We gotta get on that train."

"We don't know where it's going. We don't know where it's going to stop, or if it's ever going to stop. Maybe it's just going to keep running, forever."

waaaahhn

"The train brought us here, and it can take us back."

"Or maybe it can't, maybe it's a one-way thing. Even if it can take us home, we don't know how to drive it. We could wind up anywhere. Or nowhere."

"As long as we get out of here, I don't care. C'mon." Doesn't move: he always thinks about stuff too much. "C'mon!"

We run, my arm over his shoulder again, both of us really more like limping, toward the station. Running, and then I'm breathing hard already—Jesus, I'm so tired, I can't do this, I can't. Lurching, stumbling, hobbling, we go fast as we can, best as we can.

waaaaaaaahhhn

We run, run. Chest burning—doesn't matter—keep going. Not fast enough: run on my bad ankle anyway—SHIT it hurts! Ignore it, keep going.

We're halfway to the station when the train thunders past, horn blaring, wheels *klggklggklggklggklggklggklggklggklggklggklggklggklggklggklgg.* Cars—ten, twenty, fifty, a hundred, hundreds more—behind it, going fast, blurring, gray steel and rust, fast, too fast, and the horn fills this wasted land.

waaaaaaaaahhhn

We're not going to make it to the platform, and we wouldn't have made it even if we had started running when we first saw it. It doesn't matter. Because the train's not stopping.

klggklggklggklggklggklggklggklggklggklggklggklggklgg

Shit. Shit shit shit.

We stagger, totter, manage to stay up, but we can't keep going. Both of us bend over, gasping. The wind from the train tousles our hair. Sam watches the cars flash by, the same look on his face like he had when he kept getting up to fight Ōth.

"The only way..." he pants, "we get on...is if we jump."

"We'd...kill our...selves." I could have died climbing up on this train when I was chasing after it before, when Freydis took Sam. And it wasn't going anywhere near this fast.

"I know...but...what else...are we gonna do?"

What *are* we gonna do? Shit. Think of something. Anything!

waaaaaaaahhhn

Not as loud this time, going away fast.

"If we can't catch...the train," Sam says, "then, maybe there's another way."

"Like what?"

"Freydis teleported me across the desert." He's mostly caught his breath. "So, she must have had one of those marbles—those talismans—that Ōth did, the one he said he was going to give us so we could get out of here." He straightens up; I do, too, still leaning on him. "Did you find it on her?"

I shake my head. "I didn't think to look." I was hardly thinking anything then.

klggklggklggklggklggklggklggklggklggklggklggklggklgg

"If we go back to where you killed her," Sam says, "if we can find her body, she might have it, and then, maybe—"

I shake my head. "If it worked like that, and could bring the two of you here, why was she even on the train?"

klggklggklggklggklggklggklggklggklggklggklggklggklgg

"I don't know," he admits. "I'm just trying to get us home."

Home.

Freydis.

When I killed her.

waaaahhn

Sam, she said, as she was dying. *Home.*

Right after what I thought was a tooth fell out of her mouth.

I reach into my other back pocket, not the one with Jeremy's photo. It's still there; I take it out. The flat, white thing. Same shape but half the size of a piece of gum. Hundreds of tiny runes etched into it. Sam might call it a *talisman,* too. To me, it looks more like a ticket.

"When you were on the train with her, did she say any kinda magic words or whatever to make it stop?"

"I don't remember."

Fat lot of help that is, but I don't say anything, cuz I know he was losing his shit that whole time he she had him on the train.

klggklggklggklggklggklggklggklggklggklggklggklggklggklgg

If I'm gonna do something, I better do it quick, cuz I can see the end of the train now. In a few seconds, it's gonna go past us and be gone.

"C'mon," I tell him, and this time he doesn't argue as we start running—ow ow ow I can't believe how much that hurts!—toward the train.

waaahn waaahn waaaaaahn

The ticket—she used to carry it under her tongue. This is gonna be absolutely God damn gross. Trying—failing—not to think about anything with her putrid mouth being in mine.

I stop running and Sam stops, too, and I stick the flat white thing under my tongue, almost make myself barf, almost spit it out, but I keep it in, then shut my eyes.

It's magic, I told Sam. *You hold this, think about where you want to go, and it, like, takes you there. You and whoever's with you.*

This is stupid. It's not going to work. *I'll teach you the ruling rune,* Ōth said. Except he didn't, cuz he was just lying. And I got no idea

This Wasted Land

what you're supposed to say or do to make this *talisman* work. If it even does.

Stop, I think. Don't know if I'm telling the train that, or me that. Or both. *Just, stop.*

Everything, all at once, goes totally silent. No horn, no wheels on the tracks, nothing. Nothing for a second or two, and then, I hear myself breathe out through my clenched teeth as I try to keep this this gross-as-shit magic ticket-thing, that's making me want to actually gag, under my tongue.

"No way," Sam whispers.

I open my eyes. The train is stopped. Dead-ass stopped, like it didn't move another inch after I told it not to. Which is impossible, cuz nothing can do that. But there it is, with the last car right in front of us.

Every door on the entire damn train slides open—*THWM*—slamming metal echoing off those huge spiky boulders.

We stand there for about ten seconds. Nothing comes off the train, nothing moves. Not even the wind.

The last car is that empty freight one that I climbed up on before. Even with a busted up-ankle and Sam's issues, it's a lot easier to get up there now.

A squeak, not a proper meow. A little black cat, not much more than a kitten. Thin, its tail too long for its body, huge yellow eyes, round irises. Huddled there in the farthest corner from us.

Sam steps in front of me. "Relax," I tell him. Mike's voice in my head again, about not trusting anything, and blah blah blah, and all that. I'm so over this. "I've seen her before. She's nothing horrible. Just a cat."

Slowly—oh my God, everywhere on me hurts like I can't believe—we sit ourselves down on the cold, steel floor, in the corner across from the kitten. She comes over, rubs herself against me—my arms, and chest, and face—and then Sam, and then back to me, and then she curls up in my lap and yawns, tiny needle teeth.

"See? Told you."

In horror movies, this would be the part where the cat turns into a monster and kills the Stupid Bitch and her Geeky Boyfriend, and the screen goes black, and then the credits start going, and you walk out of the theater all shaky and messed up cuz you thought it was all gonna end okay, but no, it all turned to shit right at the last second.

But that doesn't happen.

What actually happens is that when I look up, they're standing there, dozens of them, just outside the train car.

Smooth white heads—for real, all-white, like the lady from the Duran Duran album cover—and where their faces should be is just straight and flat, actually flat, like if you took a block of wood and sliced off part of it with a power saw. Like that.

Instead of eyes and mouths and noses and ears, they got lots of holes, some big, some small, some not so round—more like rips or tears—scattered random all over. Empty black holes—no blood—in ragged, fish-white flesh.

They stand there, dressed in regular clothes: some in shirts and pants and some of them with jackets or ties, some in dresses, some in coveralls or uniforms. They stand there and stare at us, somehow.

Where did they come from? Were they on the train?

The cat sees them, hisses, squirms in my arms to get away, and I fight to hold on to her. Sam tries to get up, but his feet slip out from under him and he thumps back down on the floor. He looks up and over at the latch for the other sliding door, across from the open one.

Black sand starts to trickle out of the holes in the faces of some of them.

Sam trying again to stand up. "Alyx, we gotta get out of here." The cat's clawing me, biting me, trying to get loose. More black sand running, spilling out of more and more of their faces. Long white hands—two fingers and two thumbs on each—slap the steel deck as slowly, the ones at the front start to climb onto the car.

"Alyx!" Sam's up, tugging at the latch, the door starting to slide open, not fast enough. "Alyx, c'mon!"

I can't. Can't even get up. I'm done.

The first of the monsters gets all the way onto the edge of the deck, stands up, sways there for a second, keeps its balance. Sam yanks the door behind us all the way. "Alyx! Get up!"

Sam, she said, as she was dying. *Home.*

And *home* is what I say in my head as I press the cat against me, close my eyes, clench my teeth to keep the ticket-thing under my tongue.

The train jolts forward. I hear the monster fall to the floor, then tumble out of the car and slam into some of the others, knocking them down, and then there's this horrible wet squashing sound as the train's wheels go over some of them. Both of the huge flat doors of the car slide shut—*THWM*—and the train keeps speeding up.

*klgg klgg klggklgg klggklgg klggklggklgg klggklggklgg klggklggklggklgg
klggklggklggklggklggklggklggklggklggklggklggklggklggklggklggklg*

I open my eyes, ease up on the death grip I got going on with the cat, expecting her to jump out of my arms. She stays against me. Sam stumbles over, sinks to the floor next to me. Hangs his head, sighs real deep. He's got nothing left, either. I take his hand.

klggklggklggklggklggklggklggklggklggklggklggklggklg

"Is it happening?" he asks. "Are we really going back?"

Squeeze his hand cuz I don't know what to say. I want to spit out the ticket, but I'm worried that if I do, then the train will stop, or it'll take us somewhere else, or something else shitty will happen. So, I don't.

I lean back against the wall of the car, put my head on his shoulder, shut my eyes again. He rests his head on mine. The wheels are really frickin' loud, but maybe I'll try to sleep. It's not so cold in here anymore, and I have Sam, and the cat's purring on my lap. Sleep, just for a minute. Just—

skeeeeeeeeeeeeeeeeeeeeeeeeeeeeeeeeeeeeeeeeeeeeeeeeeeeeeeeeeeeeeee

377

This insane squealing screech that no-shit stabs my ears, like actually physically hurts, and rips me awake when I only just closed my eyes not even ten seconds ago. If it's another monster, we're completely screwed, but it's only the brakes on the train as it slows, slows...

klggklggklgg klggklggklgg klggklgg klggklgg klgg klgg klgg klgg klgg

...slows...

klgg klgg klgg klgg kl

...stops.

Nothing. And then, a high, faint trilling from outside. Feel like I should know what it is, but I can't quite tell.

"You okay?" Sam whispers.

I ache and I'm stiff, like I haven't moved for hours, which is impossible. But other than that, I'm okay, I guess. My mouth feels like it's full of cotton; I run my tongue around inside, don't feel the ticket-thing. God, I hope I didn't swallow it, cuz that would be beyond disgusting.

Wincing, Sam hauls himself up one more time as the car door in front of us slams open.

THWM

Nothing horrible waiting outside. No spooky people with holes in their faces. No witch with silver eyes. No metal tree with glass leaves and hanging baskets made of trash and bones. No ugly, twisted thing that came out of the dark and wanted to be a god, and to be a king, and to be loved, and wound up none of those.

No gray desert. No wasted land.

It's warm, and green, and that high trilling, I recognize it now. Birds, real birds, not toys that move and talk and watch.

The cat's gone, somehow, vanished in my sleep, like she did in the phone booth. It's okay. Everything's going to be okay.

We're home.

Track 37. Little by Little

"This is Jennifer Franciotti reporting live outside Christiana Hospital in Delaware, where two missing Eastern Shore teenagers—Samuel Patterson and Alexandra Williams—were taken this morning after being found injured but alive an incredible 16 days and approximately 35 miles from where their motorcycle crashed near Centreville, Maryland."
—*from WBAL-TV 11 News broadcast, April 19*

* * *

It was an early Friday morning when two guys—Jimmy, a big, loud dude in his mid-fifties, and Hugh, a little white-haired guy with a Southern accent—out hunting wild turkeys spotted me and Sam. We were stumbling along some railroad tracks—real ones—not far from the woods where the train stopped and let us back into the world before it started up and drove away.

They recognized us from the TV news segment that had run the weekend before, and they called 911 and stayed with us until the EMTs came. We were a quarter mile from Golts, Maryland, near the Delaware line; if we had headed left instead of right when we started walking, we would have gone into the center of town.

The EMTs took us to the ER, and they admitted us for cuts and bruises, exposure to wind and cold, and dehydration and malnourishment. Come to find out, my ankle was sprained, not broken: two weeks in a walking boot, and I'd be okay. All the hundreds of pinholes where the needles from the vines stabbed me—none of those were there. They asked about all the blood on my shirt and all over me, and I just played dumb, like I didn't know where that came from.

They put us in beds next to each other, and they made calls while they ran tests on us. About an hour after we were checked in,

Sam's mom came with Cynthia, who was up from Richmond. The two of them lost their shit when the nurses brought them back to us. I didn't think Cynthia liked me all that much, but she about crushed my damn neck pressing me up against her while their mom bawled her eyes out over me and Sam. I was a little weepy, but was otherwise okay—I didn't have much left after everything with Ōth and Paddoch and Sam and what I thought was Sam—but I melted down when my uncle and my mom got there.

She had flown in two days after the cops had told Uncle Tony that we were missing. He had sent her some money, and she had taken the high-speed train from Daegu to Seoul, and then a 15-hour direct flight on Korean Air to Dulles, outside DC, where Uncle Tony had picked her up. I couldn't believe she did that. It was the first time in my life that I could ever remember her crying.

Me and Sam gave vague answers to the EMTs and the nurses and the doctors about what had happened. Eventually, they decided that we had gone into shock or suffered head injuries or emotional trauma or all of the above, and that we'd wandered away from the "accident," and that only just that morning had we stopped losing our shit and mentally gotten it together to go find help. We didn't say anything to let them think otherwise.

Sherriff Hoffman drove up from Queen Anne's County, and questioned us—gently—about what had happened, but by then, we had our script down pat. He asked us if there had been problems at home, or school, or with each other. He asked why we didn't try calling anyone, and I said my phone broke and Sam's didn't have any battery. He said there were search parties out for us for like, two weeks, and hadn't we seen or heard anyone? At least it wasn't a lie when we told him that no, we hadn't.

He played us back my call to 911, where I was going off about railroad tracks that weren't there, and an old woman who beat us up and snatched Sam onto a train. I pretended like I didn't remember saying any of that, and that I must have had a really bad concussion, cuz I had sounded totally out of my mind. He couldn't argue with that.

We found out later that he had talked to Sam's mom and mine (as best he could; her English isn't good), and Uncle Tony, too. I got the impression that he wasn't entirely sold on our story—that maybe there was something else, like drugs, or running away from home, or even that someone had tried trafficking us—but he didn't push it. We were alive and were going to be okay, and that was good enough.

* * *

After a few hours, the docs transferred us out of the ER and admitted us to the hospital proper for observation. We spent the rest of Friday, all day Saturday, and a good chunk of Sunday morning there, too.

Sam's dad flew in from Chicago, but when the staff told us he had come, Sam said not to let him in.

Hospital food supposedly sucks, but it was so good after the scraps that I'd had here and there during my time in that wasted land. When they weighed me and saw that I was about 96 pounds, I told the nurse that I had been about 103 before, when really I'd been 115. There's no way I could explain that much weight loss if I had only been gone two weeks-and-change, like everyone thought we had, instead of the months it had felt like.

That Friday night, I had my first shower since the motel, and that made me think of Mike and Tyra and those three stoners, and then it hit me that they're dead now, all of them, and I curled up on the floor of the shower and cried. The motel felt like it was a whole other life ago. I guess it was.

On Sunday, Sam's mom and mine and Uncle Tony brought us clothes—we told the hospital staff to pitch what was left of the dirty, torn-up stuff we came in there with—and the five of us (Cynthia had had to go back to Richmond for work) rode to Kent Island in my uncle's big black Yukon. Sam and I sat on the middle bench, holding hands the whole time.

We pulled up to Sam's house to drop them off, and people had left dozens of balloons and stuffed animals by his front door, and there were handwritten posterboard signs on his lawn, saying, WELCOME HOME, SAM! and WE MISSED YOU! and all that. I didn't want to ever let him out of my sight again, but we were going to have dinner together that night, so it was okay.

Nobody had left anything at our place, but that only figures, because it's hard to find, and not well-marked, and my uncle's really private, so hardly anyone on the island knows who he is or where he lives.

When we got inside, Uncle Tony went to his office so me and my mom could talk. I don't know why he bothered shutting the door, cuz we just spoke Korean to each other the whole time, so it's not like he was gonna understand anything. We talked for a long time, about her and me, and her and my dad.

I don't think we're ever going to be close: we're too different. She's real reserved, doesn't usually show a lot of emotions. When she talks, she doesn't say much, and what she does say is real careful, formal even. And me—well, I'm me. But even if we're never going to be friends, I felt a lot better about us after we talked, and I think she did, too.

Then I went upstairs to my room and took a nap, the first decent sleep I'd had in forever, cuz they never let you sleep good at the hospital. When I got up, it was about four thirty. We met Sam and his mom at Kentmorr, a casual seafood place by a marina. My mom and I split a crab pizza, and though she'd never had Maryland crabs before, she really liked it.

There's a little sand beach behind Kentmorr, and after we ate, all of us went there to watch the sun go down over the Bay. Me and Sam took off our shoes—I got out of my walking boot—and held hands and waded in the water, away from the others. The water was cold on our feet and ankles for the little while we were in, but not too bad. We'd been a lot colder for a lot longer.

I leaned in close. "Should we tell them what really happened?"

"No," he said. "They'd think we're crazy, or that we're making it all up."

I took Jeremy's photo out of the back pocket of my jeans, looked at it—and him—again. "But we wouldn't be making it up. This proves it was real."

"It's over. It doesn't matter anymore."

"I don't like keeping it from them. And I don't know if I can keep it to just us. You say it's over, but for me, it's not, not even close. I can't just flip a switch in my head and have everything be all good. Can you?"

He looked down, squeezed my hand. "No, I can't. The whole time I was there, I had weird dreams of you walking across the desert, or being chased by monsters. Scary stuff, more scary when it dawned on me that the dreams were real."

He looked out across the Bay again. "She had me locked in a dark, little room at the far end of that hospital, where she thought no one would find me. Until Ōth did. I didn't see what he did to her, but I could hear her screaming, and even though I hated her, I wished it would stop. But it didn't. Not for a long time.

"Then he came back to the room, and said he was going to go find you and bring you there. And then I was really scared."

"So, it's not over for you, either," I told him.

"No, it isn't. But it's not like we can tell anyone."

"Ms. Custer, at school, says I can tell her anything."

"I don't think Ms. Custer's degree covers witches and monsters. If I was going to tell anyone, it'd be Fr. Paul. Hopefully, he wouldn't think I'd lost my mind."

"You can if you want, but I don't know him. I like Ms. Custer, and I think she likes me."

"Okay, but can you trust her?"

Considered it. Mike used to tell me, *You can't trust anything*, and lots of times, he was right: I couldn't trust what I saw, or thought, or even did. But I guess you can't live your whole life like that. Not even Mike did. If he had, we never would have come close to finding Sam. It took a while, but eventually, he trusted me, and I trusted him.

"Yeah, I think I can."

***

The next day, Monday, me and Sam went over the bridge to Annapolis to get me a new phone; I had given him back his, of course. They have phone stores on the island—there's a Verizon right across from the Dairy Queen—but we didn't want anyone to recognize us. Even so, I think the girl who worked at the store did, especially when I gave her my name. At least she didn't say anything.

When we got back to my uncle's house, I remembered to give Sam Cynthia's phone, to give to her, and he said that she hadn't even mentioned losing it. It wasn't until a really long time later that I told him where I'd found it. It wasn't until a really long time later that he told me the reason why his sister hadn't noticed her phone was gone.

It was cuz the night before we went missing, this baby with all kinds of medical issues just flat out vanished from the ward where Cynthia works, and everybody on duty that night, including Cynthia, was freaking out, until they found some paperwork saying that the baby had died in the night and been taken to be cremated. But nobody at her work knows who made out the report.

That night, I finally got my period, and it hurt a lot. Yay. Welcome back.

The next day, Tuesday, Sam picked me up and we drove to school. Mike had said that maybe time passed different in the waste land, but I didn't really notice that until we pulled into the parking lot. All the same cars were there, all the same kids—nothing had changed for them. Everything had for me.

Sam parked, shut off the car. Looked at me. "You okay?"

"Yeah. No." Monsters had tried to kill me, Freydis almost did, I'd watched Mike die, and Paddoch or Ōth or whoever he was.... I didn't even know where to start with figuring him out. And now, I was supposed to go back to English class? Like none of that had ever happened?

"I don't think I can do this," I said.

He nodded. "I know what you mean."

"What if we just don't? What if we just leave, and never come back?"

"Then, we don't graduate."

"So?"

"Then, I don't go to college."

"Screw college. We could go get our stuff from home, and we could drive somewhere until we run out of gas, and then we could just stay there. Get jobs at 7-Eleven or Eat'n Park, or something. I don't know."

"Then we don't go to prom. And you said you wanted to."

I smiled, just a little. "Yeah, I did, didn't I?"

He opened his door. "C'mon. We're going to be late." Got out.

I didn't move. He walked around to my side, opened the door. Held out his hand.

"I'm a little freaked out, too," he said. "But we can do this."

I took his hand. Followed him in.

If being home was weird, school was a million times more weird. I used to think that everybody stared at me all the time, but that morning, they really did. As me and Sam walked past the gym and the cafeteria, toward the front office, lots of people I don't even know came up to us, up to me, and asked if we were okay, if I was okay. Said they'd been sad when they'd heard about what happened, and they'd worried about us, about me, and how relieved they'd been when they heard we'd been found, and how happy they were now that we're back. That I'm back.

I couldn't think of anything to say except, "I'm all right," and, "Thanks," and, "I'm glad to be home."

We checked in at the front desk, and Shrek, our principal (his real name's Mr. Schrecongost, but everyone calls him "Shrek") came out of his office and hugged us, and I swear to God, one of the ladies who works there started crying. It was like everyone forgot that the last time I was in the office, Ginger Cop had me in zip ties on the floor.

And then it was time to go to class, Sam to AP Bio, me to Modern World History, where Ms. Magin talked about the 1947 war between India and Pakistan, and the ongoing conflict over the Kashmir Valley.

I went through the day like I went through the *tsingy* after Mike died. The next thing I noticed, I was walking out with everyone else, out to the parking lot. To Sam's car, where he was waiting for me.

"How was that?" he asked.

"I…" Got no idea. "Okay, I guess."

"I tried to pay attention, to just get back into it, but I wasn't registering anything."

"Yeah. Me, either."

He drove me back to Uncle Tony's, and he came in with me, and my mom was making *gaeran mari*, rolled egg omelets, for dinner, so Sam stayed.

The four of us sat and ate and talked about nothing much—I translated for my mom a lot—and Jake, my uncle's Rotti, lay under the table right by Sam the whole time, cuz he was slipping him scraps when he thought nobody was looking, and by the end, we were laughing about something—I forget what now—and it was great, the food and just hanging out and everything. It was a nice way to say a proper goodbye to my mom, cuz she was going back to Daegu two days later.

* * *

Intent on settling in Vinland (modern-day Newfoundland), Erickson returned there with his wife Freydis (some accounts list her as his sister), his lieutenant Thorvald, and his advisor Ōth, a practitioner of **seithr***, or Norse rune-magic.*

After skirmishes with the native Beothuk (in his journals, Erickson referred to them as "skraelings," meaning, in the Greenlandic Norse dialect, "savages"), Erickson negotiated a truce, probably through the common practice of marrying off women between the two groups.

The peace does not seem to have lasted more than a few years, and this, combined with the Norsemen's other difficulties in maintaining the colony, persuaded Erickson to abandon his settlements in the New World.
   —*www.en.wikipedia.org/wiki/Leif_Erikson#Discovering_Vinland*

This Wasted Land

* * *

On Wednesday, I brought my old backpack and some stuff along (*Let's play* **Show and Tell**, Mike had said), and me and Sam blew off 1st Period to go see Ms. Custer. We took turns telling her everything. Well, almost everything: I still hadn't told Sam about the creepy Pelican bird toy, and I wasn't gonna, cuz it still freaked me out. When we were done, it was ten minutes into 2nd Period.

She said she wanted to believe us, but she asked us, didn't we think it was more likely that the trauma of the accident had been too much for us, and that it was all in our heads? *Temporary shared psychosis*, she called it. It had happened to other people who were really close and went through something terrible. That none of it was real, that everything had been just hallucinations: the waste land, the monsters, Ōth, Freydis. Even Mike—after all, Sam never even saw him.

I showed her Jeremy's photo, the one Mike kept in his pocket. The one I took when he died. That didn't convince her, so I took out the book with the leather cover, the kid's book in the strange Spanish dialect. With the drawings of the little flying lizard shooting lightning bolts at the six-legged flying snake that's breathing laser beams back at it. That, and the one of the naked woman with the coyote's head, where's she's eating a baby. And then I told her to look at the front of the book, where it said it was published in 1909. In Cuidad de Agustin, in the Empire of Ysparria.

She asked what that was, so I said she should google *Ysparria*, and she did. Except there is no such place. Not in this reality, anyway.

For a while, she didn't say anything. Then she told us that she's had students tell her all kinds of bad shit—their parents were beating them, or their cousin was molesting them, or, like, they were cutting themselves—and in those cases, she had to, by law, file a report with the principal or the cops or a doctor or all of them. And because what we had told her was so messed up and not-okay, because going through that had so…*damaged* us, she felt like she had to report it. But she couldn't. Cuz who would believe any of it?

Then Sam asked her if *she* believed it. She said she did. And that we should come back tomorrow. And every day until graduation. And any day over the summer, if we wanted to.

* * *

Despite what I had said, I hadn't really wanted to go to prom. Too much hassle, too princessy, too many people, too expensive. But Sam wanted to, and my Uncle Tony said I should.

"Some things, you only get one shot at," he told me. "If you go and you don't like it, then it's just one bad evening. Won't be the first you've had, won't be the last. If you go and you like it, then you'll look back on it for the rest of your life. But if you don't go, you'll never find out how it would have been. And someday, you'll wish you had."

So, I told Sam I would, and his mom took me around to all the consignment stores on the island, because I didn't want anything too fancy. Or slutty, Sam's mom insisted. She told me that when Cynthia went, a lot of the girls were dressed like they weren't *saving anything for marriage,* as she put it.

It took a while, but we found a floor-length gown with a wine-colored skirt that had a bow at the waist. The top was sleeveless and black. Sam's mom thought it was kinda plain, but when I tried it on, I liked it, and it was only thirty bucks. I got a pair of low-heeled satin shoes that Sam's mom dyed to match the skirt.

The night of the prom, Sam picked me up at Uncle Tony's. He had a charcoal tux with a wine bowtie and vest. Sam's mom had let me borrow these dangly diamond earrings that I probably could have bought another Kawasaki with. I asked her if she was sure, cuz what if I lost them, and she said that Sam's dad had given them to her as an engagement present, so she didn't care what happened to them. And so, we went.

As soon as we walked in, I realized what "Bollywood" meant. The cafeteria and the courtyard right outside it were all decorated in all these colorful drapes and lanterns and India-style decorations that Ms. Martin and some of her other students had been working on for months. Looking around, I wished I had volunteered to do some, instead of blowing it off when she mentioned it back in January.

Posters and cutouts of dancing girls in saris, or men with turbans. You could put your face through some of them and have your picture taken like that. Mandalas stenciled onto the floors and walls. Paper lotus blossoms hanging from the ceilings. A painting of a weasel or something fighting two cobras—I didn't get it, but Sam said it was from a really well-known story. Not well-known to me, but okay.

At one end of the room was this massive seven-foot tall papier mâché elephant in a blue and silver mosaic pattern, with "jewels" hanging off its tusks. Shrek spent most of the night standing by the elephant to make sure no one messed with it or—just as likely—tried to climb all over it and fall off and break their heads.

My favorite was the mural painted on a long piece of plywood. Under a blazing sun, a desert of yellow sand. A handsome warrior with powder blue skin, aiming a bow and arrow at a huge tiger-headed guy with a long, curved sword: a rakshasa, like Sam's card and my drawing for art class. Chained up at the bad guy's feet was a beautiful woman in pink silks. I found out later that Ms. Martin painted the whole thing in like a week, after school and over a three-day weekend. Badass.

No Indian music, just current stuff. No Indian food, either, just catered Chick-fil-A; I don't know why people on Kent Island are obsessed with that place, cuz 5 Guys is a million times better.

We ate and danced and hung out with all of Sam's gamer and band friends, who weren't as dorky as they usually were. That Rachel girl that I thought had been hitting on Sam at the mall was there, and she said how much she liked my dress, and I said, "Thanks," and she and her date (this Josh guy I don't know) hung out with us, too. She and I had our hands done at one of the henna tattoo stations: I got this cool, intricate design that sorta looked like peacock feathers. I took a picture of it on my phone and sent it to my mom.

We stayed the whole time, and after prom ended at 11:00, we went with a bunch of other people to the Denny's in Grasonville, off Route 50. We sat with Dylan and Holden and their dates. I had these awesome salted caramel and banana cream pancakes that I didn't need syrup for.

We sat around, stuffing ourselves, and Dylan told this embarrassing but hilarious story about how when he and Sam were at North Bay (this week-long camping thing that everyone in sixth grade around here goes to), they somehow got stuck inside a porta potty together, and it took Mr. Chermak and Mr. Ricketts a half hour to get them out. He told it with a totally straight face the whole time, like he was talking about the weather, but I thought I was gonna pee myself, mostly cuz Sam turned almost the same color as his tie.

We hung out there 'til almost two in the morning. When we got in the car to leave, Sam noticed I wasn't smiling anymore. At first, I didn't want to talk about it. He waited in the parking lot with me, until I did.

"Mike told me that if we made it back home, we'd be different people, that what we'd been through would change us. And that maybe even though we love each other now, that might not be enough."

"You're enough for me," he said. "And if I'm enough for you, you can have me as long as you want."

"You promise?"

He nodded. "I promise."

We kissed. Then Sam started the car, drove us a couple miles to the Hilton at the Narrows, where he'd gotten us a room. Where we could finally be together.

* * *

The little that is known about the religious practices of the Beothuk comes from oral accounts that were recorded by European settlers of Newfoundland before the Beothuk were officially declared extinct in 1829. Chief among their deities were the sun, the moon, and Aich-mud-yim, the "Black Man From the Water," who demanded human sacrifice, especially stillborn infants or those with birth defects.

—*www.en.wikipedia.org/wiki/Beothuk#Religion*

This Wasted Land

* * *

I'd thought that missing two weeks-and-change of school would tank both our grades, but Sam took his AP exams on time, in the first two weeks in May, and got 5's on all of them. Then he crushed his finals.

Not so much me. My grades weren't all that to begin with, but I busted my ass that last month—Sam tutored me, just like he had all year—and I went across the stage. No full ride to Loyola, like Sam got, but I did get some scholarships—based on financial need, because they considered my mom's income—to Anne Arundel Community College, a half hour from Kent Island, and another half hour from there to the north end of Baltimore, where Loyola is.

Uncle Tony said I could live with him as long as I wanted to, and he'd let me borrow his other car, a white Ford Focus with all the acceleration of an old lady with a walker, to get there and back. No wonder he never drove it. Damn, I missed my Ninja.

But before school started in the fall, I spent some hours looking up stuff online. And then I told Sam that me and him had to take a road trip.

* * *

"Finally, tonight, it's been three months since the missing Kent Island teenagers Samuel Patterson and Alexandra Williams were found about two weeks after—and more than thirty miles from—the scene of a motorcycle crash on the Eastern Shore. The couple has refused all requests from the media—including this station—to tell more about their remarkable story, but Alexandra's guardian, Anthony Williams, issued a statement saying, quote, 'They just want to go back to being regular kids.' Sources from Stevensville, Maryland, say that's exactly what's happening. Here's wishing them well now, and into the future.

"This is Stan Stovall for WBAL-TV 11. Good night."

Track 38. Love Song

"Hold on," Sam tells me. He takes the turn off Beeline Highway a little too sharp—seems like the exit came up right after the sign for it—but we make it okay, onto a two-lane road. Waze says that in a quarter of a mile, we'll turn onto a dirt road. Then it's a few more miles to the house. Trailer, it's a trailer, not a house. Doesn't matter.

"You okay?" he asks. "You're really quiet."

"You're driving too fast."

"You like driving too fast."

"I like when *I* do it, not you."

He chuckles. "Now you know how I felt on that motorcycle."

* * *

Sam parks his car in front of the trailer, and we get out. A desert again, but super bright and about a million and twelve degrees. "So, this is that 'dry heat' people talk about," he says. "You know what else is a 'dry heat?' A pizza oven, but nobody wants to live in one."

I don't say anything. Look at the paper in my hand, with the address I'd found. I saw this on the satellite view of Google Maps, but here it is in real life, a nice-looking doublewide—American flag flying from the porch, a little garden out front, potted plants in the windows, a big glass mason jar of sun tea brewing on the front step—a few miles from Payson, Arizona. A place I'd never thought I'd go.

"You want me to come with you?" Sam asks.

Shake my head.

"You don't have to do this by yourself."

"Yeah, I do. He was my friend."

"All right then. I'm going to wait in here."

Nod. "I won't be long."

"Okay, then."

He gets in the car, turns it and the AC on. I take the photo out of my back pocket, where I always keep it. Walk to the house, up the steps, onto the porch. Open the screen, knock on the door, close the screen.

A guy opens the house door. In his thirties, I guess. Curly blond hair, brown eyes that aren't right. Down's syndrome. I almost lose it when I see him. Keep it together somehow.

"Hello," he says.

"Hey, Jeremy, is your dad home?"

He turns around. "Da-doo, somebody here."

Tall guy comes to the door. Mint-green golf polo, shorts, flip flops. Mid-to-late fifties, bit of a gut. "Can I help you, Miss?"

Mike.

"Yeah, um...." Blow out a big breath through my teeth. Turn away for a second. Don't cry, goddamn it.

"You okay?" he asks. Looks at Sam in the car. "That your boyfriend?"

"Yeah, yeah, his name's Sam."

His voice, lower. "Everything all right with the two of you?"

"Yeah, yeah, we're good."

"Okay, then." Nods. "What can I do for you?"

"Mr. Fernandez, you don't know me, but my name's Alyx, with a 'y,'—"

He smiles. "That's unusual."

"—and this is gonna sound really odd, but I found something of yours—your son's, I mean. I thought you'd want it."

"Absolutely," he says, opening the screen door. "Where are my manners? Come on in."

"Thanks." AC blasting. Nice place: tidy living room with comfy chairs and couches, and just enough clutter—books and games and papers—on the shelves so it looks like people actually live here.

Jeremy settles into a recliner. Looks at me, smiles, waves. "Hello."

I wave back. "Hi."

"This is our son, Jeremy, and this," holding out his hand to the lady coming out of the kitchen, "is my wife, Cathy. This is Alyx-with-a-'y.'"

A tall woman, older but still pretty, blond, though I can tell she's dying the gray. "How do you do, dear?" she asks, shaking my hand. Big-ass diamond on her finger. "It's awful hot out: would you like something to drink? Maybe some pop?"

I grin. "I don't know anybody else who calls it that."

"Cathy's from Pittsburgh. They talk funny there."

"I used to live near Philly, and everyone there calls it 'pop,' too."

"Ask her to say, 'wash,' like 'washing machine.'"

"He's always making fun of my accent. It's *warsh*." Looks at him. "Happy?" she asks him, but she's smiling. "What kind of pop you want, sweetie?"

"Oh, I can't stay long. My boyfriend's out in the car and we're on our way to the Grand Canyon. I, umm, before I got here, I found this picture." Hand it to Mike. "Out in the desert."

He frowns. "Around here?"

"No, a long way away."

"What were you doing out in the desert, dear?" Cathy asks. "That can be dangerous."

Tell me about it. "You know, just…walking around. It was okay, Sam was there." Not a total lie. "I wasn't by myself." No reaction from Mike.

"You found this?" Mike asks. Looks at me like I'm crazy. "And you came all this way just to give to us?"

"Yeah, I thought, umm, it's a shame that this photo's just lost out in the middle of nowhere. I thought maybe the people it belonged to would want it back."

"Huh. Well, that's awfully nice of you," he says. "Hey, Jeremy, look at this, pal." Holds it out to him. "You know who that little boy is?"

Jeremy looks at the photo, looks at Mike, looks at me, back to the photo, back to his dad. "Jeremy," he says.

"That's right," Mike says. "That's you when you were...." Turns to Cathy. "What, two?"

"Seventeen months. We got that done as a set for my folks, for Christmas."

"She does all the thinking," Mike says, "I'm just here to look sexy." Swats Cathy on the butt. "She can't keep her hands off me. Don't blame her a bit."

"This is why I can't take you out in public."

Mike turns the picture over. "There's nothing on the back. How'd you find out it was Jeremy, and where we live?"

"Honey, you can look up anything online these days," Cathy tells him.

"Right," I say.

"I don't need to look up anything," Mike says. "If it's not in a book, I don't need to know it."

"He doesn't even have a cell phone. But he's a big reader. Reads to Jeremy every night."

"Yeah, that's—"

And then I lose it.

"Honey, what's wrong?" Cathy says, wrapping her arms around me. "Why are you crying, dear?" She looks over at Mike; he

395

shrugs. Jeremy gets up, hands me the box of tissues on the end table next to where he was sitting.

"Here, Alyx-with-a-'y,'" he says.

"Thanks." Wipe my face. Get it together, you're freaking them out. "Sorry, I'm…I'm really sorry. I…a good friend of mine passed away recently, and…."

Mike puts his hand on my shoulder. "I know how you feel. I lost my dad when I was about your age. There's not a day goes by that I don't miss him."

"I bet he was a really great guy," I say.

Mike nods. "Yeah, he was. Worked hard—he was a mechanic, fixed those big trucks and pavers and things they use when they're laying down roads and painting them and such. Was always good to my mom. Never raised his voice or his hand to her, never went to the titty bars—"

"Mike!" Cathy says, glancing at Jeremy.

"Sorry." Jeremy doesn't seem to have noticed. "He never touched another woman. Coached me and my brothers in Little League."

"Did he like Gilbert and Sullivan?" I ask.

Mike furrows his brows. "Yeah. How'd you know?"

"Just a guess. My uncle's an older guy, too, and he's a big fan." Total lie.

"That must be a generational thing," Mike says. "I'm pretty much a country-western guy, though I like some old rock-n-roll, Eighties stuff. Geezer music."

"Yeah." Dab my eyes one more time, jam the tissue in my pocket. "Listen, I don't want to take any more of your time, and Sam's waiting, so, thanks for letting me come in. I'm really glad to see you, and that you're all right."

Mike, puzzled. "Yeah, we're fine."

"Well, nice meeting you, Jeremy." I shake his hand.

"Bye-bye."

"And it was really nice meeting you," I tell Cathy, both of her hands in mine. "My folks are divorced, and so are Sam's, so it's awfully sweet when I meet people who have been together a long time."

"Well, it hasn't always been easy," Mike says, putting his arm around Cathy. "Sometimes, she's a real Witchiepoo." Winks at her; she rolls her eyes. "But I guess we've made it this long because when I gave up on her, she didn't give up on me, and the other way around."

She kisses him on the cheek. "We never gave up on each other at the same time."

"That's...that's great," I say.

Cathy's eyes bore right through me. "Are you gonna marry that boy, Sam?" she asks.

"Christ on a stick," Mike says, "you can't ask that, you just met her, like, five minutes ago. This is why I can't take *you* out in public. Or let anyone come visit." Grins at me. "And that's why we live way out here in Shithole, Arizona."

"Mike!"

"Well, I gotta go: Sam's gonna think I moved in. I'm glad I could get Jeremy back for you. His picture, anyway." Keep it together. "I'm glad I met you, Mr. Fernandez."

"Call me Mike. So, where you headed after you go see the Canyon?"

"Back to Maryland. That's where me and Sam live. And then, you know, school in the fall."

"And what are you gonna study at that school in Maryland?"

"Art, I think. Graphic design."

"Well, good luck, then." He goes the door. "Nice meeting you, Alyx-with-a-'y.'"

Try, fail, start tearing up again. Throw my arms around him, squeeze him real tight. "Yeah. Take care, Mike. You got a real nice family."

And then I throw open the screen door, run off the porch, jump the steps, get in the car, slam the door, tears running down my face. Tell Sam, "Get me out of here before I have a freaking meltdown."

They come out on the porch, Mike with this confused look on his face, as Sam turns the car around. I watch in the side mirror while Mike and Jeremy and Cathy wave goodbye as we drive away, a plume of dust behind us. I watch them until we're gone.

"What happened?" Sam asks.

"It's him. He's older—the age he should be—and he's not skinny, but it's him. And he's still married to Cathy, and Jeremy's all grown up and lives with them. Everything's perfect for him. Ōth, or Paddoch, or whatever he called himself, said there are nine realities. And in this one, this Mike never lost what the other Mike, the guy I knew, had been looking for all that time."

Take tissues, a lot of them, from the center console where Sam keeps them. He gives me some time to get myself mostly back together.

"So, what's wrong?" he asks.

"He doesn't know me." Shake my head. Damn it, I am done crying. "Doesn't recognize me at all."

"Why would he? And isn't that a good thing? For him, anyway."

"Yeah, you're right. It just sucks for me."

We're coming to the end of the dirt road, where there's a wire fence around a big field for someone's horses.

"Let me ask you something," he says. "If the Mike you knew was from another reality, is there an Alyx in that one? And if so, is she just like you?"

I thought about it for a second or two. "Well, if there is, and she ever shows up here, she better not start something with you, or I'll tell her what happened to the last bitch who tried to take my man."

He chuckles, puts on his blinker to turn left onto the two-laner that will take us back to the highway. Rolls to a stop at the intersection. Looks left, looks right. Gets a funny look on his face.

"Check that out," Sam says. "Isn't that weird."

I never told Sam about it—still freaks me out—but there it is, on the corner post of the fence. A toy stuffed bird, yellow beak, tufts of fake blue and green and yellow hair sticking up all over it, huge googly eyes, itty bitty wings, big orange feet.

"I wonder who would leave that there," Sam says.

"Dunno." Death grip the door handle, fight the urge to lock it.

The toy bird doesn't say anything. Just turns its head and watches us drive away.

DISCOGRAPHY/LINER NOTES

The chapters (or "tracks") of ***This Wasted Land*** are named after some of Alyx's favorite rock songs from the 1970's, '80's, and '90's. Each relates to its chapter in some way, whether it evokes the mood, mirrors events, reiterates themes, or simply was the inspiration for it.

Below, I list information about each song, so that you may seek them out. If you were to collect each song and assemble them into a playlist—for your personal use only—as an unofficial soundtrack to this book, I feel certain the recording artists would appreciate your purchases.

Some of the songs listed are cover versions, and in those cases, I listed the artists who redid them, not the original artists, because those were the versions that Alyx had on her playlist.

- "You Could Be Mine"—Guns 'n' Roses, from the album *Use Your Illusion II*, released 1991
- "The Wanton Song"—Led Zeppelin, from *Physical Graffiti*, 1975
- "Ladies Room"—KISS, from *Rock And Roll Over*, 1976
- "Sign of the Gypsy Queen"—April Wine, from *The Nature of the Beast*, 1981
- "No One Like You"—Scorpions, from *Blackout*, 1982
- "In the Dark"—Billy Squier, from *Don't Say No*, 1981
- "Plush"—Stone Temple Pilots, from *Core*, 1992
- "Sixes and Sevens"—Robert Plant, from *Shaken 'n' Stirred*, 1985
- "Atomic Punk"—Van Halen, from *Van Halen*, 1978
- "Paranoid"—Black Sabbath, from *Paranoid*, 1970
- "Toys in the Attic"—Aerosmith, from *Toys in the Attic*, 1975

- "Do You Wanna Touch Me (Oh Yeah)—Joan Jett, from *Bad Reputation*, 1981
- "The Thing That Should Not Be"—Metallica, from *Master of Puppets*, 1986
- "Where Have All the Good Times Gone"—Van Halen, from *Diver Down*, 1982
- "Sick Again"—Led Zeppelin, from *Physical Graffiti*, 1975
- "Don't Know What You Got (Till It's Gone)"—Cinderella, from *Long Cold Winter*, 1988
- "Dust N' Bones"—Guns 'n' Roses, from the album *Use Your Illusion I*, 1991
- "Plowed"—Sponge, from the album *Rotting Piñata*, 1994
- "Humans Being"—Van Halen, from *The Best Of – Volume I*, 1996
- "Innuendo"—Queen, from *Innuendo*, 1991
- "In the Evening"—Led Zeppelin, from *In Through the Out Door*, 1979
- "I'm Gonna Crawl"—Led Zeppelin, from *In Through the Out Door*, 1979
- "Why Can't This Be Love"—Van Halen, from *5150*, 1986
- "Would"—Alice in Chains, from *Dirt*, 1992
- "Foolin'"—Def Leppard, from *Pyromania*, 1983
- "Love Lies Bleeding"—Elton John, from *Goodbye Yellow Brick Road*, 1973
- "Ain't Talking 'bout Love"—Van Halen, from *Van Halen*, 1978
- "Still Loving You"—Scorpions, from *Love at First Sting*, 1984
- "Don't Cry"—Guns 'n' Roses, from the album *Use Your Illusion II*, released 1991
- "Photograph"—Def Leppard, from *Pyromania*, 1983
- "Estranged"—Guns 'n' Roses, from the album *Use Your Illusion II*, released 1991
- "Master of Puppets"—Metallica, from *Master of Puppets*, 1986
- "Too Late for Love"—Def Leppard, from *Pyromania*, 1983
- "God of Thunder"—KISS, from *Destroyer*, 1976

- "Heavy Metal (Takin' a Ride)"—Don Felder, from *Heavy Metal: Music from the Motion Picture*, 1981
- "Little by Little"—Robert Plant, from *Shaken 'n' Stirred*, 1985
- "Love Song"—Tesla, from *The Great Radio Controversy*, 1989

* * *

I began working on what would become *This Wasted Land* in the spring in 1988. After doing extensive research and attempting several drafts over the next few years, I put it aside after realizing that I didn't have the skills or experience to successfully put on paper the story I had in my head.

After publishing two other novels—*Dragontamer's Daughters* (in 2012, revised and reissued in 2015), and *Lost Dogs* (in 2014)—I finally felt like I was up to the task. Nevertheless, it still took three years, many drafts and edits, and quite a bit of assistance. I'd like to thank the following people for helping to make this novel happen:

To my wife Joni, and my daughters Elise and Alexandra, for their encouragement and patience as I spent countless hours (even on summer vacation!) tapping away on a keyboard.

To my awesome beta readers—Liz Brewster, Paul Briggs, Patrick Eibel, Bo Gott, Elise Kilgore, Tara O'Brien Elliott, Janet O'Mahony, and Gareth Topping—who waded, with a short turnaround time, through the manuscript that I sent them. In addition to catching typos and awkward sentences, they offered numerous great suggestions, especially for strengthening the original ending. They also surprised me with how passionately they fell in love with this story and its characters.

To Matthew Margolis of Logotecture (logotecture.com) for the fantastic cover art.

To Verlyn Flieger, the late Jack Salamanca, and all the other excellent teachers I had along the way.

This Wasted Land

To Ann Collins and the real Ms. Custer, for when I was lost.

To authors Brent Lewis and Robert Bidinotto, for mentoring and invaluable professional advice.

To the Jungle fanboys and fangirls, who encouraged and stuck with me even when I was taking time away from my Warhammer 40K site (fightingtigersofveda.com).

To all the readers of *Dragontamer's Daughters*, and *Lost Dogs*, and to my followers on social media, for all their support, kind words, and telling others about my works.

To the musicians and singers—especially Led Zeppelin, Guns 'n' Roses, Van Halen, and Def Leppard—whose songs gave inspiration and voice to this story.

If I May Ask a Favor

Thank you for reading *This Wasted Land*. If you enjoyed it, I'd be very grateful if you would please leave an honest review on Amazon.com. Leaving a review is more than just a pat on the back: it helps other readers find new authors and new books, and decide if they'll take a chance on them.

Also on Amazon, you'll find my other works. As of this writing, I have published the following:

For young adults (and adults who are still young):
Dragontamer's Daughters
Lost Dogs

For children (and their parents):
Our Wild Place (with Patrick Eibel)

You can find my website and blog at kentonkilgore.com, follow me on Facebook and Instagram, and subscribe to my newsletter.

Thanks again for letting me take you there.

Kenton Kilgore
November, 2018

Made in the USA
Middletown, DE
22 January 2022